REDEMPTION

THE SPADES TRILOGY
BOOK ONE

MIKE SCHLOSSBERG

Redemption

Mike Schlossberg

Ellysian Press

www.ellysianpress.com

Redemption
© Copyright Mike Schlossberg 2018. All rights reserved.

Print ISBN: 978-1-941637-49-4
First Edition, 2018

Editors: <u>Jen Ryan</u>, Imagine That Editing, Maer Wilson, M Joseph Murphy
Cover Art: M Joseph Murphy

DEDICATION

To Brenna, Auron & Ayla
My Redemption

CHAPTER ONE

It wasn't actually the high-pitched, hysterical shrieking that woke Asher Maddox. It was the air. He knew right away that something was wrong because the air around him felt far too icy and sterile. Drowsily, since he was just waking up from a deep sleep, it dawned on Ash that it was much colder than he remembered; he usually preferred the cold, but not quite this sharp. That, and the smell. It smelled like the first night he slept in a dorm in college, many months and a lifetime ago. The brief sensory input of too-clean air, combined with the off-putting chill, was just enough to stir Ash's sleep-addled mind. He was blinking slowly when the screaming started.

Ash bolted upright in his bed. No, cot. A hotel-type cot. The screaming emanated from across the room, where a copper-skinned girl was shrieking at a pitch so sharp and high it sounded like the noise was coming from a wounded animal, rather than a person. Ash's eyes started to focus as the girl brought her hands to her mouth, as if trying to summon the courage to stuff her cries back into her larynx. Light spilled from a hallway on Ash's right. It cast a pale glow over the rest of the room, barely illuminating the girl's wide-open eyes.

It was with that dim illumination that Ash found his second shock of the past thirty seconds.

Two rows of cots lined the area. A quick look to his left and right revealed bodies of various shapes and sizes, all in various stages of awareness, and like Ash, various stages of shock.

Ash had definitely not gone to sleep in this room last night. He had gone to sleep in his own bed, in his room at home, hoping that when he woke up in the morning, he would be able to push through yet another day.

A second girl let out a high-pitched shriek, resonating with terror. A third voice, this one male, joined the growing chorus. Ash blinked a couple of times, trying to shake himself out of his bizarre nightmare, but he only succeeded in waking up further. That was fine; he needed to be awake.

Somewhere in Ash's head, the engine behind his brain turned over and started to function. *Okay. This is . . . very bad. But someone needs to do something here. Where the hell am I?*

Other people were starting to move. A glance in the dim light revealed ten beds in each row, for a total of twenty. In the far-left corner, a short young man around Ash's age swung his legs over his bed and rapidly scanned the room, his eyes tight and his fists balled. He looked more angry than afraid, and Ash felt his breath catch in his throat when he realized that the young man's name was shimmering off his shirt: "Anton" glowed in a garish neon yellow.

Two beds down from him was the original screamer, whose blanket had fallen to reveal her name shining as well: Exodus. Another girl looked like fear of embarrassment was the only thing that kept her from joining her neighbor in expressing her terror, this one apparently named Miranda. A blond girl with curly hair framing a small, fair-skinned face – Echo, Ash saw as he squinted into the distance – had a hand on the shoulder of a crying boy, and appeared to be trying to talk to him.

Ash looked to his immediate left, where a tall, dark-skinned girl was propped up on her elbows, looking completely confused. She made eye contact with Ash and lowered her eyes, her mouth forming a silent "O" of shock as she focused on his name. Mirroring her stare, Ash found the girl's name: Blondell. Eyes moving upward, they stared at each other for a heartbeat before the girl raised her eyebrows as if to say, *Well, what's this?*

Ash smiled for a millisecond before noticing a pale girl

with raven hair and a million freckles, her eyes wide with concern, but not fear. She turned back to Ash, clearly disoriented, then scanned the room for some clue about what to do next.

The lack of helplessness shown by the two women were all Ash needed.

"Hey!" he shouted. To his own disbelief, that actually shut the room up. The panicked cries stopped on a dime and faces turned to him expectantly. It was not what Ash anticipated, and his mind stumbled for something to say that would make it sound like he knew what he was doing. "Anyone know how we got here?"

A chorus of shaking heads from the assembled mass.

"Anyone know where we are?" More heads shaking.

"The floor is vibrating," said a freckled red-haired boy in a bed against the corner. "In fact, everything's vibrating. I think we're in motion."

Tentatively, Ash touched the cold steel frame of his cot and felt the smallest tremor. The redhead was right. There was a hum throughout the . . . wherever they were. Ash nodded vigorously. It felt good to have some sense of reality, however tenuous.

"My clothes!" screeched a girl all the way at the left side of the room. There were other whimpers of terror at the raised voice. "I didn't go to sleep wearing this! And these pants! They're. . ."

And whatever she was trying to say was swallowed up by sobs, but it was enough to make Ash look down, revealing a pair of black track pants that Ash had also not worn last night.

At that, Exodus began to cry again. Echo moved from the boy, who was calmer, to Exodus. Putting a hand on her leg, Echo spoke in soft, soothing tones. Ash shook his head a couple of times, trying to clear the cobwebs. He felt increasingly useless.

Aside from the cries of the more emotional, the room fell into an awkward, vaguely sickening silence. Slowly, unsteadily, Ash swung his legs over the side of his bed. He looked again at the raven-haired girl on his right, who appeared to have somehow grown paler in the space of two minutes. Their eyes met.

"You okay?" asked Ash quietly.

"Fantastic," she said wanly. A small smile crept over her face. "Couldn't be better. Great way to start the day. Who the hell are you?"

Ash couldn't help but smile as he tentatively swung his legs over the bed. "Ash. You?"

The girl patted her nametag, while nodding to Ash's own. "I'm Alexis. Nice meeting you, Ash. And by nice I mean terrifying." Ash laughed as Alexis continued, "At least someone is finding some humor in all of this."

"I wish I knew what this was," Ash said. The panic was abating and giving way to the sheer strangeness of the entire situation. Was he part of a science experiment? Hallucinating? Had an aneurysm exploded in the deep recesses of his brain, leaving him to die in the comfort of his own bed?

Realizing that Alexis was still staring at him, Ash spoke again. "What's the last thing you remember?"

"Falling asleep, listening to music," said Alexis. "I think I was out . . ." Alexis' voice trailed off and her eyes focused on something in the distance. "Actually, wait. Now that I think about it, something weird did happen last night. The last thing I remember wasn't listening to music. It was a . . . some kind of . . ."

"Woosh!"

Ash turned around as Blondell joined the conversation.

"'Woosh' is what you are looking for. You felt like your stomach disappeared from under you. Like you fell into a black hole and the rest of your body followed."

"Yes! Exactly!" cried Alexis. "Like everything was sucked out from under me, as if I was on some kind of roller coaster or something."

Blondell cocked her head and scrunched her eyes while Alexis looked expectantly at Ash.

He closed his eyes and tried to recall his last memory, before he woke up in this . . . place. *Last night, okay, I was upset because I didn't get as many hours at work as I would have liked. Facebook showed everyone partying in their dorms while I was stuck at home. And that's . . . No.* That wasn't the last thing he remembered. It came back to him; the last thing he remembered was feeling grabbed. "Woosh. Yeah, okay. This I remember."

"Well, at least that explains something," said Blondell.

Alexis nodded and peered around the room. Most were talking in groups of two or three, but two were simply curled up in bed, covers to their chins. A few beds down from Ash, he saw a form, coiled under the blankets, completely unmoving except for a soft rise and fall of their chest.

"Someone should probably check on them," said Ash, gesturing to the prostrate form hiding under the blanket.

Blondell followed Ash's gaze and nodded. She walked over to the bed.

Ash turned back to Alexis. "So, I'm guessing you have absolutely no idea what happened or where we are?" he asked.

"None. You?"

"Definitely not," Ash replied.

Alexis nodded, raised her eyebrows, pursed her lips and shifted her gaze downward, appearing scared for the first time. They lapsed into silence, punctuated only by the muffled cries of an assortment of terrified teenagers. Slowly but surely, Ash felt fear creeping into his lungs, filling them like black ice: cold and unforgiving.

From the back of the room, the angry-looking boy moved forward, toward the hallway light. "Hey," he said to Ash. Ash looked up at the short, stout figure in front of him. His shoulders were as square as the buzzcut that crowned his head, and his face was locked in a scowl. Ash felt a moment of pity for him before spotting the angry tilt to his eyes. He looked like a kid who had tried out for the football team and hadn't made the cut. Ash lowered his eyes to his nametag again: Anton. "Any idea what's going on?"

"No. Nothing," Ash responded. He didn't even bother to ask the same question in return and was surprised to discover that there was no fear on Anton's face . . . just a clenching of his jaw and a narrowing of his eyes.

5

Anton tilted his head and looked at Ash. "So what now?" he asked, an edge in his voice.

Gripped by an increasing fear, Ash shrugged and stood. "I have no idea, man."

Alexis seemed to pick up on Ash's mood and pulled herself up. "Maybe you want to help out Blondell?" she asked, tilting her head toward the other girl.

Blondell was gently rubbing the shoulder of the cot's occupant, but whoever was under the blankets was holding tight.

Anton shook his head violently. "She doesn't need help." He turned to a corner where three scared figures – two girls and a boy – huddled together. "I'm gonna go talk to them, see how they are feeling." He looked directly past Ash and at Alexis. "Want to come?"

Alexis almost looked offended. "I'm good, thanks," she said.

Anton shrugged and walked away, leaving a perplexed Ash and Alexis behind.

Alexis looked back at Ash, appearing more confused than scared. "Wonder if anyone else here has an 'A' name," she said with a smile.

The little joke made Ash chuckle. "Wonder if anyone else has issues like that guy," he said.

"Oh, relax," Alexis responded, lightness creeping into her voice. "Not like this is a situation that any of us have ever experienced before."

"Fair enough," Ash responded.

The fear in the room was palpable, thick like fog on a humid day. Others were in bad shape: barely stifled sobbing, bewildered looks and some borderline catatonic teenagers.

"Come on. Let's see what else is going on. That guy in the corner seems to have a vague idea of how to figure this out," Ash said.

Alexis nodded. "Better than any idea I've got."

The two stood up and walked to the end of the room, toward the redhead who had noticed the vibrations. They passed a dozen kids along the way. Ash tried to take mental snapshots of who else seemed to have fallen through the looking glass with him. There was the Hispanic girl who had started the screaming, still being comforted by Echo. The short, tanned, black-haired girl, huddled up in the bed, knees covering her name tag, looked absolutely terrified. She kept groping behind her, like she was trying to grab something that wasn't there. A thick African-American boy, with a closely-cropped haircut, stared mindlessly into the distance, not looking ready to move just yet.

Ash and Alexis reached the redhead. He had been standing at the foot of his cot, scanning the room, a look of quiet concentration on his face. He nodded when Ash and Alexis walked up.

"I'm Jameson," he said. Ash and Alexis introduced themselves.

"What makes you think we're moving?" Ash asked.

"It's not like I haven't done this before," said Jameson. "There's a slight pressure, a push that's almost unnoticeable, but this feels different than anything else I've ever experienced." Before Ash could quiz Jameson further, Blondell walked over to them.

"Sorry, no luck with that kid," she said. "At one point I tried to pull the cover back, and I'm pretty sure he actually growled at me. And I mean that literally. He actually growled."

Ash and Alexis shook their heads.

"This is really bad, and I'm worried about him. And a couple of others. Everyone here looks like teenagers, but whatever is happening is making a bunch of them act like scared little kids, and I don't blame them." Blondell looked back over her shoulder, where Echo continued to comfort the increasingly hysterical young girl. "We're going to need to do something."

Ash felt a flash of indignation. "Do what?" he snapped, a little more irritated than he intended. "None of us know what is going on, or where we are, or how we got here, or . . . well, pretty much anything. Let alone how to comfort people who are hysterical. It's a small miracle there are a few people who are even functioning right now."

"You're not asking the more immediate questions,"

Jameson said, with a frost that spurred the rest of the group to face him.

"What?" asked Ash, trepidation seeping into his voice.

"If we are in motion, what are we on, and where are we going?"

That was a new concern, and one that was at least three steps removed from Ash's thoughts. He looked at Alexis. Her eyes started to widen as the floor shook from a massive explosion.

CHAPTER TWO

It felt like they were inside of the cymbal of a drum set; the explosion was massive, metallic, and reverberated around their entire room. The lights flickered and stayed dark for a few moments before kicking back in. Jameson crouched on the floor, hands over his ears. Alexis backed up a few steps and looked around wildly, trying to locate the source of the explosion. Blondell spun around, as the rest of the room's occupants went into various states of unmitigated panic. Ash slammed his hands to his ears and tried to keep his balance as the room shook around him. It didn't work, and as the floor lurched to the left, he lurched with it, crashing into a bulkhead and falling to his knees, his face narrowly missing Jameson's shoulder.

Ash looked at the hallway where the light was coming from. It might have been his panicked mind, but the room wasn't shaking as much. The light was steady. Ash righted himself and tried to ignore the metallic *pings* snapping off around him.

"Come on!" he yelled at the top of his lungs, waving his hand forward. For the second time in the past ten minutes, Ash's loud voice carried over every other sound of hysteria. Sensing escape, others in the room scrambled out of their beds and raced to follow. Not waiting for anyone to change their mind, Ash grabbed Alexis' wrist and raced for the doorway, Blondell and Jameson hot on their heels.

A second crash brought more shouts, but this one was not nearly as violent as the first. As Ash sprinted forward, he caught the first markings that he had seen since opening his eyes: A horizontal infinity symbol, with a "U" and a "G" lodged in each of the loops. As quickly as Ash noticed it, it was gone, as he rounded a corner, with at least a dozen others racing to keep up.

"Where are we going?" Alexis wrested free of Ash's grip as they continued to run.

"No idea!" Ash shouted back. "But anywhere was better than feeling trapped like a bunch of sardines!"

"Agreed!" They came to a T-intersection and, for the first time, saw signage:

← *Bridge*
Cafeteria →
Engineering →
Conference →
Docking Bay ↓
Labs ↓

"Bridge?" Blondell exclaimed, catching up. "There's a blasted *Bridge* here?"

"Apparently!" Ash said, staring at the signage in disbelief. It was official. He had to be in a coma.

"Which way?" Alexis asked, frantically looking at Ash.

"Gotta go to the Bridge there, Captain," said a voice behind him.

Ash turned around, and there was Anton, the slightest of smirks on his face.

"Absolutely," Ash said. "That's the only thing that makes sense . . . as if any of this makes sense. Alright, let's go!" Ash took off running, and the rest of the group followed. With one exception.

"I'll see you soon!" Jameson shouted over his shoulder, racing the opposite direction.

"Jameson!" cried Alexis, turning around, but the redhead was gone. Whether it was the idea of separating or one more pressure on the already chaotic situation, Ash wasn't sure, but Jameson's sprinting had triggered something in Alexis. She tried to chase after Jameson, only to be blocked by the big African-American that they had walked past earlier.

"You only run in that direction if you know what you are doing," he said, his glowing nametag identifying him as Daniel. "He's all right."

Alexis looked up at him for a moment, and back to Ash for reassurance.

Ash nodded. "I think Daniel's right. Let's get to the Bridge." The words felt alien in his mouth and left his tongue feeling like sandpaper. Regardless, they began to sprint again.

The narrow hallway was straight now, with more light at the far end. With one last burst of speed, Ash crossed through another doorway and entered the Bridge.

He stopped so sharply that the next three people who entered crashed into him, only to gasp when they realized what Ash was looking at.

Space.

More specifically, space as framed by the most bizarre collection of technology Ash had ever seen.

They were clearly on a spaceship; that much Ash was able to deduce. But from there, it was a mystery. Directly in front of him, on a slightly elevated platform, stood a console that featured a series of tablets, with various lights, buttons and a touch-screen keyboard.

Below and in front of the platform, Ash made out a straight-backed chair which had a large joystick, surrounded by other knobs and an old-fashioned control panel which looked like it had been borrowed from a *Star Trek* episode.

Further survey of the room revealed six other stations, all surrounding the center chair. But what didn't make any sense was the varying nature of all of the stations; some had computers which looked recognizable to Ash. At least one had what looked like a miniature projector, facing the ceiling, and nothing else. Another looked like something out of a cheap 1980s war movie.

But it was the front of the room that presented Ash with the most stunning sight: a massive window, which arced around half the Bridge, held in place by two large, gun-metal panels. Outside of the window Ash only saw blackness and stars.

Space.

To Ash, the sight of space, cold and infinite, was the last straw, and it brought down a white wall between himself and reality. He no longer felt as if he was truly seeing life through his own eyes, but was instead detached, watching a movie of someone else. After all, that was the only thing that made sense. The idea that he wasn't really there was the only possible way he could even begin to explain away the vastness of space and infinity of the stars which lay before his very eyes. It was the only way he could accept that he was standing in the middle of a *freakin' spaceship,* with a hodgepodge of different technologies.

The wonder of the moment began to overtake him. Ash fell into a chasm of disbelief and wonderment at the exceptional sights in front of him.

Seemingly from nowhere, a brilliant white light wheeled from an invisible spot in front of their ship, hitting the window head on. More lights, more vibrations. Arcs of electricity shot across the assembled equipment, crackling and sparking, while the front window morphed into the various colors of the rainbow. From the area of the blast came a distortion in space, shimmering like a ghost, soaring through the void. The spectral blur raced to Ash's left, behind the ship.

The shock of the iridescent colors and bright laser brought the last of the stragglers into the room, pushing forward others who had arrived first. One of those last arrivals was Anton, whose head whipped around the room, freezing when he caught sight of something on the left-hand side of the Bridge. Anton's face immobilized so suddenly that Ash followed his gaze and discovered three more chairs, one in the front, two behind. This was one of the barest of the stations, featuring only an L-shaped metallic stick that seemed to be attached to a pivot.

"Now this I know!" said Anton, cracking a smile for the first time. He raced over to that console and expertly kicked the pivot, unlocking it and pulling the metallic attachment toward him. He ran his left hand over the top part of the bar, and using his pointer finger, poked the middle of the air and pulled his finger upward. An electronic interface materialized, and Anton expertly poked a series of icons. The display shifted to space, framed by a series of crosshairs.

Almost all of the room gasped as two others pushed forward, sitting behind the matching stations. They didn't touch anything and seemed content to sit behind someone who knew what he was doing. Anton turned around and looked at the rest of the group.

"What?" he asked, seeming genuinely confused. No one else answered; they only stared blankly at him. "Someone had to do something."

Clearly, Anton wasn't the only one with that thought, as others began to edge their way forward, their attackers momentarily forgotten in the discovery of new technology. Their mystification evaporated, however, as the attacking ship sped in front of the Bridge's window. A series of screams followed, and virtually everyone jumped back.

"Yo, someone do something!" said Daniel, his voice lurching toward unhinged. And again, just like before, that was all Ash needed. He moved forward, past the elevated chair and to the joystick, extending his right arm and stopping just before he touched it. After a second's hesitation, he poked the heavy control, ever so slightly. Correspondingly, the ship moved marginally to the right.

We can fly this, Ash thought, and he looked back to the rest of the group. "Anyone have any flying experience?" he shouted. Much to his surprise, it was Alexis who shot forward, her curly hair bouncing across her face.

"Civil Air Patrol!" she said, literally shoving Ash out of the way and expertly gripping the joystick with both of her hands. "Ah, that's better!"

Ash didn't give Alexis a second look and went to the panel next to Anton. Two large blue circular screens showed a large red dot with a streaking red one racing across the right panel.

"Okay, anyone have any idea?" Ash questioned.

13

Instantly, the group went silent. "Come on, someone, anyone, what the hell is this thing?"

This time, there was the slightest of whispers, so faint that Ash almost didn't hear it. "What? Come on, we don't have time, who said that?"

A short Asian boy, blocked out by Anton's bulk, took a small step forward, still almost hiding behind one of the terrified young women. "It's X-Wing. It's the radar in the X-Wing computer game. You know, from *Star Wars*."

And, just like before, everyone standing stared blankly at the short kid, as if he was speaking a foreign language. The gamer swallowed tightly.

"I have no idea what you are talking about, but you do, so get over here!" Ash cried.

The short kid bounded forward to the two screens and started poking buttons, rapidly cycling through displays. Ash couldn't keep up, but this kid could, and Ash kept moving.

On it went. Blondell understood the next station, which seemed like a sleeker version of Anton's location. A tall, olive-skinned teen named Tidus, whose bizarre name was matched only by the most ridiculous feathered hair that Ash had ever seen, raced up to a paper-thin computer and started poking symbols before extending an invisible line from the screen to his ear. Miranda, the girl with short black hair who Ash had walked passed earlier, seemed to understand the various flat screen monitors at another station.

One of the back two posts held the oldest looking equipment, including a bulky computer, blocky keyboard, and of all things, a massive utility belt. Daniel stared at that station and gingerly touched the keyboard, caressing its keys like a lover touching the face of his betrothed.

"Uh . . . you okay?" asked a mystified Ash.

Daniel slowly glanced over at Ash, a pensive smile splashed across his face. "Never better, buddy."

Ash shrugged and raced on to the next station, which was . . . a bookshelf. With physical books. *What the hell?* But, to his surprise, Echo gingerly stepped forward, looking reverently at the hardcovers.

"Books," she whispered, her voice barely audible. Delicately, almost as if afraid of startling the bookshelves into running and hiding, she took the tiniest of steps, stretching out her left hand and caressing the spine of a thick volume labeled *DSM-IX*. Tears brimmed in her eyes.

"Oooookay," Ash said, moving on. And just like that, all the stations were full. Job complete, Ash turned his attention back to the movement of the ship, which he realized had been increasing gradually. Alexis was cautiously piloting the ship, apparently getting a feel for it, moving the massive beast like a baby elephant trying out its legs for the first time. Ash moved back to Alexis and stood over her shoulder. "What do you think?" he asked.

"I think this thing is absolutely huge," said Alexis. "Huge and weirdly agile. I mean, I've flown Sikorskis before, but this is nuts. I've never seen anything like it. And more to the point, I'm not a spaceship pilot!"

"Can you get us out of here?" Ash quickly asked.

Alexis turned around and looked at Ash as if he had six heads. "Out of here? Ash, I can move up, down, left, and I think I just figured out right. But I don't even know where here is, let along how to get us out of it."

"I think I can help with that," said Blondell, her voice eerily sterile and cool.

Ash moved forward to her position. "What you got?"

Blondell methodically poked at the translucent screen in front of her. "The display. It's easy, actually."

Ash and Alexis both stared at Blondell in disbelief.

"What? It is. I've used this kind of system before." She spread her fingers above the computer, zooming out the map, grabbed the edge with both hands, and pushed it forward to reveal a three-dimensional map. "We're here," she said, jabbing at a miniature ship. Her fingers dropped down to a series of coordinates labeled X, Y and Z. "Give me a few seconds, and I think I can figure out a safe place to go."

"Okay, I think we can do that!" Ash spun around to go back to Alexis, but before he could move, caught the absolutely terrified look on the short kid's face, who was staring at his equipment as if it had just told him his mother had cancer.

"What?" Ash snapped.

No response. The kid kept staring blankly, eyes frozen.

"What? You gotta tell me what's going on."

Ash realized he wasn't helping and slowly walked over. "Okay, sorry, sorry. Hey, what's your name?" Ash asked. He tried to bend forward to see the kid's name, but the young man was frozen to his equipment, and Ash thought forcibly moving him to stare at his chest would not do him any favors. "Okay, I'm gonna call you Radar, since that's what I think we are looking at now. Radar, what's up?" Ash asked gently.

That did it. Radar pointed at a bright red dot on the second panel, moving his mouth but emitting no sounds.

A beeping occurred behind Ash. Spinning around, Anton was excited, and standing at his station. "I've got a lock on them!" he cried, pulling downward on the translucent panel in front of him. Anton brought up a new screen and appeared ready to hit a bright red button.

"That's not them," said Blondell, her voice seeming to dip an octave or two. "Look!"

Turning back around, Ash saw a ship . . . the third spaceship in the area. "Who the hell is that?" he asked, staring at the new arrival. Squinting, Ash tried to make out some of the ship's features. It was big and chunky, clearly designed with no consideration for form or attention to function. It looked like two blocks that had been combined: A smaller one in the front, and a larger one in the back. The rear of the ship bore two, heavy-duty wings, and the entire exterior was replete with a series of cranes, hooks and beams that Ash couldn't make out.

"No idea, chief, but I think we better blow it up!" Anton said back.

"No, no, wait!" Ash shouted. "You can't just blow things up! Can we try to talk to them?" There was silence. "Anyone?" Unfortunately for Ash, the only response came from the mystery ship itself. The ship, which had been drifting, abruptly turned and started making a beeline for

16

Ash's ship.

"You sure I can't just blow this thing up, Ash?" said Anton, his hand hovering over the red button, practically chomping at the bit to press it. The new arrival opened fire, spewing green bolts of energy.

"Dammit!" cried Ash. "Fire!"

Anton hadn't waited. The ship shook as three separate turrets opened up on the new attackers, catching the ship front and center. The ship shook violently before listing dramatically to the left. An instant later, boosted from an interior source, the smaller block separated from the larger one, which exploded into a million pieces, ejecting debris and gases into the vacuum of space. The entire ship was suddenly quiet.

"What in oblivion was that?" asked Anton.

Another beep, this one from Radar's station, was the only answer. Radar pointed and tried to speak. "Ship! Ship!" he said, choking out his words.

Ash, thoroughly confused, spun back to Radar, and sure enough, there was another red dot, blinking unsteadily.

"Alexis, move us, quick!" he ordered.

Alexis, abandoning caution, brought her hands up and pushed down on the joystick, hard.

For an instant, the ship pitched forward, threatening to turn the level ground of the Bridge into a steep hill. Ash tumbled forward and fell to his knees, quickly flinging his hands forward to arrest his fall. Instead, however, the ground shifted back downward, returning level.

"Huh?" Ash said, pulling himself up and spinning around the Bridge, finding a slew of disoriented faces staring back at him. An abrupt shake of the ship returned his attention in front of him.

"Up, up!" Ash said.

As Alexis continued to pull, a brightness illuminated the window. Ash turned around just in time to see a white laser scream past the window, coming within feet of hitting the ship directly from behind. A distortion – the same one as before – bulleted past their ship and began to turn left, setting up for another pass.

"Hang on, hang on, I think . . . Yes!" shouted Anton, as he literally punched through the screen in front of him. With a jolt, a miniature blast shot from the left side of the ship and what could only be described as a missile fired forward.

Ash stared in disbelief at the large white cylinder, which rotated as miniature rockets fired from the device, steering it on course in the direction of their assailants.

"Holy crap, that's something!" Ash yelled, pumping his fist in the air as white-hot adrenaline shot through his veins. The rest of the room cheered in delight as the weapon raced after the other ship. "Blondell, anything?"

"Maybe?" Blondell was flinging the map and keyboard in front of her, flicking through screens faster than Ash could track. "Something's not right here, and I'm not quite sure what."

"What do you mean?" Ash moved over to Blondell and tried to make sense of the screen in front of him. Blondell flicked the lower-right corner of the display.

"I keep hitting this function, here," she said, pointing at the glowing yellow icon that she had just tapped. "I think it's supposed to get us out of here, and it's flashing like it's important, but nothing's doing on that front. Every time I hit it, the computer stutters and returns to normal." To demonstrate, she pushed the button again. Sure enough, the entire map froze for an instant, before blinking and returning to the previous screen. "Something's not right, I don't know what, and I'm not sure how to fix it."

Ash spun around and looked at the rest of the group, all of them were nervously staring at him. For the first time since he had charged onto the Bridge he looked at the back of the room, where everyone who didn't have a station was standing.

"Anyone have any ideas?" A series of nervous head shakes was the reply. "So we got nothing."

"No one in here has the answer," said Anton, a hint of impatience creeping into his voice. Ash hated to admit it, but Anton was right. No one there had the answer.

"No, but I bet someone else does!" Ash yelled. "Uh . . . you! Teedus!" The kid with the feathered hair spun around, looking annoyed.

"It's Tidus," he said, drawing his shoulders up. He rhymed it with "eye."

"Fine, Tidus! That computer, what's happening?" Ash moved to the station in question. Before Tidus had a chance to explain anything, Ash studied the screen, discovering an outline of the spacecraft. For the first time, Ash was able to get an idea of the spacecraft's shape: It was straight and narrow, with stubby, triangular wings on each side.

"This is obviously a diagram of the ship," said Tidus, his voice practically oozing contempt. "I've been hitting the various sections in here and all I hear is static, except for here," he said, pointing at a section labeled "Engineering. I swear to God, someone in there is talking to themselves and humming."

"Jameson!" realized Ash. "Put me through to him!"

Tidus responded by reaching to his left ear and yanking something out of it. Ash looked closely at Tidus' hand for some sort of small ear piece and saw none, but the next second, Tidus flicked his wrist and appeared to throw an invisible Frisbee at Ash.

It was as if someone had placed earmuffs over Ash's head. The world became instantly and completely silent, save for a small echo and the beating of Ash's own heart.

"Hello? Hello?" Ash heard himself talking but the sound felt projected ... like he wasn't hearing his own voice coming from his mouth, but instead, from inside his own head. "Okay, this is weird. Hello?"

"Hello??" replied a surprisingly strong and high-pitched voice back. "Who's there??"

"It's Ash! Who's this?"

"Ash, it's Jameson. I'm just getting settled down here. What's up?"

"Where's here?"

"Engineering, obv. I ran down here, and I'm trying to figure out the engines. Ash, you need to see these things, they're—"

"Don't care! Not now anyway. Jameson, Blondell thinks she knows how to get us out of here, but said that something is missing. She keeps hitting some yellow button, but her insane map just freezes. You got anything?"

There was a pregnant silence for a good ten seconds, and as Ash was about to repeat his question, Jameson spoke again. "Yes, I think so. There's a couple of buttons here . . . hang on, let me switch this on." Before Ash could ask what "this" was, a screen lit up mere feet from Ash's face, giving him a bird's eye view of Jameson's line of sight. It took Ash a moment to realize that the screen wasn't coming from any piece of technology on the Bridge, but was actually being projected from inside his eye, then reflected back into his vision. The realization made Ash's eyes water and he blinked, trying to focus on the highly disorienting vision in front of him.

"Ash, see this panel here?" A finger glided into sight and ran across a thin row of heavy, multi-colored buttons. "I need you to go back to Blondell's station and tell me when you see something that looks familiar." Ash obeyed, but realized something wasn't right. Everything at Blondell's screen was digital, and the buttons in Ash's face were large and physical.

"That's not it . . . hang on," Ash whipped around and looked for an older station, finding it on a panel to the right of Alexis. "I think I got it!" He moved to that panel and saw that it was a duplicate of the vision in front of him.

"Okay, good! Try the button marked 'P-B.' If it works like it does on the ships I've read about, you have to hit the button, then I follow." Without waiting a moment, Ash slammed the fat button with his fist, finding the sensation oddly satisfying. To his surprise, the ship shuddered slightly. On the screen in front of him, a small light activated on the corresponding button in Engineering.

"That's it!" Jameson yelled, and he hit the same green button as well.

Ash didn't need to be told what to do twice. "Blondell, hit it!"

Blondell started to respond, but Ash couldn't understand a word she was saying, since Blondell was only moving her lips and not actually speaking.

"Huh?" Ash said, bewildered.

Blondell stopped and started over, but still, nothing.

"What the hell?"

Sighing with impatience, Tidus walked over to Ash. He reached up and took Ash's ear with one hand and stuck three fingers near the opening and pulled. Ash's hearing promptly returned.

"Oh . . . right then," Ash said. "Thanks. Anyway, Blondell, go!"

Blondell's fingers were flying across her computer. "Give me a second!" she said.

Ash pulled his head back, surprised at the response.

"I need like a minute to recalibrate this thing." Blondell spun back toward her display and began rapidly tapping out keystrokes.

"Uh . . . Ash?" said Radar, his face contorted in fear again.

Ash was starting to think that everyone on this ship pretty much had only one facial expression: terror.

"Ash, can you please hurry? That red dot is—"

"Alexis!" Ash wrapped his arms around the panel closest to him. He was relieved to observe that just about everyone else did the same thing, some crying softly as they tightened their grips on whatever object was available.

"Okay, okay, let's try *up!*" said Alexis, pulling her stick back. The ship responded and they began to move upward.

"Not working, not working!" said Radar, who, like Blondell, had been smart enough to strap himself into his seat. "They're still on us back there!"

"Hang on!" Alexis said, redoubling her efforts and grunting as she did so.

Once again, the ship sloped upward, and for the second time, Ash crashed to his knees. An instant later, a solid mass landed on Ash, complete with a pointy elbow that drove into the back of his skull with a cry of "Oof!" A sound similar to a gong echoed through Ash's head, and he struggled to look up as Daniel regained his balance and pushed off Ash, crying "Sorry!" as he scrambled back to his station.

"Come on, Blondell!" Ash said desperately, holding his

head with one hand and the edge of Blondell's chair with the other.

"Just a few seconds," she responded. But as she did, a scorching white laser beam appeared above and to the right of them, and a second bolt closer after that.

Their attackers had overshot their mark but were moving to correct, and at their current rate would be able to hit their ship in a few seconds.

Ash's eyes widened with horror.

"Sorry!" Alexis threw the yoke on an angle and to the right.

The ship lurched, whipping everyone and everything on the Bridge to the left. This included Ash, whose arm made solid contact with Blondell's temple. Instantly, her eyes unfocused, her hands went limp and her head slumped forward. Ash gasped in horror as Alexis turned the ship, causing him to lose his balance and topple against a wall.

"Crap! Blondell! Blondell! Wake up!" Ash cried. No luck. Blondell stirred ever so slightly but didn't move. Ash frantically looked at Blondell's station. The yellow function – the one that Blondell had been struggling with – had changed colors. It was now green, and had gotten larger, as if to say, "Push me."

With no options remaining and time running out, Ash pushed himself into a standing position and raced toward Blondell's station. He caught a swirl of bright lights in his peripheral vision as the enemy ship fired again. The ground disappeared from under his feet as the angle of the ship's turn intensified. With one last desperate push of his feet, Ash launched himself into the air, arm extended toward the green button that could take them to safety.

Time moved in slow motion as Ash tumbled mid-air, his mind catching fragments of images as he spun. Scorching plasma arced into the vast emptiness of space. His dive continued and brought into focus the pure fear etched into Tidus' face, the haughtiness of mere moments ago evaporated. An angry yell framed Alexis' small mouth, her face contorted with intense rage. And at last, as his head moved past Blondell, bringing into focus the innocuous control panel that could bring them to safety.

With a blind stab, Ash shifted his hand right, pushing his fingers through the digital screen but unquestionably connecting with the all-important green button as he did so. There was no hesitation, no delay; the stars in front of them evaporated, bathing the ship in a bizarre mishmash of racing lights and drowning out all of the screams with the roar of the engine. There was the sound of bone on metal, a crack as Ash's head slammed into a bulkhead. Reality folded in on itself, and there was nothing.

Chapter Three

For the second time in thirty minutes, Ash woke to the sound of hysterical screaming. A grogginess pressed on his forehead and his temples, and an aching pain was just beginning in the back of his head. Using one hand to push himself up and the other to rub the back of his neck, Ash opened his eyes and saw that he couldn't have been out for more than a few seconds. The screaming, meanwhile, was coming from the same girl as earlier. Blondell was still unconscious, and everyone else on the Bridge was staring at him.

"You all right?" Alexis said, concern etched into her face.

"Yep, great. That was fun. Should do that again." Ash continued to rub his head before shaking it roughly, sending warning bolts of pain into his skull. "I'll be fine. What happened?" Silence was the response. "Right. I'm not too sure either." Ash looked over at Blondell, who was stirring. "She alright?"

"She'll be fine," said Echo. "Anyone in here know where a go bag is?"

"A what?" Ash asked.

Echo ignored him and began stomping around the Bridge, riffling through various compartments Ash hadn't noticed before. "Alright. Forget it. You . . . you do you."

Ash looked back out the window and discovered it was impossible to make out any sense of direction as stars whizzed by so brightly that he couldn't determine any sort of position. "At least we're moving. Radar, those guys . . . whoever they are. They still on us?"

Radar turned to face Ash, having run back to his position as soon as the ship had righted itself. "No. I don't think so. The screens are clear." His expression was relaxed and not immobilized with fear, and for the first time, a trace of a smile crossed his face. "I think you got us out of that. Nice job."

Murmurs of agreement followed from the rest of the Bridge.

Ash shrugged. "Got us out of what, though? That's the question."

At that, a groan came from Blondell. Echo stood over her. Blondell was slowly blinking and staring at the small tablet in front of her nose.

"Smelling salts!" said Echo cheerfully. "How you doing?"

"Been better," said a woozy Blondell. "Thank you."

"Glad I could help," said Echo, gently tilting Blondell's head. "You're going to have one heck of a bruise, and a headache. We should test you for concussion symptoms, too. Don't worry, I can handle this without any equipment."

Blondell nodded slowly while the rest of the ship stared, bemused.

Ash turned back to the rest of the group. "Okay, we need to figure out what to do next. Any ideas?" Not for the first time since the journey started, Ash was greeted with silence.

"Ash . . . I think they need a minute." Alexis unstrapped herself and walked over to join him. Ash sighed and made eye contact with her, noticing the fear in her face and her wide-eyed, unblinking stare. He stared at her for a moment before looking back down.

"Yeah. Probably." He looked back at the rest of the group. "Okay, never mind. Hold that thought for a second."

No one acted as if Ash had even said a word. While the rest of the crew stared and blinked, Daniel joined Ash and Alexis.

"Hey man, good work today," he said, extending a large hand.

Ash shook it and was struck by how massive Daniel was. Ash was tall, just a shade under six feet, and Daniel towered

25

over him. He was thick too; not overweight, but built like a wall.

"Thanks," Ash said, staring up at Daniel. "You have any ideas?"

"I do," said Anton, walking up to him. "We need to figure out what we are doing here. Let's walk the ship and see if we can find anything that actually shows us where we are."

Ash raised his eyebrows and tilted his head to think. That wasn't a bad idea at all . . . still . . . He jerked his thumb at the rest of the group. "What about the rest of them?"

"And what about flying this thing?" Alexis added.

"They'll be fine. Sia here can watch them. Si?" Anton turned over his shoulder and looked at one of the two girls who had taken a seat behind him. Since Alexis' last desperate maneuver, she hadn't moved and was still splayed across a bulkhead, gazing vaguely at the group. She looked no more capable of taking responsibility for anyone's well-being than an eight-year old did of chaperoning a fraternity party.

"I'm not sure about that," Ash said. "Sia? You okay?"

Sia blinked. "Great," she said dreamily.

"Yeah, no," Ash said. "Someone needs to stay in here who is fully conscious."

"I'm good," said Echo, wrapping an arm around Blondell and helping her out of her seat. "She's okay too. Just a little woozy."

"Okay, great," Ash said, as Alexis and Daniel nodded appreciatively. "Sorry about that, Blondell."

"No worries," Blondell said, smiling weakly. "Next time you save us, try to avoid knocking me unconscious."

Ash laughed. "Will do," he said.

Echo led Blondell to a seat. "I'm gonna keep an eye on her here for a minute, but she's okay. She and I will try to talk to everyone. It will help keep her awake too, just in case."

"Thank you," said Ash. "Seriously, thank you. I have no idea how to take care of anyone who is injured, and I don't know if anyone else does."

Anton and Daniel shook their heads; Alexis took a slight

step backward.

"You got it," said Echo.

Ash turned back to Daniel, Anton, and Alexis, waving them over to Tidus' station, which featured the diagram of the ship. "Okay, Alexis and I will take this side of the ship," Ash said, pointing at the left hallway and its various branches. "Anton and Daniel, you guys want to take the other part?" Both nodded.

"Cool," Daniel said, smiling. He started walking, not waiting for Anton. "Let's go, little guy!" Anton hustled to keep up, taking three steps with his short legs for every two of Daniel's. It reminded Ash of a Chihuahua chasing after a Mastiff, and he had a laugh before turning to Alexis.

"After you," he said, exaggeratedly gesturing toward the closed door at the back of the Bridge.

Alexis chuckled before walking to the door and into the dimly lit hallway. "Good that we are laughing," said Alexis. "And, you know, not worried about things like what happened, who any of us are, how we got here, how we get back, or who is flying the ship right now." The last part of Alexis' statement was easily the most pressing, and it made Ash pause.

"Damn. I didn't even think of that," he said, pulling up. "Do you think we should stay?"

"No, I don't," Alexis said, shaking her head. "It's fine. Blondell, whatever she did, she got us going the right direction. My controls locked the second you hit that green button, and I mean really locked; I couldn't move them at all. Whatever this ship is doing, me sitting in that chair won't do anything."

"Fair enough," Ash said. "Lead on."

Alexis did, walking back to the T-Junction where they had first walked toward the Bridge.

"Let's try Engineering, see if we can catch up with Jameson," said Alexis.

"Good call," Ash said. They moved on another thirty feet before Ash abruptly stopped.

"What?" Alexis asked.

Ash stared at the wall in front of him, brightly lit from

an unknown light source. He was staring at the sideways infinity symbol again, with the "U" and "G" lodged in a loop. What he was just noticing, however, for the first time, was the text underneath it:

U.G. Redemption

"U.G. Redemption?" Alexis said, staring incredulously at the words in front of her. "That mean what I think it means?"

Ash nodded. "It's the name of the ship."

They walked on, and after a few more feet, Alexis spoke again. "That's an interesting name."

"How do you mean?" Ash asked.

"Redemption. That is a really interesting name for a ship which seems to have pulled a group of teenagers out of their beds and into space."

"I guess," Ash said. "I don't know. Seems like that's an overreach."

"Nope," Alexis said stubbornly, with a conviction that gave Ash pause. "There's a reason for that." They came to another door, the first one they had seen since they left the Bridge. It was simply labeled "12" below an infinity symbol, and the text seemed to levitate off the door. The door, however, had no knob or handle. Tentatively, Ash reached out and touched the cool metal. Upon contact with his fingers, the door opened with a soft *hiss* of hydraulics. Ash and Alexis stepped inside.

They were inside of a sleeping quarters. It wasn't a huge room, maybe ten feet by ten feet, but it made use of its limited space well. A bed was lofted in a back corner with a desk and dresser placed underneath. On the other side of the room stood a small closet; opening it, Ash saw a series of plain white t-shirts, made of a synthetic fabric that he had never felt before. Fingering the shirt's collar, he found it flexible and cool to the touch. Even more bizarre was the collection of casual, colorful shirts, next to the white one. He stared thoughtfully at the open door, trying to make sense of what he was looking at.

"Don't you go rifling through the dresser," Alexis said with a smile.

Ash snorted. "Don't worry, checking out underwear is way, way at the bottom of my priority list," he said. "But this is interesting."

"What is?" asked Alexis.

Ash was looking at the back of a shirt, which had a logo sewed in. He had expected to see the infinity symbol, but closer examination made Ash gape in disbelief. He handed the shirt to Alexis, making sure to hold it so that she saw the logo.

"Old Navy? The shirt has a brand name?" she asked.

"Yeah . . . this is getting weirder by the minute," Ash said, alternating his glance between Alexis and the shirt, unable to avoid noticing a slight tremor that started in Alexis' fingers and travelled up her arms. "What is an 'Old Navy' shirt doing—"

"I have no idea. But I do know this is really freakin' creepy. This metal furniture seems like a dorm from the future, and I want to get out of this room, now." And with that, Alexis turned on her heel and marched out of the room. Ash wasn't more than a step behind her.

"You want to go back to the Bridge?" he asked gently.

"Go back to what, the island of misfit toys? Come on. We need to keep walking and try to figure out what the hell is going on here. Let's move." And Alexis kept walking, not stopping at the next room, which Ash noticed was labeled with a "13."

They walked on, passing computer screens embedded in the walls. Upon closer examination, Ash realized that the screens were from all technological eras, becoming more modern as they moved. They walked past models labeled "Amiga 3000," "PowerMac 6100," a husky "Dell Latitude" laptop and a series of increasingly small flat screens which transitioned to iPads of all sizes. Around that point, the models became less familiar to Ash, and he couldn't help but notice that Alexis seemed to be staring in disbelief. But it was only when they arrived at a computer that seemed to be projecting from a flexible, translucent piece of paper held to the wall by an unknown force that Ash had to stop walking.

"I'd love to know how they do this," he said, looking at

the paper computer in disbelief. "Have you ever seen anything like this?"

"No way," Alexis said. "This is brand new. Hey, sorry about that?"

"What?" Ash stared in confusion.

"Snapping before. I'm sorry. This has to be the strangest thing I've ever experienced. I didn't mean to make it worse."

"You're kidding, right?" Ash asked incredulously. "You're apologizing for yelling at people who weren't in the room at the time? You have to know I get it. Anyone would."

Alexis nodded, biting her lip before brushing a loose strand of curly hair out of her eyes. "Thanks. I appreciate it."

Ash nodded empathetically. "I get it. Really." *And I don't know when my time to snap will come, so you better forgive me when it does,* was what Ash wanted to say next, but he couldn't. Not yet. They moved on.

"What's in there?" Alexis said a few moments later, noting the presence of a large, metallic box. It was attached to the nearby wall and seemed to be made of the same material as the cabin door. Ash touched the box lightly and its top sprang open from unseen hinges. Inside, handle facing upward, was the unquestionable outline of a gun.

"Whoa!" Ash exclaimed, delicately pulling the weapon out of its container, holding it away from his body as if it was a deadly virus. Ash was no expert with weapons, but he knew enough to know that this was not like anything he had ever seen. For starters, when he pulled it out of its case, it detached with a small, almost magnetic click. The handle was light and maneuverable, not heavy, and Ash realized what this meant right away: No bullets. The barrel of the gun was almost pencil thin, and the trigger had been replaced by a button. Gingerly, studiously avoiding a top switch he imagined to be the safety, Ash turned the weapon over in his hand.

"Do you have any idea how to use that?" Alexis asked.

"None," Ash said, trying to figure out the way to put the gun down.

"That's not the right question," said a voice from down the hallway.

30

Ash and Alexis both looked in the direction of the voice. They were relieved to discover Jameson walking toward them with what could almost be described as a strut. Alexis spun and ran to him, hugging him with such force that they almost fell over.

"Why are you so happy to see me?" asked Jameson.

"Because right now, anyone who looks even a little like they have an answer to this feels so good!" Alexis said.

Meanwhile, Ash walked up to the two, a slight smile on his face at Alexis' honesty.

"So what is the right question?" Ash asked. Jameson, who had successfully detached himself from Alexis, looked at the gun held loosely in Ash's hand.

"Why would we need a gun in space?"

At that, the trio fell silent. After a moment, Ash sighed. "That is a good question," he said quietly. The prospect of violence terrified him. He was alright with the earlier dogfight; that was more like a video game. But the idea of an actual fight, one that could end in injury, bloodshed or worse, absolutely horrified him. Ash had never been a fighter. He was in decent shape, but while some of his high school friends had gotten into weapons, or cars, Ash had found salvation – at least while he was capable of doing so – in a decent book or an addictive video game. Violence was a foreign concept, one reserved for people who had no better way of resolving conflicts. Ash had shed himself of those primitive pieces, and he had no desire to become reacquainted. "Here's to hoping we won't ever find out why."

Jameson nodded curtly. "Agreed. Now, here's this." Jameson reached into his pocket and pulled out a tablet. It was small, no bigger than a coffee mug, and on it was only one line of text, displayed digitally:

Y: 7643.4

The group looked at the tablet, then each other. "Have you seen this on the Bridge?" Jameson asked.

"Not the number, no," Ash said. "But it's ringing a bell and I can't remember why."

31

"Think. This is important," Jameson encouraged. "The number doesn't matter as much, but I suspect the letter does."

"Sorry, I've taken a few blows to the head today," Ash said, smiling wanly.

At that, Alexis smacked Ash on the shoulder.

"Ow! What the hell?" he asked.

"Blows to the head!" Alexis said. "I remember where I saw that. It was on Blondell's computer thingie."

Jameson arched his eyebrows.

"Thingie?" Jameson said. "Is that the technical term?"

Alexis punched Jameson.

"Ow!"

"I know, right?" Ash said. "She's got a hell of a punch."

"Anyway!" said Alexis, mock impatience slipping into her voice. "That Y. It was on Blondell's computer. Ash, I remember it, because when you took your miniature flight through the air, your fingers dragged through a Y."

"Flight through the air?"

"Don't ask," Ash responded. "But she's probably right. Blondell was playing with a map. Maybe it's a coordinate or something?"

Jameson shrugged. "That makes about as much sense as anything I've been able to come up with," he said. "Still, that alone can't be meaningful. We're in space. We're travelling in three dimensions. One coordinate isn't going to get us anywhere. We've got to get the rest of them, wherever they are."

"Back to the Bridge?" Alexis asked. "Maybe Anton and Daniel found something."

"Maybe," Ash said. "But maybe we look around a little more first. See what other surprises this thing has in store for us."

"Yeah, I want to see this place anyway," Jameson said. "What else have you found?"

The three walked in the direction of the Bridge. Ash and Alexis filled Jameson in on what they had seen so far, Jameson asking questions as they moved. "This whole thing sounds preplanned," he said, as Alexis concluded telling them about the cabin, leaving out the part about how she briefly lost control.

"What do you mean?" Ash asked.

They reached a branch in the hallway, and instead of walking straight, Ash gestured to his left, and they walked toward a new section of the ship.

"Well, when we first woke up, I thought this might have been a science experiment gone wrong. But now, I don't think so. That doesn't make sense. There's the clothing. There's stuff like this tablet which would seem to indicate intentionality. It's like we're on a weird scavenger hunt."

"Don't take this the wrong way, but I miss my bed," Ash said. "And my house. And . . ." Ash laughed. "Earth. Getting back to Earth again would be just fantastic."

There was silence before Jameson, his voice barely a whisper, asked the most bizarre question anyone had proposed that day. "You want to go back there?"

Ash and Alexis both stopped walking and stared at Jameson.

"What?" Ash said. "Are you kidding?"

"As opposed to what, heading off to Mars?" Alexis said. "Though, now that you mention it, we could probably get there in a few hours."

Jameson looked from Alexis to Ash, then back to Alexis, as if he was seeing them for the first time. And to the surprise of both, he smiled, ever so slightly.

"Of course I'm joking," he said. He walked past both and waved an arm over his shoulder. "Come on," he said, moving forward.

Ash and Alexis took a moment to look at each other, both confused, before they continued.

The hallway they were walking down terminated with a door labeled "Junction," and below that, the infinity symbol with a U and G. Without hesitation, Ash tapped the door, which opened with a sigh. All three entered the cramped space.

"Good thing we're skinny," exclaimed Alexis, and indeed, she was right.

The space was barely big enough for the three of them.

The entire room was filled with computers, colorful, glowing and translucent wires and various forms of hardware that Ash didn't recognize. Looking around the room in awe, Ash also realized that the ceiling of the room was high, probably thirty feet in the air, with handholds in the thinly-wired fence that someone could climb to the ceiling. Following the path of handhelds, Ash gazed at the ceiling of the massive room, where he saw—

"Space? There's a skylight in here?" Alexis said, unable to keep the skepticism out of her voice. "That doesn't make any sense. Why would there be a skylight in a closet?"

"Solar power, obv," Jameson said, practically snorting.

Ash looked up at the ceiling again and was even more confused. The only sources of light he saw were the small pinpricks of reflected stars at a distance. Not wanting to seem stupider than he already felt, he remained silent. But, as he brought his head down to look at Jameson, his eyes froze, and he jerked his arm up and pointed.

"Look!" he cried. "There!" Alexis and Jameson each turned around and followed Ash's finger, quickly spotting what had made him so excited: a tablet with a glowing screen that clearly wasn't native to the room.

"Ha! Awesome. Good job, Ash," exclaimed Alexis. "Hang on, I got it." Alexis scrambled up the fence, kicking Ash and Jameson as she did so. When she had climbed out of range, Ash and Jameson glanced at each other. Jameson raised his eyebrows.

"I can't remember the last time I was punched and kicked in under five minutes," he said with a slight smile.

"That's probably a good thing," Ash said, smiling back. He liked Jameson. There was no guile, no mystery; just the mission.

"Got it!" cried Alexis as she snagged the tablet from a shelf which contained a series of small, triangular lights and computer chips. She sped back down and hopped off the fence, knocking both Ash and Jameson out of the room and creating enough space to bring her arms up and hold the tablet up for all three to see:

X: 19482.6

"Think that's enough?" Alexis asked.

"No," Jameson and Ash said at the same time. Jameson looked at Ash with surprise.

"What?" Ash said. "You said it yourself. Space is three dimensional. We probably need Z."

Jameson nodded. "Let's get back to everyone else. Hopefully the other two will be back and everyone will be doing better."

When the three arrived back at the Bridge, Ash discovered that his hope was just that: a hope. The Bridge's occupants had barely moved, save for Blondell, who leaned against a railing. Next to her, Echo was smiling and looked relieved.

"She's okay," Echo said. "Much better than I thought."

"Awesome," Ash said, looking at Blondell. "I'll try to avoid kicking you again."

"Good to know," Blondell said with a tired smile.

Echo walked up to Ash and took his arm, leading him to an unoccupied part of the Bridge. "She's not the one I'm worried about," Echo said quietly, her face tight with worry. "We've been the only ones even speaking. A lot of them are really not doing well." Echo looked to the back of the Bridge at the eight people still standing, four males, four females. Two of the girls were desperately holding hands, and as Ash glanced at their fingers, he saw that their knuckles were white with strain. The other six looked as stiff as planks of wood. When Blondell walked up to one and gently touched his arm, he jumped.

"I can see that," Ash said, noting the presence of tear tracks on multiple faces. He looked back at Echo.

"Try talking to them," Echo said. "You saved our lives before. I think they'll appreciate anything you have to say."

With those two sentences, Ash felt a familiar digging and rumbling in the pit of his stomach. His heart started to accelerate, ever so slightly, and his head felt like it was deflating, as if all the air was being let out. He managed a weak smile and a nod. "Okay, thanks." Ash felt the weight of responsibility on his shoulders. But before he could do anything, Ash heard the thumping of footsteps from the entrance to the Bridge.

Daniel and Anton came jogging in. Daniel, looking as if he didn't have a care in the world, thrust his hand into the air. "Look what we found!" he cried triumphantly.

Catching up with him, Anton looked into Daniel's large hand and smiled. Ash smiled too: they were looking at a third tablet.

"Blondell!" Ash cried, marching back to her station. Blondell turned around to look at Ash, albeit slowly. "Did anyone explain to you—"

"Yes, coordinates, absolutely, and you're right," Blondell said. "That's what they are and that's what I inputted earlier. That Z?" she asked, gesturing to the tablet in Daniel's hand. Daniel responded by holding the tablet at chest level:

$$Z: 729.0$$

Snatching the tablet out of Daniel's hand, Blondell walked to her station and punched in the three numbers. Abruptly, the green button appeared in the lower-right corner again. Blondell turned around and looked at Ash, who had followed her to her post, joined by Daniel, Anton, Alexis and Jameson.

"Want to do the honors?" she asked as a mischievous smile spread across her face.

"Wait, wait," Jameson said. "This seems like a terrible idea. We have absolutely no idea what we are dealing with, or where these coordinates will take us." He looked at Blondell's map. "Where does this take us?"

A young girl with short black hair and light brown skin piped up. "I'm on that, actually." She was the girl who had been too curled up in her cot for Ash to have caught her name. She took a tentative step forward. "I'm Sierra and I've been working on this thing." She jerked her thumb over her shoulder to a flat-screen computer that actually looked familiar to Ash. "The information in here is organized like Wikipedia. I figured out the mapping system about an hour ago—"

"Lady, that would have been really helpful when we were trying to figure out how to get out of here and where to go," said a perturbed Alexis.

Sierra shrugged. "Well, I got it now," she said testily.

Ash took a step forward. "Okay, great," he said, trying to change the subject. "Can you look up what's there and confirm if it's clear?"

"Yes. Absolutely. Hang on." Sierra turned back to the computer, sat down on a stool, and began racing her fingers across the keyboard. After a moment or two she smiled. "Got it. Here's where we are going." She jabbed a finger at a three-dimensional map that looked like a less-advanced but more information-heavy version of Blondell's. "It's empty."

"No one's there." That voice came from the opposite end of the Bridge, from Radar. As the entire group looked at him, he seemed to physically shrink. "Sorry. It's just that . . . Blondell, when you brought up those coordinates, my radar changed. I hit these buttons here and the map reset . . . and no one's there."

Ash starred in disbelief. How had this kid, who looked afraid of his own shadow, figured out what he was doing? How was Radar functioning, when Ash felt like he had been run over by a tank? "Nice work," Ash said tightly, nodding slowly. And, the more important question was this: What was going on with the equipment in this ship? The computer Sierra was using looked familiar, maybe a little speedier than he was used to, and the monitor was a touch thinner, but it was something he thought he could use. Radar's equipment looked twenty years old, like it was from a bad computer game. And Blondell's map? That was something entirely different.

"Middle of nowhere," Blondell said. "No other planets around. Just empty space."

As if that sentence makes sense, Ash thought.

Alexis verbalized what Ash was thinking. "Sure, no other planets, just a routine trip through space. Good thing that doesn't sound completely insane."

For the second time in twenty minutes, Jameson looked at Alexis as if she had six heads, but this time, that look was joined by Anton and Blondell. Jameson only held the stare for a moment before looking back at Ash, but Blondell and Anton held the look longer.

"Ash, we have to think about this for a second," Jameson said. "We have no idea where these coordinates will lead or who put them there."

"Yeah, and we also have no idea of what else to do," said Anton. "Really, guy, what are our other options here? Sit around with our heads up our asses? I say we do something. You heard the quiet kid over there. It's empty. There's nothing. Let's shut up and go."

A frost spread across Jameson's face as he looked coolly from Anton to Ash. As Jameson's stare shifted, Ash realized he had a more pressing issue: the entire Bridge was looking at him again.

"Jameson, it's clear out there. What do you think?" Ash asked.

Jameson's hands were glued to his hips. "Ash, there's a lot of risks with this."

"There's a lot of risks with space," Alexis snapped. Catching her breath, she paused. "Sorry. I know what you are saying. But, however we got here, whoever put us here, I doubt it was to put us in a super-expensive mouse trap and watch us die. You're all about logic. Does that make sense?"

Jameson's hands relaxed and went loose around his sides. "No. Then again, none of this makes any sense." He looked at Ash. "Up to you, boss."

Ash barely suppressed a shudder. "Up to you" was the last thing he wanted to hear. But the crew was looking at him, and they needed an answer. He looked at Blondell. "Hit it," he said.

A smile spread across Blondell's face as she used her fist to smash the massive green button. And again, with no hesitation, the ship raced into the deep reaches of space.

CHAPTER FOUR

The ship lapsed into an uneasy quiet, and for the first time, Ash had a new problem to deal with: time. Specifically, too much of it. According to Blondell, they were at least two hours away from their destination, leaving many of the crew with nothing to do. Sierra went back to her computer (she had tried calling it *Redemption-pedia* a few times before realizing how awkward that sounded) and experimented with it to try to learn more about their ship. Elsewhere, Blondell fiddled with her map, while Anton toyed with his weapons systems, chatting with Sia and Pike, the only person on the ship bigger than Daniel.

Some talked in small groups. Alexis chatted with Blondell and said goodbye to Jameson, who was headed back to Engineering to get a better idea of how the engines worked. Others sat wordlessly, their faces fastened in various stages of terror and confusion.

Ash, feeling at loose ends, tried to talk with various members of the "Back Brigade," the name he had given to the group which seemed to stick to the back of the Bridge. They looked more scared than Ash would have thought possible. Maybe they were picking up on how he felt, could somehow sense the thudding of his heart or the flipping of his stomach. But of the Back Brigade, not a one was able to hold eye contact with Ash for more than a moment. Not one could answer a question with more than a monosyllabic grunt, and one couldn't even manage that.

It was after his third fruitless attempt that Ash realized

why he felt so helpless. He was talking to a small kid with round glasses – he didn't look a day older than fifteen – when he realized that the kid's hands were twitching at a speed so fast that Ash couldn't even make out individual fingers. Looking down, Ash saw his own hands, strumming against his chair to the beat of a song that only he could hear. The thought crashed into Ash: *This is like looking in a mirror.*

With the sensation of failure sinking in his gut, Ash gave up and went back to Echo, who had started paging ravenously through a thick book with a multicolored cover. She was startled when he stepped in front of her, blocking her light, but she recovered and smiled.

"How's it going?" she asked.

"The Back Brigade. You said you were worried about them. I can see why. They won't even talk to me," Ash said, exasperated, staring at the mixture of scared teens that comprised the group. "They're just sitting there. They haven't moved. I don't even think they've gone to the bathroom."

Echo shrugged. "I've seen enough of this to know that it doesn't mean much," she said. "Everyone handles stress – extreme stress – in their own way. The important thing for you, given your position, is that you keep trying." Echo paused and scrunched up her face. "It's pretty clear you're the leader here."

Ash said nothing. He stared at the ground. "I don't want to be," he whispered.

"You're good at it," Echo responded patiently. "All things considered, we're doing pretty well so far, and you deserve credit for that." Another pause, as Ash kept staring down. "What do you need?"

That answer was easy. Ash raised his head and made eye contact with Echo. He held her glance, searching her face for signs of recognition. Did she know what he was feeling? There was no malice in her returned stare, no narrowed eyes or sneers of detection. Her face radiated patience while his legs practically vibrated with a desire to escape, sending waves of fear into his knees, threatening to buckle them at any moment. A glance down from Echo and a knowing smile crossed her face.

"Sure, Ash, check for other tablets. It's probably a good idea for you to check the rest of the ship," Echo said, her voice an iota too loud.

Ash, dumbfounded, stared blankly at Echo. "Thank you," he said, his voice nearly empty.

Echo smiled, turning back to the book while Ash practically ran from the Bridge.

The monster was escaping, and that last conversation with Echo had been the final straw. He was past the point of damage control. Barring a pill that he clearly didn't have, he was going to have to ride it out. And as he stalked down the hallway, so sick with anxiety that he was literally weaving, Ash came to a terrible realization: despite the new, dramatic and unexplained circumstances in his life, nothing had changed. Nothing.

For Ash, the anxiety attacks hadn't "started" at any time. They just always had been. When he was a kid, he thought he was scared. Weak. In middle school, every kid snuck a cell phone into the school. Ash was the only one he knew who used the phone, not to text friends or tweet, but to call home in desperate search of a temporary reprieve.

The anxiety attacks followed a similar script: they started as a twitch, but enough. Enough to make him think, "Hey, is this an anxiety attack? Do I need to start worrying now?" And from there, the familiar sensations. The stomach upset, feeling like his bowels were going to uncontrollably evacuate at any given moment. The heart palpitations. The dizziness. The nausea. And all of the symptoms did nothing but create more symptoms, so by the time they were at their peak, Ash was a sweaty, twitchy, non-functioning disaster.

The medication started in high school and gradually increased. For a time, it was under control, and it was in high school that Ash learned a new coping strategy: sublimation. Anxiety didn't have to be beaten with calm thoughts or pharmaceuticals; it could be ignored with school work and clubs. And Ash had launched himself into every club, every class and every job he could get his hands on. There could be no free time, because free time meant that the gates of his mind would crack open, eviscerating any sense of temporary peace he had managed to obtain. Time to think was bad; thinking was the enemy. There could be no feelings, only action.

It was in college when the depression started.

Ash had no illusions that the switch to college would be easy. Accepted to Cornell on a scholarship, Ash knew that he would have a rough transition. What he did not realize was exactly where his struggles would lie. His roommate was fine. School work was hard, but he could deal. Sleeping was a breeze.

What was new for Ash was just how separate he felt from the rest of the world. The sensation that everyone else in school was there and excited about it . . . and he had been left behind. That feeling that, since he didn't like to party, didn't see anyone else who was as depressed as him, that he was wrong. That he didn't belong. That he wasn't supposed to be there.

The depression began as a gnawing feeling that, coupled with accelerating anxiety attacks, trapped Ash in his dorm room. The pressure of grades began to build. Ash was no longer one of the smartest kids in school; he wasn't special anymore. Now, he was just another face in the crowd, another over-achiever on a campus full of rich, smart kids who just knew they were going to succeed. Kids who didn't need any encouragement, or assistance, or reassurance that everything was okay in the world.

So, Ash fell apart.

Anxiety attacks didn't mean some dramatic collapse or the need to be buckled into a straight-jacket. They didn't mean an instant transition from a functioning human to a weeping ball of goo. Ash knew that. They just meant pain, fear and shame. Anxiety took you and placed you in a box, and gradually, that box shrank on you. As the walls closed in, it took everything from you: your friends, your ability to form meaningful relationships, your hope for a better day, and apparently, your college education.

That was where Ash was the night before: depressed,

anxious, contemplating the future of a college drop-out, and alone. And then *woosh.* And then the *Redemption.*

None of that mattered on the ship. All that remained was a bizarre and hopeless future, surrounded by people who seemed to be coping with this disaster better than him. Echo knew who he was, knew he was a mess, and that had to mean that she was doing better than him. Blondell, knocked unconscious barely an hour ago, was chatting with Alexis and Sierra as if nothing was wrong. Besides, Ash felt like the ship's real leader was Anton, who had already built a following and was training himself in new ways to blow things up.

Ash, arm resting on a bulkhead, head resting on his arm, eyes tightly shut, tried to breathe like his therapist had taught him (in through the nose for four, hold the breath for seven, exhale for eight) and failing miserably.

Ash was so consumed by his anxiety attack that he didn't even hear the footsteps behind him, feel the gentle hand on his shoulder. Ash's eyes shot open, adding humiliation to the array of emotions cascading through him. Risking upsetting his stomach further, Ash turned around and saw Blondell, viewing him with caring, worried eyes.

"It's okay," she said.

Ash thought, *Well, at least, she didn't ask if I was alright.*

"You're allowed, you know. How could you not react this way?"

Ash licked his dry lips and tried to speak but no words followed. Instead, he swallowed tightly and nodded. They stood quietly. After a solid minute, Ash was able to compose himself enough to speak. "Do you mind if we just stand here for a second?" he asked.

"No, of course not," Blondell said. "Do you want me to go? I don't know if you want privacy or a friend."

"Stay. Don't say anything, but please stay," Ash said, a lilt of desperation slipping into his voice.

Blondell stayed.

CHAPTER FIVE

The anxiety attack did abate. They always did, eventually. After ten minutes, when his heart-rate slowed, Ash lifted his head off his arm, wiped his sweaty brow, and turned around. Blondell was still there, and still standing.

"Little better?" she asked.

Ash nodded. "Yes. Thank you." He smiled weakly, stifled back a sob, and the two hugged.

"I'm not sure why you look embarrassed," Blondell said, squeezing tight. "This is supposed to happen. No one is supposed to get through something like this unscathed."

Ash detached himself and they walked back to the Bridge. "No one else is reacting like that," he said, and he gave Blondell a rundown of his anxiety and depression problems.

Blondell was nonplussed. "First, let's get one thing straight: You cannot truly believe that you are the only one here who feels destroyed by this. If you do, you're nuts."

"I know."

"No, not that kind of nuts. I mean you're nuts if you think people aren't struggling. And I don't just mean the kids in the back." Blondell paused and gently wrapped her hand around Ash's wrist. "Ash, do you honestly think you're the only one?"

"Yes," Ash said, with a straight face.

Blondell opened her mouth to speak again, only to be stopped by a splash of voices. They were almost back at the Bridge.

"We are so going to have a conversation later," Blondell said, smiling gently. "You're just lucky this ship isn't bigger. You can't get away from me."

Echo, bless her, barely glanced at Ash and Blondell as they walked back in. Anton did stare, his face twisted with anger until he caught the look on Ash's face.

Ash and Blondell walked up to Alexis and Daniel, and were joined by Sierra and Anton. Tidus was also there, and he was projecting Jameson through that weird eyeball camera. Evidently, the group had been discussing ship logistics and reviewing the results of other people's ventures into the *Redemption*. They had gathered around a paper-thin tablet and Tidus expertly maneuvered the device to manipulate a diagram of the ship, labeling items as they were discussed. How he could concentrate on the tablet and ignore the image of Jameson projecting from his eye was completely beyond Ash.

"So here's the deal, Ash," said Tidus, jabbing at the tablet. "We've checked out the entire first floor—"

"First floor?" Ash and Blondell asked at the same time.

"There's more than that?" asked Alexis.

"There is. A lot," said Daniel. He leaned over and poked the tablet and, pressing a tab at the bottom of the map. The outline of the ship held constant, but the internal walls, hallways, doors and labels all shifted. "Anton and I got about halfway through the first floor when we found the tablet with the coordinates."

"Where'd you find it, anyway?" asked Ash, trying to ignore the rumbling sensation in his stomach as his anxiety attack cooled down. In response, Daniel pointed at a small room, located in the rear of the ship.

"This room, marked 'utilities.' We just started opening doors."

"Us too," said Alexis. "That's how we found our tablet – something called the Junction Room?"

"Junction Room?" said Daniel, looking puzzled.

"It's a central hub," chimed in Jameson, his voice sounding tinny from the projection. "Sort of like a back-up Bridge. All the wires and cables of the ship more or less run there, and it serves as secondary access. Easy repair, easy control. And it's a secondary power source; you could see out the window and into space, right? That provides solar power."

"How the hell is that enough light?" asked Ash. "You couldn't see anything in that room if not for the lighting."

"Uhh . . . have you ever heard of solar power," said Tidus, enunciating every syllable as if he was speaking to a stupid child. Jameson jumped in.

"The technology has been around in some form or fashion since the 1860s, but really took off in the—"

"We know what solar power is, you dip," snapped Anton.

Jameson held up his hands.

"Just making sure," he said. Ash couldn't help but notice the slight smile spreading across his face, and he had to work to suppress his own.

"Anyway," said Echo, picking that moment to join the conversation. "How many floors did you see?"

"We never made it that far," said Anton. "We got about halfway through the first floor, where we are now."

"We had the other half," said Ash. "Did anyone have the second floor?"

"Us," said Sierra, a mischievous smile spreading across her face. "We got bored."

Miranda nodded. "You should see the scientific equipment on this thing! I've never experienced anything like it."

"The two of us are science nerds," Sierra said.

Anton rolled his eyes at the exuberance, but Ash smiled gently.

"You gotta explain what some of that stuff was," said Miranda to Sierra.

"Okay, there's a science lab," said Ash. In his mind, a visual was forming of the ship, its composition and capabilities. "Can I grab that?" Ash gestured to the tablet.

Daniel held up his football-sized hands. "By all means," he said.

Ash took the tablet and swung it in his direction. *It's really not all that different than an iPad,* he thought, as he began to manipulate the screen to the second floor and cycle through the various screens. Information appeared about the various rooms as he poked the tablet. In addition to the lab facilities, there was also Engineering (which was massive, taking up all three stories and the back third of the ship), the Armory (the mention of which completely captured Anton's attention), ten more dorm rooms (making twenty total) and . . .

"Kitchens. That's good," said Ash, zooming in and cycling through a series of pictures. "I was starting to get hungry. This stuff looks . . . pretty professional." A shift behind him and Ash realized that, for the first time in hours, two members of the Back Brigade looked connected to reality: Exodus, one of the screaming girls and her friend, whose hand she held stared attentively at the rest of the group. Ash wasn't the only one who noticed the girls' sudden interest.

"That's interesting . . ." said Echo, her voice trailing off. She walked over to the rear of the Bridge and began an earnest conversation with the two young women. Before long, both were doing something that Ash had seen neither do during their entire brief trip together: smiling. Like a fog clearing, the mood lifted on the ship. Some of the crew was starting to come out of their shells.

"Looks like we got our team shrink," Anton said, jerking his head toward the Back Brigade. "Maybe that will snap some of these rocks back into reality."

"Christ, what's your problem?" said Alexis.

That surprised Ash, who had been staring at Blondell, hoping she wouldn't take the opportunity to let the group know about his attack from a few moments ago.

"Seriously, what the hell is wrong with you?" Alexis' words were clipped and tinged with venom. "We're in a spaceship, in the middle of nowhere, with only the faintest idea of how to fly it and not a clue about how we get home? Maybe drink a nice glass of 'shut the hell up' for a little bit?"

Ash gaped openly at Alexis, who stared directly at Anton, issuing a challenge with her eyes.

If Alexis expected Anton to be chagrined, she was wrong.

47

Anton smirked back.

"Hey girl, don't hate the man who speaks the truth." He gestured with his head, toward the Back Brigade. "These folks aren't gonna make it."

"'Girl?'" Blondell snapped. "'Make it?' Look, none of us are gonna make it to the next stop if we can't at least avoid snipping at each other. Give them some space. We can't all handle this as well as you." The edge added to the "you" was unmistakable.

Still, Anton's smirk remained. He backed up, still facing the group, and put his hands defensively in front of his chest.

"It's all good, Blondie," he said, staring definitely at Blondell, a smirk turning up the corners of his lips.

Blondell matched his stare with weighted eyes and a scowl, holding the silence for ten awkward seconds. "Blondie?" she finally spat.

"Yeah, Blondie, like . . . hair," retorted Anton, snickering. Blondell tilted her head downward and pointed at her flowing dark hair.

"Does this look blond?" Her voice was heavy, and Anton snickered again.

"Your name is," he spluttered.

"Yeah, the dark-skinned girl with a name that makes you think of blond hair, I get it," Blondell replied, inching forward toward Anton, whose haughty attitude was starting to evaporate. "I definitely thought we evolved past this nonsense." Blondell's arms folded across her chest as Anton defensively lifted his palms into the air.

"Don't blame me. I just want to separate the weak from the strong." The haughty expression had returned.

"Are you for real?" Alexis barked.

Anton didn't answer. Instead, he turned, walked away, put an arm around Sia and Pike, and started talking rapidly.

"He's fun," Ash said.

The group giggled.

"Let's move on. Nothing we can do about him for now. Daniel, what else you got?"

Daniel, who had watched the exchange with a bemused

air of detachment, looked back down at his tablet. "Third floor. We haven't been there yet. As best I can tell, it's different than the other two."

Daniel tabbed over to the third floor and Ash discovered that he was right. The first two floors had various lines and labels indicating rooms, hallways, stations, computer units and more. The third floor had nothing, save for the relatively brief outlines of Engineering and the Junction Room, which ran the entire height of the ship. There was also no label to indicate what they were looking at.

"Storage?" asked Alexis.

"Doubt it," responded Jameson. "Why would a ship this big need so much blank space?"

At that, Sierra started loudly humming a Taylor Swift tune, which set off pangs of homesickness in Ash. A few odd looks later, and Sierra was quiet.

"You're right. This is weird," Ash said, as he looked over at a computer on the main, center console. "Still, we're almost out of time at this point. We're nearly at the coordinates."

"How much longer?" questioned Tidus. Ash strained his neck to see, but from his angle, couldn't properly read the display.

"I can't tell, but it should be soon. Alexis, can you get up and read it?"

"No," Alexis said, so quickly that Ash was taken aback. "That's your station, dude. You take care of it."

"I'm good," said Ash quietly. The mere thought of stepping onto that center station made him sick. That kind of fear was the last thing he wanted to show anyone on the crew. Alexis, realizing she hit a nerve that shouldn't have been touched, climbed out of her seat.

"It's okay, I got it." She sped past Ash, brushing a hand on his shoulder as she did so. Ash nearly recoiled at the unexpected touch and tried not to react as a chill travelled up his spine. "Hey, you weren't kidding. About three minutes till we are there."

That got everyone moving. Ash was the first to stand, and in a loud voice said, "Okay, places everybody! Get back to your stations." Ash suspected that he would, eventually, be able to accept leadership. It was something he would suffer through. But he couldn't accept the trappings of it. That meant formally accepting responsibility, and that was an illusion Ash could live without. "Anton, can you be ready with the weapons?"

"Aye-aye, Captain," Anton responded.

Ash tried to detect sarcasm but couldn't find any. He moved on. "Radar, you got anything yet?"

"Not yet, Ash," said Radar. There was a flurry of clicking as Radar pounded away at the keyboard near him. "I may be wrong though. I really don't know how to use this thing yet."

"All good, Radar," Ash said gently. "Just keep at it. You'll get there. Blondell, any idea what you're doing?" By design, the quip cut the rapidly building tension in the room, and everyone laughed, even Anton and his followers. Ash thought he even heard a small snicker from the Back Brigade, which brought a smile to his face. A glance over his shoulder confirmed that a few of them were, in fact, laughing. This earned him a warm look from Echo.

"I'd probably feel better if my head didn't hurt so much!" retorted Blondell, earning more laughter, even from Ash.

Alexis gripped her controls in preparation to resume control of the ship. "Almost there," said Blondell.

All things considered, this really could be a lot worse, thought Ash.

Alexis turned around one of the displays on the center platform and counted down. "Five . . . four . . . three . . . two . . . one . . ." With the slightest jolt of deceleration, the ship stopped moving. Alexis pulled on the joystick and levelled the ship off.

Ash wasn't sure what to anticipate, but he thought he had a reasonably good idea of what not to expect. His best guess was that there would be nothing, leaving plenty of questions as to what they were supposed to do next. He supposed that there was the possibility of finding other planets, asteroids, or, in the worst case scenario, a distortion in space, followed by a blinding white light and oblivion. What he saw instead was gray and large, with a cylindrical body, two wings and an easy glide, floating like it belonged exactly in the spot it currently occupied.

It was another ship.

In the time it took Ash to process that thought and stifle his shock, Tidus jerked with surprise, reached for his ear, and jabbed his computer screen. Instantly, another voice took up all the air in the room. It was loud, deep and confident.

"Hello, strangers! This is Captain Benjamin Valliant, of the U.G. *Remedy*. Come in, *Redemption*."

CHAPTER SIX

It took Ash hearing that sentence three times before he snapped out of his reverie and whipped his head toward Tidus.

"Uh . . . say something back!"

Tidus jabbed at his computer, growing more frantic as he flung through various screens. "Uhh . . . the interface isn't where it should be!" He pounded buttons faster.

Ash walked over to Tidus' screen and took a deep breath. As Tidus kept flinging through the screen in front of him, Ash gently put a hand on his shoulder.

"Hang on. Let's go slow," he said, before letting go.

Tidus nodded nervously and took a deep breath as well. Two finger flicks later and he found the "respond" button. Tidus pressed it, looked at Ash, and nodded. Now it was Ash's turn.

"Hello, Captain!" he said, trying to sound casual. "Uh . . . this is Asher Maddox, of the *Redemption*. Apparently. How are you doing today?" A friendly laughter followed.

"I sounded like that once too, Asher Maddox. Tell your Coms Officer to hit the 'full-screen' button." Ash looked at Tidus who was, once again, flipping through his computer display at a pace too rapid to read. "It's on screen three," Valliant added.

Chagrined, with a sheepish look on his face, Tidus flipped to the appropriate screen and hit the correct button.

A face materialized, translucent and three dimensional,

in the front window of the ship. The man that appeared was clearly the Captain of the *Remedy*. He was straight-backed and broad shouldered, with a patrician face and immaculately coifed sleek black hair. Ash was instantly intimidated. Behind the man, a crew moved fluidly and efficiently. They stared at their screens, expertly manipulating the controls in front of them. More to the point, Ash noticed that they wore military-style uniforms – without the neon nametags that might as well have been a flashing sign screaming, "We're new here!" Ash turned around and tried to repress his own embarrassment at the rag-tag mix of teenagers standing behind him; only a few had the vaguest idea of what they were doing, and at least two were openly gawking at the screen in which Valliant's visage had appeared.

"Hello, *Redemption!*" said Valliant in a booming voice. "Welcome to your day one!"

"Our what now?" said Ash.

"Your first day on the ship," responded Valliant, putting his hands behind his back and somehow managing to make himself look larger. "It's okay. We were there once. You get used to it. Running the ship isn't as hard as you might think."

"Oh. Well, that's good," said Ash. "Maybe you can tell us what's going on? We all just got here . . . and we have no idea how."

Valliant nodded and smiled. His teeth were enormous and pearly white. "Sounds like what happened to us three months ago!"

The statement elicited various gasps – and, from the Back Brigade, a terror-filled shriek. Ash tried to keep a straight face but failed, and his jaw dropped.

"Three months?" cried Ash. "You've been at this for that long?"

Valliant chortled, like he was talking to a small child who had said something unintentionally adorable. "Time flies when you are stopping Spades!"

As soon as the sentence left Valliant's mouth, Ash perked up, his ears practically becoming erect, like a puppy who had been told it was time for a treat. The way that Valliant said "Spades," like it was some sort of magical element, made Ash pause. He looked over his shoulder to see if the rest of the crew had had the same reaction, and they had. Alexis folded her arms across her chest and stared to the side, not looking at Valliant. Blondell froze while bending over to tie her shoe, like the muscles in her back had seized midway to the ground, while Jameson, who had just entered the Bridge, froze, his hands locked firmly on his hips. Even Anton was caught by surprise, his mouth ajar and eyebrows tilted toward his nose.

"Spades?" Ash asked, trying to project authority that he didn't feel.

"Spades," Valliant said. "You mean you aren't there yet?"

"Aren't where yet?" asked Alexis. "Can you stop talking in riddles, please?"

Again, Valliant smiled, exposing his white teeth. "Of course. I apologize. Let's start at the basics. It's 2180."

The ship exploded into chaos as group people questions at the same time. Ash, his anxiety rising, said nothing; he merely held onto the railing in front of him.

"How?" someone cried.

"What was that?" Valliant asked, leaning closer to the screen, appearing close enough for Ash to touch him.

"How are we in 2180?" Ash asked. "Last night, I was asleep in my bed, on Earth, and it was—"

"The past, I know," Valliant said, pulling back to his last posture. "That was our story too. All of us here woke up three months ago, everyone 34-38 years old." Ash turned around and looked at the rest of his crew, and realized immediately that he wasn't the only one who looked surprised at the last statement.

"We're not that old," he said, and he turned back to the group again, gesturing to give them permission to state their ages.

When they were done, the youngest was sixteen. At twenty, Ash was on the older end of the spectrum.

It was Valliant's turn to be surprised. "Interesting. Very interesting," he said, stroking his chin. "We woke up in a similar position to you – on the ship with no real idea of how we got here." He gestured behind him. "After some time, the crew and I were able to access our computer files and figure out what was going on."

Ash spun around, ready to bark out orders to Sierra, but Valliant beat him to it. "You there, the dark-skinned girl with the dark hair, follow my lead."

Sierra's face soured for an instant, her confused expression morphing into a scowl. Valliant, either not noticing or not caring, relayed a series of file locations, and with every keystroke, Sierra's face grew brighter. Soon she was practically bouncing in her seat with excitement.

"Ash, this is it! This is everything! Our mission, the works!" Sierra's hands flew like a blur across the keyboard. She came to an abrupt stop, looking as if she had just seen a whale grow wings and fly out of the ocean.

"Ash . . . Valliant . . . huh?" she said. "This isn't right. At least, I don't see how this can be right?"

Difficult though it was, Ash tore his attention away from Valliant and walked over to Sierra. "What did you find?" He leaned toward Sierra's display before realizing the source of her confusion. On Sierra's screen was a series of text, with a header that read, "Objective(s)."

The first objective, "Destroy enemy ship," had a check mark next to it. The second, "Obtain Spades vaccine," had a blank spot next to it. Ash paused before looking back to Valliant.

"It says we destroyed the enemy ship and now need to get the Spades vaccine." Valliant nodded.

"That's what I anticipated. Our computers say the same. Earlier, they only contained the first objective. I realized we would see you when our computers alerted us to the fact that you killed the original Spades carrier. Well done!"

"Uh . . . thanks?" Ash said, his head still swimming. "But what does that mean? We're done?"

"No, not at all," Valliant said, sighing. "Here's what I know and here's what I don't. Around 2030, Earth had a series of cataclysmic climate-related events. The planet was devastated, only to reach new peaks of civilization, technological advancement, and peace. The U.G.—"

"The what?" said Alexis.

Ash waved her off, noticing the confusion spread on the faces of many of the crew members.

"The Unity Government," said Valliant. "The Unity Government, formed the same year as the Infinity Corporation—"

Ash held out a hand to stop Alexis from interrupting again.

"Was created to reverse the nearly cataclysmic effects of global climate change. They succeeded and, after a recovery period, the Earth recovered and eclipsed its former glory. Then came Spades." Valliant went silent, his fingers flying over a control panel identical with one that sat onboard the *Redemption*. "I'm sending you a recording. One moment."

Valliant faded from view, leaving only empty space in front of them. After a moment, the window transformed into a shaky, three dimensional view of the ocean. However, unlike the transmission with Valliant, this view stretched up to the ceiling of the Bridge. The camera shook, as if the photographer was too excited to hold still.

Valliant's voice projected over the recording. "This is our first contact with Spades." From the center of the ceiling – the highest part of the sky recorded by the cameraman – a large, flaming ship appeared. "We believe that the ship attacked as part of a suicide mission."

Ash's mouth hung open as he examined the flaming ship in question. It was large, unfamiliar and certainly alien.

Before the eyes of the stunned crew, the alien vessel blazed across the sky before descending toward the ocean at a rapid rate. It began a diagonal path, bending, twirling and arcing through mid-air as it did so. Alexis gently extended a hand toward the crashing craft, as if to catch and save it, but the hologram simply molded around her fingers and continued its brutal, final descent.

The alien ship smashed into the water. No water sprays were emitted; instead, a harsh fire erupted from the crash, shooting flaming debris and golden-black fire into an otherwise unspoiled evening sky. The explosion was unlike any Ash had ever seen. It didn't mushroom like a nuclear weapon or detonate in an irregular pattern. Instead, the blast was perfectly symmetrical and circular, racing across the ocean and toward the photographer, who shrieked in panic, jabbering in a language that sounded Asian. Suddenly, the flames dissipated, leaving only shocked silence in its wake.

"That was when the terrorists crashed into the Pacific Ocean," intoned Valliant. "The date was July 20, 2180 – about one month from today."

"The terrorists . . . you mean the ones we destroyed?"

Valliant nodded curtly. "Precisely. Unfortunately, that clearly didn't work."

"How can you tell?" Ash asked.

It was Jameson who answered. "Because we are still here. Had it worked, time would have been altered, and we'd have very different instructions than those that say that there is more to do. Also, the footage we saw would have been altered from what Captain Valliant originally discovered."

Valliant nodded toward Jameson. "The young man is right. We're still here and the recording is unchanged. Which means that either our computers are wrong about the original ship being destroyed, or a second ship still attacks Earth with Spades. Either way, a contingency plan has been prepared. Your new objective is to find the vaccine for Spades."

Valliant went silent. Ash shook his head in disbelief. He felt a weight burning across his shoulders, tension wrapping itself across his neck and back, a feeling not unfamiliar to his bouts with depression.

Valliant's face disappeared again, replaced by a map of the Pacific Ocean, with a large symbol of a spade at what Ash assumed was the crash site. "The ship crashed here, roughly 100 miles southeast of Japan. Spades spread from there." A series of spade symbols began to expand and multiply across Southeast Asia, extending to Russia and through every nation in the Pacific. The view zoomed out. The Spades continued to devour everything in their path: Australia,

57

Korea, China, and eventually into the United States. Alaska and the western half of the country disappeared under a wave of blackness. The camera completed zooming out, revealing a map of the world, with only western Europe and the eastern United States free from the disease. South America, Africa, Asia and Central America were all blacked out. Spade icons covered the map like a locust-infected field.

"Most of the planet has devolved into a no-man's land. The disease is not instantly deadly. Its victims can usually survive for a month. It is highly contagious, communicable across air, bodily fluids, you name it. Some of the more modern parts of the world were able to build up bulwarks against the disease, but those can only last so long. Currently, in the future which I came from, roughly half of Earth's population is dead. Of those surviving, another half has the disease. Less than two billion people remain unaffected. Eight billion are dead or dying. There is no known cure, no known vaccine. Industry and commerce have ground to a halt. Earth has a few surviving modern pockets of civilization, which is where our ship came from. But, at the current rate, barring a miracle, human life is expected to cease within the next five years."

No one spoke, no one moved. The only sound was the gentle vibrations of the engine. The heavy silence lasted for a solid thirty seconds, as the unbearable heaviness of the collapse of modern day civilization – humanity – fell upon the *Redemption*.

When, at last, he found his voice, Ash spoke. "What do we do?" His voice sounded like a whisper caked in gravel.

"Stop Spades," said Valliant decisively.

"Yes, I get that, but how?" Ash asked.

Valliant gestured back to Sierra. "Young lady, are you exploring the computer files related to the secondary objective of developing a Spades cure?"

Sierra didn't even bother to look up. "Way ahead of you, Valliant. Ash, we'll talk, but this has everything we need. Mission coordinates, ship tutorials, the works."

Valliant nodded approvingly. "I see you are in good hands there. As you now know, Spades came from space. So does the cure. Space travel has come a long way since your time. Thanks to the combined efforts of the Unity Government and Infinity Corporation, we can now travel great distances across the galaxy. At the same time, scientific progress has advanced to the point where we are able to detect and locate the specific compounds of any disease. As such, it would seem that our job is to travel through space to collect pieces for a vaccine."

"So why not look on Earth for the cure?" That question came from Blondell. As she finished, Valliant disappeared and was replaced by what appeared to be a crudely drawn spade. Upon closer inspection, Ash realized that he was actually looking at a digital record.

"This is a molecular examination of Spades," Valliant said. "If you have even the most basic understanding of science—" Valliant continued over Alexis' snort, "Then you understand that no other molecule on Earth has this unique spade shape. Hence its name. To answer your question, tall girl . . . "

It was Blondell's turn to raise her eyebrows and look disgusted. "We can't find the cure on Earth because the disease is not of Earth. It's from somewhere in space."

Jameson spoke next. "This is, without a doubt, the stupidest plan I have ever heard in my life." He did not even attempt to hide his antipathy.

"Why?" Valliant asked, eyes narrowing.

"Well, for starters, why not send a crew from their own time period? Why waste all this time on time travel?"

"And how did we even travel through time to begin with?" snapped Blondell. "Time travel sure as hell wasn't a thing in my home."

Valliant sighed deeply before speaking, staring at Jameson. "My dear boy, that wasn't an option," began Valliant. Valliant again disappeared, replaced by the map of Spades showing the spread of the disease across the world. It remained stationary for only a moment before zooming in on Washington, D.C. Here, Ash noticed something which he hadn't before: small spades icons. "No isolation zone is foolproof; the U.G. has been able to keep much of Spades out. They are usually able to stop a flare-up before it becomes major, but keeping a disease like Spades out of an area is completely impossible. More to the point, not only is the disease highly communicable, but it has a long incubation period, followed by a rapid decline. Diagnosis during this incubation period is imprecise, which means that you can't tell who has Spades and who does not."

Jameson nodded. "Okay, I get that. There's no such thing as a perfect determination of who has Spades and who doesn't, so the U.G. had to leave modern times to find people they knew didn't have it."

Valliant, who had reappeared in front of them, nodded.

Alexis went next. "Are you going to be searching for the vaccine as well?"

Valliant shook his head. "I'm afraid not. We have other plans."

Alexis gaped. "Other plans? What could possibly be more important than hunting down this vaccine?"

Valliant locked his hands behind his waist. "Watching your back," he said coolly. "Or perhaps I am mistaken in assuming that the fluctuations in your shield's power came from an attack?"

The crew of the *Redemption* was silent.

Valliant continued. "During our three months here, we were unable to determine the exact location of the Zero Patient ship – the ship which contained the Spades virus. We patrolled the likely areas of its location, based on the information from the Unity Government, but have found nothing so far. Meanwhile, we have been consistently harassed by another ship, an invisible one that is only briefly viewable on our radar. Your arrival, and the configuration of your ship, including its docks, shuttle bays and scientific equipment, makes it clear that you were designed to find the Spades cure. Our ship, which is more weapons-heavy, is a warship. We're going to hunt down that ship which attacked you. Unless, of course, you have any better ideas?"

Alexis, chagrined, said nothing.

The discussion of the ship's equipment caused another question to surface in Ash's mind, but before he could ask, a klaxon erupted to Valliant's left. There was a commotion, and Valliant looked off-screen and barked a few orders that Ash couldn't follow.

"Ash, I'm afraid we have to go," Valliant said. "We found something." His voice showed more excitement than it had in their entire brief conversation. "There's more to tell you, and I'm sure you have more questions. We'll communicate with you soon. For now, go to the closest location, and find the pieces of the vaccine." With his last sentence, Valliant made a fist in front of his own face. Abruptly, he disappeared. The window returned to a view of space.

As Valliant faded from view, the *Remedy,* located directly in front of the *Redemption,* also changed. The ship banked hard to the left and up. With the acceleration of a bullet, it disappeared, shooting forward, leaving only a bright white scar across space.

There was silence. No one moved on the *Redemption.*

Ash spoke first, in a desperate effort to get his crew moving again. "Sierra, what have you got?" he asked. He kept his voice low in recognition of the booming silence occupying the *Redemption,* yet his words still sounded like a cannon firing.

Sierra, who had been gawking at the screen, abruptly began typing again. "Working on that," she said. "I think I figured out how to grab the map coordinates and determine where we are going first. Looks like we have some kind of advanced computing capabilities and Valliant sent us a few locations for retrieving these vaccine pieces. Give me a few minutes, and I should have our next location locked in."

Ash nodded and looked to the rest of the crew. He held his hands extended from his body, palms facing upward. "So . . . what do we do now?" he asked.

Pandemonium broke out. More than half a dozen voices erupted almost as one.

"Go get the first part of the vaccine!" yelled Anton.

Alexis, Pike and Sia reiterated the cry.

On the other side were Blondell, Tidus and Echo, who were rapidly shaking their heads.

"Not yet, Ash," said Blondell. "I get what they are saying.

I really do. But we need to give this some thought here. We aren't in some insane rush. We have time."

"Not a lot," chimed Sierra. "I'm looking at our pathway. I think it's going to take us some time to get to these destinations. They are all pretty far away from each other. I just can't tell how far." Sierra looked extremely disappointed at her own failure.

"I see it!" said Blondell, staring intently at her computer. "She's right, Ash. Our first stop isn't far, relatively speaking, but our second one will take longer. Then, we've got to haul it back to the Moon. If we only have a month, we need to move it."

"Hold it," said Jameson "Ash, you can't go yet. There's something important you are missing, and I am not comfortable with the speed we are moving at."

Ash looked around the Bridge, which had quieted. "Jameson, there're a lot of things we don't understand. And it doesn't sound like we have a lot of time to find answers. Can't we just talk while we travel?" Ash waited for the rest of the group to inevitably chime in. However, they were listening to a loud discussion that had broken out between Sierra and Blondell.

"Why did you have that information and I didn't?" shouted a visibly shaken Sierra. "We have the same data! I should have had that too."

Blondell tilted her head, confused. "Beats me. It was on my screen." She gestured to her equipment, specifically pointing at a glowing "ETA" display. "We're working on different interfaces here . . . I don't think this is anything to get upset about."

"That's crap," said Sierra. "That's absolute crap. I should have that too. Why am I not on that? Whatever the hell that is?" Blondell gestured to her computer and spoke again, trying to keep the sharpness in her voice to a minimum.

"I don't know, Em—"

"It is Sierra, and you can get it right," said the increasingly strained young woman, making Anton smile.

Echo, observing the situation, cautiously entered the space between the two girls and extended her arms. "Hang on. This has nothing to do with the equipment. Sierra, we can all completely understand why you are upset, but it's just a computer—"

Sierra slammed her fists on the railing in front of her. "It is not just a computer!" she said, her voice rising an octave.

"Mine isn't even a computer!" Blondell said, her temper finally cracking, veins in her neck starting to bulge.

At the mention of the word "computer," Ash felt an icy wave wash over him. A thought which had been tickling the back of his mind during his brief conversation with Valliant was returning again. *Equipment,* thought Ash. *Equipment. But what about equipment?*

"What the hell are you talking about?" said Sierra.

Ash stared harder at her, trying to put his thoughts together. He saw Echo walk over to Blondell, joined by Alexis, in an effort to defuse the situation. Anton flashed a twisted smile at Sierra, nodding supportively, while Ash made eye contact with Daniel. Daniel had his arms folded across his chest and the slightest hint of a smile across his face. Ash tilted his head to the side.

"What?" he said. "What are you smiling about?" Ash walked calmly to Daniel, whose eyes were twinkling. "No one smiles like that for no reason. What's going on?"

"It's not even a computer," Daniel repeated. "She's right. Sure doesn't look like any computer I've ever seen." Daniel put a special emphasis on the word "I," and Ash understood.

Why do we all have different equipment?

His eyes met Daniel's. Daniel kept right on smiling. Behind Ash, despite the growing cacophony of an argument caused by one of the most unique situations ever faced by any member of humanity, he heard a laugh. He turned around and saw Jameson, looking relaxed, and with a knowing smile spread across his face. Ash returned it, as in his mind, the puzzle pieces clicked into place.

"You knew?" he asked Jameson.

"Yes. Figured it out when you, Alexis and I were walking the ship, and the two of you said you couldn't wait to get back to Earth. The way you said it gave it away. The sentence made no sense otherwise."

Ash's eyes narrowed, pondering the implications, and nodded grimly.

Jameson gestured to the rest of the crew. "Let them know, Captain," he said.

Ash shook his head briskly and looked at Daniel. "It was your question that made it connect. You ask."

In response, Daniel used his head to gesture to the rest of the crew, and Ash understood.

"Hold it!" Ash shouted. The arguing stopped.

Everyone looked at Ash, who was looking at Daniel, who was looking at Jameson with a wide-toothy grin.

"What year are you from, buddy?" Daniel asked Jameson. The bizarre question cut off any last sound from the voices of the *Redemption's* occupants. They hadn't been together long, but they knew from Jameson and Daniel's facial expressions that there had to be a good reason – a potentially earth-shattering reason – for such a bizarre question to be asked.

"2163. You?"

"1990," Daniel said, grinning broadly. "Ash?"

"2018. And I'm gonna guess that there isn't a single one of us on this ship who was born the same year."

Not for the first time, and not for the last, the crew of the *Redemption* stared at each other in disbelief, each with the same question on their minds: *When are you from?*

CHAPTER SEVEN

Silence held the *Redemption*. The group looked from one
to another, attempting to figure out if this was a bad joke
or if their time travel had truly brought some of them from
further away than others.

It was Blondell who spoke first. "All this strangeness, the
weird equipment . . ."

"The equipment was made for us individually," said
Jameson. "Which implies intentionality."

"Say what?" said Anton, who looked truly terrified and
three shades paler than he had a few moments ago.

"We're here for a reason," said Ash, leaning on a metal
railing for support. "None of us were randomly selected." He
looked at the Back Brigade. "Each one of us was selected for
a specific skill, with equipment customized for our needs
and from our individual time periods." As the words left his
mouth, Ash realized that he was also talking about himself.
Every one of us has a role to play, he thought, pinching the
Bridge of his nose, before the pain and anxiety that was
building behind his eyes exploded from his face.

Anton gestured to the Back Brigade, attempting to
shrink into the gunmetal walls behind them. "You too," he
said, with a surprising touch of gentleness in his voice. "You
guys, too."

Ash stared, momentarily surprised, before looking at the
rest of the crew. "Valliant was right. We have a mission and
we'll need your help."

After a handful of heartbeats, a member of the Back

Brigade spoke up. It was a short boy, all limbs, with a pock-marked face covered in acne. "Nope." He said. "Noooooooooope," and with an extra-long emphasis on the O, he bolted out of the room, running at top speed down the corridor that led away from the Bridge.

"Crap," Ash said. "Uhh ... at least one of them is moving. Echo, you got this?"

"Way ahead of you!" She chased after the fleeing teen. "Hey, come back!" Her voice ricocheted down the walls of the hallway.

Under different circumstances, Ash would have been happy to have shaken the Back Brigade out of their trance-like serenity. However, it was clear that the first member to speak had given the rest ideas. Single file, most of the group turned and followed their screaming friend down the hallway, remaining silent, exerting as little energy as possible as they left the Bridge. Only three others stayed behind, evidently still too scared to move. They simply stared vaguely at Anton.

"That went well," Alexis chirped, her voice warbling.

Alexis, like Ash, was leaning on the railing in front of her for support. Both of her hands were wrapped around the barrier with a grip so tight she looked ready to wrench the metal from its moorings.

"I think we can all sympathize," Ash said, gesturing to Alexis' hands.

Alexis looked down and jerked her head backward when she discovered her hands attached to the railing. She released her grip and blinked.

Silence spread like a metastasizing virus across the Bridge, smothering noise and hope. Ash, for his part, tried to keep as still as could be, fearing that even the slightest movement would set off a fresh wave of terror. He wasn't the only one trying to avoid moving. Seeking out Alexis, Ash found her, eyes bulging and fingers trembling while she clung to the railing.

Ash walked over to her and touched her arm. "You okay?"

"Super. Super. Been a fun day."

Ash resisted the urge to laugh and made a noise that sounded like an awkward splutter. "Me too." He paused. "We'll figure a way out of this."

"Really?" There were unmistakable traces of skepticism and fear in her voice.

"Yeah, I have no idea," Ash said, and that made Alexis laugh.

"Well, thank you for your honesty, at least," she said.

Following Ash's lead, the crew began to slip out of their trance and speak to each other.

Alexis climbed into her pilot's seat and Ash stood beside her. When they spoke again, it was in their normal voices.

"We know the next step," Ash said. "We need to get to that first location. Figure out how long it will take."

"That part I get," Alexis said. "But how do we get there?"

Ash looked at Alexis as if she had three heads. "You know what I mean."

"I have no idea what you mean," Ash retorted.

"Ash, think about this. There's twenty of us, maybe a little more than half are functional. We're in a spaceship, in case you forgot. That's something that should take years of training. We've been here for a few hours."

Ash responded by shaking his head emphatically, like a puppy trying to dry off after a bath. "Alexis, whatever is going on here, it was designed for us. You're right. Flying a spaceship should be hard, but clearly this was designed to be easy. After all, we did get out of that nasty fight a little ways back. We did blow us up some alien terrorists."

"Ash. Think this through. This ship isn't a computer mouse. You can't just point and click. We need a plan. We need a fully-functional crew. And we need training, which is going to be hard without any sort of expert."

Ash breathed deeply and collected his thoughts. "Yeah." He paused and smiled bitterly. "Good thing I'm a trained space captain."

"You're the best we got," Alexis said. She smiled sweetly. "Besides, you did okay last time."

Ash snorted and realized that much of the remaining crew was listening to him.

"Does anyone want to talk about what we just figured out?" Blondell asked. Her question was greeted with a long silence before Ash responded.

"Yes, yes, and hell yes," he said. "But we have more immediate problems. Jameson, can we actually run this thing?"

Jameson inhaled deeply. "I think so," he said. "Blondell and I were just talking, and we think we can manage the ship okay. The computer systems onboard are clearly compensating for our lack of knowledge about space flight. With enough practice and their assistance, we'll live."

At the mention of computers, Ash turned to Sierra, who seemed to have perked up. "Sierra, you've been playing with the computers, what you got?" he asked.

"It's nothing I've seen before . . . and that's why it's so upsetting."

"Why are you taking this so personally?" Blondell asked.

"Stop. We're not doing this again," Ash said, noticing Blondell's lips thinning. "After all, arguments can only lead us to mind-blowing realizations so many times."

Fortunately for Ash, the entire crew chuckled, and the tension drained from Blondell's face. The only person who didn't laugh was Alexis, who merely stared at Ash, a mixture of curiosity and admiration on her face.

"Sorry," Sierra said. "I'm not used to this."

"What do you mean?" questioned Jameson.

Sierra stuttered and took a moment to gather her thoughts. "I . . . I get computers. I've seen computers, and I know their systems, their logic, how they move, everything. What I don't understand is how to interface this with Blondell's equipment, and I think that's something I need to do."

"Okay, well, take your time," Ash said.

The crew looked at him, surprised.

"I thought we were in a rush," said Blondell.

"We are," said Ash. "But not in a rush to die." He waved a hand across his body, shaking it for emphasis with every word. "We can't go anywhere. Not until we figure this out." Much to his relief, Ash saw most of those assembled in front of him nodding, with Jameson nodding the hardest. "So here's the plan. First, Sierra, review those files that Valliant helped us find. Jameson, you and Daniel walk the ship. Get us a better understanding of what the hell we are working with here."

"On it," said Jameson.

"I'm with him," said Daniel. He marched over to his station and started equipping himself with a thick utility belt. "I'm not sure how late 1980s tools are gonna do on a 2180 ship, but let's find out!"

Jameson briskly walked out of the Bridge, and Daniel slapped his back heavily before following him. Ash stifled a laugh as he watched Jameson stumble with the force of Daniel's massive hands.

"Sierra, you—"

"Work on the ship's computers and figure out how to interface with Blondell's station. Yeah. Got it."

"One more thing."

"What?" Sierra asked sullenly.

Ash walked up to her computer. He had noticed before that it looked similar to what he had worked with at home . . . before all of this had started.

"When are you from?"

Sierra made eye contact with Ash; her eyes large, brown, and swimming with tears. "2039."

"Okay. You won't know much more than I do, but you understand this equipment. I don't. Help me find out what happened to our planet. Because you don't know much more than I do." Sierra nodded and swallowed hard before turning back to her equipment. Ash walked back to the center of the Bridge.

"Blondell, can you figure out where we are going and what we are heading into?"

At this, Blondell nodded vigorously. "Yes. Yes, absolutely." She turned on her heel and walked briskly to her station, leaving Ash and Alexis standing together.

"You can fly this thing?" Ash asked, trying to keep his tone level and banish the note of wonderment. He failed and Alexis smiled again.

"Yeah," she said, tossing her hair in a mock Valley girl way and adding an inflection to her voice to match. "You know, between going to the mall and stuff." Ash full-on laughed.

"I haven't heard a voice like that in years!" he said. "Which reminds me. When?"

"2001."

Ash nodded, and a corner of his mouth turned up involuntarily.

"Well, I've always liked older women."

For the second time in the past few hours, Alexis punched him.

"Ow! Dammit, stop that!"

"Then stop . . . oh, never mind," Alexis said, and they both laughed loudly again, only to stop when Ash caught Anton out of the corner of his eye.

"Now that's interesting," he said quietly, looking in Anton's direction.

Alexis turned around as well, and saw Anton, chatting with Pike, Sia, Tidus and the remaining three members of the Back Brigade. *I don't even know who they are,* thought Ash. *Hell, have I even spoken to half the crew? And they want me to stand in that center platform? Screw this.* Ash shook his head vigorously, trying to shake these new thoughts free.

Whatever the group was talking about, it was funny. They were all laughing, even the three remaining members of the Back Brigade who hadn't bolted from the Bridge. After a few more moments of conversation, the group turned around and left the Bridge. None of them looked back, except for Anton, who wore a smirk. Ash had a sickening feeling he was going to see that expression far too often. For a moment, their eyes locked before Anton turned forward and left the Bridge.

"Great," Ash said. The rest of the remaining crew stared at him. *No weakness,* thought Ash. He turned around and pointed forward. "Let's get to work."

Chapter Eight

The next few hours passed in an unbroken blur, moving as quickly as the stars racing by in a rainbow spectacle of colors out of the Bridge window, interrupted only by the occasional conversation or crew members shooing Ash away as he stared anxiously over their shoulders, trying to figure out what they were doing. The only real conversation Ash had during this time was with Echo, who came back about two hours after first leaving the Bridge.

"That was bad, Ash," she said. "I mean, really bad. I've seen some bad stuff in the field—"

"The field?" Ash interrupted.

Echo nodded. "I'm from 2075. It's a long story. We'll get there."

Ash shrugged, accepting her comments . . . for now. As if to punctuate the need for urgency, the ship jerked sharply downward and to the right, knocking everyone off-balance.

"Sorry!" cried Alexis. "Still trying to get the hang of this." She reached forward and adjusted dials on her yoke.

Ash sighed and looked back at Echo.

"Those kids are in bad shape," Echo continued. "I spoke with three of them, and they were just wandering the hallways. Well, two of them were. One was huddled in the corner and twirling her hair. Fortunately, their rooms are all in the same section of the ship, though I almost put one of the bigger kids in a room so pink it made my eyes hurt. I got all of them in bed and they are sleeping."

"We're all here for a reason," Ash said. "However we got

picked for this thing, I'm sure we're supposed to be able to handle it. They'll be okay, eventually."

Echo didn't react. Instead, she fixed Ash with a stare that was somehow withering and gentle at the same time.

"They may. But everyone will need time to get themselves acclimated. Everyone works on different schedules and copes differently," she said, staring at Ash intently.

Ash knew she wasn't talking about any Back Brigade member. He met her gaze and nervously flexed his fingers. "I know," he said, voice barely above a whisper. "And I am grateful for your kindness . . . and your discretion."

Echo shrugged nonchalantly. "Apparently that's my role," she said. "It's one I've been playing for years, and I'm more than happy to fulfill it." With that, Echo reached out and grasped Ash's upper-arm. Her touch was warm. "You'll grow into your job, too." After holding the touch an extra second, Echo turned around and walked out of the Bridge.

Ash realized that he had, in fact, found his role. Accepting it was another story.

An hour later, Sierra jumped and shrieked so loud that it caught the entire Bridge's attention.

"What you got?" Ash asked, practically bouncing over to her station.

"How to start the interface—"

"Yes!" interrupted Blondell, with an excited slam on her dashboard. "Great work, Sierra! Let's go!" Both women started typing excitedly.

"Um . . . can you tell me what's going on?" Ash asked docilely, sounding more like he was asking for permission than giving an order.

"No," both responded simultaneously.

"Fair enough," Ash said. He moved on, feeling oddly useless for someone who was supposed to be the ship's leader.

Minutes later, Jameson and Daniel came jogging back onto the Bridge. Daniel waved a paper computer over his head, his massive arm nearly clobbering Jameson.

"How the hell did you figure out how to use that thing?"

Ash asked, genuinely baffled.

Daniel shrugged. "It's all intuitive, and I'm brilliant." Again, Daniel's big, toothy grin came out, and Ash couldn't help but smile back. "The whole ship is mapped out on this thing, and we used it go on a nice long walk."

"Wow. Is that why you were gone so long?" inquired Ash.

"Pretty much," said Jameson. He reached up and took the device out of Daniel's hands, which required him stretching his arms completely above his head. Unfurling the equipment on a table in front of him, Jameson fired up the device and tapped with astounding rapidity. "There isn't too much more on the first or second floors that you wouldn't expect. We went through and mapped everyone's room as best we could. Ash, here's your room, room one. Alexis, you're across from him, room eleven." Jameson jabbed at the two cabins closest to the Bridge.

"How do you know where our rooms are?" Ash questioned.

"Easy," said Jameson. "First, the furniture, music, clothing. Everything is from your unique time period. Same with all the stuff in Alexis' room. Second, it makes the most sense. You two are the two most important people to the ship, pilot and—"

"No," Ash growled, with so much intensity in his voice that Jameson was taken aback, if only for the briefest instant.

Daniel continued. "Anyway, rooms are here, all along the first floor. So is the galley. The armory is here and lemme tell ya, there are weapons in there that I have never seen."

"That makes sense," said Jameson. "I think you are from the oldest time period, and the weapons in there are from across the century or so that spans our births."

"Century?" asked Ash and Alexis at the same time. They looked at each other as Jameson nodded.

"I'm afraid so. Ash, this is gonna take some catching up."

"He hasn't even gotten to the best part," said Daniel, a mischievous grin spreading across his face.

"Right. Check this out," said Jameson. Using his fingers, Jameson flung the diagram of the ship ahead to the third

73

floor. He grabbed the picture and spun it to an overhead view, allowing the crew to stare at the *Redemption* from above. "What do you see?"

Ash traced the internal bulkheads of the ship with a finger.

"Well, that's the engine room," he said, outlining the rear section of the ship which was on all three floors. "And there's the Junction Room. But the rest of this is empty. There aren't any lines."

"It's huge. Two hundred yards or so," said Jameson.

"What the hell is it, a basketball court?" asked Alexis, causing Daniel to laugh out loud.

"No, it's not a basketball court," said Jameson.

"It's a holodeck!" cried Daniel excitedly. "What? No one in here watches *Star Trek*?"

Jameson rolled his eyes. "It's a simulator." He held his fingers on the massive space which was the simulator room and the image changed. The picture of the ship dissolved and was replaced with what Ash could only imagine was an interior view of the room.

"It's completely empty," Ash said.

"Yes. And watch this." Jameson zoomed to a wall panel. "Here's the controls. That palm-shaped outline? You put your hand on it, and it simulates anything you want – anything you are thinking, doing, feeling. Just put your hand to the wall and whatever you are dreaming about becomes reality."

"Anything, huh?" said Alexis with a snicker.

Ash tried to control his eyebrows but found them crawling up his forehead.

Alexis giggled. "Sorry, sorry."

Jameson sighed impatiently.

"This thing has some real practical uses," Ash said, as the implications of Jameson's simulator began to dawn on him.

"Exactly," Jameson said.

"We played around with the thing a little bit. You can use it for stuff you are thinking, sure, but check this out," Daniel said, bringing one of his large hands above the paper computer. A moment later, a digital recording appeared, featuring Daniel. He was running his finger along a groove to the panel's right. As he did so, the groove disappeared and was replaced by text.

"Whoa," said the digital version of Daniel. "Jameson, check this out."

"I am," said digital Jameson, who appeared to be filming the scene.

Daniel began rapidly scrolling through the various files of the wall panel, seemingly picking one at random. At once, the lighting behind the two changed, becoming darker as Jameson spun the camera around. The blank, brightly lit, warehouse-like interior of the simulator room had changed, and now matched the Bridge.

"Are you serious?" cried Alexis.

"Oh yes," Jameson said.

The simulation continued. A holographic Ash was barking instructions at Blondell and Alexis, each of whom frantically operated their controls in an effort to either remove the ship from danger or attack an unseen enemy. The ship was clearly in mortal peril, with sparks flying from various panels throughout the Bridge. A small fire had erupted near Daniel's station, and three bodies lay motionless in the back of the Bridge.

"Controls are sluggish!" cried a holographic-Alexis, her eyes wide with fear.

"Captain, if Daniel can't reroute the power from the main engine to our shields, it's over!" cried Blondell, racing her hands across the panel in front of her.

"Fine, fine!" yelled hologram-Ash, while the real Ash looked on, feeling a mixture of anticipation and horror. "Just tell me how to do that!" As the words left hologram-Ash's mouth, the entire scene froze, with sparks, flames and stars all held suspended.

Abruptly, a computerized voice was the only thing which could be heard. "To appropriately remedy, enter Junction Room, Panel C6, and enter—"

There was a flash, and then nothing, as the recording cut out.

"What happened?" Ash asked.

Jameson gestured to his right eye, where a red welt which Ash hadn't noticed before was rapidly swelling. "Oh."

"Yeah, someone got a little too excited when they were flailing their arms," Jameson said.

A sheepish Daniel shrugged. "My bad."

"Uh-huh. Anyway, when he hit me in the eye, it disrupted the recording, and that—"

"Wait," Alexis said. "Hit you in the eye? What were you taping this thing with?"

Jameson tapped his forehead, eliciting gasps from Ash and Alexis.

Ash was reduced to simply shaking his head; it seemed as if a new technological wonder was shocking him senseless every five minutes. When he regained his composure, Ash asked, "Jameson, have you—"

"No. I've never seen anything like this. Whatever capabilities are on this ship, they developed after 2160. I knew that the Earth was beginning to recover, but technological development like this . . . well, it's extraordinary. Absolutely extraordinary. I cannot even begin to imagine how this happened."

"Which means that mastering some of this technology is going to be difficult, if not outright impossible," Ash said, throwing his arms into the air in disgust. "Great. Well, at least I know that all of us—" He paused as he looked from Daniel to Jameson. "Okay, most of us – are going to be in the same boat." With a smile, Ash added, "We can't all be natural born techies like you two."

Daniel appeared ready to say something smart in response, but delighted squeals from Blondell and Sierra cut them off.

"What?" Alexis said.

"We got it!" cried Sierra, practically levitating out of her seat.

"Got what?" said Ash.

"The interface. Sierra's data and my systems are now talking to each other," said Blondell.

"Great! What exactly does that mean?" questioned Ash.

Blondell sighed and looked exasperated at Jameson,

who shrugged with sympathy.

"Stop that, you two!" Ash cried, and everyone laughed.

"Let me try to explain it slowly, since this is going to be hard for you two to understand." Blondell looked at Ash and Alexis, drawing more giggles from the Bridge, even from the insulted parties. "Okay, you've got the Internet, right?"

"I'm not from the stone age," Ash quipped.

"And you've probably worked with internal networks, right?"

"Sure. Every school and workplace has that sort of thing," Ash said, although Alexis still looked confused. Sensing her befuddlement, Ash looked at Alexis and asked, "2001, right??"

"Right."

"Gotcha," Ash said, relieved that the time difference wasn't worse. "Okay, you've seen two computers hooked up to each other, right?"

"Sure," Alexis said. "I've played tons of Warcraft that way." It was Jameson, Daniel and Blondell's turns to look confused. "Game. Computer game. Come on, you've got to have those in the future."

"Sure," said Blondell.

"No," said Jameson at the same moment.

This caused more confusion, as Blondell and Jameson looked at each other in shock. In an almost tiny voice, filled with wonderment, Jameson said, "They come back?"

Ash cut the conversation off. "Anyway!" he interrupted.

"Right, sorry. Okay, so we've got two computers that are networked with each other. Depending on the time period, functionality of the machines, software, whatever, that can all be complicated enough. So, imagine what happens when you've got computing software from—uh, Sierra?"

"I'm from 2039."

"Right. And I'm from 2167," Blondell said.

"As best I can tell, you're the closest to the current time period," Jameson said.

Daniel laughed. "Congrats there, future girl."

Blondell blushed.

"So, networking computers can be hard if those

computer systems are – what, almost fifty years apart. Okay, I get you. And you figured it out?" Ash said.

Blondell smiled widely. "Even better. We enabled the software to automatically feed into each other. Sierra's got the data, I've got the navigation and other ship systems. Look." Blondell's fingers danced across her holographic keyboard, pulling up a map of their current location, the location of the first cure piece, and a variety of potential routes. This was an incredible display of technical acuity, but Ash was pretty sure he had seen Blondell manipulate her systems in a similar pattern already.

"This is what I had before, right?" Blondell said. "Now watch this." A few keystrokes later, and it became apparent that her systems had been improved greatly.

Instead of just a map of potential routes to their next location, Ash was looking at a variety of data. Using his fingers to open a text box which had appeared above the route, Ash began to read that information.

"Threat assessment, gravitational assessment, other activity, anomalies . . . whoa," Ash said, staring at Blondell. "That's incredible. This is a huge amount of information. How did you do that?"

Blondell shrugged. "I get computer systems. But I couldn't have done it without Sierra. She's fantastic."

Sierra appeared ready to float right out of her seat. "Thanks!" she exclaimed, sounding like an excited five-year-old who had just been genuinely praised by her parents.

"This prepares us," Ash said. "A lot. And it means we can all make better decisions about where we go next." He looked back at the rest of the Bridge. He was so intent on thinking through his next course of action that he almost didn't hear a small voice to his right. After a third squeak from that direction, Ash turned around.

"Hmm?" he said, trying to determine the source of the sound. Another glance and Ash realized it was Radar talking and pointing to his screens with a shaky finger. "What?"

"It's moving."

"Huh?"

"Our target. It's moving."

Ash quickly walked to Radar, put a hand on his shoulder and ducked down so he was at eye-level with the screens. "Show me."

Radar flicked a couple of small metallic switches, causing a purple dot to magnify. "I tagged this as our target—"

"Nice work," Ash said.

"Thanks," Radar said shakily.

Ash got the distinct impression that, should he ever discover his own shadow, Radar would drop dead from fear of it.

"Um . . . so I tagged our target. And once Blondell plugged in our data, it started to move."

"Move?" Ash said, suddenly alarmed. He had the impression that all of their objectives were on planets, which seemed much simpler than trying to catch a target in motion. Of course, that also meant that they would have to learn how to land a spaceship, but that was an entirely different set of problems.

"Yeah . . . move." Another switch, and the purple, blob-like target magnified again.

Ash could definitely see it – the target was moving in an almost parabolic arc. After two or three rotations, however, Ash saw the arc pattern cease. The target jumped wildly.

"It's moving in this relative pattern, except that every few cycles, it changes direction and moves randomly. I have no idea what this means." Radar traced a pattern on the screen.

Ash whipped around to Blondell, who was already typing madly on her keyboard.

"Working on it," she said.

Ash moved back to Blondell's station and stood over her shoulder.

She turned around to look at him. "Okay Ash, as best I can tell . . . we have a problem."

"What?" said Ash, as Alexis, Daniel and Jameson gathered around Blondell.

"Sierra's data shows that this is a gravitational distortion."

Sierra chimed in. "A *what*?"

"Gravitational distortion. These fields trap everything in their path. Meteors, ships, space-debris, all that good stuff. As best I can tell, this one isn't a strong one, but it's strong enough that it could give us some grief. And the entire field is moving."

"Which means . . ."

"It means we need to get there. Now. Or the field could disintegrate, and we could lose it. Or, even worse, it could compromise the structural integrity of whatever we are supposed to capture."

"Okay. Let's get there. Now," Ash said decisively.

"Wait!" Jameson cried, and everyone on the Bridge looked at him. "Captain, I understand. But we don't have a clue of what we are flying into, or how to get that thing once we get there."

Ash exhaled and nodded. Jameson had a point.

"Blondell, how long until we get there?" Ash asked.

Blondell tapped a few buttons. "Six hours, give or take," she replied.

Ash nodded. "Okay. Let's go then. We can figure the rest out when we get there."

Jameson put his hands on his hips and looked down.

"Sorry, it's the best we can do," Ash said.

"I know," Jameson replied. "I get it. But we're going to need to talk to everyone on the Bridge crew to come up with a plan."

"Everyone?" Alexis said, dread slipping into her voice. Ash knew why, and Blondell nodded in agreement.

"Everyone," she said. Ash nodded, slowly this time.

"Agreed," he said, looking around the Bridge and noting that there was just one empty station. "I'll find him." With that, Ash turned on his heel and left the Bridge.

CHAPTER NINE

The mostly-quiet ship, combined with cavernously large hallways, allowed for voices to carry. Ash found Anton with depressing ease, discovering him and another seven crew members in the cafeteria. One of them had attempted to cook a meal, using boxed pasta that they had found. It didn't look half bad.

"Anton, got a second?" Ash asked, walking into the room.

Anton, who had been sitting with his back to the entrance, turned around and faced Ash, looking scornfully at the new arrival as the conversation around him ceased. Stealing a quick glance at the others, Ash noticed that they had all been turned toward Anton.

"Sure, boss," Anton said quietly, letting the words slip slowly from his lips. "Just a second." Anton walked over to Ash.

Despite his assumed leadership role, Ash couldn't help but feel like an outsider on a ship that he was supposedly commanding. He couldn't miss the icy reception in the room, or that everyone was looking coldly in his direction. At least four members of the Back Brigade were in the room with Anton. More importantly, all of them looked as if they had been smiling, laughing, and generally having a good time with Anton and company. Ash knew he should have been happy to see some of the crew members snapping out of their funk, but the circumstances made him distinctly uncomfortable.

"What's up? What you need?" Anton asked, walking up to Ash and getting far, far too close. Trying to hide his discomfort, Ash took a discrete step backward.

"You," Ash responded, deciding to lay it all on the table. "We need your help."

"Okay," Anton said, drawing out the word, sly smile playing across his face. "With what?"

Ash sighed. *He's not going to make this easy, is he?*

"Look, we're heading to that first piece of the vaccine, or whatever." Ash tried to sound normal, casual, but he was already feeling intimidated and insecure, like he wasn't up to this entire conversation. "We need everyone's help – we need your help."

"For what?"

"To get through this thing, whatever it is."

Anton folded his arms across his chest, a slight smile still etched across his face.

"We're heading into what we think is some sort of gravity trap distortion . . . thing . . . something like that. I need everyone who was on the Bridge back there to review what we're heading into."

Ash caught Anton up on the activity of the Bridge, including the data that Blondell and Sierra's computer detective work had revealed.

"So, you think that this piece of the vaccine, this virus, is waiting for us in space, just . . . what, chilling?" Anton asked when Ash had him up to speed.

"Something like that, yes."

"What's it in?"

"Huh?"

"You said you think that it's just floating around. In what?"

"I don't know," Ash responded, his face flushing.

"Is it on a planet? An asteroid? Just a vial of something? What?"

"I don't know," Ash repeated, with his teeth slightly gritted. Again, he noticed Anton's infuriating smile.

"Okay," Anton said, once again, allowing the word to roll easily off his tongue. "Any other ships out there, like those aliens that attacked us?"

"No idea," Ash snapped, desperately wanting the interrogation to be over. "There could be a whole fleet of them, for all I know." A thought hit Ash. "That's why we need you."

"What?"

"We're not sure what is out there, or if that ship that attacked us before will be waiting for us, and that's why we need you at the weapons panel. You're obviously good, and we need your help," Ash said pleadingly.

Finally, the smile faded from Anton's face, but he acted as if it had never left. "You're going to have to do better than that," he said quietly, the words practically oozing from the back of his throat.

Ash's eyes narrowed, his patience evaporating like a puff of smoke.

"Look, man, I don't want to get blown up. You do? Chill here. Eat your damn pasta," Ash said, his voice gradually rising.

The others, who had been trying to pretend that they weren't listening, ceased their conversation and looked over at Ash and Anton, appearing concerned.

"I'm just trying to do whatever we need to keep going," Ash said.

"So, let me get this straight," Anton began. "'Keep going,' means listening to a ship we just met, sending us on some giant fetch quest across the solar system, facing an alien who can probably blow us up pretty easily, with a crew that doesn't know how to fly, to stop a disease that none of us have ever heard of. That sum things up?"

"More or less," growled Ash. "If you have a better idea, knock yourself out. I'm all ears." But again, Anton smiled. Like he knew something.

"I'm in," he said.

Ash was surprised. "What?"

"You heard me, Captain, I'm in. Sounds like you can use all the help you can get." Anton turned around to his group. "Guys, I'm gonna head to the Bridge for a while, see if I can help these guys out." As Anton said "these guys," he jerked his thumb at Ash. "You have fun. I'll be back in a bit." Without a second look, Anton walked toward the door, extending his arm forward at the threshold to the hallway. "After you, boss," he said.

Ash paused, made eye contact with Anton, and quickly walked forward.

That couldn't have gone worse, Ash thought. He reviewed the entire conversation in his head as he walked, slowly growing angrier and angrier at himself. Nothing he had said had felt right. He couldn't shake the feeling that Anton was clearly going with him to prove something to the crew: his superiority, his intelligence. That he was better. Ash felt distinctly manipulated, like a pawn in a chess game, when he couldn't even recognize the board.

Feeling incompetent, Ash skulked back into the Bridge, Anton strutting behind him.

CHAPTER TEN

The ship accelerated toward the gravitational distortion. Once again, Ash had nothing but time on his hands. Thinking ahead, he suggested Alexis take the opportunity to practice in the simulator, since the controls were completely locked and there was nothing else she could do.

Alexis eagerly ran off without another word, with Jameson chasing after her, offering to be of assistance. Blondell was left watching the helm for any emergency. Sierra furiously typed at her computer, gathering as much information as possible, while Anton cycled through the ship's various weapons configurations.

Ash, with nothing else to do, sat in a chair off of the center platform, still refusing to sit on the Captain's platform. With his adrenaline fading, he fought off the increasing urge to sleep. Desperate to distract himself, he started to talk. Blondell was closest.

"You ever think you'd be flying a spaceship?" he asked drowsily.

Blondell looked at him with a smile. "You ever think you'd be Captain of one?" she questioned in return.

Ash flinched, still stung from his last conversation with a crew member. He turned around and looked at Anton, spotting him manipulating his weapons system. Ash glared at the young man, feeling his anger boiling up at Anton's every characteristic: the way he hunched over his air computer, eyes locked in concentration, his short stature preventing him from sitting comfortably in the chair. Small, stubby fingers on his left hand danced aggressively over his display, the faintest of smiles playing across his lips, while his right hand clenched and unclenched into a tight fist.

Unfortunately for Ash, Blondell followed his eyes.

"Don't worry about him," she said quietly, walking next to him and sitting down in another empty chair. "I know his type. He's covering."

"Covering for what?" Ash repeated, genuinely confused.

Blondell pursed her lips, thinking. "There are two kinds of people. First, there are people like you. People who address their inner demons. Then there are people like him – people who hide them, either through stims, sims, or just generally being an asshole."

Ash laughed. "I understood one of those things," he said. "Being an asshole, I suspect, is a universal concept that travels across all time periods." Blondell laughed too. "But seriously, I get the point, but you're wrong about one thing. I haven't faced down crap. In fact, I get my ass kicked by my demons on a pretty regular basis. Christ, you saw me a couple hours ago. Remember, head in my arms, leaning against the hallway, not really moving?"

"You're right, I did see you like that," Blondell said, eyes focused in front of her. "See that out there? That's space. You were honest with yourself and had an anxiety attack. Space, a spaceship, a space battle . . . that would give any of us a panic attack, right?

"Maybe," Ash said quietly.

Blondell took a deep breath and rotated her neck, letting out audible cracks. Shaking her hands loose, she said, "I will confess to being a little confused. I cannot figure out why you aren't giving yourself a little bit more slack. Especially now, in the middle of all of this." She gesticulated her arms around the ship. "We are, apparently, in the middle of a fight to save humanity, and you can't grasp how that pressure may affect your mind. And remember, facing your demons doesn't always mean beating them. It just means living to fight another day." She changed her gaze and looked at the back of Anton's head. "And covering your demons up in insecurity and the need to dominate doesn't mean that you've done anything for yourself. It just means that you delay the fight."

Ash shuffled uncomfortably in his seat. The conversation had gone in a dramatically different direction than he'd intended. He had revealed . . . well, maybe Blondell had detected . . . far more than he had expected.

Shifting the conversation, Ash asked, "So, what's your time like?"

Blondell snorted. "Come on. You think I'm going to let you off that easily?"

Ash smiled weakly. "It was worth a shot," he said quietly, feeling afraid.

Blondell looked down, sympathy in her eyes. "Fine, fine," she said. "But don't forget what I told you in the hallway before. I'm not letting go of this." She leaned forward, elbows on her knees. "The future is . . . different."

Feeling free, Ash leaned forward as well. "How? What happens that we ended up here?"

"The end of the world, and the start of a new one," Blondell said.

Ash paused expectantly, waiting for her to continue. Instead, she stopped talking, the faintest of smiles spreading across her face.

"Oh, come on!" Ash said. "Don't leave me hanging like that."

Blondell brought a hand up to her chin and caressed it before looking back at her controls. "Alright, tell you what. There's a lot more of my display that I need to learn here, and I should get back to it. You get three questions."

Ash laughed.

"You do realize that this is a dream, and a nightmare, right? Three questions? About what happens one hundred fifty years in the future?"

"Oh, of course," Blondell said, her eyes sparkling. "But that's the point. This isn't for you, Captain. This is for me. I want to see what you ask."

Ash leaned back and thought carefully. "Who wins Super Bowl 100?"

"Super Bowl what?"

87

Ash laughed.

"Don't laugh too hard! One down, Space Captain, two to go."

Ash's mind started to wander and he found himself reaching into his pocket . . . which, in turn, led to his second question.

"What happens to iPhones?" Blondell tilted her head and stared at Ash questioningly. "Cell phones? Communication devices?" No change in Blondell's stare, and Ash brought his hand up to his face, miming a phone. "You know, these guys? Speaky-into-them!"

Blondell laughed. "Yeah, I know what an iPhone is, I just wanted to mess with you." Ash burst out laughing. "They get replaced and morphed into something smaller and more powerful. The Infinity Corporation takes care of that one."

Ash's laughter came to an abrupt stop. The third question was easy.

"What is the Infinity Corporation?"

Blondell nodded, and her voice took on a more even pitch. "Took you all three questions, Captain, but you finally got a good one." Blondell stopped talking and looked to the ceiling of the Bridge, gathering her thoughts, before she began to speak again, leaning forward on her elbows. "Okay. 2018 right?"

"Right."

"Biggest companies were what, Google, Facebook, Apple?"

Ash shrugged. "Something like that. I mean, that's not exactly comprehensive, but that's the right idea."

Blondell nodded. "What would happen if all of them merged?"

Ash raised his eyebrows. "I . . . I can't even imagine. A lot of people would make a lot of money."

"And a lot of barriers would be broken, right, Captain?"

Ash began to follow Blondell's line of thinking. "And a lot of technology would be shared. Holy crap. Wait, really? Big companies merge?" Ash's mind began to race. *What the hell would cause something like that to happen? And what would the end result be?*

Blondell continued to stare expectantly at Ash.

He continued, "God, the amount of money those companies would have. I can't even imagine the possibilities of that kind of concentrated wealth."

With that, Blondell smiled, stood up, patting Ash's arm as she moved. "Now you're asking the right questions, Captain." And Blondell moved on, leaving a shell-shocked Ash to close his eyes and contemplate what she had said.

CHAPTER ELEVEN

Ash jerked upward, feeling as if he had just fallen off a cliff. It took a moment to orient himself and another to cover up his embarrassment. He had fallen asleep in one of the Back Brigade seats, and someone was standing over him. It was Alexis; her face was shiny with sweat, a plate with food in her hands. She smiled gently.

"Hey sleepyhead," she said gently, as if she was waking up a classmate who had dozed off in the middle of a lecture. "Brought you something." Ash looked at the sandwich in her hand – some kind of processed meat, yellow cheese, a tomato.

"This ship has produce on it?" He pulled himself into a sitting position and wiped the drool from the corner of his mouth.

Alexis laughed and nodded. "Not sure how long it will last, but yes," she said. "Exodus and her friend were trying to make sandwiches, but were so nervous that they could barely cut the tomato. Poor things. It was either that or cold pasta. So, I figured I'd give you this." She pushed the plate further forward. "Here. Eat. I know you haven't since we got here, and you're gonna need it."

Ash took the plate out of her hand, took one look at the sandwich and proceeded to stuff as much as he could in his mouth. Alexis was right. He was starving. Processed lunch meat had never tasted so good.

"Thank you," he said. Through a full mouth, though, it came out sounding more like "Fank shoo!"

Alexis smiled. "You're very welcome," an upbeat lilt to her voice. She sat down in the seat next to Ash, who attempted speaking in between inhaling his sandwich.

"What about everyone else?" he asked.

Alexis smiled gently and patted Ash's knee. "Don't worry. We got them," she said. "You were out of it, but I was able to shift everybody in and out of here for food."

Ash nodded slowly. "Well, thank you again." He licked mustard off his fingers. "I'm glad someone was able to take care of the rest of the crew while I was asleep."

"Of course," she said. "I know you're kind of in charge here, but the rest of us . . . at least, most of us, I think . . . we get it. You didn't sign up for this. Everyone has to help." Alexis paused. "Talk to me," she said softly. "Tell me what you're thinking."

It was a reasonable question, and it took Ash a moment or two to gather his thoughts before responding. "Well, I'm trying to wake up, so let's start there," he said.

Alexis laughed.

"Once we get past my reemerging consciousness . . . okay." He shifted in his seat so he was facing Alexis, their knees touching. "A few things. First, is the immediate stuff. How long can our food last? How do we actually fight off that phantom ship if we get attacked? What do I do if we spring a leak? Can this thing spring a leak? Seriously, there are about a thousand questions that I don't know the answers to. Questions I should be able to answer and can't.

"Second is the longer-term stuff. The bigger stuff. If all of that crap Valliant laid on us really is true, we have a major problem on our hands. I mean, seriously? Who is trying to kill us? Why us, here, now? How are all of us supposed to get up to speed? And how do I manage this crew when a good portion aren't functioning? There's no way we can get to where we need to be to save the future of humanity if the people onboard this ship can't even perform.

"And last, speaking of this ship . . . I'm trying to figure out how to lead it, honestly." Here, Ash's voice began to trail off. "I'm a twenty-year-old college drop-out who suffers from severe anxiety attacks and a major depressive disorder. When I'm from, I was doing part-time in a burger place after I panicked my way out of Cornell. So now, you're going to give me a crew of twenty, a spaceship, the vast majority of which I can't even begin to understand, in a time period not my own . . . and expect me to run this thing? I literally have no idea what I am doing, Alexis, and I'm waiting for everyone else to figure that out." Ash exhaled deeply as he finished talking. He stared at Alexis, waiting for her response. There was none right away. She just sat there, simultaneously looking surprised and impressed.

"I didn't expect all that," she finally said.

A wave of embarrassment washed over Ash. "Sorry," he mumbled, trying to figure out how to take back everything he had just said.

"You don't have to be sorry," Alexis said. "That's not what I meant. I meant I didn't expect you to be so open. I had you pegged for the strong and silent type."

"I'm neither," Ash snapped. Then he sighed. "My bad. I'm just . . ."

"A mess?" Alexis finished the sentence and patted Ash's hand, leaving her own on top of his. Ash felt warmth racing through her fingers and into his, and despite it all, felt his body stirring in a way that it hadn't in months. Neither of them moved for a few moments, each staring past the other, almost fearful of making eye contact. Finally, Alexis gave his hand a last comforting squeeze and pulled away. She stood and walked away, leaving Ash with a slight smile on his face.

***

Feeling more energized than he had since the start of the journey, Ash spent the rest of the trip examining his crew. He stood over Anton's shoulder, watching him cycle through the ship's two primary weapons: torpedoes, with a bay located on each wing, and a laser bank, with one row located next to the torpedoes and another below the Bridge in the center of the ship. Anton seemed to have a good grasp on the systems and clearly enjoyed the prospect of destruction.

Next was Daniel, whose antiquated computers had been improved so that diagnostics could be made instantaneously. The remainder of his station consisted of a dizzying array of tools and equipment that looked capable of fixing almost any problem the ship could throw at them. Daniel said nothing as Ash walked by; he was too busy typing his way through the ship's diagnostic systems.

Radar sat motionless. He was sound asleep at his station. Ash smiled slightly before moving on.

Sierra and Blondell each hacked away at their keyboards, occasionally having halfway-coherent conversations which consisted of "Did you—" and "Yes," followed by long stretches of silence, punctuated only by the clattering of fingers on digital displays. Ash shook his head, stared at the two for a moment, and moved on.

Alexis sat in her seat, hands on the joystick, eyes locked on the window in front of her. She wasn't moving and appeared to be in mental preparation for when she would resume control of the ship. Reflecting on the task that was in front of them – maneuvering the ship through a gravity field that had the potential to shatter the ship into pieces – Ash thought that Alexis was likely the most important part of this mission.

Confident that the rest of the ship was far too engrossed in their own work to notice, Ash discretely stepped onto the Captain's center platform for the first time. Various panels gave Ash a bird's eye view of every one of the ship's operations and allowed him to determine what was happening throughout the *Redemption* at all times. A detachable tablet in the center of the platform allowed Ash to also assume control over any one of the ship's stations – not that he ever would, considering that it would probably result in an instant disaster. A padded, elevated chair provided Ash with the ability to sit down when the action was slow, and strap in when it got hot. There were surveillance cameras that everyone who had walked the ship had missed earlier. Ash realized, to his own relief, that the only places on the ship not covered by cameras were the cabins.

Ash stood on the platform for a moment and admired the view. It was an impressive command center. *Still not for me. Not yet.* Ash stepped down, noticing Echo had returned to the Bridge, worry stamped on her face.

"What have you got?" he asked, quietly.

Echo shrugged. "They're all still asleep," she said.

Ash raised his eyebrows. *I could have sworn I saw at least one of the folks who ran out of here hanging out with Anton.*

"I think they will be like that for a while. Honestly? Right now, those folks are the least of my worries," Echo said.

"How do you mean?"

"You. Alexis. Daniel. Anton. Everyone else," Echo continued.

Ash folded his arms across his chest.

Echo sighed. "Look, everyone here is obviously undergoing an incredible strain. We are some of the only people who have ever been in a situation like this. The human mind . . . it just isn't prepared for this. I'm worried how everyone will hold up under this kind of pressure."

Ash jammed his hands into the pockets of his pants. "How did you get like this?" he asked. "What made you understand people with this kind of insight?"

Echo smiled without joy.

"That is a fake smile if I've ever seen one. And I would know. I've given it a few times myself since we got here." Ash chuckled.

Echo laughed, and it was a genuine one. "Yes, I suppose you do understand that look, better than most." She sighed. "I was born in 2056, around the time my world started falling apart. My family lived in New York when the flooding started. We left pretty soon after. They could read the writing on the wall. When things got really bad, we started walking. We joined one of the wandering bands that travelled toward the center of the country, toward higher ground. Anyway, doing that . . . you saw things. Things you wish you hadn't. And you became good at reading people. Or else."

Ash went silent, processing. Everything Echo had said

would impact the world he came from. His family. His world. Everyone and everything he cared about.

That being said, 2018 wasn't his world anymore. 2180 was. He made a conscious decision to focus on the here and now.

"Or else what?" he asked.

"You died," Echo said bluntly. "It's pretty simple, really. Thanks to that, I have a gift for knowing people. So, back to my original point. It's everyone else on the ship I'm worried about. I know what pressure does to people, what happens to groups when they are backed up against the wall. That's something we will all have to watch out for. Particularly you."

Ash nodded. Unfortunately, he already understood what Echo was talking about.

He turned around to leave, but froze when Echo spoke again. "Remember, Ash. The Back Brigade is in bed. It's the rest of you flying this thing."

Ash nodded. "I know," he said, resignation in his voice. Ash heard Echo sit down, and he moved on as well.

According to Blondell, the *Redemption* had only fifteen minutes before they arrived at the gravity distortion. While he had been asleep, the rest of the crew had reviewed a plan, and as the ship closed in, they gathered in front of the center platform to review.

"When we hit this thing, it's going to get very bumpy, very quickly," Blondell said. "From what I can gather from the ship's specs, we should be able to handle it, but I can't say I'm one hundred percent sure that we can escape without any damage."

"Oh, we'll get damaged," Sierra said. "But as long as we keep moving, the damage shouldn't be anything extreme."

"Fantastic," Ash said. "What does damaged mean?"

"Standard stuff," said Sierra.

Ash resisted the urge to throw his hands into the air in disgust.

"Can you elaborate?"

"Well, our shields will take a few hits, and we may have some minor structural damage—"

"I got it," Daniel said, his deep voice resonating. "Look, Captain—"

There's that word again, thought Ash.

Daniel continued, "We're going to take a few hits, and we can't do anything about it. It's the only way in. But I've been reading up on this thing and run a few sims. I can handle minor stuff, I know which buttons to push and where to run. If things get real bad, we've got a problem, but we'll make it work."

"Not like we have a choice," Ash muttered. "Okay, Blondell, then what?"

Blondell tapped at her keyboard, bringing up a map across the front window of the ship. Ash saw the *Redemption* and its projected path, highlighted by a bright blue line. The gravity distortion was represented by a slew of three-dimensional waves.

"Here's where we are, and here's where we are going," Blondell said, pointing. "Sierra and Radar were able to plot out some of the weakest areas of distortion, and here's where we need to fly."

"This sounds like a really good time," said Alexis, running a hand through her hair.

"Oh, it gets better," said Blondell. The display in front of them abruptly zoomed ahead, into what Ash presumed was the gravity distortion. Different blob-like shapes took form, highlighted in various shades of splotchy red. "See those spaces?" said Blondell, pointing. "The redder it gets, the angrier the area. If you hit one of those dark red spaces, we may have a problem."

Another button pushed, and the view zoomed into the gravity distortion, with a solid blue tube showing their projected path. "Alexis, that blue line will be visible in front of us, projecting outward, like a track. You stay in there, and we'll make it to our asteroid."

Alexis nodded forcefully. "I can do that," she said. "Absolutely." Abruptly, her head froze, and her head jolted upward. "Wait, asteroid? As in, flying rock?"

"Big ole flying rock," retorted Blondell. "You'll have to get us in close enough to activate the tractor beam. You got this. Don't go all shaky on us."

As if responding directly to Blondell's exhortations, Alexis stood perfectly still. "Yep. Sounds like a fun time."

"Good, 'cause we're screwed if you can't get close enough," Blondell said. "The dangerous areas appear in bright red. You hit that, and I can't guarantee what happens to us."

"That's comforting," Ash said grimly. "Okay. We get to the asteroid. Then what?"

Blondell paused here. "Yeah . . . that's the one thing."

"The one thing?" Alexis gulped. "You mean actually getting the part of the asteroid?"

"Yes," Blondell replied.

"Just a minor, mission critical detail," Alexis said, shrugging and somehow keeping a straight face.

Ash barely suppressed a laugh.

"Oh, shut up," Anton said to Alexis. Ash was so surprised that he was momentarily speechless, while Alexis froze as a pained expression crossed her face. "I already dealt with the tractor beam."

"You did?" asked Ash, Jameson and Blondell at the same time. Anton nodded vigorously.

"Hell, yes," he said. "I rearrange my controls, which took me all of five minutes to figure out. Right now, it's configured as a tractor beam. Once we do that, we'll trap the asteroid in the docking bay."

"I think I can take it from there," said Miranda, catching Ash by surprise. He stared at her for a moment and pondered, before remembering who she was. *Right. Tall girl. Loves the science stuff.* "The ship has the equipment to decontaminate and contain the asteroid, and I've got a couple years' lab experience—"

"Of course you do," Ash said.

Miranda laughed. "Someone here had to. Anyway, once we get the asteroid, I can store it. We have the equipment."

"One more point," said Blondell. The rest of the crew turned to look at her as her fingers tapped a keyboard, bringing up a new translucent graphic on the ship's main window. A simulated image of the asteroid moved in a U-shaped path. "The reason it's following this route is because of the unique gravity field it's caught in." More typing and the view changed. The asteroid and its pattern were still visible, but the background was no longer blank space. Instead, it was a multicolored map, the colors of which varied from white to red. The asteroid was in one of the lightest spaces in the map. "As you can see, our rock is caught in a weak pocket of gravity."

"A what now?" said Ash.

Blondell gestured to her map. "See the large asteroid?" she pointed at a large jagged ball which looked like it had survived an attempted mauling from a very large animal. "That's emitting a gravitational force unevenly. Think of it like butter spread unevenly on a big piece of toast."

"And what happens when we fly a big ship too close to that pocket that the big asteroid is causing?" Ash asked.

Blondell pointed at him. "Scorched it, Captain," she said. "I don't know for sure, but I have a pretty good guess."

"The ship gets . . . uhh, screwy?"

"You got it. We either get squished like a pancake or risk getting flung into another asteroid. Either way, seems like a bad plan."

Ash nodded grimly. "Okay," he said. He looked around. "Let's not screw this up, people!"

The crew nodded.

"To not screwing up!" cried Blondell, a rallying cry which was echoed by other members of the laughing crew.

Ash, smiling, walked over to his improvised post next to the captain's platform.

Ready as I'll ever be, he thought.

CHAPTER TWELVE

With five minutes before they reached the distortion, Ash stood next to Alexis, who was strapped in and focused intently on the space in front of her.

"You okay?" he said. Alexis nodded so hard that her curly hair bounced into her face and she was forced to let go of the controls in order to restore her vision.

"Fine. Super. Just gotta keep us from dying. Why?"

"Oh, Anton's shot at you, I just wanted to make sure—"

Alexis fixed Ash with such a withering stare that he almost took a step backward.

"Ash. I deal with guys like that all the time. He's not pleasant, but he's also not going to stop me. His time will come. And so will mine." She faced forward again. "Now let's do this."

Heartened by Alexis' determination, Ash nodded and moved behind Alexis, where his vantage point was best. A voice buzzed in his ear.

"Ash?" It was Jameson, coming in via an invisible receiver that Tidus had installed earlier.

Startled, Ash jumped, before turning to Tidus and gesturing at his ear. "Is this thing stuck in there?"

Tidus shrugged and made a noncommital grunt.

"Hey? Captain?" Jameson again. The tinny quality of his earlier communications was gone.

"Yeah, Jameson? What's up?"

"You might want to strap yourself in. This is going to get bumpy."

Ash grimaced. "You're probably right, but I have to stand here."

"Not if you just go into your station. There's an awesome chair right there. I hear it's *real* comfy."

"No," snapped Ash.

Jameson sighed. "Fine. But don't come to me when you are all bruised and banged up." Abruptly, the communication cut off.

Ash pushed the thought of his prone body bouncing around the ship outside of his mind. "Blondell, shields up?"

"Aye aye, Captain," Blondell said, trying navy speak and earning an eye roll from Ash. "I'm activating our guide line and the spatial distortion overlay." With the click of a button, the view in front of them changed: gone was the solitary vastness of space, replaced by a bright blue, curving line which drifted gently into the distance. The line travelled through a bright, white background, studiously avoiding pinks and brighter reds. "The computer mapped the most efficient route through the least of the gravity distortions. Alexis, whatever you do, *stay on that line.* The darker it gets, the more dangerous the route."

"You got it," Alexis said, grip tightening on her joystick.

"Good. Because here we go. In five . . . four . . . three . . . two . . ."

With a small jolt, the *Redemption* entered the gravity distortion. *Not a bad start,* thought Ash, as the ship began to curve upward, following the guide line. It felt as if they were travelling along a badly maintained road.

No one else on the Bridge made a single noise. The air was filled with the whirl of machinery and periodic ticking sounds as Alexis made slight adjustments to her controls. Otherwise, the Bridge was silent, and it stayed that way as Alexis guided the ship forward.

"Seven minutes until we get to the asteroid," said Blondell, staring straight ahead.

Alexis acted as if she hadn't heard, save for a slight twitch of her lip.

"Nicely done. Hope it stays this easy," said Blondell.

As if spiting the ship for Blondell's temerity to hope, a

moment later, Ash sensed a sudden, jerky movement on his left.

"The distortions are shifting," Radar said, his voice tight.

"How?" Ash asked. "Actually, scratch that. More important: Where? And can we—"

"I don't know how," Blondell said, her voice unnaturally level. "I didn't see that was a thing when we were preparing for this."

Ash looked out the window and saw what Radar had picked up on his equipment: shades of white turning the color of blood, while blotches of red were morphing to pure white. Meanwhile, the guideline was shifting as well, turning to compensate.

"Alexis, can you handle this, or do we need to get out?"

In response, the ship banked downward, flinging its occupants forward and forcing Ash to brace himself on Radar's screens.

"I can't see, I can't see!" Radar yelled as Ash's body blocked his view. Ash tried pushing himself off the screen, to no avail, and was only able to move when Alexis reversed the steep dive into a milder climb. As his eyes focused on the front screen, Ash realized that he didn't need any advanced training to understand what was in front of them.

"Massive gravity distortion!" cried Blondell.

A black ball streaked across their plane of vision, obliterating the already established gravity fields. It was far away, well into the distance, but it ran right through their guideline, which faded completely away in the distance, creating a solid wall of black space.

"Alexis! Can you get us out of here?" asked Ash, his arms wrapped around the back of Radar's chair, wishing he had heeded Jameson's advice.

"No!" Alexis responded, yanking back on her controls. "Best I can do is aim right. Hang on!" Ash tumbled backward against a wall. He closed his eyes tight, listening to the ominous creaking and groaning coming from the left part of the ship.

"Getting sick of tumbling like a freakin' rag doll!" he yelled.

"Sorry!" shouted back Alexis as she strained against gravity.

Abruptly, they passed through the red space and entered into safer pink. The guide line returned, and Alexis acquired it, setting them on a (relatively) stable course again. Ash stood and smoothed out his clothing.

"Blondell, come on!" he cried, exasperated. "You didn't tell us to be ready for that!"

Blondell whipped around, having clearly lost any semblance of composure.

"Does it look like I've ever flown a spaceship before?" she snarled through gritted teeth.

Ash sighed and leaned on a railing. "You're right, and I'm sorry."

Blondell's snarl turned into a sad shake of the head. "Me too. But sorrier for not realizing this."

"No, you're right. Let's get out of here."

Another bump jolted the ship, sending Ash sprawling. He looked up to see a slow strobe light in front of him. One second, the way was completely clear, and the ship rocked – the next, it was red, and the ship jerked.

"We got a problem, boss!" Daniel cried. "The left wing keeps slipping into the distortion field. We lose that, we lose half our weapons."

Desperately, Ash turned over his shoulder to face Daniel. "What do you need?"

Ash grabbed a railing to his right, wrapped his arm around it, and hung on for dear life.

"Do everything you can to avoid moving the left wing into the distortions!" Daniel answered. "We need both sides to fire the tractor beam."

Ash looked at Alexis to relay the order, but she had heard it already.

"On it!" she said, moving her controls. The bumping and jerking of the ship continued. Bracing himself against a rail, Ash pulled himself back up and looked around the Bridge before his eyes settled on Blondell. He moved to her as fast as his legs would carry him.

"Can you get us a path out of here?" he asked, his words

broken by the turbulence.

"Too late," Blondell said as she dragged her fingers across the computer display, frantically flinging icons. "I think I can reroute us, but that wall we flew through cut off our escape route. Everything else is too dangerous. The best bet is to move forward, grab the asteroid and get out of here."

Ash bit his lip. "Fantastic." Just as he said that, another jolt nearly threw him off his feet.

A new very narrow guide line appeared in front of them, trailing to the left and expanding into a large tunnel. For an instant, Ash felt his heart leap with relief.

"Follow that guide line!" he ordered.

"It's not a guide line anymore!" said Alexis, looking at Blondell.

"I know, I know," she replied. "I figured something out . . . stay inside of this passageway. The gravitational forces are safe in here."

"I like safe!" said Alexis.

Moments later, the *Redemption* trailed toward Ash's left, following the guide line into a tunnel. Ash clambered to his seat and snapped himself into his restraints as quickly as possible.

"Uh . . . Captain?" said a soft voice. The sound was so quiet that it was almost unrecognizable, and Ash had to turn to look at Sierra's strained features.

"What?" he asked. "Why do you look so scared?"

Sierra didn't respond; instead, she simply pointed forward with a shaky finger. Ash turned and felt his hope shatter like ice on a thawing lake. The guideline remained, but rust-red blobs were eating away at the tunnel's left side.

"Alexis, you can't follow that!" cried Ash. "You heard Daniel, we can't risk damage to the left wing until he has time to repair it."

"A little late, Captain!" Alexis replied.

Ash spun back to the window in front of him and realized just how right Alexis was: straying off of their guide line steered the ship straight ahead, into a shade of red that was tainted so heavily with black that it looked like space was bleeding. Alexis was trying to split the difference between the gravity distortion and the guide path, but with minimal success. The instability of the ship was increasing, and accelerating crackling sounds could be heard coming from the left side of the ship.

Ash stared forward, watching in horror as the ship continued to streak forward, his mind racing. *This is like a bad movie. If only there was some way to slow down . . . wait, slow us down . . .*

"Can you slow us down?" he said to Alexis.

Alexis blinked and shook her head in disbelief. She grabbed her controls and pulled them toward her. Abruptly, the ship's speed slowed as the forward thrusters fired. The turbulence eased with it.

"Okay, that should buy us some time," Alexis said. "And I think I can handle this."

"How?" asked Ash.

Alexis responded by tweaking her joystick. "I can tilt this thing sideways and shift us 90 degrees. The tunnel is higher than it is wide in that section and that should make us narrow enough to fit on the guideline."

Ash's eyes narrowed. "Whoa. You want to fly this thing sideways? Won't that basically kill us?"

"Have you lost your mind?" cried a wide-eyed Anton, who was desperately clinging to the arm rests of his seat, eyes wide and cheeks flushed. "You're saying you want to tilt the ship 90 degrees, right?"

"Right."

"And have Alexis fly while we are all sideways," Ash said.

"Right."

Anton opened his mouth to protest again. Ash cut him off by drawing a hand across his neck. Anton's complaint caught in his throat, forcing Ash to hide his satisfaction.

"Alexis, can you do this?" he asked quietly.

"She can barely fly the ship normally. She couldn't even remember to slow the damn thing down, and she—"

Ash opened his mouth to speak again. He felt rage building in his chest. But, to his pleasant surprise, he didn't need to say anything. With a solid *thwack,* a flying shoe connected directly with Anton's nose.

Ash spun around and saw a smiling Alexis, who was wearing one less sneaker than she had been a moment ago.

"Shut. The. Hell. Up," she said calmly.

The ship was dead silent again, save for the snickering coming from Daniel.

"Jameson, can the ship handle that?" asked Ash.

Jameson's voice snapped over an invisible loudspeaker. "If Anton is finished, I can save you all the trouble. Everyone here has forgotten we're in space. There is no X-axis. The ship's gravity will shift with us."

With a gasp of recognition, Blondell said, "He's absolutely right, Ash. The ship will fly sideways but it won't have any effect on us inside."

"Great. Turn us then, Alexis," said Ash.

With a stiff nod, Alexis spun the ship. In front of them, Ash's eyes were treated to the dizzying sight of the stars tilting.

"That's not off-putting at all," Ash muttered to himself.

"Inertial dampeners, Captain," chimed in Blondell.

"Try again?" said Ash.

"Inertial dampeners. That's what is creating our gravity, and it's why we stick to the floor no matter what direction the ship is spinning.

"As long as it works," Ash said.

"Working so far. Shut up please," said Alexis.

Ash opened his mouth to apologize but closed it again with a pop.

Slowly, achingly slowly, the ship continued its turn. At the same time, however, it began to dip into a dangerous zone of red space.

"Alexis, pull us up!" cried Ash.

Alexis did, freezing the ship's turn at thirty degrees before she re-stabilized and resumed the ship's tilt. Ash, straining his stare out the window, caught a smattering of red in space.

"We're in the red here, Alexis," he said anxiously.

"I have eyes, thank you," snapped Alexis. "It's weak. I think we can handle it."

Ash noticed that the ship's floor was slanted, and that gravity was pulling him to the right.

With a gulp, Ash said, "Uh . . . Blondell, where are those inertial things you were talking about?" Alexis turned the ship further, and Ash swayed harder to the right.

"It's—," began Blondell. "That's – oh." Sounding like she had been punched in the stomach, Blondell began to frantically fling displays in front of her before speaking again. "I may have misread something here."

"Ash, why am I sliding into a wall? Where's my gravity?" said Jameson, his voice tinged with panic.

The ship was halfway inverted and taking the rest of the *Redemption* crew with it, with its angle extended to forty-five degrees, causing Ash to use an arm to brace himself.

"Blondell, an explanation would be really helpful right about now!"

"Trying!" replied Blondell.

"Ash, are we in one of the pockets of red?" said Jameson.

Ash pressed a finger to his ear to drown out the growing cacophony of the Bridge.

"Maybe!" he responded. After a stare out the window, he added, "Okay, yes, lots of red and getting redder!"

"I have no choice, it's where the asteroid is!" said Alexis.

"The gravity outside the ship is throwing off the Bridge's sensors!" said Jameson with a grunt.

"What does that mean?" shrieked Anton.

"It means the dampeners are not compensating correctly! It's trying to orient to the outside gravity instead of keeping the floor level," answered Alexis.

With growing horror, Ash realized she was right. The angle of the Bridge had taken Ash completely sideways; strapped to his chair, gravity crushed his arm, and with a yelp, Ash pulled it free. Ash opened his mouth to say more but was pelted with random debris – including, of all things, Alexis' shoe.

The entire Bridge rotated at a crazy angle, and Ash was so dizzy that he could not imagine how he was still conscious. Searching the space in front of him and straining his eyes, he tried to concentrate on the guide line in front of the ship. Behind him, he heard retching. Ash tried to push the sound out of his mind as Alexis eased forward on the joystick. Slowly, the ship began to accelerate, back in sync with the wider guide line.

"Keep doing whatever you are doing, Alexis!" Ash said through gritted teeth. The words felt absurd coming out of his mouth.

The *Redemption,* which only moments before had been filled with a cacophony of noises and shrieks, fell miraculously silent as Alexis guided the ship to their objective. Ash could practically picture her face: Bright red with exertion, eyebrows knotted in concentration, her hands glued to the joystick except to brush aside loose strands of her wild curly hair.

"There!" cried Blondell, her long dark hair hanging downward like branches of a willow tree.

Ash's eyes followed Blondell's extended fingers until he saw the asteroid. Sure enough, it was sliding through space, maneuvering around a series of other, larger asteroids. Squinting, Ash tried to focus on their target, but found himself distracted by the larger rocks. Most were oblong with spiked, jagged claws of mass reaching into space. Others appeared as smooth as the surface of an undisturbed lake. Looking closer, Ash blinked in disbelief at what was before him. One large rock, at least the size of three football fields, had metallic strands bored into its surface.

Wrenching his attention away, Ash refocused on their target, now highlighted in a bright-red glow created by Blondell's digital overlays. At the moment, it was curving up before abruptly braking, like a yo-yo that had reached the end of its string. Trapped in a gravity-enforced prison, the asteroid bounced back downwards.

The asteroid grew closer and larger.

"Anton, you ready?" Ash said.

Anton delayed a few seconds before responding. "Sure," he said, his voice strained.

"On my mark, and not a moment before," said Blondell. "Three . . . two. . ."

As Blondell said "two" Anton fired the improvised

tractor beam from the upper wing, sending a bright blue beam of light across space.

"You moron!" shrieked Alexis. The tractor beam, not properly positioned, nicked the asteroid, altering its parabolic path and sending it careening into space. Moving as slowly as an injured turtle, the asteroid moved into blood red space, where strong gravity distortions ensured that the *Redemption* would not be able to chase it.

Like a flash, the idea hit Ash.

"Fire the center laser bank!"

Clacking and a desperate mashing of buttons followed.

"Uh . . . hang on . . . okay, got it!" said Anton. A second blue beam shot from just below the Bridge. But this one was also moments too late. Once again, the asteroid was grazed and kept travelling downward, spinning wildly.

"Fire the right weapons bank!" Ash cried, frantic.

Anton did, and this time, he was ready. The beam connected with the asteroid, freezing it in mid-spin. A cheer went up from the entire crew.

"Stop cheering, stop cheering!" Ash cried. "Alexis, get us level, and get us the hell out of here!"

"Hold onto your seats!" she cried back, slamming the throttle yet again.

The guide line, which had been a bright, narrow blue, abruptly widened, and with a cry of victory, Alexis yanked the joystick to the left as quickly as possible. Slowly, the pressure eased.

Ash gasped for breath as the world started to right itself. Adjusting his arms against the restraints that threatened to cut off circulation to his shoulders, he leaned forward as much as possible, practically licking his lips with the anticipation of being completely level once again.

"Sierra, can you reel that sucker in once were even?" Ash finally asked when he thought he could speak without vomiting.

"Way ahead of you, boss," Sierra responded, looking like she was trying to control her giddiness.

Sure enough, when Ash looked back at the asteroid, he saw it being wound into the ship.

"Should be inside in about ten minutes," Sierra said.

"Great." For five minutes, no one spoke. The entire crew peered into the distance, searching for an unknown threat, awaiting a death-signifying chime from a piece of machinery that they barely understood. Instead, thankfully, blissful quiet reigned. When it became apparent that they were out of danger, Ash unstrapped himself and began to speak.

"Lessons learned," he said. The crew stared quizzically back at him. "Look, we're new at this. But we all made huge mistakes there. Radar and Blondell, you didn't know that the gravity field wasn't stable, and that almost got us all killed. Alexis, as unquestionably funny—"Ash found that the volume of his voice was increasing, "and *well-deserved* as that was, that was stupid. You can't throw a shoe at someone when we are all in a life-threatening situation." Ash found himself trying to suppress a chuckle. "Anton, for Christ's sake, what the hell are you doing, yelling at someone in the middle of something that tense, then not even following orders correctly?" Anton looked like he was silently fuming, but said nothing. "Blondell, I know it was an honest mistake, but we went sideways because you don't understand the Bridge's gravitational dampeners . . . whatever." Ash paused and sighed. "And me. Me too. I screwed up royally. I should have strapped my stupid ass to a chair much sooner. I could have gotten myself killed. We need to do better.

"We're gonna pause here. I don't care about time. But we nearly died because almost every one of us made terrible mistakes. We're going to set up shifts inside the simulator, we're going to look at whatever files Sierra puts together for us, and we're going to figure out how to fly this thing right. That's it. That's what we are doing. Any questions?" The crew was as still as glass.

"Good. Let's get to work. Sierra, let me know when that thing is inside the ship. I want to take a look at it."

CHAPTER THIRTEEN

Ash's first thought upon seeing the asteroid was that it was significantly bigger than he expected. In the vastness of space, it had looked small, but in person, it looked enormous: at least twenty feet tall from lowest to highest points, and roughly the same width. Studded with flecks of blue and gold, the asteroid was also peppered in bumps and pockmarks, giving it the appearance of a miniature mountain range. At the moment, it was suspended in the air, held in place by a stasis field Sierra had figured out how to activate.

From behind a pane of glass, Ash stared at the monstrous space rock in front of him. "So now what?" he asked Sierra.

Miranda had joined them as well, and she spoke first. "I need some time to figure this out. We know that Spades and its antibodies come from space. My goal is to try to figure out how I can break into the asteroid, isolate the compound we're looking for, and mix it with whatever we get next."

"Can you do all that?" Ash asked.

Miranda shrugged. "Um . . . maybe? Eventually. Look, right now, I don't want to go anywhere near that thing. Its radiation count is off the chart." Miranda rapped the glass separating them from the asteroid. "We're safe, but I need to determine how to de-radiate this thing before anyone goes near it . . . or, you know, the radiation kills us all."

The corner of Ash's mouth turned up. "Well, space hasn't done that yet, so we're doing okay on that front, at least."

Miranda smiled bitterly. "As a fan of gallows humor, I appreciate that." She sighed. "I'll get to work on this. You go get some rest or something."

Ash waved a dismissive hand. "Nah, I conked out before. I'm gonna get back to the Bridge, figure out how to start a training program."

"Okay, but don't go too nuts. We need you to sleep," Miranda responded, emphasizing the word sleep.

Ash, not wanting to hear anymore, nodded curtly and left the storage bay, intending to go straight back to the Bridge.

His second anxiety attack of the day put a stop to that. One moment, everything was (relatively) fine. Ash was walking back to the Bridge, trying to determine the best way to impose some sort of structure on the crew without coming off too heavy. The next, he visualized Anton's sneering face, and it hit him all at once.

Ash put a hand to his chest and clawed at his rib cage. *Oh, good, I'm going to die now. That's what's going to happen. I'm actually going to have a heart attack, and go completely nuts, and crap my pants, and everyone is going to have to figure out how to deal with their crazy captain.* Even thinking the word "captain" made Ash's stomach flip, and his other hand grabbed his stomach.

Slowly, looking like an old man having a heart attack, and feeling twice as vulnerable, Ash backed against a wall and slid down to the ground. He quickly stuffed his head between his legs and tried desperately to remember how to control his breathing. Moving his head like that also had the added benefit of blocking out any sound from the rest of the world, and he added to the sensation by flinging his arms over the back of his skull, holding his head as still as possible.

The world moved faster and faster, and Ash couldn't stop it. He squeezed his knees over his ears, tensing his muscles. Nothing. He felt like he was trapped in a cage, surrounded by a dozen lions, all licking their chops. The fear was uncontrollable. Even by their normal terrifying standards, this was a bad one.

Breath coming in ragged bursts and heart pounding in his ears, Ash didn't hear the approaching footsteps. He only noticed the presence of another person when a female voice gently said, "Hey." Whipping his head up, Ash saw raven hair and a concerned face. After a moment, he realized he was looking at Alexis. The realization filled him with humiliation.

"Hiya," he said, trying to sound goofy, even though he knew he was caught. "What's a girl like you doing—" The feeble attempt at a joke was cut off by a wave of nausea. Ash stuffed his head back between his legs.

"Don't talk," Alexis said. "It's okay. Blondell told me to find you. Now I see why." She ran a soft hand through Ash's thick brown hair, nails raking against his scalp.

Ash whimpered and twitched, and Alexis withdrew her hand.

"Talk when you are ready," she said.

A few minutes later, Ash tried again. "They don't usually come this strong," he said, his voice pained. "Not this quickly, not this intense. It must be . . ."

"Everything? It must be everything?" Alexis said. Ash looked up and realized, for the first time, that her eyes were a clear blue, not unlike the sky after it rained. She moved her hand over his, and Ash reflexively jerked his hand back.

"Sorry," Ash said, his voice running away from him. "Sorry. I'm sorry. I'm—"

"Stop," commanded Alexis, her voice strong.

Ash moaned and Alexis brought her hand back to his. Ash tried to withdraw his hand again, his lips quivering. He expected Alexis to let go. Instead, she held on tight. He took a couple jagged breaths before speaking again.

"Do you know what anxiety does to a person?" he asked.

Alexis shook her head sadly. "No. Other things, yes. More than I care to remember. But not this."

Ash nodded, too hard, and his head hurt. "It . . . it puts you in a box. In a little box."

"Keep going. Tell me what you are feeling."

"Hell," Ash said, breathlessly, knowing how ridiculous he sounded, and not giving a damn. "It's different for everyone. For me, heart-racing, sweating everywhere, stomach churning. You feel like you are going to die. Or go insane and start screaming. Or explode. It's just . . . fear. Panic. A . . . oh, God." Ash put his head back between his legs, an intense feeling of shame crushing him.

Alexis put a hand on his back and gently rubbed it, applying as little pressure as possible . . . to just let him know that she was there.

"This is not supposed to be what a leader does," he continued.

"No," Alexis snapped, abruptly pulling her hand off his back. The vitriol in her voice caught Ash off guard, and he lifted his head up. "Never, ever say that again. We could all go home tomorrow, and we could never see each other again. Our memories can be erased, but listen to me. You can't say that. I don't know much about anxiety, but I know that this sucks. A measure of leadership isn't what you are stuck with, but how you deal with it." Ash didn't react for a moment, and Alexis let the outburst melt into the muted light of the hallway before slipping her hand back on top of his. "Keep going. Anxiety puts you in a box. What do you mean?"

Still stunned, Ash took a moment before speaking. "It . . . okay. Anxiety attacks are hell because you become so afraid of them. You have them when you go to school . . . so you start to hate school and don't want to go there anymore. And then it happens at the movie theater. And when you are driving. And when you are more than ten minutes away from home. And it gets to be like a boa constrictor. It squeezes the life out of you. It puts you in a box, and that box keeps getting smaller and smaller. The next thing you know, there's nowhere you can go, nothing you can do. You are stuck, trapped in your bed at home, working a part-time job, when you know you are supposed to be more."

"More than what?" Alexis asked.

"Be more than you are right now," Ash said, realizing that the conversation had gently transitioned into an area much broader than anxiety. "When you know, deep down, you are supposed to be more than you think you are."

Alexis smiled thinly. "That I can understand. And I like the way you put it."

Ash nodded and realized that his heart rate had started to slow. It slowed further as Alexis put one hand on each of his shoulders and squeezed tightly, creating the illusion that Ash was wrapped in a warm embrace. He murmured gently. Both he and Alexis sat motionless, Ash enjoying the cooling sensation of his anxiety starting to melt away.

"Come on," Alexis said, slowly pulling Ash up.

Ash started to groan but stuffed the noise back down his throat. Alexis wrapped an arm around Ash's waist and he returned the favor; not out of closeness or affection, but because he simply needed Alexis' balance to help him walk. His knees felt like Jello that had been left in the sun for too long.

"I found your cabin," she said.

"Oh, yeah. Great," Ash said, forcing a smile and making Alexis laugh.

"It's just around the corner from the Bridge. Blondell and I talked. We can fly this thing for the night. You rest. We'll go from there."

Half a minute later, they arrived at Ash's cabin. Gently taking Ash's hand, Alexis opened his palm and pressed it against the door. When it opened, revealing the room inside, Ash gasped and slammed a hand to his chest.

It was his room. He was practically in his room from home. There was the same model of television, complete with an Xbox One. The same picture collages, and astoundingly, the same pictures, from home. The same poster Aunt Rebecca had given him: Super Mario, goofy, plastic smile, arms stretched into the air, soaring into the sky.

Even the bedspread was the same. It was brand new, without the wear and tear, but it was there.

Alexis looked as dumbfounded as Ash. "How do you think they did this?" she asked.

Ash shrugged. "No idea." The weariness began to smother him. Sensing this, Alexis took Ash's arm and led him to the bed. Ash collapsed.

"How do you sleep at home?" she asked.

"Terribly," Ash said, voice muffled by the pillow.

"Even after a day like today?"

"Especially after a day like today," Ash said. "Lemme tell you, anxiety and depression are awesome." A bitter laugh followed.

"Okay, hang on," she said, marching off.

Ash heard the small sound of a door opening, then a smaller door, and the sound of items being shuffled. Shortly, Alexis returned. "Turn around," she said, and Ash did so. There he saw Alexis, holding a small, yellow pill, and a glass of water. "Klonipan, one milligram. To be taken as needed for anxiety. That sound right?"

Ash's mouth fell open. "How did you know to look for that?"

"I just did. Take it." Alexis extended the pill and water glass.

More shocked than ever, Ash took the pill and popped it under his tongue. "No water," he said, sucking on the chalky tablet. "Quicker if it goes in like this."

Alexis nodded. "Okay." She pointed back at Ash's pillow. "Lie down. Now."

Ash obediently collapsed back into the bed and was dimly aware of Alexis taking his shoes off. She covered him with a soft, blue blanket.

Normally, the pills took at least twenty minutes to work. Ash knew he wasn't going to need that long. As sleep's claws pulled him into a tight embrace, Ash saw a jumble of images flash before his eyes: the Back Brigade, looking scared and alone; Anton, sneering, laughing at Ash's weakness; Echo, seeing through him; Blondell, staring thoughtfully at her computer; Daniel, looking as carefree as could be; and Alexis tenderly gazing at him from above, stroking his hair, as sleep finally captured him.

Chapter Fourteen

Slowly, Ash blinked his eyes open. He had no clue how long he had been out, but he realized right away that the light in his room was brighter than it had been the previous evening. Perhaps the ship's lighting system was designed to mimic the sun?

Ash removed the covers and stood up. His head felt foggy. His sleep had been anything but restful, but he also knew from his ample experience with tranquilizers that the sensations would clear – eventually. All things considered, he felt okay; after difficult days like the one he'd had yesterday, things could have been a lot worse.

Ash padded over to the small bathroom Alexis had been rooting around in yesterday. He noticed the small medicine cabinet, complete with the small white pills that he was supposed to take daily. He skipped them, for now. After all, hadn't yesterday been bad enough? Disorienting enough? Wouldn't it be better to reintegrate his medication once he had gotten used to this place?

Ignoring the small voice warning against the decision to put down his medication, Ash stripped. He turned the shower on. Stepping under the water, he immediately blasted the heat and let the warm steam envelope his senses. All of yesterday felt like a dream: a long, long dream, with several days of action compressed into far too little time. Ash tried to review yesterday's events, but found himself completely overwhelmed. Everything jumbled together, from the first moments of being awakened by a screaming young woman to being led into a strange bed by Alexis last night.

Alexis. Crap. That could get complicated. Under normal circumstances, Ash would go running in her direction as fast as he possibly could. She was . . . well, she was difficult to describe, but Ash was pretty sure she could take him in a fight. The thought made him laugh. Then again, there were very few relationships on this ship that didn't give him at least a snicker. Whatever was going on it was one of the few things keeping him functioning. Besides, they had barely known each other for twenty-four hours, and she had already seen him at his worst. She could never be romantically interested in him. Hell, she had just tranquilized him and dropped him into bed. Women wanted real men, right? Not big anxious balls of goo?

Ash turned off the water and grabbed a thick white towel. How could he go on like this? He'd had two major anxiety attacks yesterday, and he was theoretically *in charge* of a ship tasked with saving the future of humanity? This was ridiculous. The people in charge of making these decisions – this Unity Government – must have been drunk when deciding on a crew roster, because this was insane. *I'm a twenty-year-old college drop-out,* Ash thought. *They couldn't get a freakin' submarine commander or something?*

Ash opened his closet and stared in disbelief, yet again, at the neat row of slate-gray uniforms which hung loosely on a row of shiny metal hangers. He tentatively reached out and pinched the fabric of one of the shirts. The top was astonishingly cool and thin; pulling harder, the uniform stretched, but when Ash released the shirt, it automatically returned to the same form as before, looking as if it hadn't been touched. Sighing wearily, Ash flung the shirt over his head, followed by a dark pair of flexible black pants over his legs.

A few steps later, and he was on the Bridge, his hair still wet.

"Morning everyone," Ash said, trying to sound as chipper as possible. A few mumbled greetings were the best he got back. Most of the crew – at least those on the Bridge – were either too engrossed in their stations, or too dazed to care.

There was one exception.

"Morning," said a smiling Alexis, looking well-rested. "How'd you sleep?"

"Uh . . . fantastic," Ash said. He wasn't going to pretend that last night hadn't happened. Alexis had been there. What did he have to hide at this point?

It was the right response; Alexis laughed. "Well, good," she said. "You look a lot better, though." She waved Ash over and he walked next to her. She stood, and with a brief, conspiratorial glance around the Bridge, she leaned toward Ash, looking ready to trade secrets. "Hopefully, a good night's sleep will put you in a better place?"

"Yeah. Hopefully." Ash looked down for a moment, gathering his thoughts, and connected with Alexis' warm stare. "Thank you. I can't exactly figure out any other words for it, but thank you. I'm glad it was you that found me last night."

"Me too," Alexis said. She furtively glanced around the ship, and Ash followed her glance, relieved to discover that no one was looking in their direction. His eyes found Alexis' again, and she returned his stare. Ash flinched, expecting to find judgment on Alexis' face. Instead, he saw sympathy.

She wrapped a hand around his wrist. "You're okay," she said.

Ash's heart skipped a beat. She withdrew her hand and her voice perked up again.

"Blondell covered for me last night, so I'm going to relieve her. Go get some breakfast in the cafeteria."

"Will do," Ash said. "I'll meet you back here. We've got to figure out a plan moving forward."

Alexis nodded. With a snap of her head (which almost resulted in Ash getting whipped by a mass of curly hair), she walked back toward Blondell.

Ash left and went to the cafeteria, curious about what kind of food he would find. There was a pitcher of orange juice and a large tray of floppy pancakes set in the front of the room. Ash walked closer to inspect them and picked one up; they were toasty warm.

"They're from the microwave," said a voice behind him.

Ash jumped, startled, and turned around, coming face to face with Exodus, the infamous screamer from their arrival.

"I'm sorry!" she cried, putting her hands in front of her chest. "Sorry, sorry!"

"It's okay, it's okay." Ash smiled and extended a hand. "Don't worry about it. I've been there too. I'm—"

"Ash, I know," the girl said. "I'm Exodus. We met when I was going insane." Ash got a good laugh about that. "I'm really sorry—"

"Stop apologizing," Ash said.

"Sorry about—" Exodus caught herself and smiled a little. "Okay, I gotcha. Just a little nerve-wracking, is all."

"Believe me, I understand," Ash said.

Exodus' eyes narrowed. "You do?"

Ash paused, unsure of how to answer. "Just trust me. I get it more than you know."

Exodus looked unhappy with that answer, but shrugged.

"Breakfast is here." She gestured to the pancakes. "Mercury found the food. I found the orange juice." Ash surmised that Mercury was the other girl he had seen with Exodus. "Sorry this is all that we have right now. We're working on it though. Maybe later we can make a nicer meal for everyone."

Ash shrugged, smiled, and dropped four pancakes on a nearby plate.

"Exodus," he said, tearing off one of the pancakes and popping it into his mouth, chewing with genuine delight. "This is one of the best meals I've had in a long time. Thank you. And keep up the good work here. Lord knows we need all the help we can get."

"Thanks," she said, standing little straighter.

Ash nodded, walked by, and jammed another pancake into his mouth.

"Thank you!" he said, leaving the cafeteria, an extra bounce in his step.

CHAPTER FIFTEEN

Back on the Bridge, Ash found Blondell, Alexis and Daniel locked in an intense conversation, with Anton, Pike and Sia watching intently.

"Nice timing, Captain." Daniel looked up at Ash as he walked in. "We were just debating what to do next."

"I say go for it," Blondell said. "We've got about four days until we can even get to our next stop."

"Before we go any further, what is our next stop?" Ash asked.

Blondell walked over to her station, tapped out a few commands and brought up a large map on the front screen.

"That would be this." She pointed at a planet. The front view zoomed in, revealing a large, rocky mass. "Kepler 438b. NASA of the old United States found it in 2015, so Ash, you might remember this."

"Not a clue, but keep going. You seem to know what you are talking about," Ash said.

Blondell laughed before continuing. "The space program bit the dust around the time that the Earth's ecosystem started collapsing, so we don't know a ton about Kepler. It's 470 light-years from Earth, but it won't take us too long to get there, given the ship's engines."

"About four days," said Jameson. Ash, Daniel and Alexis looked at him in disbelief.

"Four days. To travel 470 light-years?" asked Ash.

"Give or take," said Jameson.

Ash shook his head. "Okay, that works, I guess. Anyway,

Blondell, what are we doing on this thing?"

Blondell zoomed in on Kepler 438b.

"This mountain range, here, is our next target. According to the information Sierra was able to dig up, we're going to need to go into it. There is organic matter in here that needs collecting. We can't determine specifics yet, but Sierra and I think we'll be able to figure that out as we move closer to the planet."

"Organic matter?" asked Anton. Pike and Sia flanked him. "You mean we have to go onto the planet?"

"Yup," said Blondell. "We combine that with the chunk of the asteroid that we were able to get yesterday, and we're green."

"Green?" asked Daniel, looking confused.

"Yes, golden, ace, good, whatever," said Blondell.

Ash shrugged. "Okay, we get onto the planet, get this organic matter, whatever it is, and go to our next objective."

"Right," Blondell responded.

"And we can get there in four days?"

"Right again."

"That's not enough time!" Anton said. Ash stared at the ship's troublemaker and noticed something for the first time: he looked sick. Anton, who wasn't exactly loaded with color to begin with, seemed to have grown paler since yesterday. He was certainly more jittery.

"What do you mean?" Ash asked, suspiciously.

Anton wheeled on Ash. "You almost got us killed yesterday."

Ash's heart leapt into his throat at the accusation, which was almost instantly cut off by the objections of everyone assembled.

"*You* almost screwed that one up, you idiot!" yelled Alexis. "You are too stupid to follow orders and fired our weapons too early. If Ash hadn't thought quickly—"

"To save your rear, because you didn't prep enough and the gravity almost killed us!" Anton retorted, his voice rising in pitch. "Remember that part? When you couldn't navigate worth a damn? Or should I be yelling at Blondell for misjudging the gravity distortions' danger?"

"Why are you doing this?" asked Blondell, her voice level. Ash marveled at her relaxed stance; how she gestured with her palms open while his hands were balled into fists. "Everyone made mistakes yesterday." She took a step closer to Anton and kept her voice soft. The response from Pike and Sia was to draw closer to their friend. "Anton, no one was perfect yesterday. None of us have gone on a world-saving mission before. We can learn from what happened. Make it better for next time."

"You are both right," Ash said, drawing nasty looks from everyone assembled. "What? It's true. We all made mistakes yesterday that could have gotten us killed, and that includes me. That's not the issue. The question is this: how do we go forward from here?" A thought, sharp as a lightning bolt, hit Ash. "Anton, what do you propose?"

Recognizing the moment, Anton said, "We wait. We've got a few weeks at least, right?"

"Right," said Blondell. "We've got about four weeks until the ship is supposed to crash into Earth."

"I don't want to rush," Anton said. Was that pleading in his voice? "Can we just take our time?" The crew became quiet. *I still don't know what the hell we are doing,* thought Ash.

"Let's try this," Ash said. "We've got the simulator, right?"

"Right," said Daniel. "That thing is the bomb."

"Ew," said Alexis. "'The bomb?"

Daniel laughed.

"Alright, so we've got the simulator," Ash said, rolling his eyes. "We train. We take a few days and train. All of us. That includes me. We train, figure out where we are going, what we have to do, and we are better prepared for this next stage. Agreed?"

A chorus of nodding heads was the response.

"Okay. Let's get to work."

CHAPTER SIXTEEN

Ash and the rest of the crew spent the next few hours working out a training schedule. Using the pre-programmed material, crew members engaged in training simulations based on their various roles. As Jameson had also pointed out, they'd need to work in shifts in order to get some sleep, and the training would at least enable all of them to have a rudimentary understanding of the ship's various platforms, in case they needed to operate them in an emergency. Meanwhile, Blondell, Sierra and Radar would keep trying to get information about their next mission. That would be fed into the simulator in an effort to prepare them.

Ash also realized there was an added benefit to taking a slower route: it would give the crew a chance to better know each other, work together, and, hopefully, bond. Furthermore, it gave them time to get used to the new surroundings. He was asking a lot of the crew and himself. They were just kids, all of them, from time periods spanning nearly a century, trying desperately to save a planet which generations previous and future had destroyed. Ideally, this added time would give them a chance to build relationships, trust each other, and learn what the hell they were doing.

When the schedule was agreed to, Ash and Daniel walked down to the sim together, since Daniel actually knew how to operate it.

"I still don't understand how this thing works," Ash said. "How does it create matter out of thin air?"

"It doesn't!" cried Jameson from the Bridge, his scientific sensibilities offended. "That's not possible! Not possible!"

Ash sighed. "Fill me in, will ya?" he asked a smirking Daniel.

"Sure, boss," Daniel said. "Look, I'm not a scientist, and I don't think Jameson gets half the stuff that he says he does."

"I heard that!" said Jameson from down the corridor.

"You were supposed to, airhead!" called Daniel over his shoulder. "Anyway, I said the same thing to him earlier. What he said – and this makes sense – is that it doesn't create matter. Just rearranges it."

"Huh?"

"Don't ask me," said Daniel, pausing to look Ash's way and scan his face. "You're doing alright, Captain. Just keep it together," said Daniel. The word "Captain" made Ash pause, involuntarily, for just a moment. He tried to keep walking, as if nothing had happened, but Daniel noticed anyway. "Why do you keep doing that?"

Ash replied, "Doing what?"

"Hating your responsibility. You're in charge, boss, and you know you've done alright by us so far. You got us out of a couple of scrapes back there. We may not be alive if not for you."

"Luck, my friend," Ash said. "Pure, unadulterated luck. I don't know what we are doing—"

"Do you think anyone expects you to?" Daniel snapped, instantly dropping his happy-go-lucky attitude and replacing it with a sharp edge. "You act like we are demanding that you know exactly what you are doing, all the time. Seriously, snap out of it. We're in the middle of *space*. It's 2180. A bunch of us – myself included – are long dead! We don't expect you to do anything but what you have already done."

"I can always do better," Ash said quietly. "Especially if I am really the captain of this thing."

"What's the alternative?" said Daniel. "That nut job Anton?"

"We're all a little nuts here, in case you haven't noticed," Ash retorted, earning a snort from Daniel.

"Sure," he said. "That's because we got sucked up from our beds and thrown in the middle of space. But crisis reveals character. I truly believe that. That's why I like you. It's why I like most of the crew. But Anton – that boy is off. Keep an eye on him. There's something angry and fearful about him, and that is a dangerous combination."

They reached a stairway that took them up to the third level of the ship, where the simulator was. "This is fun," Ash said. I wish I was always put in a life-or-death situation to save the human race and got to play babysitter to people with more issues than me. How are you doing, anyway?"

Daniel turned over his shoulder, the left half of his mouth turned upward. "Never better," he said. "Come on, don't be stupid. We're all in a bad place now. I know that means you, too."

"You don't seem to be," Ash countered. "In fact, of all the people on this ship, you might be doing the best."

"Doing the best of hiding it, you mean." Daniel held a railing as they walked past the second level. "Look, Captain – no, I am going to keep calling you Captain, it's what you are, don't even try to act like you aren't – you gotta look past the surface. Everyone here is struggling. Some are just better at hiding it than others."

"Yeah, well, I've never been good at hiding my emotions."

"Maybe that's a strength," said Daniel. "Maybe that means you're better at facing them head on."

Ash waved his hand dismissively before speaking again. "Where you from, anyway?"

"1990."

"No, no, not when. Where?" Ash asked. "We've all been so caught up in this when crap – I don't know much about anyone's lives."

Daniel seemed to perk up. "Sandusky, Ohio," he said. "I was about to start my senior year of high school."

"You know your way around computers and mechanics."

"The two go hand-in-hand."

"What do you mean?"

Daniel looked over his shoulder at Ash and gave him a brilliant, knowing smile. "See, that's what these shop jocks don't understand. They go, 'Oh, look at me, I can use a wrench, I'm gonna be a kick-ass mechanic.' It don't work that way." Daniel took a finger and jabbed his head. "You gotta have brains if you ever want to do more. I get repairs, that's the easy part. The harder part is computers, electronics, all that stuff. Me? I'm going into Engineering. Mechanics and computers combined."

"Oh yeah?"

"Hell yeah. Lehigh University. I got the grades, my parents have the money, and this time next year, Sandusky can kiss my ass goodbye." Adding emphasis to his last point, Daniel executed a perfect spin move on his toes.

"Whoa, calm down there, Michael Jackson," Ash ribbed good-naturedly. Much to his surprise, and showing a degree of grace his large body would imply he didn't possess, Daniel balanced on his toes and flung one hand into the air, held the stance for a moment, and spun his way back to a normal position.

Ash froze, almost as shocked as he had been the first time he saw the Bridge of the *Redemption*.

"What?" asked a smiling Daniel. "Never seen a big man move?"

"Not like that!" cried Ash.

Daniel's smile got bigger before he pounded Ash on the shoulder with an open palm and kept moving. Fortunately for Ash, he had seen the movement coming and had time to plant his feet; otherwise, he might have fallen over.

As they approached the simulator doors, Daniel said, "By the way, don't think you are getting away with not telling me your story too. I bet it's more interesting than half the people here. You're just lucky we're at the sim." Before Ash could say anything else, Daniel brought his hand to the door. With an easy glide, it slid open. "After you, Captain."

Ash entered the room and felt as if he had walked into a massive, vacant airport hangar that had been stripped bare. The room's ceiling and walls were black. The only markings

126

at all were repeating square indentations on the floor. The ground, Ash noticed, was porous. He stared.

"Best I can tell, that's where the holographic imagery comes from," said Daniel, who was fiddling with a wall panel. "Check this out Captain: what's your favorite animal?"

A pang of homesickness rang in Ash's chest, resounding like a perfectly struck guitar chord. "A six-year-old golden retriever," Ash said quietly. "With a small chunk missing from its right ear."

"Oh, okay. Well, here's a giant bear!" Daniel responded, and in a flash, a six-foot black bear rose from the spongy ground. Frothing at the mouth and roaring like a train, the bear lifted its arms and moved to strike.

"Gah!" cried Ash, diving away despite the fact that that his brain was telling him that the bear wasn't real. Abruptly, the bear disappeared and was replaced by a baby chick.

"What? Just a chick, dude. You're jumpy," said Daniel.

From the ground, Ash looked up and smiled. "I hate you. Only a little bit, but I definitely hate you."

"Gotta relax there before you give yourself a heart attack, buddy," replied Daniel. "Here, have some sunshine."

The lighting in the room changed from an industrial florescent to a natural orange and yellow glow. Streaking white clouds covered an orange-yellow sky, making the newly-appeared ocean reflect a ginger glow. Birds and waves echoed across the chamber as imaginary sand clustered around Ash's feet. Ash extended his arms, taking in a deep breath of air, which was somehow salt-tinged and windswept. He knew he wasn't really on the beach, and he didn't care. Ash sat down and closed his eyes.

"You're good, man," said Ash. "By the way, congratulations. You're also now the Captain. I'll see you in about a week."

Daniel laughed but said nothing else, and the two enjoyed the silence, filling Ash with the first non-chemically induced sense of peace he'd felt since arriving on the *Redemption*.

After a minute, Daniel said, "You'd be surprised what

happens when everyone works together."

"How do you mean?"

"The Unity Government, man. Haven't you talked to Blondell about them?"

Before Ash could respond, the ocean disappeared as the door to the simulator opened. Turning around, Ash saw a bobbing head of curly blond hair.

"What's up, Echo?" he called across the room. Echo's chest was heaving, as if she had gone running down the hallway.

"Talk to you for a sec?" she asked.

Ash looked back at Daniel, who nodded.

"Do what you gotta do, Captain. I'm gonna prep this thing for Blondell."

Ash nodded and stood up, slapping Daniel on the shoulder as he walked past. "Give her a bear scare," he said, joining Echo. They walked back toward the Bridge. "What's going on?"

"You seem better," Echo said, staring at Ash briefly as they walked.

Ash shrugged. "Eh, a giant bear has that effect on people."

"What?"

"Never mind."

Echo smiled slightly. "I'm glad. On the list of people I'm worried about, you're still high up there," Echo said. "But that's why I think you can help me." Echo began to slow and Ash matched her pace.

"How?" he asked.

Echo stopped and leaned on the railing of one of the stairs. "The Back Brigade? There's about three of them left at this point."

"Left?" asked Ash, incredulous. "What do you mean?"

Echo sighed heavily. "The good news is that two of them are functioning. They are running around – I've got Blondell and Sierra working with them. It's just menial stuff right now – you know, running errands, exploring the ship, all that stuff. The bad news is that one of them has a new best friend: Anton."

128

The image of one of the quiet, scared kids talking to Anton, smiling, laughing, bonding . . . Ash sighed heavily as well. "Okay, understood," Ash said, holding back from ripping into Anton. There was truly nothing about the guy that he liked. In their brief time together, Anton had shown an instant love of turning objects to debris and flames, attacking other crew members and undermining Ash at every turn.

Echo's next words confirmed Ash's fear. "Look, Ash, these guys are scared, impressionable, and looking for a leader." Echo lowered her voice and said, "That needs to be you."

Ash folded his arms over his chest and didn't say anything for a moment. He'd never been in charge of anything in his life – not really. And as he had spun into the cycle of anxiety, loneliness and guilt that was his depression, he had barely even been in charge of his own affairs. He was feeling like an unabashed failure, leading a ship that was responsible for saving the future of humanity. More than ever, he understood something which he had never fully grasped before: Why the burden of leadership was so heavy. His own emotions didn't matter.

"Okay. Where am I going first?"

Chapter Seventeen

"Robin? Robin?"

Echo rapped lightly on the door to Cabin #13, and the only answer was silence.

"Robin? You awake?"

Echo knocked louder this time, but the door didn't budge and no noise could be heard from inside.

"Fantastic. Just great. We can't get in unless he opens the door. Do you have a master key or something?"

Ash wracked his brain. "A master key? No." He placed his hand on the cabin door. "Maybe we can check with Daniel, he seems—"

To both of their surprise, the door *wooshed* open. Ash tumbled against the side of the door, falling on his shoulder.

"Ow! Dammit!"

"Oh yeah!" Echo said brightly. "Forgot about that. Guess you are the master key, Ash."

Ash stood up and brushed his pants. "Just what I always wanted," he grumbled.

The door started to close and Echo waved. "See you in a bit!" She turned to walk down the hallway as the door closed behind her, leaving Ash alone in the room with its occupant.

Ash cleared his throat, searching for his voice. "Hi Robin," he said, looking at the room's occupant.

Robin was the small, pockmarked boy who had spoken up on the Bridge the day before. His cry of "Noooooope" still rang in Ash's ears. When Ash had last seen him, Robin was running away from the Bridge. Apparently, his bed was where he had fled. Currently, Robin was staring straight at the ceiling, eyes wide open and unblinking. The covers on his bed – still firmly tucked into the corners of the mattress by his feet – were pulled up to his chin, giving Robin the appearance of a puppet which had been cast aside in the middle of a boring children's show. On the table next to the bed was a bowl of some kind of soup, half eaten. Looking closer, Ash saw that there were soup stains on Robin's pillow.

Ash sat down heavily on the chair next to Robin's bed, feeling weariness into his bones. Robin, for his part, didn't react to Ash's presence.

"I hope the ceiling is interesting," Ash started. "Looks like you've been staring at it for a while."

No response. Ash sighed deeply and crossed one leg over the other.

"Yeah, I don't blame you. That was a pretty stupid joke. Honestly . . . I don't blame you for any of this." Ash tried to keep the emotion out of his voice but found that impossible. "This sucks. This all sucks. I mean, who are we to get this burden? And why us? There are so, so many questions that really need to be answered, and I'm the last person to answer them, let alone be given the responsibility of saving a planet. And who are you, right?" Ash, who had been facing forward, turned to look at Robin, whose eyes remained locked on a point above him. "You don't have to respond, but I know exactly what you are thinking right now. 'Why me? Who am I to be here? What did I do to deserve this?' You can tell me I'm wrong, but you won't."

Still nothing.

"I don't expect you to move, Robin. Not until you want to. But I do know this much: it's a miracle that I'm not in bed, every bit as catatonic as you." Much to his surprise, that worked.

"You?" croaked Robin.

Staring in disbelief, Ash found his vision drawn to the boy's chapped lips. Horrified, Ash stood and walked to the bathroom. He filled a glass with cool water and came back to the room. Robin was struggling with the blankets, which remained firmly tucked into the bed, hotel style. Ash bent down, freed the covers, and handed Robin the glass of water, which Robin drank in two gulps. Putting the glass on the table, Ash noticed that Robin was following him with his eyes.

"Absolutely," Ash continued. "Robin, I've been depressed for years. It's getting worse. The medication feels like it's barely working, and I'm lucky I'm not stuck in my bed, pissing my pants. And now we're here. That's life, or something, I guess. Look, I know being stuck here is making this worse. Lemme ask you something: Were you happy at home?"

It was a solid ten seconds before Robin answered: "No." His voice made the "no" sound more like an admission of guilt than a response to a question.

"Didn't think so. Me neither. And isn't it funny? We're thousands of miles, and decades, away from where we came from. And it doesn't mean a damn." Ash shook his head. "You can't out-run your troubles. The only thing you can do is live. And try to get through the next day." At the mention of "the next day," any momentum Ash had been building with his new friend broke. Robin's face stiffened, like he had been shot. Ash sensed Robin pressing the back of his head deeper into the pillow, making his already small frame appear even more miniscule.

"Fine. Forget it," Ash said, feeling like a failure yet again. "Talk to me. Tell me about your life. Tell me something about you. Get out of your own head a little." Ash tried to keep the bitterness of his own inability to help a crew member – *his* crew member – out of his voice, and found himself failing miserably. Robin replied to Ash's question with silence, and Ash found himself wanting to find his own bed to sink into. "Robin?"

The smallness in Ash's voice reached Robin, and he turned his head ever so slightly to Ash. "1998."

Ash nodded. What a strange thing to have to say in a conversation: not where you were from, but when.

"Wyoming." That explained the slight twang in Robin's voice.

132

"Farm country?" asked Ash.

Robin shook his head in a movement so slight that Ash had to squint to see it. "Kinda. Cheyenne. Closest thing to a big city we have." A small smile crossed Robin's face. "Wish I could say I got out of the state. Cheyenne is the biggest city I've ever seen."

Ash began to tug at the strand of conversation which had appeared. "What do you do? What are you into?"

At that, Robin shrugged. "Stay small," he said quietly.

Ash rolled his eyes. *Good Lord, do I sound like this to others? To Alexis?*

"Come on," he said, and Robin shrugged again, this time meeting Ash's stare.

"No, I mean that, staying small," he said. "If you can stay small enough, no one can notice you."

Jesus, Ash thought. *Try something else.*

"Okay, I understand that, but you must like to do something other than duck people." For fifteen seconds, Robin seemed lost in a silence which threatened to stretch into oblivion. Just as Ash thought he would have to say something else, Robin spoke again.

"Fixing things," he said quietly.

Ash raised his eyebrows.

"Really?" Ash said. He smiled slightly. "You don't strike me as the type."

"I get that a lot," Robin said bitterly, making Ash instantly regret his words. Seeing the cloud that had come across Ash's face, Robin quickly added, "No, it's okay. I don't mind. I set myself up for it, to be honest. Surprising people can be fun." Robin stared into the distance, his eyes seeming lost. "I played with legos a lot as a kid. I still remember the sets that my Mom would get me. She'd put them at her feet and say, 'Now, Robbie, how fast can you put them together?' And it would be a race. And she'd always be so proud." A sniffle, followed by a wet, heaving noise that came from somewhere in Robin's small chest. "I miss her." And Robin shrank into the bed yet again, but before he could move more than a few inches, Ash put a firm hand on Robin's shoulder.

133

"Stop," Ash said quietly, and with a soft smile. "I miss my Mom, too. But you can't do this. You can't allow yourself to retreat into a pillow."

"Oh, I can't?" said Robin sarcastically, showing a fight in his voice that Ash had yet to hear. "Oh, alright, I'll just go for a walk outside and clear my head . . . oh yeah *we're on a spaceship and nothing matters.*" And Robin sank again.

Stung, Ash withdrew his hand.

"Yeah, this sucks." He sat back, combing his mind for some comforting words or a way to reach the small, depressed, scared boy in front of him. An idea flashed through his overwrought brain. "Hey, want me to take you to Daniel? He can probably use some help with some of the stuff he is doing." Robin shook his head imperceptibly.

"I'm good, thanks," he whispered, staring straight ahead.

Ash sighed and stood up. "Fine. Just fine," he said, brushing his hands on his pants before leaning on the chair he had been sitting on. "Look, there's not a lot of reason to hope right now. I've been there . . . actually, scratch that, I'm there right now. All I know is that we have to keep going. We, as a ship and as a crew, have to do something, or we lose everything, including our own lives." Robin didn't react, and Ash stepped forward and knelt at his bed. "Do you honestly think that sitting in bed is going to fix anything?"

"Do you honestly think I care?" Robin shot back.

Ash sighed and put his head down for a moment, cursing his own inadequacy and trying to figure out why this hurt so much. "There's only one way to move forward. And that's to actually try to move," he mumbled. "This is just me, but the second I stopped moving, stopped thinking, stopped *living,* depression got me. But if I kept moving, kept trying to accomplish something . . . I did okay. I'm not stupid enough to think that having a type-A personality cures depression. And I know that the meds and the therapy have helped, even if that hasn't completely worked yet. But I do know that if you ever surrender, that's when depression gets you. I also know that as long as you breathe, there is hope."

Robin didn't react.

"You can't work through depression, anxiety, whatever, by force of will alone. But if you surrender to it, you've already lost." Ash reached out to supportively squeeze Robin's arm, but found himself hesitating.

Robin had walled himself up again; his face was slack and his eyes, with remarkable speed, had regained their glassy stare. Maybe he was sinking into himself again. Or maybe he was just thinking. Either way, he shifted so he was looking up again, back at the ceiling.

Ash sat and stared at the prone, scared boy, and saw nothing but his own face.

CHAPTER EIGHTEEN

Staring at the Bridge from his perch on the captain's platform, one thought kept repeating in Ash's mind: *Anywhere is better than those rooms.*

The visit with Robin had gone the "best" of his visits with the three remaining crew members who weren't functioning yet – the other two hadn't appeared to have heard a thing Ash said, and they remained locked in their beds, unable to even make eye contact. One young girl literally whimpered every time Ash spoke, and eventually he just squeezed her hand and left the room. It seemed to be the most merciful thing he could do.

Back on the Bridge, Ash and Alexis established the training schedule for the rest of the crew. Sierra and Blondell had some success at gathering information about where they were going on their next stop and were starting to design a mission profile for the planet. While they did that, the rest of the crew cycled in and out of the training simulator.

The good news was that, according to Blondell, the enhanced data gave them a better idea of what they were expecting. Using an air computer, she diagramed where they were going and what would happen next.

"We're here," she said, jabbing at an icon of the *Redemption* while blowing a few loose strands of hair out of her face. She dragged the *Redemption* to the planet, and the view abruptly changed; they were looking at an overhead shot of a rocky, craggy ground, with peaks and valley's overlapping haphazardly. "This is Kepler, about four days away, and that large red dot in the center of that cave network is our target."

Seeing an immediate problem, Ash asked, "How are we supposed to land there?"

"Easy. We don't," responded Blondell. "At least not in this thing."

"Not in this thing?" Ash looked at her quizzically. "So . . . beam me up, Blondy?"

That earned Ash a dirty look. "No, Ash, there's no beam onboard this thing, at least not one that I am aware of. We'll fly in these." Blondell slid the current screen aside to reveal two smaller space ships that looked like deformed spheres with stubby wings and little feet as landing gear. "You're right. The ground is too rocky for us to land the *Redemption*. So we take these: shuttle craft designed to land in tight spots. Depending on how many of us go, we take more than one. The good news is that we can program them to land exactly where we want. All I have to do is manipulate the map a little bit."

"Well, that's something," Ash said. "Then what?"

"Then we run into these caves." Blondell zoomed in on a small hole in the mountainside that Ash hadn't noticed earlier, revealing a small entrance. "Our target is located in there."

"What exactly is our target?"

"Eggs."

"Beg your pardon?"

Blondell sighed faintly and altered the screen again, revealing blue oblong eggs.

"According to the information Sierra and I were able to gather—" Sierra squeaked happily in the distance, which Blondell ignored. "The eggs are native to some kind of animal which lives on Kepler."

"Alright," Ash said. "Do we know where this animal is? How many there are? If they're hostile or not?"

"Of course not," Blondell replied. "That would be too easy." Ash opened his mouth to speak again, but was interrupted by the far louder Anton.

"You're not very good at plans, are you, Blondy?" he snorted, a viciousness in his voice which had become all too recognizable.

Ash rolled his eyes, and sensing a fight, started to speak, ready to interject himself between the two.

Alexis beat him too it. "What's your idea, genius? I haven't seen you do much except screw up around here. All together now . . . three . . . two . . . one . . . you remember one, doncha?"

Instead of getting quiet, as Ash expected, Anton simply sneered and stood up, brushed past Alexis and walked to a spare computer. He typed a few keystrokes and brought up the same overhead map of Kepler that Ash was using, but this map looked different: a large target overlaid the main cave.

"Easy. We blow it up." Blondell, Alexis and almost the entirety of Bridge practically screamed in horror; Ash could even make out cries of protests from the normally quiet Radar.

"You want to blow up a critical piece of the cure for the deadliest disease ever to hit humanity?" asked Alexis, her eyebrows raised

"Not the whole thing, you hag," retorted Anton, his voice increasing an octave.

"Hey!" Ash interjected. Anton ignored his protests.

"Ash, I cycled through our weapons, and I have the right kind. A medium intensity torpedo will hit the top of this cave ceiling and allow us to land on the top, here. Then, one of us drops in, grabs the eggs, and gets back into the shuttle. Less people need to go, we don't need to follow Blondy's convoluted route, and there's less risk. Piece of cake."

"Unless you fire too hard and destroy the cave!" said Alexis, her voice dripping with sarcasm. "Then what? We just go back to Earth and say 'Oops.'"

"This is the only option!" said Anton, hammering his fist into a railing. The intensity in Anton's voice was unmistakable, but there was something else there too, a timbre that didn't quite match his usual arrogance. Anton's cheeks were flushed, and a shiny layer of sweat appeared on his forehead. His bottom lip was quivering ever so slightly. So were his hands.

Near Ash, Echo stood, arms folded over her chest. Ash realized that her eyes hadn't moved from Anton since he'd started to speak, and her eyebrows were scrunched so tightly that they were practically touching the top of her nose.

Ash decided it would be better to play diplomat. "Anton, I understand what you mean, and I appreciate your alternative idea. That being said, I think Alexis and Blondell are right."

"Of course you do," retorted Pike, speaking the first words that Ash had heard him say since they arrived on the ship. Ash ignored him.

"It's too risky, and if it goes wrong, it leaves us with no alternative. We'll have failed everything."

"Too risky? Your way can get us killed!" Again, Anton's high-pitched voice sounded like a wailing child.

"And your way can literally end humanity!" shot back Alexis, as she took a step toward Anton.

Ash looked surprised and seized the opportunity, standing between the two with his arms extended.

"Knock it off. Both of you."

The entire Bridge was looking at him, and Ash took a very loud, deep breath and froze for a moment. He watched Alexis' features soften as he did so. The ship was deathly quiet, save for the hum of the Bridge's machinery. Anton said nothing. He simply stared at Ash for a moment, disgusted, before spinning on his heel and marching out of the Bridge.

Sia cried, "Anton! Wait!" and raced after him.

After ten seconds of silence, Blondell spoke. "That was weird."

"Very," added Alexis.

Ash looked at both of them before turning his gaze to Echo.

Watch him, she lipped.

Ash gave the briefest of nods, and looked back at the rest of his crew, feelings of incompetence and regret starting to seep into his brain.

I could have done that a lot better, he thought. *Maybe I should have given Anton more consideration? Still, that seems like the dumbest idea ever. None of us want to face the risk like that, but . . .*

Brushing the thoughts out of his mind, Ash turned to Sierra, who had been silent for the entire conversation. She was looking at Alexis, her mouth slightly agape.

"Can you keep feeding the simulator?" Ash asked.

Snapped out of her reverie, Sierra jerked her head toward Ash and rapidly nodded.

"Definitely," she said.

"Good. Then let's do it."

***

The first group in the sim insisted on going together: Pike, Sia, Tidus and a far-less-agitated Anton. None, except Tidus, came back to the Bridge upon the completion of their sim, and Tidus' face was red and glossy from sweat and exhilaration.

"They had sims in my time, but nothing like that!" he exclaimed, practically gasping for breath and shaking from adrenaline. "That thing crushed! Everything felt so real . . . it practically smelled real!"

Ash stared on, hands on his hips, in disbelief. He hadn't seen Tidus this animated in the brief time he had known him. Maybe this sim could help unite the crew around their mission?

Daniel and Blondell took the next run, though it took all of Daniel's charm and wit to pry Blondell away from her precious computers.

"Come on, girl, I know you've been wondering what you are doing all this typing into!" he had said.

"Girl?" said Blondell, shifting her body into a fighting stance. "Alright, tough guy. You want to see a girl?" She playfully advanced on Daniel, who surprised everybody by charging Blondell, picking her up, and slinging her over a shoulder. Blondell yelped, startled, but started to laugh.

"Okay, you know what? Fine! Let's go! Giddy up, horsy!"

Their laughter echoed down the hallway and was contagious; the entire Bridge found themselves laughing.

"I'm next!" shouted Ash after the two, and the crew laughed harder.

All bets were off, however, when the pair returned. "I don't know what Blondell was feeding into that computer, but man, that was not easy," said Daniel. For the first time since Ash had known him, he realized that Daniel was not smiling.

"What do you mean?" Ash asked intently.

Blondell, her face ashen, responded. "Ash, I've been giving the computer all the information I can gather and preparing it for the worst-case scenario: The creatures who laid the eggs are there, they are hostile, and they are large. If that's the case, we've got a problem."

Silence. Fear and worry cascaded over Ash, which he tried to bury. "Okay. What did you do on the sim?"

"We went in," Daniel responded. "It was just the two of us. The mission Blondell and Sierra set up had us advance like we will in a few days – through the cave, through the passageways which Blondell thinks we're going to have to move through, and into the nest to get the eggs. Only . . ." Daniel's voice trailed off, and he looked at the floor. Eyes locked on his feet, he continued. "We never even got that far."

"It was an ambush," Blondell continued. Ash and Alexis exchanged worried looks. "I inputted some generics about the animals based on the make-up of the eggs. The eggs are larger than I anticipated, so we can assume the animals are as well. That, combined with the makeup of the planet, allowed the computer to create a simulation of what we are dealing with."

"We were literally beaten to death," Daniel said quietly.

Blondell immediately stepped in.

"It was a simulation . . . well, obviously, we're still here," she added. "But, Ash, that thing is awful. Those things are awful." Blondell shivered.

Ash didn't say a word for a moment, searching in his mind for a solution. He whirled toward Sierra. "I may be grasping at straws here, but Sierra, come on . . . is this accurate?"

Sierra shrugged and put her hands in the air.

"Sorry, Ash, but I'm not smarter than these computers," she said, tapping her own flat screen monitor. "Just about all of the data we've fed this thing has proven to be correct so far. If this is what the computer says, I think it's legitimate."

No one spoke on the Bridge.

CHAPTER NINETEEN

After two hours of relative silence, it was Ash and Alexis' turn. Ash still felt smothered in hopelessness.

Alexis was overly upbeat. "You know, this may not be that bad," she said, energetically walking down the hallway.

Ash followed a few steps behind, hands in his pockets. "How do you mean?"

"I know Sierra's a computer genius, but sorry, she's wrong. That thing isn't perfect. If it was, that disaster while we were trying to get to the asteroid wouldn't have been nearly as bad. It missed that the gravity distortions were shifting, including the one which almost got us killed and messed up our left wing . . ." Alexis' voice trailed off, and she slowed to a stop.

Ash halted next to her.

"You do realize what I'm saying, right? We can beat this," said Alexis.

Ash merely shrugged. "I guess."

Alexis' features tightened. "What do you mean, 'you guess'? Come on, Ash. You're the Captain! Inspire me or something!"

"Haven't we had this conversation?" Ash retorted, more sharply than he meant to. But he could feel a combination of rage and hopelessness bubbling up inside of him, seething like lava inside of a volcano, yearning to be released. "I don't want this."

"Well, it's either you or Anton," Alexis said, her voice rising. "Do you not get that? Look, I get that you feel messed up, but we need you."

Ash snorted. "No one needs me for this. Look how far I've gotten us."

"Oh, please," Alexis said, her voice taut. "I can't believe I have to yell at you to convince you of this, but have you been paying attention? Not just living in your own head? Ash, we got the first vaccine piece! We have a third of the vaccine for a disease that will otherwise kill Earth! And that was under *your* leadership! You saved this ship! You came up with the plan to get us there! You saved us when Blondell, Anton and I almost screwed up! Can you not see that?"

"And look where I got us!" said Ash. The entire experience felt surreal, detached. Like he was outside of his own body, having an argument with someone who wasn't really there. "I'm actually leading us to a potential death at the hands of vicious aliens on some planet that no human has ever been on."

"What you are leading us to may save the entire human race! Are you so myopic that you can't see what kind of impact your actions – our actions, that you are leading – may have?" By that point, the arguing pair had reached the metal stairwell which would take them to the third level of the *Redemption,* where the simulator lay in wait. Accelerated by anger, the two thundered up the steps, ignoring the slam of boots on metal as they hurried up.

"I appreciate the thought, but that's crap, and you know it. It's a miracle I haven't gotten any of us killed yet," Ash said. "I get it, you're trying to buck up the crazy captain—"

Much to Ash's surprise, Alexis' arm cocked back, like it was controlled by a rubber band. Just as quickly, Alexis froze, and the arm dropped.

"Did you just start to hit me?" Ash spluttered.

"Ash, I swear to God, I'm going to punch you in the face," Alexis said.

Ash opened his mouth to speak, but Alexis cut him off. "Don't you dare say anything else. Not another word. I'm done." Alexis' voice trembled and Ash realized that she was near tears. A deep breath later, and Alexis spoke again. Her voice was much softer now. "I get it. You don't want this.

144

And I don't mean wanting to be the Captain. You don't want to hear how good you are. But you have to know. Somewhere, deep inside of you, in a place where your depression and other issues can't reach . . . you have to know, to believe, that you're really good at this."

Ash immediately shrugged. This answer was easy. "I lucked into the good. And I may be leading us to our deaths, and I can't figure out a way around it, short of forfeiting humanity. So no, Alexis, nothing I've done means a damn thing."

Alexis' anger, which had seemed to have burnt itself out, rose like a phoenix. "Fine," she said, through gritted teeth. "Fine. I accept. And you're an idiot." And she stomped off toward the simulator.

Ash, dizzy at having alienated the closest real friend he'd made on the ship, hustled to keep up. "Alexis," he started, catching up to her. He tried to put a hand on her shoulder, but Alexis threw it off.

"Don't," she said, her jaw still locked and feet still moving.

"Alexis, wait, please," Ash said. "I know what you are trying to do, and it means so much—"

"You don't know anything," Alexis retorted, her voice like venom. By now, they had reached the simulator door. Alexis made a fist and hammered, causing the door to open with such speed that it seemed afraid of Alexis' hand. Alexis stormed in and Ash followed, their footsteps echoing across the spacious room.

"Look, you don't know what this is like—"

Ash was cut off as Alexis whirled on him, her face a surprisingly intense mix of anger and pain. "What? You're the only one here with an issue? Life sucks. I get it. But I can't understand why you can't accept what you are." The volume of Alexis' voice increased with every word she said, until she was practically screaming. Like a dam breaking, her emotion broke; her face relaxed and went slack, and her arms fell limp at her sides. "Let's just do this sim, okay? We'll talk when we're done."

Ash was stunned into silence. "Okay," he finally

muttered, when he felt capable of speaking again. Alexis turned away from him and looked at the ceiling.

"Daniel, fire it up," she said.

Daniel's booming voice echoed across the chamber. "You got it," he said. "First things first, grab those guns by the door."

Turning around, Ash picked up the two heavy weapons and handed one to Alexis; she took it from his hands without making eye contact. Ash tried to pretend the awkward interaction hadn't happened and concentrated on his gun. It was large, blocky and gray, resembling a traditional automatic weapon. However, instead of the magazine, a small, electronic battery connected to the gun's barrel. A green display indicated that the weapon was full charged.

"Good. Okay, hold on tight, this is gonna be a little disorienting at first."

Abruptly, the scenery changed. Gone was the warehouse-like space, the porous ground, the harsh lighting. In its place was a hazy, blue-purplish sky that resembled a fresh bruise. Beneath the sky lay a craggy, rocky series of alps, peaks and rock stacks. The brown mountain was dry and dusty; Ash swore that, if he approached it and ran his fingers across the stone, it would crumble beneath his touch. The ground, too, was sandy, and as Ash took a tentative step forward, it crunched softly beneath his boots.

After a few moments of shocked gawking, Ash felt himself begin to sway; the dizziness was kicking in. Alexis must have been having a similar reaction, because Daniel said, "Yeah, it's a bit of a trip. Just hold still for a few seconds and don't close your eyes. That helped Blondell and me when we ran this. Try focusing your vision on a fixed point."

"This didn't happen last time," Ash said.

"That's because you were nice and calm, Captain. Now you're freaking out at what's to come." Daniel's chuckle was gleeful. "Now, listen to Daniel, and stare at something."

Ash locked his head and focused on the dark, dank cave opening in front of him. He couldn't see more than a foot into the black maw; however, he drew comfort from that. At least the darkness was the same here as it was anywhere

146

else.

Daniel's voice returned. "The sim assumes that you have landed in the shuttle craft about one hundred yards back. This is the cave in which our eggs are located. The nest is about half a mile and downhill, located in a central pod in the middle of this cave system." Daniel paused, ominously. "The sim has been updated since Blondell and I ran it. She was able to find one of their bodies in the cave system and the computer's used that to extrapolate their physical and intellectual capabilities. It's not good. This sim should give us a better idea of what they are like, so if they beat you, don't panic too much, we can figure out how to do better later."

"Beat you?" Ash asked meekly.

"Yeah, kill you. I was just trying to be nice."

Alexis groaned.

"Don't worry, you won't actually feel anything if these guys do get you. The sim will start to flash and simulate physical damage," said Daniel.

"Well, better than getting beaten to death, I guess," Ash said. He looked at Alexis, waiting for her to laugh, but she froze, apparently trying to pretend she hadn't heard him.

"Yeah, try to avoid that part," Daniel chimed in after a moment. "Go get 'em, kids."

"Yeah. Thanks," Ash said. Silence was the only reply. The swaying had stopped, and Ash took a few tentative steps forward. "You ready?"

"Ready," Alexis said evenly, without turning. "Let's do this."

Ash moved with Alexis, and side by side, they entered the darkness.

Ash heard a crackling noise to his right. A moment later, a bright, white-blue electronic light burst out from the top of Alexis' weapon. Ash groped the same part of his gun until he found the appropriate switch and flicked it. Seconds later, the same light shot from his weapon.

"Well, that's good to know," he said, a slight smile playing across his face. Even in the darkness, he could sense that Alexis' expression hadn't changed. Ash could

147

practically feel waves of cold emanating from her. "Look, you want to talk about this?"

"Nope," Alexis said, her voice unchanging. "I want to run this sim. We can talk later."

"Yeah, but if you are pissed at me, this isn't going to go very well," Ash responded. "Maybe we should—"

"Freeze here, lovebirds," Daniel said.

In the glow of the harsh light, Ash saw Alexis' facial expression finally shift, morphing it into a look of sheer disgust. Ash's heart sank, and once again, insecurity bubbled up inside of him.

Great. Real professional, Captain. I'm sure that won't become part of the crew's gossip. Even better that Alexis looked so nauseous at the thought of caring about me.

"Here's where it gets tricky. Ahead of you are two paths; take the one on the left. The one to the right leads to a pit. The one to the left will spiral downhill. From there, it's a straight path to the central pod with the eggs. We don't know a ton, yet, about what you are up against. We think they are alerted by noise, not sight, so whatever you do, be quiet."

Both Ash and Alexis froze for a moment before Ash took a tentative step forward, feeling the crunchy surface beneath his feet. Alexis slowly followed.

"Amazing," Ash whispered, desperate for a conversation with his friend.

"Hmm?"

"This. It feels like we are actually there. Can you tell that we aren't on a spaceship?"

"No," Alexis said.

After a beat, Ash realized she wasn't going to say anything else. Meanwhile, the ground shifted beneath them, leading to one of the more bizarre sights of Ash's life. Looking down, his vision told him that he was going downhill, as his feet gently tilted to simulate walking on a gentle incline. However, it still *felt* as if he was walking straight forward. The sensation was just the latest disorientation Ash had felt over the past two days and he paused.

Alexis, who seemed to be struggling as well, also froze.

"Weird, right? Keep walking, you get used to it. Oh, and again, shut up, will you? They can't hear me, but they can hear you. Practice like this is the real thing." There was a playfulness in Daniel's words, but Ash knew he was serious. He tried to keep quiet as he resumed walking.

Gradually, the ground levelled out. Ash's vision and physical sensations again matched as he and Alexis were walking on even ground.

"Here's the fork. Make a left," Daniel said. Ash and Alexis obeyed. "Good. Now, you'll walk about fifty yards ahead, and the hall is going to keep getting wider, like a funnel. Go slow. Walking should be free and clear until you get to the center of the chamber. Once you do, you've reached the eggs."

"Doesn't sound too hard," Ash said, quietly.

Next to him, Alexis snorted.

"Unless you want to stop to bitch about something," she said.

Ash pulled up, stunned, feeling as if an icicle had shot through his heart. He turned on Alexis and tried to summon up the words to express his anger.

"Excuse me?" was all he could muster, and even then, he only sounded hurt.

Perhaps that got to Alexis; in the thin light coming from their weapons, he saw her blink and briefly bite her bottom lip. However, before she could speak, a roar cut through the darkness. Ash and Alexis both whirled toward the sound, which was high-pitched, choppy and malevolent.

"Did you—"

"Of course I heard it," Alexis snapped. "How could I not? You'd have to be deaf to miss it."

"What the hell is your problem?" Ash sniped.

"Hey, morons!" Daniel cried. "Bad guys inbound. I know it's just a sim, but will you please pay attention?" Being yelled at by the second person made Ash lose his cool.

"Then tell this one to shut up!" Ash jerked his thumb at Alexis, who dropped her weapon in outrage.

"I'm not the one ready to . . ." Her voice trailed off.

"Ready to what, Alexis? Ready to what?" Ash shouted,

resisting the urge to get even closer to Alexis.

"They're coming!" Daniel yelled.

A pale form swung between Ash and Alexis, extending its freakishly long arms around their necks.

Ash barely had a moment to think, *Wait, this is a simulation, it can't actually hurt me,* before an unseen force from behind dragged him down by his neck, slamming his shoulder to the ground.

Answering the question that Ash was to stunned to ask, Daniel said, "The sim alters gravity to simulate combat. It's not going to hurt you. At least, I don't think it's going to hurt you."

His panic rising, Ash squinted in the dark and wildly swung his weapon before finding the pale form of the monster lying on the ground, prone. Alexis stood over it, her weapon upside-down, having apparently used the gun to club it to death.

"Damn," Ash said. "Remind me not to piss you off. Again."

Another high-pitched, broken roar rocketed through the hallway, echoing off the walls, giving Ash the impression that he was trapped inside a movie theater from hell. A second roar joined the first, followed by a third and a fourth.

Ash, now truly frightened, forgot about his surroundings, forgot about his mission, and sought shelter; the best he found was a thick rock which reached his thighs, and he quickly dove behind it.

"What the hell do we do?" cried a frightened voice. Ash turned his lit weapon toward Alexis and found her situated behind a rock almost identical to his own. Like him, she was curled into a ball, hastily trying to make herself as small as possible. Like him, she was failing.

"I don't know!" Ash whispered, as more roars bounced around them. Abruptly, the noise stopped, save for the remaining echoes. What replaced them was even more terrifying; the gentle scraping of nails on rock, followed by the dragging of something else.

"There are at least six of them," Daniel said. The pattern of the monsters remained unchanged. "The grinding noise you hear? That's not a weapon. Those are their arms dragging across the ground. They are massive, and they are strong. Trust me on that."

Ash tried to turn around his rock and get a better view, but couldn't see anything in the inky blackness. The only sense of his working right now was his hearing, which registered the various noises of long nails meeting rock. The eerie sounds, playing across Ash's ears at various pitches sounded like a symphony of the damned, multiplied the cacophony of terror firing through Ash's every nerve.

"What do we do?" Alexis said, louder than she should.

Abruptly, the noises stopped.

"Quiet!" Ash whispered, even louder. It only took him a moment to appreciate irony, as the roars started again, sounding more aggressive.

"Great, just great!" Alexis yelled at full volume. Abruptly, she stood up and aimed her weapon.

Ash followed. The sight that greeted him was horrifying. There were, indeed, six of the monsters. They towered over Ash and almost hit the ceiling of the cave, at least eight feet tall. They were covered in splotchy, matted fur, the color of snow covered in car exhaust on the side of a busy highway. Their arms, which, indeed, dragged along the ground, appeared to be elongated spaghetti noodles. But, as soon as Alexis raised her weapon, their stance changed: almost impossibly, the arms hardened and rose, controlled by muscles of power and precision so great it reminded Ash, absurdly, of the locking jaw of a pit bull.

Alexis was able to fire one laser bolt, catching one of the fiends directly in its sloping skull, before another got close enough to swing one of its monstrous arms. She ducked and the arm swung harmlessly through the air, smashing into the rock wall behind Alexis at an impossibly fast speed, spewing up dirt, dust and pebbles.

"Alexis!" cried Ash, forgetting the need to be stealthy. No longer thinking, Ash charged forward, firing his gun twice and extending both of his arms as he tackled one of the beasts. To Ash's surprise, the behemoth was more agile than it looked. It juked to the left and flung Ash like a discarded children's toy, his gun flying off in the opposite direction.

"You moron!" yelled Alexis, firing her weapon all around him. She managed to catch the beast towering over Ash squarely in the chest.

Ash heard a grunt, followed by silence from Alexis' direction. For a moment, Ash was too stunned to move, but that didn't last for long. Another beast took the place of the one Alexis had smashed. Instead of roaring in Ash's face, it merely bent down, inches from Ash's nose, looking at him with an almost detached sense of curiosity. Ash's weapon was well out of arm's reach, but the light shone in their direction, and Ash saw the monster's pig-like snout, black eyes and rancid fur. Terrified, Ash tried to push his head backward into the ground, but only felt simulated rock for his effort.

Abruptly, the monster's facial expression tightened and contorted. It roared again; not its high-pitched roar from before, but a growl resembling a lion's. The monster brought its massive hands together, clenched them, and swung them like a hammer toward Ash's head, ready to smash it like a grape. Ash cringed and brought his arms up to protect his face . . .

A switch was flipped, and the cave, monsters and darkness were no more. Ash and Alexis were back in the simulator, each lying prone on the ground, gasping desperately for oxygen which couldn't come fast enough.

After fifteen seconds of his chest heaving and contacting, Ash began to consider speaking. Before he could, however, the ground vibrated. *The simulator isn't running,* was Ash's first thought. *Why . . . oh no.* The ground shook again, this time enough to bounce Ash out of his prone position and onto his side. His veins were flooded with new adrenaline.

"Daniel!" Ash screamed, sitting up. "What's happening?"

There was no response. Ash ran over to Alexis, who looked confused and pained.

"Come on, get up!" Ash urged. "We need to get to the Bridge!"

Bewilderment swamped Alexis' face, but only for a

moment, as the pieces clicked for her as well.

As Ash helped Alexis to her feet, Daniel's voice returned. "Guys, get to the Bridge, now!" he cried.

With the floor shaking beneath them, they raced for the exit, running back to the Bridge at top speed.

CHAPTER TWENTY

Ash and Alexis said nothing as they bolted down two flights of stairs and through the hallways to the Bridge. Instead, they practically raced each other, silently challenging the other to run faster, each unwilling to let the other arrive first.

They arrived at the same moment, squeezing through the door simultaneously. Ash catapulted himself into his elevated captain's platform, while Alexis wordlessly moved Sia out of her pilot controls.

"What have we got?" Ash asked, his chest heaving.

"Our invisible friends are back!" said Blondell. "Two o'clock, high!"

It took Ash a moment to remember what that meant. He looked out the Bridge's windows, where a speedy, shimmering shape accelerated toward the ship.

"I see them," Ash said as he followed the shimmer.

Abruptly, it completely disappeared, and Ash realized that nothing good would come next. "Alexis, move it!"

Alexis floored her controls, sending the ship into an abrupt climb, and not a moment too soon. White bolts of energy shot out of a position close to where Ash had last seen their nemesis. For a terrifying moment, Ash heard the mechanical roar of an engine soaring over the *Redemption*. Just as quickly, the noise reached its peak and dulled to a whisper, followed by silence.

"They flew over us!" Anton said, his voice high-pitched again.

"Everybody strap in!" Ash cried, fumbling with his own harness. "Blondell, can we get out of here like last time?"

"It's not that simple," Blondell responded with unnatural calm, not bothering to look over her shoulder as her fingers rapidly played across her air computer. "I need time to plot a solution. At least five minutes."

"Can we have that on standby from now on?" Ash cried.

Blondell's response was to turn around, with a raised eyebrow and upturned lip, as if to say, *There's gonna be a next time?*

"Okay, fine. Just get us out of here as quickly as you can!"

"On it," Blondell said, turning back around and giving her full attention to the computer.

"Alexis, move us around! Zig zag, up, down, I don't care, do something!"

"Way ahead of you!" Alexis said. "I'm trying to alternate the timing as much as possible . . . bring us up and down, left and right. It's the best I got right now."

"Better than nothing. Anton, do—" Ash's next question was cut short by a familiar whir, which grew progressively louder. "Alexis! Move!" Again, Alexis yanked the ship forward, but not fast enough; sparks erupted from multiple panels and the Bridge jolted.

In front of Ash, he heard a cry of pain. Sia's panel had shorted and burst into flames, touching the left side of her face before burning out. Pike unbuckled himself and ran to her, while Anton focused desperately on the panel in front of him.

"I can't find the thing!" cried Anton. "It's not like last time. The ship is less visible. I can't do anything unless you can find it."

"I think I can help with that," said a voice in Ash's ear. Jameson.

"What have you got?" Ash asked, bracing himself and stuffing down a wave of nausea as the ship turned rapidly to the right.

"Daniel is in Engineering with me. We've been tracking the distortion in space caused by our new associates, and we think we can track its wake. It won't show you where the ship is, per se, but it will show you where they have been. Have Radar cycle through his systems."

"Radar, can you do that?" Ash said.

Radar, his hand touching his ear, nodded rapidly and began to turn dials.

"And Tidus, while we are at it, try and get the *Remedy*. Maybe we'll get lucky and they are close by," ordered Ash.

Tidus, without acknowledging the order, brought a hand to his ear and began to talk. "*Remedy*, this is the *Redemption*, do you copy? Hello? *Remedy*, this is the *Redemption*, can you hear us?"

Ash tuned out Tidus and turned back to his immediate task.

"Got it!" whooped Radar.

Sure enough, a bright orange path now illuminated the space in front of them. The orange trail of doom arced, spiraled and circled across the area in front of the *Redemption*, looking as if a toddler had gotten his hand on a magic marker and colored excitedly on a piece of paper.

Ash unbuckled himself, stood and searched desperately for the end of the trail which would indicated where their attackers were at that moment. He soon found it, circling on their left, apparently lining up for an attack.

"Alexis, you see that?"

"Absolutely. What do you think?"

Ash paused.

The obvious move was to fly away from the ship, put as much space between them as possible and give Blondell enough time to get them a course out of there. But obvious didn't seem to be working so far.

"Go toward them!" Ash said.

"What?" Alexis turned around and looked up at Ash, confused.

"You heard me! Go right at them. They aren't expecting it, and they won't have time to react." Awareness crept across Alexis' face. She turned back to her controls, giving Ash just enough time to re-buckle himself before she yanked the joystick to the right.

In front of them, the orange path changed, and the wisdom behind Ash's decision was clear: their attackers had accelerated, and they were much closer than Ash realized. Turning toward them cut off any time that the enemy had to track the *Redemption*. Anton fired blindly, but missed wildly. The *Redemption* soared past the alien ship, causing whoops of joy from the entire Bridge crew.

Ash pounded his fist into the railing in celebration. "See! We can beat this!" he exclaimed. "Blondell, how much longer?"

Blondell's response was to put her hands to hear ears and squeeze, instantly throwing cold water across the brief celebratory atmosphere of the Bridge. "No idea," she said, clearly frustrated. "Every time I think I'm getting somewhere, the computer decides it has other ideas, and I have no idea how to fix it. All the turning of the ship is throwing us off. There must be a way to compensate for it. I'm still trying to figure out what."

"I can't do anything about the shaking!" cried Alexis, her eyes searching desperately for the orange trail. "You're gonna have to figure it out."

"I know, I know," responded an exasperated Blondell. For a brief moment, silence prevailed on the Bridge. "I'm sorry, Ash. I need more time."

"We all do," said Ash. "Just do what you can. In the meantime, everyone hold tight and keep an eye out."

"Daniel and I are trying to adjust our radar systems in here," said Jameson. "I'm sending him back up to you. He'd be more useful there if we take another hit."

"Okay, good," Ash said, barely paying attention as he scanned the horizon. The tablet computers in front of him flashed, begging for his attention, but Ash forced his eyes to trust the cold reality in space.

The distortions from the other ship were disappearing. Space was starting to clear. Enough time passed that Ash was starting to wonder if, perhaps, they had finally gotten lucky and had somehow outmaneuvered their foes. That belief started to grow in his chest, sprouting like a seed of hope, getting stronger by the moment. Ash debated saying something about their newfound luck.

A crash rocked the Bridge, filling the ship with a cacophony of sound and light.

"They came from beneath us!" wailed Radar, pounding on his display.

Abruptly, the lights on the Bridge blinked, eliciting screams of terror from the voices around Ash.

"They're making a tight turn. Every time I get a lock on the ship, it disappears the second they change direction," said Radar.

Ash needed to tell Alexis to turn the ship as quickly as possible, knowing that there was nothing they could do, knowing that they were about to die . . .

The biggest explosion yet rocked the *Redemption*. Sparks, klaxons, sirens, explosions and tremors all shook the Bridge. The noise overloaded Ash's already congested mind. He buried his head in his arms, waiting for the final ripping sound which would signal that the ship's structural integrity had failed.

That moment didn't come. Ash opened his eyes and peeked from behind his hands. The Bridge was completely dark, barely illuminated by emergency lighting hidden in the corners of the room. Main power had failed, which explained why the Bridge had grown so eerily quiet. Save for the occasional button or switch, it looked like most of the instrumentation had crashed as well. Crew members appeared to be in similar positions to Ash, desperately looking around at each other, hoping that one of them held the answers they were seeking.

A brief scan of everyone's faces told Ash the truth: no one knew what was going on. His next step was obvious. He had to get the ship's power back on. And that meant finding Jameson or Daniel.

"Blondell, take the Bridge!" Ash unbuckled his harness and ran out of the room, barely hearing the cries of surprise or pained call of "Ash!" from Alexis. He raced down the darkened hallways, focusing on a dim red light at the end of the hallway to keep his orientation as straight as possible. After barely fifty steps, the red light disappeared. Before Ash could register its absence, he ran into a solid mass of flesh and fell to the ground in a heap of tangled limbs.

"Ow!" he yelped.

"Ash!" said a scared male voice. It took Ash only a moment to register who it was: Daniel. "I was coming to you."

"I got that!" Ash cried, dusting himself back off. "I was trying to find you or Jameson. We need to get the power back on."

"I know," said Daniel. "That first blink was the Bridge almost losing electrical power. That weakened the shields, and our backup power went next." The ship swayed suddenly under their feet. A familiar whisper streamed by overhead. Evidentially, Alexis still had limited flight abilities.

Ash heard Daniel's hands clattering around on the floor, searching for something, which he found. The flashlight was on in an instant. It was only when Ash saw Daniel that he truly realized how much trouble they were in: fear was etched on his friend's face. Daniel, who had never been anything but happy-go-lucky, looked terrified. His eyes were wide, his eyes pools of brown swimming in a sea of white. That was what struck Ash the most at that moment: Daniel's wide, wide eyes.

"Okay," Daniel struggled to gain his composure. His expression locked and his body went as stiff as granite; it was only for an instant, but Ash knew something had happened.

"What?" he asked.

That seemed to snap Daniel out of his trance. "I know what to do," he said, body still but eyes scanning the hallway. "I'm heading to the Junction Room."

"Huh? Why?"

"Jameson and I tried to rewire power in Engineering, but it was no good. The wiring must be shot. I can reroute it from there."

Hope surged through Ash. "Okay! Great! I'll get back to the Bridge. We'll be ready for you."

"Okay," Daniel said. He didn't move.

"What? What am I missing?" Ash asked. Again, Daniel shook his head, like he was trying to clear the cobwebs.

"When I get the power back on, have Anton fire. As soon as possible. Even if it isn't close to the ship, have him fire."

"Why?"

"No time, Captain."

Ash cast Daniel a sideways glance, but Daniel merely waved his hands.

"Okay. Go! I'll see you when we get out of here."

Daniel didn't respond. Instead, he tore his glance away from Ash and bolted down another corridor to the right, footfalls echoing as he disappeared into the darkness.

Ash turned around and ran back to the Bridge. He barreled through the doorway. His eyes readjusted from the near blackness of the hallway to the emergency lighting of the Bridge.

The first person to greet him was Alexis. "That was fast! What happened?"

"I found Daniel, and he's gonna get the power on. I'll explain the rest later. Anton?" Anton whipped around, his features taut.

"Yeah?"

Ash scrambled next to Alexis, turning to Anton as he moved. "Get ready to fire something the instant the power comes back online. We should have it any second."

The sound of screeching engines in the distance grew louder with every moment, heralding death.

"Ash?" Alexis said, her voice barely audible over the roar of the other ship. Alexis was breathing heavily, evidentially from the strenuous task of desperately moving the ship away from their attackers. Ash hung his head, no longer able to hold his eyes up to meet the stars.

Reflected off of the clear panel that met Ash's stare was empty, shimmering space, the distortion which denoted the position of the alien attackers so visible that Ash felt as if he was looking right at it. The shimmer grew larger, preparing death for the *Redemption* and its crew. There was no time for final wishes, no time for final prayers. Ash felt Alexis slip a hand inside his, felt their fingers knot together, as his mind focused on one thought: *the past two days have been for nothing.*

The boom which presaged the end of their own lives came. Ash pressed his eyes tight, his heart leaping, preparing to face oblivion . . .

The power surged back on, light temporarily blinding the crew of the *Redemption*. Ash blinked and realized they were still alive. Without thought or hesitation, his hand, intertwined with Alexis', grabbed the ship's controls and pushed down, harder than he had ever pushed anything in his life, and the ship entered a steep dive. This flung everyone on the Bridge forward and caused those who had unbuckled themselves to careen toward the front window.

"Anton!" Ash bellowed, not even attempting to hide the desperation in his voice. "Fire something!"

Anton found the right button and pressed it. Lasers from the *Redemption's* armory spat white-hot death in the general direction of their attackers. The orange trail, which had appeared directly in front of the *Redemption,* no more than a few hundred yards away, transformed from a line painted with a brush to a wall shot by a paintball. The invisibility which had characterized their opponents failed. A thin white ship, joined by two wings, could be seen with the naked eye. Just as quickly, the ship vanished, leaving Ash with the mental sensation of having noticed something important, only to forget it once again.

The orange trail returned and took evasive action, barreling in the opposite direction, into the depth of space. The enemy was on the run. Silenced reigned on the Bridge as the entire crew watched their attackers flee. The orange line grew thinner and thinner, before fading into nothingness.

The crew burst with joy and began to cheer, arms in the air, high-fives and hugs all around. All except Ash. His eyes were locked onto the window in front of him, not believing that they had driven off their attackers, completely befuddled at what had happened. *Why?* He thought. *Why did that do it?*

Abruptly, Ash became aware of a background noise

which was calling his name.

"Ash? Ash? *Ash?* You there?"

Ash put a finger to his ear to better hear. "Yeah, Jameson! I copy. What's up?"

Jameson's voice, normally calm and steady, had a timbre of panic to it. "Where is Daniel? Is he on the Bridge?"

"No, he ran to the Junction Room. He got the power back on!"

There was silence on the other end.

Before Ash had time to react, another ship burst into space in front of them. The celebrations onboard the *Redemption* froze until the rest of the crew recognized the *Remedy*. The cavalry had arrived.

"Captain Maddox? This is Benjamin Valliant of the *Remedy*. Are you alright?"

The prim, proper pronunciation behind every one of Valliant's words sounded like nails on a chalkboard to Ash, but he had never been so glad to hear another voice in all his life. Like a ghost arriving from the ether, Valliant's face appeared, his face tight with concern.

"Yes, Valliant, we're alright, thank you!" Ash allowed relief to seep into his voice for the first time. Someone else was here; someone who knew what they were doing. They were going to be alright.

"You're lucky we weren't far away!" Valliant cried. "We got here as fast as we could. What happened?"

Ash explained their brief encounter with the unknown enemy ship. Valliant put his chin in his hands and rubbed his face when Ash finished.

"Hmm. Interesting. It must be the same ship we've been chasing. Incredible that you got a look at them. That must have been an amazing shot."

Ash resisted the urge to groan. All he needed was Anton's ego further inflated.

"Which direction did they head?" asked Valliant.

A whoosh from behind stopped Ash from answering. He turned and discovered Jameson, standing in the doorway, frozen. He was leaning on the wall for support.

"Ash?" he said, his voice so quiet that it silenced

everyone in the room.

Ash stepped closer to Jameson and saw that his complexion was pale, approaching gray; his first thought was that Jameson had been injured and had stumbled up to the Bridge seeking aid, but Ash couldn't see any obvious wounds.

Five steps later and he was next to Jameson. "What? What happened?"

Jameson looked up at Ash. Their eyes met, and Ash saw urgency and pain in his friend's face. Without another word, Jameson turned around and left the Bridge.

Ash followed. They walked at an awkward speed, as if Jameson wanted to break into a run but at the same time was unwilling to reach his destination. Ash took the right toward the Junction Room without even thinking. He didn't even know how, at this point, his feet were moving, but they seemed to be walking of their own volition, taking Ash to a sight he knew he didn't want to see.

Within twenty feet of the room, it hit Ash for the first time: the smell. Like burnt meat. It made Ash freeze in his tracks and sent a frost through his veins. "Please," he said quietly. "Please don't tell me." Ash knew how desperate he sounded. How small. He also didn't care.

Jameson, who had been in front of Ash, didn't turn around. "He died for all of us," Jameson said. Ash groaned and put his hands on his knees. He didn't want to hear this. He didn't want any of this. "I went in . . ."

At that, Ash lifted his head and tried to stand upright. "I'm sorry."

Jameson didn't acknowledge that Ash had said a word. "The connections that supplied power from Engineering to the rest of the Bridge were severed. I knew that and I said it to Daniel."

Ash stared at the back of Jameson's head, noticing the way that his red hair clung together in sweaty chunks. Jameson's head seemed to expand and swell in Ash's vision, coming into vivid detail. It struck Ash as ridiculous, given the heat of the moment, but he couldn't move his eyes from the back of Jameson's head.

"Daniel said he would repair it. And he did." Jameson turned around, slowly, taking each step deliberately. "He did the only thing he could do."

Again, the smell of burnt meat struck Ash. With growing horror, he realized what had happened.

"He fixed the wiring," Ash gasped.

Jameson nodded, head moving imperceptibly. "And electrocuted himself in the process."

Ash whimpered again and began to cry.

Ash had known depression before. It had been his neighbor, his constant companion, for years. Depression had always felt like a rope which bound Ash to a sadness that was indescribable, inexplicable and inescapable. But nothing, nothing, had ever felt like grief. Grief, which Ash knew, deep down, was his fault, and his fault alone. He should never have let Daniel go to the Junction Room.

Depression led to loneliness; Ash knew that. But he had never felt so alone in his life. His mind travelled back to being a small child, of being safe in his mother's arms; of getting beat up by bullies and being able to cry with his father; of being rejected by a girl and having people to talk to . . . of having safety, security, others.

But he was all alone. There was no adult who could absolve him of what he had done. No teacher who could give him punishment to make him feel like he had paid for his sins. There was no counselor who could comfort him, no pill that could excise the image that bounced around in his head like a pinball: Daniel, sweating and scared, holding a clump of wiring and cables, staring at them in his final seconds, before plunging them together, followed an instant later by a storm of blue lights and sizzle of electricity. There was nothing, just Ash, responsible for a crew he had never wanted, stuck with a mind that worked against him, and judgment that had failed him.

The silence, at that moment, was suffocating.

CHAPTER TWENTY-ONE

The ceiling looked familiar to Ash. It was, after all, the same color of his bedroom at home, and he had spent more days than he cared to remember in a similar position, with a similar view. Even in his massively depressed state, Ash couldn't help but notice the irony. Two days ago, he had been trying to coax other crew members out of bed. Now, here he was, confined to the same space he had been trying to help others escape.

Others had come to visit him. He vaguely remembered Blondell, Radar and Sierra stopping in. Jameson had even come in, his eyes red and swollen. He had been closest with Daniel, more than anyone else on the ship. He had said kind words, urging Ash to realize that Daniel's death was not his fault, but they were for naught. Ash suspected that, deep down, Jameson blamed him for what had happened, blamed him for not going with Daniel and finding another way.

Alexis hadn't come by yet.

Or maybe she had. Ash hadn't noticed. The world seemed to be fading in and out, as if he was in a foggy dream. Only snippets of reality stuck with him, like a ping pong ball hitting a wall. *Ping.* Sierra was there, leaving a sandwich, trying to coax him to eat. *Ping.* Blondell was there, trying to explain the difficulties with setting the course to Kepler. *Ping.* Jameson was there, crying softly.

Pong. And Ash faded inside of his own mind.

***

Despite the gray that had enveloped Ash on day two, he knew that his bed could not become a new home. A break from reality was certainly a welcome vacation, but he couldn't stay there. Sooner or later, he had to come out and face the consequences of his actions. More to the point, he needed to face the rest of the ship and get them to their next location.

As Ash mulled over the concept of moving, a soft hiss on his right indicated his door was opening. He had a new visitor. He tilted his head ever so slightly, and there was Alexis, looking pale and withdrawn, raven hair framing her gentle features. Right now, she looked like she wanted to be elsewhere. Or maybe that was just in Ash's mind.

"Hey," she whispered, a small smile creeping across her face.

"Hey back," Ash responded, barely louder than Alexis. "Come on in."

Alexis sat in a chair on the opposite side of the room. She stared at Ash and nervously licked her lips and folded her hands together, only to rapidly unfurl them.

"I don't know what to say to you," she began, stuttering her first words. "I know I helped you before, but I don't know if I can help you now."

"How come?" Ash asked.

Alexis looked down. "Because I know."

Ash stared quizzically at her. Alexis shifted uncomfortably in her seat. Despite the fact that he had barely eaten or slept over the past two days, Ash recognized that Alexis wasn't making eye contact with him, something she always did. Alexis was direct. But she looked like she was the one being challenged.

"About a year ago . . . well, a year from when I was taken, I guess . . . I killed a man. His name was Kevin Thompson. He was thirty-five, he had three children, and he was a fitness nut." Alexis shifted and sniffled. If she noticed Ash's mouth agape, she didn't say anything about it. "He was running. That's all he was doing, he was running. And, unfortunately for him, he was running down the same street

that I was driving on. I'd had my license for three months."
Here, Alexis raised her hand and began to diagram the road
she had driven that day. "There was a trick curve and a rise
in the street . . . it always looked easy and it was fun to take
while speeding. And I did. Except I took it too fast. I
overshot where I needed to turn. I thought I had
time . . . and there was Kevin." Alexis raised both of her
hands and crushed one with the other.

"My first thought when I hit him was that time was
fragile . . . it was so fragile, that I could go back, just reverse
that one second. It was irrational, but it's all I could think.
He went over my car, and I never saw him." Alexis turned
and looked at Ash. "Is that strange? That I never saw the
man I killed? Only the pictures in the paper afterward?"

Ash, mouth closed, shook his head. "No."

"I thought it was," Alexis said, detached, sounding like
she was telling someone else's story. "I thought I needed to
see him, to make myself realize what a moment of
carelessness had done. I cost some poor woman her
husband, his children their father. And all for one moment
of bad luck, one random second.

"In court, his wife said that her husband didn't usually
take that road. She said inspiration must have hit him, and
that road ultimately killed him. I don't remember a lot, but
I remember that part very well. She blamed the road. Not
me. She said I was just some kid who had made a bad
mistake, and pled for leniency for me. She said her husband
wouldn't have wanted to add to the lives lost." Alexis paused
in her story to stand up. Hands on her hips, she turned
around. Ash watched her shoulders heave as she tried to
control her breathing. When she turned back around, her
face was wet.

"And at that time . . . I was mad at her. Can you believe
that? Mad at a grieving widow, because I felt like I needed
my share of the blame. I didn't deserve to get off easy, with
community service and a letter of apology. And I was *furious*
at him, even though it clearly wasn't his fault. And I was
furious with myself . . . for more reasons than I can count."
Alexis paused, brushed the hair out of her eyes and crouched

next to Ash in bed. "This make sense to you? Why I got so mad at you the other day when we were walking to the sim. Do you get it now?"

"Some of it," Ash said, realizing that the few words he'd said to Alexis were the most he had spoken in the past forty-eight hours.

Alexis licked her dry lips before continuing.

"I think it's because I do understand depression that I got so angry. Because I know what it's like to be trapped in your head when you actually have something to feel guilty about. When I was at my worst over Kevin, I would have given anything to escape my own mind. Watching someone like you imprison yourself . . . that's not right." Alexis' hand crept over Ash's arm, reached a bicep, and squeezed tight. "Ash, you had nothing to do with Daniel's death."

Ash rolled over, away from Alexis. He knew she had just opened her heart to him; knew what a slap in the face that action must have been. He also, at that moment, didn't care. He didn't want absolution. He wanted condemnation. Punishment.

"Ash . . ." Alexis' reaction was surprising, all things considered. Ash felt her hand slowly moving across the fabric of his shirt and awkwardly slip over his shoulder, pressing against his chest.

"Ash, listen to me." The pleading in Alexis' voice was unmistakable. "First and foremost, you had no idea what was going to happen when Daniel went to the Junction Room. I don't even know if he did, but I know you didn't. Second, even if you did, what Daniel did saved the ship. He was trying to save nineteen, and maybe billions more."

Ash remained motionless. Alexis hadn't said anything new to Ash. But that didn't make the burden any more difficult to deal with.

"How long have you been like this?"

Ah. There was the real question, one that a normal person wouldn't even blink about. They weren't just talking about Daniel's death anymore. This question he could answer. Slowly, Ash turned around, his tear-covered eyes meeting Alexis' tear-streaked face.

"Years," Ash said.

"Are you taking your medication?"

"I'm supposed to," Ash said, "but no."

Alexis looked at the ground and shook her head rapidly. "What about the tranquilizer from before?"

Ash shook his head, pillow rustling beneath his ears. "That's for an emergency. The anti-depressants . . . those are different."

"That's a terrible answer," Alexis said.

A wave of familiar shame washed over Ash. He hated his pills; hated the fact that he needed to take them. They represented everything weak about him. And once again, he hated himself: this time, for telling Alexis his secret.

"I know," he said. "I'm trying to get off of those things. The pill I took the other day was for anxiety attacks – I haven't touched the anti-depressants since I got here." Alexis looked at Ash with growing horror.

"You haven't taken them?" she said, shocked.

"No . . . they're in the bathroom, with the tranquilizers, but—"

Alexis shot up and marched into the bathroom. For the second time in their brief relationship, Ash heard her rifling through his medicine cabinet. A moment later, she burst out, a vial of pills in hand.

"You need to take these. Now." Alexis made no effort to disguise the urgency in her voice.

Ash stared, confused. "But I thought you said—"

"I said that what you said was a 'terrible answer' because you said you were supposed to take your pills, but weren't. The fact that you aren't taking the pills is the terrible part, not that you need them." Alexis dropped down to her knees and extended her hand, gently stroking Ash's face. "Needing medication to cope isn't something to be ashamed of. Ash, how many people take pills for a heart condition and are alive because of it?"

Ash briskly shook his head, bouncing Alexis' hand.

"This's different, and you know it," he said.

"Why?" Alexis shot back.

Ash's mind turned but found no answer.

"Because I shouldn't need pills to survive," he stammered.

"You and I both know that this isn't about weakness. This isn't about you being wrong. I needed them to get me through the aftermath of the accident. You may need them for the rest of your life. But you need them to function, and we need you." The last part of Alexis' sentence made something click inside Ash's tortured mind.

"The ship . . . who's flying this thing?" he questioned.

Alexis sighed. "I was hoping to wait on telling you that, but it's Anton. He took charge when you left. Pike and Sia are his enforcers, and we're . . . well, let's just say that a bad captain who leads is better than no captain at all."

The news hit Ash like a ton of bricks. Anton may be able to lead, but he couldn't stay calm and he made decisions by fear, a dangerous combination for a captain if there ever was one. *Still, who am I to judge others for poor decisions or not staying calm?* Ash thought. With that, he slid down in the bed.

"Never mind," he said, his momentary spike of energy fading back to black.

Alexis stared at him for a second and patted his shoulder.

"Come on," she said, standing up. "I want to show you something. And for the love of God, before we go anywhere, you freakin' stink. Take a shower."

Despite himself, Ash laughed.

Chapter Twenty-Two

Thirty minutes later, showered (and having taken his fifteen milligrams of Lexapro, under Alexis' watchful eye), and dressed, Alexis led Ash to the cafeteria. "I get that you think we don't need you, but there is something you need to see."

Together, the two walked through the empty corridors of the ship, Alexis slightly closer to Ash than she would have walked otherwise. Ash wasn't sure if the reason for Alexis' closeness was because she was afraid he would turn around and run back to his cabin or that she was worried he would need to lean on her for support. Or both. Probably both.

They walked into the cafeteria. The first thing Ash noticed was the smell. It was something Ash hadn't smelled in days. Something good. Pleasant. Reassuring.

Alexis must have noticed Ash sniffing the air, because she said, "Hang on, we'll get there." She took Ash by the shoulders and turned him slightly to the left. "Here. Look at that." And, even though Ash's depression still clung to him like a magnet to metal, he found a new reason to smile: Robin, the small boy who he had tried comforting days ago (though now it felt like weeks), sat at a table, eating tomato soup. He was alone, and he wasn't smiling, but he was out of his bed.

Without even thinking, Ash sped toward Robin. Robin looked up at Ash as he drew closer and smiled.

"Ash!" he said, looking flustered. "It's really great to see you! Here, have a seat." Robin spastically stood and jumped to another chair, knocking his food over in the process and covering the table in a red, creamy soup. "Gah!" he exclaimed, flailing for napkins and dabbing the mess. "Sorry about that."

Exodus, Mercury, and two other members of the Back Brigade looked in their direction.

"It's alright," Ash said, grabbing a fistful of napkins and joining Robin in the cleaning. "It's nice to see you, too. When did you get up?" Ash replied.

Robin shrugged and kept eating. "About a day ago. I haven't done much, but Alexis has me trying a few things. Turns out the mechanical stuff I knew from home actually carried over to the ship. We should talk too, by the way. The joints that are keeping the left wing sealed to the ship are really stressed."

That's when Ash noticed something else, something familiar: Robin was wearing Daniel's toolkit. The straps had been adjusted, of course; Robin must have been a foot shorter than his predecessor. But there it was, in use again.

They looked like they belonged.

Ash nodded, in a daze. *It's terrible and it's tragic, but necessary.* "Yeah, sure, absolutely. I'm just starting to get moving again. Give me a few on that."

Robin nodded eagerly.

"Sure," he said, smiling. "I'll see you soon?"

That question made Ash pause. He opened his mouth to answer, but no words came out. Instead, he smiled weakly, stood up, and turned around.

Alexis was there in a flash. "He told me what you said to him. About how you had to keep going and not surrender."

Ash said nothing.

"That has to mean something. You have to know that your words mean something to these people. They mean something to me. Ash, we need you. Badly."

Ash sighed, heavily.

"You've been alright under Anton."

Alexis rolled her eyes.

"Come on. Cut the crap," she said, with a directness that startled Ash. "You know you did that."

"Did what?" Ash demanded.

Alexis used her head and gestured in Robin's direction. "Got the little guy moving," she said. "I don't think he'd do it without you."

Ash pointed past Robin at two of the Back Brigade members. "They did just fine on their own," he said.

Alexis snorted. "I'm not talking about them. I'm talking about Robin. Yeah, maybe those two got out alone, but Robin told a bunch of us that he wanted to try working, if only to distract himself." Alexis pointed at Robin. "Look at him, Ash. He's eating and he's reading."

Ash hadn't noticed it before, but Alexis was right. Robin was completely absorbed in a small tablet which was sitting on the table next to his tray, so absorbed that he didn't notice a blob of cheese which had dripped from his sandwich to the table.

"He's reading about the ship, in case you were wondering. Trying to figure out how to do what you told him to and learn how to function here." Alexis put a hand on Ash's shoulder. "That must mean something to you."

Ash responded by sighing heavily, and Alexis tore her hand away from Ash's shoulder. In an instant, Ash regretted his sigh, even if he couldn't show it. He felt the absence of Alexis' hand like a burn.

Hands on her hips, Alexis said, "Here, you want proof? Okay, Ash, let me ask you this. If you are on the Bridge, back in that center platform that Anton stole from you, what are you telling us to do?"

That answer was easy. "We're practicing in the sim non-stop and moving full speed to Kepler. Everyone who isn't in the sim is practicing their stations for when we get attacked again. Then we launch the raid. And I'll listen to any other better ideas along the way."

"Why the rush?"

"Because we don't know how much time we have, and we don't know when the bastards who hit us will come back. Whatever we do, we have to do it immediately, or we leave ourselves wide open to attack."

A slight smile spread across Alexis' face. "That sounds like my captain."

Ash twitched involuntarily, and Alexis pretended not to notice.

"Okay, next question. What do you think Anton is doing?"

Here Ash was stumped. "I don't know . . . same thing but slower?"

"Well, you're not far off. We're going slower. A lot slower."

Ash's eyes narrowed.

"How slow?"

Alexis folded her arms across her chest. "He says he'll let us know when we're ready. But it won't be for weeks."

A firework exploded behind Ash's eyes. "Weeks? We don't have more than a few weeks before that ship crashes into Earth and Spades destroys the human race!"

Alexis shrugged.

"What about the sims? Are you still doing that? Practicing grabbing the eggs?"

Alexis shrugged. "We're doing target practice, Ash. Captain Anton seems to think that some of us are a little dangerous with the fancy laser guns."

Ash's jaw unhinged, falling into an "O" of disbelief. "This guy's afraid of his own shadow, and he's going to kill us all," Ash said, his voice constricted by horror.

"Maybe you should tell him that, Captain."

Ash didn't need to think twice. As the white-hot anger flashed over him, he turned on his heel and stomped to the door.

CHAPTER TWENTY-THREE

"Ash!" cried Anton from the center platform. "I'm so glad you're back!" Anton turned his lips up, but the smile didn't reach his eyes.

"Anton," Ash said, his voice clipped. "Thanks for taking care of the ship. I'll take it back now."

Anton looked confused.

"Take it back?"

"I'm in charge again. Get out."

Anton looked offended. Ash knew better.

"Ash, I'm sorry, but that's just not possible," Anton said.

Ash felt the anger bubble up inside of him. He struggled to control his raw emotions. That challenge was magnified by Anton's new attitude. He seemed . . . contemplative? Was he that much of a chameleon, capable of changing his personality so easily?

"The crew took a vote. Given your . . . convalescence . . . we felt it was best if I was in charge."

Ash heard contempt in the way Anton said "convalescence," and felt shame wash over him anew. He paused to gather his thoughts before responding and stared at the ground.

"Well, let's vote again," he said, so quietly that the rest of the crew had to strain to hear his voice.

"Sorry?" Anton said, learning forward. "I didn't catch that."

"Let's. Vote. Again." This time, Ash's voice was clear, and he looked directly at Anton as he spoke.

After a moment's hesitation, Anton asked, "Oh . . . Ash, do you really think that's a good idea?" There was a saccharin sweetness in his voice, so thick and syrupy that Ash had to suppress the urge to retch.

At the same time, Ash realized that Anton's hesitation, however brief, meant that he wasn't sure what the result of such a vote would be. Ash pressed his advantage. "What, you don't? If I learned anything during my brief time as leader, Ant, it's that you can't be afraid of anything." Ash stopped here, waiting for some explosive refutation from Anton. Instead, he got another sweet smile.

"You're absolutely right," Anton said, surprising Ash. Anton kept talking as he walked across the captain's platform, slowly dragging his fingers along the railing. "Real leadership means getting help from everyone on the most important decisions that this crew will face . . . like who will lead them to safety, and who will lead them to their deaths. Again."

Ash took a deep breath, shuffled his feet, but said nothing. Anton, expecting a reaction out of Ash and seeing none, paused again, but for a second time, the hesitation was short-lived.

"Fine," Anton said, his voice testy. "Here's the deal, folks. Previous to this, we've had no plan. We've had no way forward aside from blindly following whatever whims these idiot clues have supposedly shown us. Look where that's gotten us. One of us is dead. The ship is damaged, and we're millions of miles from home. I'm tired of barely staying alive. It's been four days." Here Anton paused, and when he started up again, his voice was a touch higher. "You're afraid. I am too. How could we not be?"

This surprised Ash. He hadn't expected this kind of candor from the younger man.

Anton continued, "Did you know that fear has an evolutionary purpose? Fear is supposed to let us know when we are in a dangerous situation, one that could pose a threat to our lives and help us find our way out of it. That's why we are all afraid right now, and we need to react to that fear with more caution."

Across the Bridge, heads were nodding, almost all of them. Much to his chagrin, Ash saw that even Blondell's head was bobbing slightly up and down.

"So, here's my plan. We move with that caution. We practice in the sim. We give Sierra and Blondell more time to figure out the information around us. And, if we're convinced that it's the best plan, we go to Kepler and try to get the piece. Otherwise, we take as much time as we need."

More nodding and assorted clapping. The response was startling enough that it gave Ash pause.

But only for a moment.

Ash lifted his hand up to quiet the crew, fiery anger boiling inside of him. It felt hot, like lava that was ready to erupt.

With some still applauding, Ash said, "That was, without a doubt, the biggest load of crap I have ever heard in my twenty years alive." The applause ended, and there was a giggle or two. "Seriously. I'm not even trying to joke right now. Anton, you're standing twenty feet away from me, and I can smell the manure you are shoveling from here."

The ship fell into an awkward silence as Anton's face went from amused to enraged.

"Okay, tough guy, what's your plan? Run back to your room?" spat Anton. "Cry some more? Get back under your covers? That part you did good at, I'll give you that."

Ash smirked. "Hell yes, I might just do that. And if you stay as captain, that's probably the safest bet." Ash stopped here, surveying the room, trying to look each of the dozen or so assembled crew members in the eyes. "In the four days I have been here, I've learned so much. And I have made mistakes. I don't dispute that for a minute. We should have taken more time.

"But weeks? Seriously? Anton is right about one thing. Fear does serve a purpose. But it's about more than making you stop doing what you are doing and run. If you are afraid, you don't just stop and retreat. You recalibrate and repeat. Sierra and Blondell have confirmed that Spades is real and that we have limited time. And Anton, you seriously want to just hang out, drink some tea and practice in an overgrown computer? Are you nuts?"

Ash moved into Anton's personal space, nose to nose.

"Fear isn't about making you run. It's about making you find your weaknesses and reinforcing them."

Anton flashed a sneer again. "You would know something about weaknesses, wouldn't you, Ash?"

Ash froze and tensed. Pike and Blondell leaned in, ready to separate the two if the adversaries turned into combatants. But Ash spun around.

"You see that? He acts like a weakness is a bad thing. Hell no, it isn't! Any of you want to tell me that you haven't been afraid? That you haven't found your own flaws? That our four days on this ship haven't kicked you, up and down, back and forth, side to side? Made your own worst nightmares real? Anyone? Of course not!" Ash felt his emotions running away from him, but was totally unwilling to reign himself in. He had spent two days sitting in bed, and this was what greeted him?

The crew was stone still as Ash pointed a finger back at Anton. "But pay attention to what this man is telling you. He wants to stop something that he cannot stop. He wants to trade fear for power. That fear has clouded his judgment, and he wants to let the rest of the world suffer as a result." Ash paused, took a deep breath, and tried to slow his voice.

"Before, I thought I had to show no weakness. Now I get it. Of course I'm weak. Of course I'm flawed. Of course I'm afraid. But so are the rest of you. I'm just smart enough to learn from it." Despite himself, Ash felt his control evaporating, again. "But what I am not is so cowardly that I want to run out the damn clock! We may die in the middle of space. Or we may die of some terrible disease. Or we may save the world and never figure out how to get home. But anything is better than waiting for our worst nightmare to end humanity." Ash paused, but only for a beat. "Who's with me?"

There were nineteen crew members onboard the *Redemption*, Ash knew. It appeared as if all of them were on the Bridge, having been brought in by either Alexis, Sia or Pike. They crowded the hallways and the entranceway to the

Bridge, with shorter members peering over the taller ones, trying to get a glimpse of the drama. And when Ash asked his question, their hands went up.

Some of them.

Ash and Alexis spun around the room, counting. Radar, Blondell, Miranda, Sierra, Robin, Echo, and Exodus all had their hands up. Including Ash and Alexis, that made nine.

Anton, who was counting as well, said, "Who wants to live?" More hands: Pike, Sia, Mercury, Tidus and four other Back Brigade members. Plus Anton: also nine. And Anton smiled.

"Tie," he said. "Majority is needed for change. I'm still in charge."

"What?" Ash said, and a cry from his supporters followed. "That's crap, and you know it."

"Not so fast," said a disembodied voice which silenced the whole ship. Ash took a moment to try to identify the voice, and when he did, a chill washed over him. He smacked his own forehead. Of course. Nine and nine equaled eighteen.

"Who is that?" said Anton.

"Jameson," said the voice coolly. "If you want to be captain, you should at least know your own crew, Anton. I'm still in Engineering, and there is no way I'm leaving, even for this. But, now that you asked, I'm with Ash. The only chance we have is to try."

Slowly, all eyes in the room turned back to Ash and Anton, standing feet away from each other, bracketing the small stairs which lead to the center platform. After an awkward stare, Ash stepped forward, closing the distance between them, with only one thought in his mind: *I have one chance to try to put this back together.* He extended a hand, palm outstretched.

"Help me," he said. "Help me lead."

Anton stared at Ash, disgust and contempt spread across his face. Anton held the stare until his face turned an almost comical shade of crimson. He brushed past Ash's outstretched hand and stormed off of the Bridge. Pike and Sia followed after a moment's hesitation.

Ash blinked and moved on.

"Okay, back to work. Sierra and Blondell, we need to refine the sim. Alexis, slow down the course, by two days, we need more time to train. Robin, what's up with the left wing?" Blondell started barking out orders as well and the Bridge turned into a hive of activity as a beaming Robin bounded toward Ash.

"Hey, Ash?" Alexis said over the cacophony. "Talk to you for a second?" She gestured with her head, out of the Bridge.

"Sure," Ash said, stepping off his platform. "Gimme a second, Robin." Robin nodded and began talking to Blondell. Ash followed Alexis off of the Bridge, following her to the hallway outside. After few feet, she stopped and turned around. Her face was lit with a small smile, her arms slightly spread open. Ash stepped into the warm embrace.

"Nice job," she whispered, holding the hug before stepping back. Slowly, Alexis reached up to Ash's face and brushed his cheek with the back of her hand, tracing her fingers over Ash's two-day stubble and sharp jaw lines. Her fingers moved slowly, achingly slowly, and Ash wanted more.

He also knew he didn't have time and sighed heavily. "Thank you," he said. "Thank you for everything."

Alexis held the touch for a last fleeting second before reluctantly pulling away, a sad smile spreading across her face. "It's okay," she said, eyes cast downward. "For everything. It's okay."

Ash bit his bottom lip and nodded.

"You know I'm not over this, right?" he said to Alexis.

She nodded, understanding, and reassuring in her grip. "I never expected you would be," she said. "I know enough about depression and anxiety to understand that a good pep talk and beating a jerk doesn't erase it."

Ash laughed, quietly. He thought of Daniel laughing too and the smile was erased from his face. Alexis, seeing this, reached up and touched his cheek again. "You aren't supposed to be over anything. You just give it everything you've got, and you move, as best you can. Until then, let the idea of a better day fill you up. Fill you up like . . . oh, wait!"

Abruptly, Alexis pulled out of Ash's arms and started racing down the corridor. "I'll be right back! Go sit down!"

Weird, Ash thought, moving back onto the Bridge. However, Alexis was good to her word. A few minutes after Ash sat down, Alexis had raced back into the Bridge.

"Here," she said, plopping a tray on Ash's lap.

Ash smelled the steaming bowl of thick soup before he saw it, and with a downward glance, he saw a piping hot bowl of tomato soup and a sandwich wrapped in aluminum foil. Ash eagerly unwrapped it, and his smile crew wider. A grilled cheese sandwich.

Alexis smiled from ear to ear. "The ultimate comfort food."

Ash looked at Alexis and met her eyes. They were wide, shining as brightly as her smile. As best he was able, Ash returned the grin, hoping that Alexis' heart was beating as fast as his was at that moment.

Taking the sandwich in his left hand and the spoon in his right, Ash began to eat. Vociferously. Like someone who hadn't eaten in years.

CHAPTER TWENTY-FOUR

Their course set for Kepler, the crew had assembled in a large conference room off the Bridge. A large screen was situated in the front of the room, and if not for one critical detail, Ash would have thought he was back in college, about to receive a lecture from a professor. However, there was no projector that he could see. Instead, a gorgeous, detailed-rich representation of Earth spun from a small hole in the center of the sturdy table.

Jameson, who had been coaxed out of Engineering, began with a provocative opening: "Here's what happened to Earth."

The presentation began with information familiar to Ash: climate change, rising temperatures, weather disturbances, and an inability of the world's leading governments to deal with the change. As Jameson detailed the data, Ash's mind started to wander.

"Up until about 2030 or so, the Earth was in bad shape, but most people didn't notice. Sure, it was a little bit warmer but, by and large, no one cared. They had their big screen TVs and their iPhone 19s or whatever. Fat, dumb and happy." Jameson tapped a button in the middle of the table and the display rapidly changed, moving from graphs which explained climate change to a three-dimensional model of the East Coast of the United States. At least, Ash thought it was the East Coast. You couldn't really tell, because much of it was covered by a massive circular hurricane.

"Meet Hurricane Ayla from 2030," Jameson intoned.

"Then the largest on record. Like its little sister, Katrina, this was a monster which tore up the East Coast, but this one did more damage. Katrina killed around 1,800 people; Ayla 4,000, most of whom were in New York, which was totally unprepared for this level of devastation. It knocked out power to the East Coast for as long as a month in some places, and it brought total devastation everywhere it touched."

As Jameson spoke, one horrifying image folded into the nest: huddled refugees on the top of slanted roofs in suburban neighborhoods; the Empire State Building, in total darkness, with half of its windows shattered; and peaceful main streets completely inundated with water, brick facades having been torn up as though smashed by a giant, angry toddler.

"Ayla was a Category Five when she hit, and she killed more people than Harvey, Irma and Maria *combined*. And it was nothing compared to the next year, when Hurricane Auron attacked the East Coast. Auron was the first ever Category Six. It made Fives look like a cloudy day. Keep in mind, much of the former American South was built for resilience against storms like this. The East Coast wasn't. The two hurricanes permanently drove a million people out of New York City. Auron destroyed the Lower East Side and much of the World Trade Center complex."

The images which appeared as Jameson spoke were devastating; the World Trade Center complex, sheered in half as if by a meat cleaver, reminding Ash of a gutted pig, glistening innards shining on display. More pictures brought more horror: water which had reached the second level of the New York Stock Exchange building, and the famous bull had come loose from its moorings and was bumping against the façade.

Jameson paused for a handful of seconds before continuing, waiting for the rest of the crew to regain their composure. Ash could only imagine how those from that time period felt. It wasn't just a history lesson for them – they lived it.

"At that point, it became apparent that climate change

was real – as if there was really any doubt before – and the government put in place contingency plans. The capital of the U.S. was moved from Washington, D.C. to Denver, which was on higher ground and further away from the increasingly volatile coast."

Ash whistled lowly at the image of the president, his face stern and mournful, waving stoically to a crowd as he walked out of the White House.

"As you can imagine, it only went downhill from there. Huge chunks of the West Coast of the United States began to burn. Agriculture became unreliable, and food was scarce. This led to skyrocketing prices which threw the entire U.S. economy off kilter. In less advanced parts of the planet, governments collapsed. Most of Africa and South America became failed states and reverted to middle-age fiefdoms. India and Pakistan nuked each other in a fight over some disputed territories. China nuked itself after Tiananmen Two. Corporations dissolved overnight. Sea travel became impossible. You get the idea."

"It couldn't have been that fast," snapped Miranda.

"It was," Jameson said. He put his arms down on the front of the conference table and glared at the assembled crew. "You are all forgetting, take away the veneer of civilization – the laws, the guns, the courts – and it all falls apart. Civilization is artificial. Power is all that mattered. And when you have a government that denied climate change was even happening, this was the end result."

Jameson gestured grandly to the model in front of him, showing a slew of solid red lines, dotted blue lines, and in one very confusing case, a series of question marks. It took Ash a moment to realize that he was looking at a map of what had once been the United States. Unable to resist, he peered closer and saw state boundaries merged and torn. Disconnected heaps of the South were labeled "New Confederacy," New Jersey and New York had merged into "Hudson," the entire state of Pennsylvania had an X through it, and the West Coast, save for the northernmost portions of Washington state, were covered by a sandy brown.

As Ash stared, Sierra, Pike and Sia, became increasingly

184

horrified. Sia tried covertly to wipe tears from her eyes and failed miserably at stifling a loud sniffle. Pike tried to place a comforting hand on her shoulder, but Sia shrugged it off.

"The economy had largely collapsed and communities shifted to nomadic tribalism, wandering from place to place, staying as long as they could, scavenging off of the remnants of Earth." More images now: shaken families, battered children in tattered clothing, babies with bloated bellies and visible rib cages. Ash had to look away.

"So how the hell did you fix this?" Alexis snapped, her nerves frayed. "Earth came back?"

Jameson nodded. "I'll turn it over to Blondell, who's from a little closer to our current date of 2180." With that, Blondell stood up, smoothed out her pants, and walked to the front of the room, trading places with Jameson.

"It was in 2080 that the governments finally realized what they had to do. Create a massive unifying force, combining all available public and private sector resources. So, the North American Union and European Union combined – forming the Unity Government. Others followed suit, and eventually, most of the civilized world was part of the U.G."

Ash raised his eyebrows.

The letters "U" and "G," glowing silver, rose up from the table, circling silently.

"At the same time, the biggest businesses in the world realized that there was no money to be made if the Earth was destroyed. It started with Apple and Google—"

"Huh?" Ash said. Jameson paused, and the interruption stirred the room's occupants out of their trance-like state. "Echo just said she spent a lot of time—"

"Years, Ash," said Echo.

Ash swallowed and continued. "Right. Echo said she spent years wandering the planet looking for food. How are Apple and Google still a thing?" A dour look crossed Jameson's face, and he turned over his shoulder to Blondell, who had her arms crossed against her chest. She stared downward for a moment, her face still, before bringing her neck back up and facing the group.

"When civilization collapses, it doesn't collapse evenly," she said, voice steady and stare even. "We learned this the hard way."

Ash opened his mouth to ask more questions, sensing more behind Blondell's words, but a warning look from Jameson and a smoldering fury from Echo stole his voice. Ash nodded once toward Jameson who continued.

"Gradually, and encouraged by the government, the largest corporations on Earth began to merge, with the purpose of combining resources to develop the technology to save the planet. They called themselves the Infinity Corporation." A new logo emerged from the table: a silver infinity sign, which wrapped itself around the floating "U" and "G," completing the ubiquitous logo.

Echo snorted. "This just started when I got taken, but I don't get it. How can we be here, now, if these were the people involved?"

"What do you mean?" asked Blondell.

"The Earth was destroyed by greed. Business loved money, and politicians loved their money. And that's why the Earth was ruined. We all thought it was just a matter of time. So, what was the purpose of the Infinity Corporation? Rape what was left?" Echo's bitterness was so strong, and so out of character, that Ash's jaw dropped.

Blondell, however, seemed to expect – or at least understand – the visceral anger. "2075, right, Echo?"

"Right."

"Yeah," said Blondell, her eyes faltering. "My Dad works for the U.G. – he's Director of Technological Advancement. He told me how bad it got. You were more or less in the worst of it when you were taken." Echo folded her arms over her chest.

"Well, please thank your Dad for his sympathy, but that's cold comfort," she said, her face icy. Like a wave, her anger broke. "I'm sorry. That's not fair. But you have to understand what it was like."

"Were you in one of the nomad camps?" asked Blondell.

Echo nodded. "Yes. We loved the Earth, because no one else did. Please continue."

186

Blondell looked at her feet. "It's difficult to, knowing what you went through, and where we may be headed again." But she went on. "Anyway, the U.G. and Infinity Corporation began to work hand in hand, so closely, that it became hard to tell where the government ended and the corporate world began. Gradually, more and more businesses, or at least what was left of them, joined in an effort to push back against what we'd done to the planet. And, slowly, Earth began to recover.

"By 2167, around the time I was taken, renewable energy became sustainable. It became possible to power the earth without simultaneously destroying it. The tide started to turn. Back in 2146, weather control had become possible. By 2150, they turned the Sahara Desert into a farm. Do you have any idea how exciting that is?"

Ash felt compelled to nod his head, but it was almost out of a sense of obligation to Blondell – his mind felt like it was swimming in a pool of Jello.

With an exaggerated sigh, Blondell continued. "Using this newfound power, the effects of climate change were reversed. The U.G. was able to pool its expertise and invent the technology to expand outward, exploring space for new resources. It was like the cork had been removed for human progress. The world was alive again." As she said her last sentence, Blondell's fist closed, and her face flushed with excitement.

But Ash was suspicious. "Business and government are besties?" he asked, incredulous. There were a few snickers from those taken around his time period, but mostly a confused silence. "Uh. Best friends?"

Blondell nodded. "Yes. Still. At least when I left."

Ash nodded. "That can't end well."

Blondell sighed heavily. "A few years ago, the demands of an increasing population and skyrocketing energy consumption meant that we needed new materials. Materials that could only be found off-planet. Every single one of our scientists – well, at least those that hadn't been bought off by Infinity – warned that off-planet mining had the potential to cause major disruptions. They said the

187

material could be unstable – that more testing was needed if we wanted to avoid unintended consequences. Like, you know, death." Blondell abruptly stopped and rubbed a hand to her forehead, as if the pain from the memories was suddenly too much to bear.

"My Dad begged them to stop. He begged them. And no one listened. With business running the government . . . there's an old saying that my grandmother used to say. 'It's like the wolves running the hen house.' Something like that. Regular people fought back, but they don't have the money the richest do. My dad told me some of what the U.G. was hiding. We knew that off-planet mining could be dangerous for Earth. And no one was listening."

Ash rolled his eyes at the comment, not out of disgust, but because it seemed so familiar.

"So, let me get this straight," Ash said. "Government and business actually saved the planet. And now the people on your Earth are destroying it all over again."

Blondell nodded rapidly.

"Yup. Pretty much," she said. "It's frustrating beyond comprehension. We were given a gift, and we're going to piss it away all over again."

There was silence, broken by Anton.

"So, why exactly are we trying to save Earth?" The bitterness in his voice was palpable, and for the first time, Ash saw Echo nodding in agreement with something Anton had said.

Blondell stuttered and licked her lips, her gaze fastening onto Echo. "You're why," she said, and Echo tilted her head.

"I don't understand."

Blondell stroked her face for a moment, gathering her thoughts. "You're the reason. Your experiences. What you and your family endured. The U.G., for all its flaws, is still proof that some semblance of order and civilization is better than none. It is fundamentally flawed. Maybe fatally. But it is still a government that has saved a dying planet and accelerated technology at a rate previously unseen in human society. It brought us back from the brink."

Echo's eyes narrowed. "Yes, but at what cost?"

Ash caught Blondell's hands balling into fists and extended a hand upward. "We can debate the merits of a planet-wide government later," he said. An awkward silence settled uncomfortably over the room. Ash felt like a Band-Aid had been ripped off. They now knew what had happened to the planet they called home, and Echo's question was bouncing around Ash's mind like a ping-pong ball: *At what cost?*

An even more uncomfortable question reared its ugly head next: *Was the good that the Unity Government brought worth the pain they had now inflicted upon the planet?*

And then a third question: *What is the alternative?*

Ash's mind quieted down after that.

Chapter Twenty-Five

After talking with the crew, and armed with a newfound sense of urgency over their mission, Ash realized he needed help. Valliant was the only one in any sort of position to provide it.

At Valliant's insistence, and after an awkward conversation with Tidus, Ash had the conversation privately, in his own cabin. He spent the first ten minutes catching Valliant up on what had happened on his ship, including Daniel's death and Anton's brief time as captain. Valliant peppered Ash with questions about the events, including the time Ash had spent buried in his own bed. Upon completing the story, Valliant spoke again.

"It speaks volumes about your leadership that you were able to get control of the ship back. You clearly have the command of your crew."

Ash snorted derisively. "Not by much. I only came back by one vote."

A thin smile appeared on Valliant's face. "Ash, before I was a captain, I worked in the government. I frequently had to cater to the needs of an asinine city council. There were seven of them. I realized when I first started that, more often than not, I didn't need to count to seven. I only needed to count to four. Same applies to you. You got to ten. That's enough."

"How can I lead with ten?" Ash asked. "I'm not asking that to be obnoxious, I'm asking because I literally have no idea."

Valliant shrugged. "You seem to be doing pretty well. You got one of the pieces we need and are well on your way to the second."

"If I don't get all of us killed first," Ash said. "Which reminds me, why don't you stick with us? The aliens have attacked us twice now. I know your main concern is killing them before they can launch their attack on Earth."

Valliant shook his head. "In a perfect scenario, that would be great. But, Ash, you have to understand. These aliens are much smarter than us."

"Sure, but what does that have to do with anything?"

Valliant sighed. Again. "These terrorists . . . whatever they are, they have been able to outsmart us at every turn. We lock on to one of their thermal signatures, they change it. We figure out how to track their engines, they start alternating speeds to throw us off. Anytime we get a lock on them, we lose them almost as quickly."

Ash knitted his brow. "So?"

Valliant pursed his lips. "Here's my concern: On the one hand, if we stay with you, the attackers may leave you alone, yes. But they may also accelerate their attack pattern. As long as we fly separately, they may try to attack us – and that keeps them off of Earth. We need to do everything we can to keep our friends on the original timeline. Ideally, that gives you the time you need to find the cure."

Ash opened his mouth to protest, but found no reason to do so. As uncomfortable as the idea of using his ship as bait made him, he couldn't think of any better ideas.

"Fine," he said. "But there is another way you can help us."

"Name it, Ash." Valliant sat forward and looked closer at the camera which was transmitting his image.

"I need two of your crew. The strongest ones you got."

***

Three hours later, Miranda had figured out how to activate the ship's docking system, and a shuttle from the *Remedy* landed safely in the docking bay of the *Redemption*.

191

The door opened and Valliant walked out almost immediately. He looked even more impressive than he had appeared in all of their communications: tall, broad shouldered, muscular, and with a walk so precise it could have cut metal.

"Hello, Captain Maddox!" he exclaimed, thrusting a hand forward.

Ash shook it with genuine enthusiasm. For all his quirks, Valliant knew what he was doing and had been eager to help with the raid.

"It's good to meet you in person, Captain Valliant," Ash said, the formal title rolling off his tongue awkwardly.

Valliant gestured back to his shuttle as his crew members disembarked.

"Allow me to introduce you to the two members who I think can assist you the most." He gestured to the young woman who had walked off first. "First is Larissa. She's the only one of us who was actually in the military. The United States Marines, I believe."

Ash took one look at Larissa and felt immediately intimidated. It was one of the first times he had ever met someone who, on first glance, gave the impression that she could easily have bench pressed anyone on the ship. Her eyes, cold blue, scanned the ship as she walked down the ramp to shake Ash's hand.

"Pleased to meet you, Captain." She shook Ash's hand. Her grip was as solid as concrete.

"Thank you for doing this. We need someone with combat experience."

Larissa nodded. "Combat without an experienced leader can turn deadly, quickly. For a cause like this, I am happy to lend a hand."

Ash nodded in gratitude, and Larissa moved on to meet Alexis, Blondell and Jameson, who had been coaxed out of his Engineering cocoon by the promise of getting technical advice from one of the engineers on the *Remedy*. Ash's eyes found the next unfamiliar figure, a brick-shaped soldier who was the size of Daniel. Ash's first thought on seeing him was that he was going to stand behind him for the entire raid.

Surely the big guy could absorb any damage that the aliens could throw at him.

Valliant gestured back toward the shuttle at the young man walking down the ramp. "This is McDonald. We just call him Mac."

"Uh . . . nice to meet you, Mac," Ash stammered, extending his arm.

Mac looked at the hand like a caveman staring at fire for the first time before awkwardly thrusting his own hand to Ash's. "Thank you," he said, stalking off.

When Mac turned his back to the two captains, Valliant shrugged.

"We're working on his social graces," he said quietly. He placed a hand between Ash's shoulder blades and steered him away from the rest of the crew. In a low voice, Valliant said, "As for your Anton problem, I understand your concerns. You can't attack Anton directly, but you have to prove your leadership. That puts you in an awkward position, especially since half the crew wanted him to stay as Captain."

"Tell me about it," Ash said. The two men stopped walking and Ash put his hands on his hips. "I'll take any advice you can give me."

Valliant nodded thoughtfully. "That's the mark of a good Captain. I suspect that's also a capacity which Anton lacks. That being said, here's your best path. Keep your ten loyal."

"What about the rest of the crew?" Ash asked, surprised.

Valliant shook his head. "Ash, what's most important to you is that the ten who supported you keep doing so. Give them your time, your energy, and your loyalty. Let the other nine go. They'll come around on their own." He placed his hands behind his back and somehow found a way to stand straighter. "This isn't an easy job."

"It's even harder when you never wanted it in the first place," Ash said.

A thin smile appeared on Valliant's face.

"I'm well aware," he said. "I was a bureaucrat. Now I'm a spaceship captain. But we only have one chance to save humanity."

Ash nodded. "It's too important to let anything get in the way. Even someone named Anton."

Valliant laughed. "That's the spirit. Come on. Let's go talk about this raid."

Chapter Twenty-Six

The next two days were a blur for Ash, and, he suspected, for the rest of the crew. Everyone participating in the raid rotated in and out of the sim, which was essentially perfected by Blondell and Sierra. When not in the middle of an active sim, Larissa and Mac ran practice drills with Ash and the rest of the crew, perfecting communications, weapons and defensive techniques. Each crew member did their best to learn a specialty as well. For Ash, that meant learning to better visualize the entire battlefield, taking command of a chaotic situation, and giving orders. For Alexis, that meant perfecting combat with a knife. The blood-thirsty look that appeared when she stabbed digital enemies gave Ash chills.

The sims were a struggle. Larissa and Mac's first task had been to determine who would go on the mission. Some crew members were immediately weeded out. In the first sim, Robin accidentally shot Miranda; in the second, he shot Sierra. In the third run, Anton panicked and ran the other way, only to be stopped by a strong, barred arm from Mac. He finished the sim with gusto, though, even coming close to grabbing one of the eggs, only to be felled by a watermelon-sized fist from one of the "armies" (as they had christened the monsters) at the last moment. To Ash's annoyance, Anton was the only one who actually made it into the "throne room" which contained the eggs.

After five failed attempts, all Ash had to show for his effort was a battered and bruised crew. His body vaguely resembled a used punching bag. Though the simulator was capable of ensuring no real pain accompanied the damage, Larissa hadn't allowed it. "You can't learn without pain!" she'd said. She had insisted the body armor that they wore in the simulator created real injury. Fortunately, Ash was able to convince her to keep the beatings they took at the hands of the simulated monsters to a minimum. Bruises, he could work around. Broken bones, however . . .

Meanwhile, the crew continued to morph into a fighting unit. Though still deeply shaken by Daniel's death, everyone seemed to have their role. Alexis and Sia each worked toward perfecting the art of flying the shuttle craft and the ship. Blondell and Sierra worked side by side to gather data for their current mission. Anton continued to take an almost sadistic pleasure in learning the ship's weapons systems. Ash tried desperately to learn everything he possibly could about the *Redemption*. He read every file on his tablet, intently watched the crew operate their stations, and even tolerated Valliant's long-winded-but-value-packed lectures about the capabilities of his ship.

Those conversations taught Ash that the ship was far more complex than he had first realized. Everything, of course, fit ergonomically, and each member of the crew seemed to have been drafted with a specific position in mind, with backups for every role and the technology to match. This even applied to the backup crew. Robin, who had taken over for Daniel on maintenance and Engineering, was taken in 1998, a mere eight years after Daniel.

One night, over a brief dinner with Jameson and Alexis, Ash discussed the issue. "There are two things I don't understand," Ash began, awkwardly shifting an ice pack that was haphazardly taped around his shoulder. "First, if the technology was designed for us, then that means that whoever took us, however they took us, meant to take us specifically."

"I would think so," Jameson said. "What's not to understand about that?"

Ash looked from Jameson to Alexis, both of whom stared blankly at him.

"You know, you look ridiculous with two black eyes, right?" Ash smiled.

Jameson dismissively raised his eyebrows over his swollen skull.

Ash continued talking. "Why us?" he asked. "I mean, we seem good at this, but are we actually the best that humanity has to offer? You'd think that the U.G. would have grabbed a Captain who didn't suffer from a major depressive disorder and need medication to function."

Alexis started to give Ash a nasty look at the self-deprecation, but Ash waved her off. "You know what I mean," he said.

Alexis sighed. "I do. And you've got a point," she said, looking expectantly at Jameson, whose mouth was full of chicken.

After a beat, Jameson said, "What? I don't know everything." He took a large swig of milk to wash the food down. "Clearly there is more going on here than we understand. Forces at play that we can't grasp. We don't have all the information, guys. That's going to make figuring out why we are here even harder."

"Fine," Ash said. "But that just leads me to other questions. Why is everyone on the ship sixteen to twenty years old? And why the hell are we all from different time periods?"

"You're asking different questions, but I have the same answer: I don't know. Whatever it is, it's beyond us. And, by the way, keep in mind, you're not even scratching the surface of the questions that we have to address."

Ash's eyes narrowed, and Jameson continued, ticking off questions on his fingers as he asked them. "Why is this ship no harder to fly than a video game? How is it that we supposedly stopped the ship that brought Spades, but we're still going, even though the so-called alien terrorists were destroyed? If the U.G. has invented time and space travel, why don't they send warships back in time in order to defend earth on S-day? Why don't they send a message, warning the government of the 'past' about the alien attack? Why are they making this so needlessly complicated? Oh, and there is one more particularly scary issue that needs to be addressed."

"What?" asked Alexis.

Jameson took a deep breath and said, "If time travel is a thing, why haven't we heard from the future? And I mean the distant future? Maybe helping us on the way?"

"Isn't it possible that they know we succeed and don't want to mess us up?" Ash asked.

Jameson shrugged.

"That's one possibility. But they could also swoop in with their advanced, twenty-fifth century weapons and blow up the aliens right now. An alternative possibility is that they aren't coming to save the day because they can't. Because we failed our mission."

Jameson shoveled another forkful of salad into his mouth and chewed loudly, leaving a perturbed Ash and Alexis to stare at him.

"You're a ray of sunshine," Alexis said.

Jameson shrugged.

"How can you eat after saying that we fail and the future is gonna get wiped out?" she asked.

Jameson pointed a fork at Alexis. "I never said that it was going to happen. But it may. Ash's hypothesis is highly possible as well. Either way, we can't do anything about it. And I'm hungry."

Ash stood up, took his tray with him and shook his head. "I'm done with this theoretical stuff. Let's concentrate on the mission. Come on, Alexis, we got a sim in an hour."

Alexis stood up with him. "Don't be mad because you can't keep up with Jameson," she said, ribbing gently and poking Ash in the ribs.

He playfully smacked her hand away. "I swear, I will cover you in mashed potatoes," he threatened, and they both laughed.

It took more time, many failed raids and additional scrapes and bruises, but by the time the last sim rolled around, the group had the mission profile well memorized. In the final battle, Ash and the rest of the crew positioned themselves perfectly, mowing down their foes with simulated laser blasts, their weapons transforming their enemies into clouds of dusty fur and pink, coagulated blood.

With a victorious "Whoop!" Ash had stowed the last of the eggs in a pouch made by Larissa. His eyes connected with Alexis' and found a triumphant stare that only spurred on his own joy.

They were ready.

At least, as ready as they could be.

Chapter Twenty-Seven

The next day, the ship orbited Kepler, roughly two miles above their landing zone. The crew of the raid was set: Ash, Alexis, Anton and Pike in one shuttle, joined by Larissa, Mac, Sia and Blondell in the other. Anton had insisted on going on the raid, and eventually, Larissa relented. Despite Valliant's advice, Ash's gut told him that intentionally alienating just less than half of the ship was a bad call. The crew nervously marched down to the docking bay. Larissa had laid out gear for everyone.

As they climbed into their full-body suits, Larissa described the equipment. "This is your full body impact armor. It's customized for your size. The number on your gear corresponds with your room number."

Wordlessly, each member of the team marched forward. Each suit bore the Infinity logo. Ash's was numbered as "1."

"Don't ask me what they're made of. What I do know is that they are impact resistant. Ash, come here. Anton, you too."

Ash cautiously stepped forward, staring at Anton with a wary eye. With a quick gesture, Larissa said, "Anton, punch Ash in the stomach for me."

Before Ash could protest, Anton turned the corner of lips upward and said, "Happily," before executing a lightning punch to Ash's gut. Ash's muscles tensed but relaxed just as quickly when he realized he felt as if his stomach had been hit by a fluffy pillow. Anton, meanwhile, appeared to have taken the brunt of the force, and he shook his hand in obvious pain.

"Sorry about that, but you get my point," said Larissa. The smallest trace of a smile threatened to break through. "This thing is hard and will protect you. That's why it covers almost all of your body, but it is weak in the joints, so be careful there. It is not blast repellant, so don't get caught in the line of fire."

Tentatively, Ash bent down and handled his weapon, picking up a futuristic gun which was nestled between two knives. Even though he had trained with it for days, he still marveled at the sleekness of its design, the coolness of the extended barrel.

"Remember," Larissa said. "Your gun has the power of a small cannon and is semi-automatic. Hold down the trigger and it will fire a burst. Keep holding, more fire. But you will run out after five hundred shots, and yes, it goes much quicker than you would think. So maintain battery charge at all time, because your life may depend on it. Any questions?"

A few minutes later, they were ready. The crew separated into their preordained shuttles. They were sent off by Miranda and Valliant, who had agreed to stay behind and command the ship. No one had needed to say the obvious. As the more experienced Captain, it made more sense that he stay behind to fly both of the ships in case the mission failed catastrophically.

"You'll do great!" said Miranda, twitching her arm spasmodically in a forced attempt to appear casual.

"You'll be fine," Valliant said, with more sobriety. "We'll be in your ears and will keep an eye out from here. Good luck, Captain and crew!"

Ash met Valliant's firm gaze, which was reassuring, and glanced around the interior of the shuttle bay for what he hoped wouldn't be the last time.

The ship flew smoothly out of the docking bay and into empty space. Sailing out of the *Redemption* on a small shuttle made Ash feel closer to the massiveness of space than he ever had onboard the *Redemption,* as if it was only the most gossamer-thin strand which stopped Ash from touching the great unknown.

Anton and Pike looked similarly touched, and stared out the front windows, mouths slack and jaws slightly unhinged. Despite the circumstances, Ash found himself enveloped in an odd sense of peace.

It didn't last. Minutes later, Alexis guided the ship in for a smooth landing on the dusty surface of Kepler. Almost as soon as the shuttle touched down, Larissa's voice was in Ash's head.

"Masks on," she said brusquely. "Don't open the doors until we're cleared to go."

Ash obediently snapped his oxygen mask into place, causing a built-in light on his helmet to blink from red to green.

Moments later, Alexis used her fist to pound a large red button next to the shuttle's rear doors. "Here goes nothing," she said, looking up at Ash, eyes wide.

Despite the fact that their faces were largely obscured by their helmets, Ash tried to muster a smile. "We'll be fine," he said, unconvincingly, voice muffled by his oxygen mask.

Anton bounced on the balls of his feet, waiting for the doors to open. At last they did, and the four gingerly walked onto Kepler.

It looks like a desert from hell, thought Ash, his boots crunching the dusty ground under his feet. Ash looked upward and instantly found himself too overwhelmed to move on. No amount of simulator runs prepared him for the real thing. From above, an inscrutable star cast a purple, yellow hue, throwing a bizarre, shifting glow across the planet's grimy surface. Underneath the alien sun, the brown sand which caked Kepler's surface appeared ready to glide into the darkness. Shadows bounced across Ash's vision, caused by mountains of various shapes and sizes which jerked across the horizon.

Their shuttle had landed in a small clearing, no more than a few hundred yards in diameter. They were surrounded on all sides by solid, towering rock. The only break in the off-putting surroundings was a series of jagged, metallic beams which cut into a hole in the ground, roughly fifty feet to their left. Analysis had showed that the aliens had been capable of building some rudimentary exits to their cave system. The hole they were looking at was likely an escape hatch. The entirety of the view, combined with the unnatural light coming from the planet's sun, gave Ash the impression that he was caught at the nexus between dreams and reality, and would slide into a nightmare at any moment.

Coming back to his senses, Ash felt a moment's fear that the rest of the crew would have continued walking toward their destination, leaving him in their wake. However, much to his relief, Ash found all other seven members as frozen to the ground as him.

"Incredible, isn't it?" whispered Larissa, her voice sounding small. There was no response from the assembled group.

In an effort to get the group moving again, Ash cracked, "One small step for man, one giant leap for a bunch of teenagers." The joke fell flat. "Sorry."

"No unnecessary chatter," chirped Larissa, awareness returning to her voice.

Ash pursed his lips. "Sorry. Wait. Was that unnecessary chatter?"

"Yes."

"Sorry."

Silence followed as the two shuttle crews merged and continued forward. As per the mission plan, they had landed roughly eighty yards from the entrance to the cave which held the eggs.

Off they walked, two by two, toward the entrance. They moved cautiously; none of the Armies had been seen outside, but they were taking no chances.

When they were just in front of the cave's entrance, Ash snuck a look at Alexis, only to and discover that she was already looking at him. She raised a gloved hand for a high five as Ash gave her a fist bump. He laughed at the confusion on Alexis' face as she tilted her head.

At the front of the line and just before the cave entrance, Larissa threw up her arm perpendicular to the ground. The group froze.

"Hold here," she said. She crept forward, ducking her head to look inside the cave, which seemed to swallow her whole.

A moment passed. Two. Three. The silence over the comm system stretched.

Ash kept his head frozen forward, his fingers itching with tension, ready to raise his weapon and mow down a pack of white-fanged Armies.

A click on the comms system, followed by Larissa's voice. "Clear."

The crew moved forward and, two-by-two, stepped into the blackness. So far, it was exactly as they had run it in the sim. Ash followed the dim light shining on top of Larissa's weapon and activated his own. The bluish beam cut through the darkness in front of him, illuminating the path ahead. Mac, the raid's designated navigator, flipped open a panel on his wrist and fingered the controls.

"All clear," he said.

Larissa nodded, shadows caused by eight beams of light illuminating her bobbing head. "Alright. Remember the plan, people, and we will live through this. Take your marks."

The group fanned out into two rows of four, and walked cautiously forward and downhill.

Even with their masks on, Ash could sense the heat and stillness in the air. If their readings were correct, the Armies rarely ventured up here, leaving the ground untouched. However, the veracity of their intelligence was compromised when Ash's light bounced off a cave wall and revealed a series of long, perpendicular scratches. He gently elbowed Alexis to get her attention and gestured to the cave wall.

"You see that?" he asked, his question going out across the open comm system.

Larissa spun around, her movements sharp and angry, before becoming perfectly still when she saw the scratches.

"I do," she said. "Those have to be Armie made."

"I thought they weren't supposed to be on this level?" Anton asked. The group was silent, looking from one to the other.

"They're not," Alexis said.

More silence followed, until Larissa spoke. "Come on, there's nothing we can do. Let's get a move on. If they are up here, I don't want to be waiting for them."

The group continued to walk. As per the simulations, the hallway forked, and the group chose the left pathway, which spiraled down. They moved, two-by-two again, weapons pointed forward.

It was during that walk that they heard their first sign of an Army in the form of a barely audible roar. Straining to hear, Ash felt his blood run cold. However quiet it was, the roar was unquestionably high-pitched. As alien as it sounded, there was a tension to the noise which was impossible to mistake. Soon, a second roar joined the first, and a third joined the chorus a moment after that.

The group had frozen upon hearing the Armies' howls. No one moved again until Larissa spoke.

"Mac, can you get a read on their location?"

MacDonald began poking around his wrist panel. "No. As we go lower it's messing with our signals. As best I can tell, though, they aren't near us, and they aren't in the throne room yet."

"Okay, let's keep moving then. Captain?"

"I'm here," said Valliant, making his first appearance on their comms since the raid had begun.

"Any help you can give us in getting a fix on the Armies would be greatly appreciated."

"Roger that. I'm working with young Radar here. He seems to have a good idea of how these systems need to work. But the metallic composition of the cave is denser than we expected, and we are struggling to break through and get a signal. Will be back with you as soon as I have something."

Despite the circumstances, Ash smiled with pride at the news of Radar's competency.

"Thank you, Captain. Out." Larissa waved her gun forward. "Let's keep moving."

Down the spiral they went. The surface was as smooth

as glass, evidentially worn down by the heavy bodies of the Armies. To Ash's left, he caught the occasional break in the rock. The holes were relatively uniform: short, stout, and wide enough so that an Armie could get in and out with relative ease.

In front of him, Larissa's feet had evidentially reached level ground. She took a few steps ahead and motioned the rest of the group forward, stopping at a cave wall. "We're going through here," she said, gesturing with her weapon into the darkness.

The throne room was a giant funnel in reverse, with the nest that contained their eggs located against a back wall. Scattered around the room were rocks which appeared to have been carved for seats. Next to all of those rocks were smaller pillars, which Miranda had theorized were for the Armies to rest their massive arms."

"Keep moving," Larissa said, entering the throne room.

The group followed, one by one. As the funnel widened, Ash squinted to see if he could detect anything, but there was nothing for him to see. No rocks, no thrones, no eggs; at least, not yet.

Larissa reached into a back pocket and snapped two glow-lights on. She placed one at her feet. She chucked the other deeper into the chamber. The stick landed, but revealed more of the same: nothing. *Maybe we get lucky, for once,* thought Ash.

However, as he crept forward, Ash realized that something was off. The sims had been remarkably faithful to reality thus far, but this room didn't feel right. For starters, there were two entrances off to one side of the room instead of one, and a third, smaller space between two massive rock panels. There were also more thrones than Ash had seen, including smaller ones toward the front of the room, complete with smaller arm rests. And there was the center of the room . . .

"The eggs!" Larissa raced forward and the rest of the group followed. And sure enough, there it was: the nest for the Armie eggs was there. But the eggs were not.

"Where are they?" Larissa asked, searching the ground

and finding nothing. "Captain Valliant! Come in!"

"We see what you are seeing, Larissa, and we are working on it. Stand by. Radar is searching for them now."

A high-pitched howl cut through the darkness, and the crew bunched closer together, near where the eggs were supposed to have been.

"I don't know if we have that kind of time, Captain," Larissa said.

Another roar. Closer this time. Ash shouldered his weapon, squinted and looked toward one of the two entrances he had noticed.

"You don't. Radar has them coming. Looks like ten . . . no, make that twelve, and they are motoring."

"Cover! Now!" ordered Larissa. The group scattered behind large rocks, and Ash found himself in the same position as he had been the first time he ran a sim: two thirds of the way from the front of the room, gun in front of him, and Alexis on his right.

"Well, this went to hell pretty quickly, huh?" Alexis said.

Ash pounded the side of his gun, lowering a built-in tripod.

"If this is it, I'm going down swinging," he said. "And what a way to go."

Alexis snorted. "I'm with you, Ash, but I'd prefer not to go down at all." Alexis slammed her weapon, bringing down her tripod. "That being said, I swear to God, I'm going to kill me one of these bastards."

"Have I said remind me not to piss you off recently?" Ash asked, adrenaline flowing. At that moment, there was no fear, no depression, no anxiety. There was only the gun, acting as an extension of Ash's arms, and a desire to kill as many of these long-armed, white freaks as possible.

With a roar and a splatter of boulders the size of toddlers, an Armie burst through the crack in the wall that Ash had noticed earlier. All eight crew members turned their fire on the monster, as Larissa said, "Watch the second entrance!"

Whirling, Ash and Alexis spun and redirected their fire as four more Armies poured into the room. One of them was shot and stumbled, but the next one reached the closest human. Using its arm like a golf club, the fiend whipped forward and spun, crushing Pike and sending him spinning through the air like a rag doll, crashing into Anton. One strike, from one monster, and two crew members had gone silent.

"Dammit," Ash muttered, training his weapon on the beast who had wrought the damage. Ash found that the Armie's hides were much thicker than he had anticipated, and it took multiple shots to slow the creature down, to say nothing of disabling it.

"Aim for the eyes!" shouted Larissa.

At that, Blondell redirected her fire at the monster's head, connecting multiple blasts and causing the attacker's head to sizzle and smoke. With a growl and one of its arms clutching its head, the Armie fell forward, landing directly on Larissa, pinning her.

"Larissa!" bellowed Mac, his voice slightly higher-pitched than normal. He darted from behind his rock toward Larissa. However, to Ash's horror, his foot caught a smaller rock, and he went down in a sprawling heap. Behind him, another Armie growled and began to raise its gigantic arms. Ash and Alexis aimed their fire its way, catching the monster in the face, and its cries of terror filled the small chamber.

"We're gonna have to do something here!" called Ash.

"Ash, it's Captain Valliant. Look to the right. We're watching something interesting," said Valliant with an astonishing calm. Swinging his weapon, Ash saw what Valliant was looking at. One of the smaller Armies that had come barreling into the throne room was now leaving, but not by the way it came. Instead, to Ash's disbelief, it seemed to suck its massive arms into its shoulder blades, retracting them as if they were controlled by hydraulics. Much smaller, it squeezed through the smaller crack between two slabs of rock.

"Where is that guy going, and why is he leaving?" Ash asked, firing his weapon at the Armie near Mac as the *Remedy* crew member tried desperately to right himself and take cover.

"That is a very good question!" answered Alexis, who had followed Ash's glance to the escaping Armie.

Ash stared and blinked. He knew what he had to do. "Cover me!" he yelled at Alexis. With a vault, Ash pushed himself over his rock cover and raced to the right, attempting to follow the small creature.

At once, three guns turned and blasted forward, attempting to stop the Armies who had turned and now lurched in Ash's direction. Three Armies stumbled, but a fourth roared forward and swung its club-like arms in Ash's general direction. Ash ducked and the Armie grazed the top of his helmet with a long fingernail, ringing Ash's helmet like a bell. Off-balance, Ash fell on his rear, and the Armie crouched down, roaring in Ash's face. The sound threatened to transform his eardrums from functioning organs to mushy paste. Recovering, Ash tried to scoot backward, but instead backed into cold, hard rock. Out of room, Ash brought his arms up to his face, preparing for impact.

Instead, the room got quieter; the Armie seemed frozen in time, froth hanging from its massive jaw and spaghetti-like arms hanging limply at its side. It collapsed, a knife handle buried in its neck, revealing Alexis, her hand outstretched as she let the sharp weapon drift out of her hand, falling with the Armie.

"What?" she said, staring at Ash's surprised face. "Its neck is the weakest point in the hide. God, don't you read, Ash?"

Despite the sheer terror of the moment, Ash found himself unable to bite back the laugher.

He launched himself up and raced toward the hole in the rock, Alexis hot on his heels. Holding his breath and clutching his weapon at his side, Ash squeezed into the opening. The rocks pressed against his ribs and his spine, filling his limbs with a fiery panic. Ash imagined himself stuck and the crew abandoning him, leaving him to starve to death in a tomb of rock, with nothing but Armies as his guardians . . .

And just as quickly, Ash stumbled forward, free of his

confinement. He fell into an open space, gasping. The room was almost perfectly circular, with a large, gaping hole in its middle. Surrounding the seemingly bottomless pit was a ledge of rock, barely wide enough for one person.

Seconds later, Alexis burst through the crack, gasping for breath but managing to stay upright. As soon as she recovered, she began swinging her weapon around, searching for any sight of the Armie which had scuttled into the room. Ash did the same. Both beams of light bounced around the small, enclosed space. Their search came up empty.

"Where the hell did you two go?" yelled Larissa, her voice strained and difficult to hear over the laser fire.

"We may have found something," Ash said. "We followed one of the Armies through the crack in the wall and are searching for the eggs now."

"Well, hurry the hell up!" cried Larissa. "I don't know how long we can hold them off, and now they're keeping their freakin' heads down when they charge!"

"Great, they're adapting," said Ash. He looked at Alexis. "We better move it." He began to traverse the circular pathway around the room, careful to watch his footing.

"Where did that thing go?" questioned Alexis. "And where are the eggs?" She continued to flash her light around the room, bouncing from wall to wall and occasionally dipping into the pit directly to their right. However, after a few feet, the bright light trailed off into a dark void.

"Not down there," Ash said. "That's too far down. Even for one of those things."

Behind him, from the direction they had come, Ash could still make out the muffled sounds of gunfire and hand-to-hand combat. His heart ached to return to his crew, but he knew that he could end this battle quickly if Alexis and he could find the damned eggs. That being said, they didn't appear to be anywhere in the room. Ash and Alexis had made a full circuit and found nothing but gray, dusty rock in front of them and a bottomless pit below. Unless . . .

Realizing that there was one place they hadn't looked, Ash whipped his flashlight to the ceiling. An instant later, a high-pitched roar followed. An Armie, who had been suspended from the ceiling of the small chamber, released its grip and dropped down twenty feet, landing with surprising grace between Ash and Alexis. Alexis dropped her weapon in surprise and Ash barely had time to shove her backward before the Armie lashed a monstrous arm forward, crossing the space where Alexis' head had been an instant before.

Another deadly roar filled the small space. The white, furry alien lunged toward Alexis, pounding it fists on the ground like a hammer. Alexis rolled out of the way, again missing certain death by inches. However, Ash had moved closer. He struck out with his foot, connecting solidly with the middle of the Army's leg. It fell in a heap. Alexis kicked the behemoth in its gut. A roar of pain filled the room, so loud it seemed to acquire a physical presence. Alexis launched to kick again, but the monster rolled away . . . off of the ledge. Its roar screeched through the space, becoming softer and softer, until it faded into nothingness.

There was no thump to indicate that the Armie had landed.

Gasping for breath, Ash looked from where the Army had dropped. The rocks which lead to the monster's former perch were craggy and easy to grip.

"Boost! Now!"

Alexis dropped to her knees and cupped her hands. Using her head for balance, Ash stepped in and Alexis lifted him up. Ash connected with the first set of handholds and began to climb. Upon reaching the top, he stepped onto a rocky beam which ran the length of the chamber. In the center of the beam was a small, circular platform, and on that platform, nestled in a series of small rocks, sat four blue-green eggs, each roughly the size of an iPhone.

"I got them!" Ash exclaimed, running forward as best he could while crouching. He cautiously lifted the closest egg and found it to be surprisingly heavy. As quickly as he dared – he had no idea how fragile the eggs were – he placed all four in a shatter-proof pouch and began the return trip back down.

Alexis was on the radio explaining the situation to Larissa when Ash's feet touched solid ground again. Moving his hands as gently as possible, he detached the pouch of eggs and handed them to Alexis. In a blur of movements, she fastened them to her waist securely.

The plan was simple: get the hell off of Kepler. Ash and Alexis raced back to the small passageway which would lead them to rejoin the rest of the group, with Alexis in the lead, ready to fight off any Armies which blocked their path. As best he could, Ash tried to ignore the crushing claustrophobia which enveloped him as soon as he squeezed through the rocky surface. Before he knew it, he burst out into the main chamber once again. The combat had largely slowed down, with humans and Armies alike staggering, lying wounded against the rocky thrones, or lying still on the ground. Scrambling behind the largest rock he could find, Ash spoke again.

"What have we got?"

"We have everyone," said Larissa. "It's time to get out of here."

"Then let's go!" Ash stood up and fired a spray of wild shots in front of him. At that mark, the attack force leapt up and began to sprint out of the chamber. Larissa jumped up and fired shots of her own, attempting to join Ash in holding off their enemies.

Ash stepped backward, noticing another two Armies stepping out from one of the main entrances which must have led deeper into the cave system. He fired wildly in their direction, catching one Army directly in the face. The other ducked behind a rock and began to move forward, its gait sluggish. Two more new Armies followed the first. Ash missed both of them. Two more came after that.

Larissa grabbed Ash's arm. "Let's go, Chief! The eggs are secured and everyone else is out." With a brief nod, Ash bolted from the chamber at full speed, leaving only an echoing cry behind him.

"We're right behind you!" Ash yelled, reaching the spiral and racing upward.

Seconds later, Ash crossed the threshold of the cave and

burst into the purple-yellow sunlight. The clouds, dim sun and bizarre desert surroundings were instantly disorienting. As Ash sprinted, he forced himself to lock his eyes onto the figures in front of him. He blinked enough to clear his head and count.

"Yeah!" Ash shouted. "Larissa, we're all here!"

"Keep moving!" was the response. In front of them, Larissa skidded to a stop. She turned around, knelt down, shouldered her weapon, and fired a burst, stitching the air with white-hot plasma. With a roar, two chasing Armies staggered, but more took up the slack. Larissa kept firing until an empty *click* filled their communications system. Wasting no time, Larissa turned back around to run, waving her hands wildly over her shoulders as she did.

"Go! Go!"

Ash kept running but pulled his gun out to fire blindly over his shoulder. The final forty yards were completed in what seemed like an eternity's worth of time. Ash clattered up the ramp and into the shuttle; Alexis a millisecond behind him.

A larger form carrying a smaller one staggered up a few seconds later. As soon as all four were onboard the ship, Ash pounded the digital display which would close the door. Alexis, strapped into the pilot seat, madly flicking switches and displays.

"Everybody hang on. This needs to be fast!"

Sure enough, two large *dings* on the shuttle doors followed. The Armies had reached the door and were trying to pound their way in. The ship lurched forward, choppy at first, but smoother as they gained more altitude until it became an easy glide. It was only then that Ash whipped off his helmet. Mac did the same and leaned down to remove Sia's helmet. She had been knocked unconscious and was bleeding from a deep gash on her forehead.

"She's alright," Mac said. "She's going to have one hell of a headache, but she's alright."

Ash smiled and looked down at Sia, who looked rather peaceful, save for the bleeding wound and rock-shaped lump between her eyes. Another look at Mac, then back to

Sia, and Ash realized what could have been.
His hands began to shake uncontrollably.

CHAPTER TWENTY-EIGHT

A short time later, the shuttle landed safely in the *Redemption*. Alexis popped the shuttle doors and Ash saw the smiling faces of Radar, Jameson, Miranda and Valliant.

Stepping off the ship, Alexis handed her egg-filled pouch to Miranda, who squeaked with joy as she ran off to her science station.

Ash looked at Valliant, whose arms were as wide open as his smile.

"Well done!" said Valliant, hugging Ash tight. Ash happily returned the gesture. He was trying to calm down, and the enveloping presence of someone who seemed to know what they were doing was incredibly comforting. "I must say, for a while there, I wasn't sure if you were going to make it. It all looked rather bleak."

"Agreed, but we did it," Ash said.

Behind him, he turned around to greet the other shuttle crew, who had just disembarked. Blondell smiled, taking long, easy strides off the ship. Larissa marched off, past everyone else and out of the docking bay, looking perturbed. Pike stumbled; his head was oozing blood from the large gash to the left side of his face. He nearly fell to the ground, paused, and consented to being led off the ship by Radar. Mac easily hoisted Sia, brushing past Robin's awkwardly extended arms.

Anton barely made it off the ship and leaned on the railings for support. Unlike Pike, he didn't appear injured. Instead, he simply looked pale, as white as a sheet, as if he could barely take another step. Ash took a step toward Anton, who suddenly found the ability to move and stuck a hand forward, palm extended, indicating that he wanted Ash to stop. Ash froze and tried to make eye contact with his crewmate. Anton didn't respond. He had ceased moving again and stood as still as a statue.

Ash stood, awkwardly, trying to figure out his next steps. Did he try to comfort the obviously-terrified Anton? Ignore it, as if nothing had happened? Something in between? As his mind raced through the possible consequences of each action, Ash felt a hand on his shoulder and heard a quiet voice say, "Ash?"

Ash turned around to see Valliant, his face kind.

"Give him a moment."

Ash nodded and walked back with Valliant, who put a hand on his back.

"I have an idea for you."

"Go for it," Ash said, feeling lost and angry at himself for the sensation. Wasn't this a cause for joy? Why did he feel so . . . sad?

"I think everyone here needs a break," Valliant began. "We've got three weeks until Spades is supposed to make its arrival on Earth, and that is more than enough time for us – and you – to take a breather. Your crew is exhausted, and you need a morale boost. My advice is this. Celebrate tonight."

"Celebrate?" Ash responded. The word rolled off his tongue like it was an alien language. Celebrate?

Valliant took a step closer. "Ash, trust me on this. I've paid the price . . . a greater price than I could have imagined . . . for driving my crew too hard. They need a rest. You are on the clock, certainly, but that doesn't mean you can't stop and unwind. After all, look at all you have done. You're a group of teenagers who are this close to developing a vaccine which may save the world. Take a moment to appreciate everything you have accomplished."

Ash shrugged. "It doesn't feel like we've done enough. And look at us. Daniel's dead. Sia's hurt, badly. Anton is stuck. I mean that literally. He's actually stuck and not moving." Ash gestured back toward the shuttle to Anton, who had remained frozen in place. The corner of Valliant's mouth upturned into an ironic smile.

"I've seen that before. He'll be alright. It's a bit of shell shock. But, given your relationship, I don't think talking to him will accomplish anything right now." Valliant paused to gather his thoughts. "Ash, I understand that you don't see it right now, but you are an extraordinary group of teenagers, every one of you. But you all have your limits. Take tonight. Appreciate your success. And let me help. I'm sure the ship has plenty of provisions to have some sort of party."

Ash considered. Valliant had a point. The crew was bone tired. He had seen it over the past few days – the zombie-like stares. The way people hadn't been eating and had been too tired to sleep. The way that even simple actions took time. Even with his medication, and position of authority, and close relationship with Alexis, Ash was drained. He knew the rest of the crew had to feel the same. Perhaps taking the pressure off, even just for the night, would do everyone some good. But, even still, how could they begin to contemplate a party? What if the alien ship attacked them again? Staying close to their equipment was an absolute necessity.

"Fine," Ash finally said. "But we're doing it on the Bridge."

CHAPTER TWENTY-NINE

Three hours later, the entire crew of the *Redemption,* as well as their guests from the *Remedy,* were lodged firmly on the Bridge. The first thing that Ash noticed as people entered were the smiles. No one had smiled on the Bridge for days, save for the occasional lame joke or bad pun. The tension had been so thick on the ship that Ash could feel iron bands of pressure wrapped around his every muscle and tendon.

For a group of teenagers who, by and large, had been trapped on an interstellar warship for days, they didn't look too bad. When word of the party had gone out, Mercury and Exodus had sprinted off to their rooms. Some of the crew looked relieved; others terrified. When they emerged from their cabins, the physical change was evident. Hair which hadn't been touched by a brush was now gelled and in place. Guys had shaved, and girls had found make-up, leading Ash to the latest discovery on his ship: whoever had put them there had given them make-up from the era in which they had been taken. Ash laughed mirthlessly. He realized this explained why Echo looked virtually the same: makeup was a scarce resource which had long been depleted in her time.

Exodus and Mercury, once back from figuring out what they were going to wear, had dashed into the kitchen and managed to turn the ship's significant provision store into a slew of party food, including mini-sandwiches and pizza, veggie's with dip, a ton of cheese, and pigs in a blanket. What pigs-in-a-blanket were doing on a spaceship was beyond Ash.

At the appointed hour, the crew had begun to wander in. No one was quite sure what to expect. Ash had a feeling that no one onboard was a party animal. By and large, Ash suspected that they were all misfits and outcasts from their homes.

It wasn't in his nature, but Ash took it upon himself to be as friendly and gregarious as humanly possible. Pike walked in, wearing a cross between a tank-top and a polo shirt. Ash cheerfully slapped him on the shoulder.

"Glad you made it!" Ash said excitedly, forcing the phrase to sound as natural as possible, and realizing how ridiculous it sounded. Pike's grunt of acknowledgement let Ash know his efforts were futile and he moved on.

Next to walk in was Robin, who seemed to be adjusting well to his new role as the ship's fix-it man.

"Hi Ash!" Robin said, bounding over to Ash, who was standing by the Captain's chair, still smarting from his failed attempt at a conversation with Pike.

"Hey Robin," replied Ash, smiling genuinely this time. "It's good to see you here."

Behind Robin, Mercury and Exodus walked in, both looking surprisingly dolled up in casual dresses that were skin-tight on top but awkwardly puffy on the bottom. It took Ash a moment or two to stop openly gawking.

"Hey, we really need to talk about the left wing some more," Robin said. "It's not an emergency, and I know that now isn't the right time, but maybe later?"

Ash nodded absentmindedly.

Next entered Blondell, staring around awkwardly.

"Hey, Blondell!" cried Ash, waving her over. "Over here!"

Blondell, looking relieved, joined the conversation. When she got close enough, Ash stared in disbelief. Fashion from whenever Blondell had come from had evidentially looped back to around to the 2000s: Blondell wore a simple, low-cut tank-top, and again, Ash was struck by how different she looked. He also noticed her arms for the first time.

"Uhh . . . Blondell . . . you're. . . " Ash's voice trailed off

219

as he tried to finish the sentence but couldn't find a way. Fortunately, Blondell finished it for him by flexing.

"Huge. I know."

Blondell was *ripped*.

Ash gaped. He tried to find the words but couldn't. He had seen Blondell countless times over the past few weeks, but he had never noticed how muscular she was. Most of the rest of the crew stuck to clothing from their own time period, but Blondell was one of the few on the ship who wore a crew "uniform" which was a simple gray shirt with the U.G. and Infinity Corporation logo.

Clearly enjoying the attention, Blondell rotated through a series of poses, her biceps practically rippling. "I had entered a few competitions at home but couldn't win. You have no idea how much it's been killing me. I haven't been able to work out here."

Ash continued to stare in disbelief, while Robin looked ready to start giggling.

"How much can you bench?" Ash asked.

Flexing her arms above her head, Blondell replied, "About 190. Was pushing 200 before this happened."

Robin, who couldn't have been a hair taller than five feet, brought a knuckle up to his mouth and smiled.

"I'm 120 pounds," he said.

Blondell froze in mid-pose and smiled.

"You make do with what you got! Get over here!" she said, clearing off a bench toward the back of the Bridge and laying down, face-up. Robin, looking like an excited kid in a candy store, ran over to Blondell. In one fluid motion, she scooped him up as if he was a toy and flung him into the air, arms straight.

"Gah!" screamed Robin, his voice pretending to sound terrified, but his smile and laughter apparent. Blondell, moving her arms with surprising ease, began to move Robin up and down.

"Count off, skinny!" she cried, and Robin began to loudly count with each rep. More people were filing into the Bridge. They were greeted by the sight of one of the toughest members of the crew lifting one of the smallest as if he was an overgrown sack of feathers. A crowd gathered and Ash smiled.

"What the hell did you do?" said a voice behind him.

Ash turned around to see Jameson, arms folded over his chest.

"Apparently I helped Blondell get back into her workout routine," Ash said, without missing a beat.

Jameson paused, considering, and dropped his arms to his side and smiled.

"I'm glad you came. I was afraid I was gonna have to send a search party to pry you out of Engineering."

"Even I need to get out of there every now and then." Jameson watched Robin bob up and down in Blondell's arms. "I didn't get what you were doing at first, but now I do."

Ash gestured back to Valliant, who stood on the opposite edge of the Bridge talking with Larissa. The two appeared to be in the middle of a heated conversation, one which didn't match the burgeoning spirit of the room. Ash ignored it.

"It's his fault," he said. "But I'm glad I listened. We needed this. No one should expect to go non-stop without having a little fun." Ash's eyes travelled back to Mercury and Exodus and their body-hugging dresses.

"Yep," said Jameson, his eyes still following Robin, who had finally been put down by Blondell and was staggering around the room, laughing. Ash felt his own tension easing, his muscles unwinding. He was starting to feel like a human again.

As the night continued, Ash felt more at peace. He floated from conversation to conversation, taking the time to get to know crew members who he had barely had a chance to talk with. One of the few things worrying Ash, for very different reasons, was the absence of two people from the party: Alexis and Anton.

Anton not attending meant he was either not feeling up to attending, or he was planning something. Either way was cause for concern.

Alexis not attending meant time in a casual setting lost. It also may have meant that Alexis didn't want to spend time with anyone on the crew. With Ash. Yes, they'd had many special moments, but Ash could easily chalk them up to two people becoming close under pressure. It probably wasn't real.

But that sucked. They felt like a team.

Ash was still mulling over what Alexis' absence meant when she finally walked in. The festivities were in full swing. Groups of conversation, peppered with food and drinks, were scattered around the Bridge. Everyone was smiling. The din of conversation could clearly be heard over the music mix which Sierra had put together.

"I have songs from every decade! Well, not much from the 30s and 40s. Slim pickings then – just a lot of wailing and sadness," she'd explained.

Ash made eye contact with Alexis as soon as she entered the Bridge. Her face seemed to unfreeze when he did so. Weaving through groups, Ash made his way to the door, stopping abruptly when he reached Alexis.

"Hey," he said, with a gentle smile.

"Hey back," she said. They both laughed a little in recognition. "I'm glad we can say that in a better place."

"Me too," Ash said, but even as the words left his mouth, he felt himself thinking back to the two days he'd spent in bed, lost in grief and sadness.

Alexis instantly picked up on Ash's changed mood. "Sorry, my fault. This is a day to celebrate. We're almost at the point where we can stop this thing. And then maybe go home."

Ash nodded pensively, trying to bring himself back to the present.

"Can you even imagine going home?" he asked. Home seemed like years before . . . in more ways than one.

Alexis shook her head. "Nope. I think about what I left behind. I'm not even sure I want to go home."

"Not much waiting for me there either," Ash said. "Well, that's not fair. My parents are wonderful, and my dog needs to be played with. And I guess there are some friends who'd miss me. But, by and large . . ." Ash's voice trailed off. He and Alexis walked over to two empty chairs.

"Yeah. I understand. Remember, you're talking to someone who killed a man." Ash opened his mouth to protest but Alexis stopped him. "I know, I know. It was an accident, but you know what I mean. That haunts you."

Ash's mind went back to Daniel.

"I do," he said. "Unfortunately, I do. All too well."

And they both fell silent, locked in shared grief until Alexis sighed deeply and threw her hands in the air.

"I also know that at some point, you move on. And you do not begin conversations with the most depressing opening in the world! Come on!" She reached over and rubbed Ash's leg, sending a jolt of electricity through his spine. He laughed and made eye contact with Alexis, and allowed his gaze to drift across the rest of her body.

Unlike Blondell, Alexis had dressed more casually. She had put on make-up, but still looked natural, with blue eyeliner and a pale-pink lipstick serving as the only noticeable additions to her usual look. Her sweater was casual and blue; it looked comfortable, and Ash found himself with a nearly irrepressible urge to wrap an arm around her waist and hold her tight. He found his thoughts drifting elsewhere, to happier, more wanton places, followed by a lurching feeling in the pit of his stomach when he and Alexis made eye contact again. An awkward smile followed.

"Difficult in these circumstances, don't you think?" Ash asked, shaking his head, trying to bring his awareness back to the conversation.

Alexis shrugged in response. "Sure," she said. "But didn't you tell me that, when you were talking to Robin, you told him that he couldn't just sit there?"

"Of course."

"The same applies to tragedy. Even to death." Alexis paused, gathering her thoughts, before continuing. "I don't think that you ever move on from something that big. Doesn't your depression work the same way?"

"Yes," Ash confessed. "When I've been okay, I've never really been okay. It's always there, floating around. The threat of an anxiety attack, of slipping into a funk. It never completely goes away."

"Then, how do you function? I think I know the answer. But you need to say it."

Ash sighed, recalling the words which his therapist had taught him, even though he hadn't believed them before. "That recovery isn't an end state. It's a progression. And that sometimes you succeed and sometimes you fail, but you always move back the same way."

Alexis nodded and discretely slipped a hand into Ash's pocket. "Exactly," she said, her eyes sparkling.

Were they really talking about depression right now? About anxiety? About death? And flirting at the same time? Ash couldn't believe it, but they were; there was a flash of recognition on Alexis' face . . . she knew what she was doing. Ash's heartbeat began to accelerate. Cautiously, slowly, and insecure despite the fact that all of the signs were there, Ash surreptitiously slid a hand across Alexis' back, fingers brushing across soft fabric and warm, smooth skin.

Alexis' lips, which Ash found himself paying very close attention to, curled upward in a smile.

"Not here," she whispered, slowly extending her front teeth over her bottom lip. "Later."

Ash knew that tone of voice . . . he was depressed, sometimes, but he wasn't crazy. "Later" wasn't an absent phrase. It was a promise.

Gradually, regretfully, Ash withdrew his hand, returning the smile.

"Okay," he said.

Alexis moved her hand back, cleared her throat and brushed off her jeans, using sharp, bird-like movements. Even so, she looked over her shoulder as she walked away, and did something unforgettable: she winked. Dumbfounded, Ash put a fist to his chin (more of an effort to stop his jaw from unhinging than anything else) and watched Alexis leave, noting the ever-so-subtle sway to her hips as she walked away.

Ash sat for a solid minute, smiling to himself, until Echo slid in next to him.

"Hey, Chief!" she cried, her voice too loud for the

surroundings.

Ash, who had hated college parties, knew that voice. Despite it, he smiled. "Have you been drinking, Doc?" he asked.

A boozy smile crossed Echo's lips, and she gestured with an empty cup toward an unoccupied corner of the ship. "Meh, only a little." From the slur in her voice, it was more than a little. "One of them, over there, they gave it to me."

Ash followed Echo's fingers to Larissa and Mac.

"You know, this is my own fault," he said. "I did tell everyone to unwind a bit." Concern flashed through Ash's mind. After all, he had insisted on having the party on the Bridge because it allowed everyone to stay near their equipment in the event they were attacked. Still . . . Echo was more the ship's shrink than anything else. Her role in combat wasn't vital. Ash patted Echo on the back.

"You're done with the booze, right?"

Echo's features froze, and she became as serious as she was capable. "Yeah, definitely. One is plenty for me."

"One? You've only had one?"

"It's my first ever, and it's so much fun!" Echo grasped Ash's wrists in both of her hands, too tight, and giggled. "I get so much more about your time now!" Without warning Echo leapt up, as if her seat had been electrified. "Jameson! Hey! Jameson! C'mere!" And off staggered Echo, leaving a laughing Ash in her wake.

The party went on. Ash had never relaxed easily, but the events of the past week had forced him to a point where relaxation or collapse were his only two options. Ash, trying to live, chose the former, and found himself carefree – if only for those precious moments. The crew of the *Redemption* – well, at least most of them – felt more like home than any home he had experienced during college.

A tap on the shoulder indicated the latest person who wanted Ash's attention, and for the first time during the night, Ash found himself speaking to Valliant. Ash had never seen Valliant out of uniform. Like Blondell, he was surprisingly muscular, a fact accentuated by a tight black T-shirt and black jeans.

225

"She alright?" the other captain asked, gesturing to Echo.

"Oh, yeah, she'll be fine," Ash said, watching Echo hold onto a startled Robin like she was about to fall over. "And besides, what trouble can she get into in the middle of space?"

Both men laughed.

"You know, Ash, I know how difficult this has been for you. It was for me too," Valliant began. "Being the captain is a thankless job. If things go right, you give the credit elsewhere. If they go wrong, it's only you. It can be lonely at the top."

Lifting his cup, Ash clinked glasses with Valliant and took a deep gulp of water.

"Ain't that the truth," he said. "Still, this could have gone a lot worse. All things considered, we're doing okay. And I owe a lot of that to you."

Valliant nodded. "I'm happy to show you what I've learned." He gestured toward the bulk of the party. "By the way, you need to say something."

A cold flash raced through Ash.

"What? Why?" He hated public speaking.

Valliant stepped a little closer and lowered his voice. "I know this is casual and social, but the crew still needs to hear from its captain," he said. "You are always the leader. Take the chance to inspire. You've still got to get to the moon, and you'll need them all now more than ever."

"Right. Well. Crap." Ash paused and nervously licked his lips. "What the hell do I say?" Valliant poked Ash in the chest and smiled knowingly. "That's not helpful," Ash said.

"It will be," Valliant said. He took two fingers to his mouth and blew an ear-piercing whistle, instantly seizing the attention of the crew.

Sierra sped over to her computer and shut the music off, leaving the Bridge in silence.

"Thank you!" Valliant said. "Now, for a few words from our captain. Captain Maddox?" Ash sighed. All eyes were on him.

"Thanks, Captain," he said, awkwardly gesturing behind

him to Valliant. Silence followed. "Uh . . . how's everyone doing?" No response. Not even a cough. "Right." Ash closed his eyes and tried to visualize what a poised, mature, experienced captain would say. What Valliant would say. Channeling a confidence Ash didn't think was there, he began to speak again.

"I'm still not sure how we got here. And I know that each and every one of us has so many questions . . . like what's going to happen next, and whether or not what we are doing is even going to work. And if we are ever going to get home again." Ash paused, nervously licking his lips and staring at the crew – his crew. To his pleasant surprise, they were all looking right back at him, their attention rapt. Ash spoke again, his voice a touch stronger.

"I do know this much. For the past week or so, we've done more than anyone ever could have imagined. A group of sixteen to twenty-year-olds—" Ash gestured to Valliant, Larissa and Mac. "With a few exceptions, of course – should never have been expected to do this much. How we have, and why we were chosen, we may never know."

A few crew members began to nod. Blondell broke into a wide smile, and Jameson uncrossed his arms, his face softening. Larissa, in particular, looked animated by Ash's remarks, and she made her way to where Ash and Valliant stood.

"If I've discovered anything about all of us during our time together, it's that every one of us have secrets. Every one of us has pain, has shame. Many of us have seen that pain multiplied by this journey." Ash sought out Alexis and found her, staring intently at him. "Many of us have also begun to fight our way out of the darkness." Alexis smiled so brightly that Ash felt it.

Raising his glass in the air, Ash said, "So, two toasts. First and foremost . . . to Daniel. May we be deserving of his sacrifice." The crew murmured their agreement and drank. "And second, to us. May we find redemption . . . for all of us, and for Earth." It sounded corny coming out of Ash's mouth, but it was the best he could do.

Regardless of the words, the crew seemed to get his

intent, and appreciative cheers and applause followed.

Ash, surveying the scene, decided had he'd enough and found the one person he was looking for, hiding in the back of the Bridge. Alexis stood alone, hands in her pockets, still smiling. Ignoring the compliments, back-slaps and attempts by both Miranda and Larissa to stop him, Ash weaved his way through the crowd.

"Nicely done, Captain," Alexis said as Ash drew close. "You looked like you felt pretty good doing that."

"I didn't," Ash said. "Not even slightly. I just tried to fake it."

"You know that's what makes a leader, right? Saying the words everyone needs to hear, even when he doesn't believe them?"

"No," Ash said. "But I'm learning."

Silence fell, until Alexis asked, "Go for a walk?"

"God, yes," Ash said.

Others, taking Ash's speech as a sign that things were winding down, began to make their way off the Bridge, leaving Larissa, who had volunteered to take charge for the night. Ash and Alexis joined the crowd and followed. The hallway lights, dimmed for nighttime, made for the perfect camouflage, and Alexis again slipped her hand back into Ash's pocket. Ash responded by snaking his finger into one of Alexis' belt loops, pulling her tight against him. Alexis giggled her assent.

They walked mindlessly, eventually losing the crowd, and found themselves aimlessly wandering the ship, comfortable in their silence. Ash found his heart galloping with equal parts butterflies and anticipation. Unhooking his fingers from Alexis' jeans, he wrapped an arm around her waist. Alexis reciprocated and moved a hand into Ash's left, rear jeans' pocket.

"Oh," Alexis murmured, giving Ash's butt a playful squeeze. Ash pretended to jump.

"That's ... yup, that's all right," he said awkwardly, savoring the feeling and fumbling his hand down, mirroring Alexis'.

"I've never been the person to wait for the guy," Alexis

said, looking at Ash with hooded eyes.

Ash became aware of his surroundings as he and Alexis slowed to a stop. The dim light, the cool air, the echoing sound of his footsteps and his own heartbeat. Sensations became more powerful: the skin on skin of his hands sliding under Alexis' shirt, caressing her waist, drawing her closer. They were mere inches from each other, pelvises touching, hands roaming.

"Here?" she gasped, mouth open.

As she said it, Ash whipped his head around, trying to identify where on the ship he was. Recognizing a nearby room, he stepped backward and took Alexis with him.

"Here," he said, hands fumbling behind him to touch the door. With a familiar hydraulic *woosh*, the door opened, and Ash and Alexis stumbled backward. Ash tried desperately to control his face and body, desperate to feel his lips on hers. They fell, Alexis on top of Ash, legs hanging off of the conference room table. Desperately, greedily, Ash took both of his hands and wrapped them in Alexis' hair, enfolding his legs around her waist, pressing her onto him. Alexis, teasing, smiling, drew up, and Ash followed intently, eyes burning with desire, craving skin on skin, lips on lips.

And that was when they heard a frantic fumbling to the side of them.

Like a glass shattering, the moment broke as Ash and Alexis spun to see the source of the sound. In the virtually non-existent light of the conference room, Ash couldn't see who, but the jangle of belts and the panicked, hushed whispers made Ash immediately realize that he and Alexis weren't the only ones who had the idea of using the conference room for an evening rendezvous.

A pair of feet made contact with the floor, and a mad dash of skittering later, harsh lighting filled the chamber. Ash lifted his hands to shield his eyes, blinked, and identified the source of the noise: Jameson and Robin, both shirtless. Jameson was standing at the light panel, looking horrified, but still better than Robin, who, unlike Jameson, hadn't managed to get his pants on.

"Uh . . . hi Captain!" Robin said, waving spastically from

the other end of the table. "We were . . . uh . . . nope, we were making out. Definitely making out." Robin's chest was heaving and his hair was mused. He looked back at Jameson, who seemed to have recovered from his own shock to realize that he was staring at the captain and pilot of their ship, one on top of the other. Ash and Alexis still hadn't moved and were both staring, mouths agape.

"Okay," Alexis said.

"Yep, didn't see that coming," Ash said, arms still wrapped around Alexis.

"Nope. Not even a little," Alexis replied.

With that, Jameson walked forward and joined Robin. It was the first time that Ash had ever seen Jameson's hair messed up, and even in the circumstances, the thought brought a smile to his face.

Solemnly, Jameson said, "This never happened."

Ash wasn't waiting another moment and started to speak, only to be interrupted by Alexis.

"Great!" She leapt off of Ash, grabbed his hand and pulled him with her. "We're out of here. You two have fun!" With that, she marched out of the room.

Ash barely had time to smile and wave as he allowed himself to be led out. A metallic clicking sound followed their exit; evidently Jameson had been smart enough to lock the room this time.

Ash and Alexis looked at each other, composure cracking, and both burst into hysterical laughter.

"Did you know?" Alexis asked, a hand on Ash's shoulder for support.

"No idea," Ash said. "Good for them!"

Eventually, the laughter died down. As it did, Alexis slipped her hand into Ash's. "Come on," she said. Off they went, ambling at a comfortable, relaxed place. Ash knew where they were going next.

They arrived at Alexis' cabin and Alexis touched the door open, using the hand that was still holding Ash's. In they walked, door shutting gently behind them. Ash took a moment to take in the surroundings. Alexis' room looked like a mash-up of multiple people. A football sat on a shelf next to a Spice Girls poster. Nail polish next to a baseball glove precariously balanced on a Louisville Slugger baseball bat. A Super Nintendo system next to a Barbie collection. Pink on black everywhere.

Alexis stepped closer to Ash, touching his chest before returning her hands to his waist. "I've wanted this for a while now," she said. "I'm glad you did too."

They were nose to nose now. Ash brought a hand up to Alexis' face and tenderly stroked her cheek. Alexis leaned into the caress.

"I did," he whispered. "I'm . . . happy. Happier than I've been in a long time."

Alexis pulled back and moved her arms up to around the back of Ash's neck. "You do know you deserve this, don't you?" she asked. Ash kept stroking her face and gently shook his head.

"No," he said, truthfully. "I can't believe that much. But I'm willing to trust you on that one." Alexis flashed a megawatt smile again.

"That's when I knew you were ready."

"Huh?" Ash said, pulling his hands back, genuinely confused.

"Before. On the Bridge. When you said that recovery is a progression. After the accident . . . I couldn't live until I realized that what I did to Kevin Thompson would always be with me. Like your depression. The only way you move on is by acknowledging that, but making a pledge to live." She paused and looked deeply at Ash.

Ash looked into Alexis' own light-blue eyes and found himself falling.

"I had to hear you say it." Slowly, Alexis drew him in again.

"What else do you want me to say?" Ash whispered. Their lips were on top of each other, grazing . . .

"Nothing." Finally, Ash pressed in, drawing his mouth down on Alexis', kissing her hungrily, with abandon. Alexis returned the favor, their tongues connecting, breaths coming in jagged gasps as they fell toward Alexis' bed.

REDEMPTION

***

Afterward, for the first time since he had arrived on the *Redemption,* Ash slept through the night.

CHAPTER THIRTY

Ash woke up feeling a warmth and a tickle on the right side of his body. The warmth was from Alexis, her naked body pressed against his own. The tickle was from Alexis' long brown hair, which was draped over Ash's face. He sneezed, and Alexis half sat up with a start. She looked at Ash and was confused before a dreamy smile crossed her lips. She laid back down, nestling in the crook between Ash's arm and chest, taking care to comb her hair out of Ash's face.

"Hey," she whispered, still content in the afterglow.

"Hey back," Ash said, feeling the same. Reaching over, Ash brushed hair out of Alexis' eyes, then kissed her on the forehead. "Thank you."

"For what?" Alexis asked, peering up.

"Besides the obvious?" That earned Ash a playful smack on the shoulder, and he laughed before lowering his voice again. "Thank you for last night. Besides the obvious."

Alexis shrugged. "What can I say . . . I love a man with authority." She giggled. "Okay, that's not true. What I do love is how good you make me feel. And how good you've made me feel since we first got here."

Ash looked at Alexis with genuine surprise. "How good I make you feel? Alexis, I didn't believe that you cared about me nearly as much as I cared about you. A piece of me still doesn't."

"You know that's nuts, right?" asked Alexis incredulously.

"I guess," Ash said, not attempting to hide the disbelief

in his voice. "Seriously, I don't understand." Alexis paused and pursed her lips before speaking again.

"Well, I guess it's a few things. Many things. Okay, more than I can count." Her voice dipped softly. "More than anything else, I think I love that you do the right thing. Instinctively. Always. And that for everything bouncing around inside your own head, you try to push on. There is nothing sexier than a man who doesn't give up."

Ash caught Alexis' hand in his and held it before looking into Alexis' eyes. He knew he was a sucker as soon as he saw them, and Ash found himself drifting toward Alexis' face, kissing her deeply. Ash felt his arms, practically of their own volition, wrapping themselves around her waist, pulling her in tighter . . . taking him higher . . .

Abruptly, and with regret openly visible on her face, Alexis broke off the kiss. "Whoa there, cowboy," she said, leaving Ash wanting. "Come on. Let's get a move on. We should really get to the Bridge."

Ash leaned across the bed, playfully grabbing for Alexis as she stood up. "Save some for later," she whispered seductively.

"Later?" he said. "You know I'm twenty, right? Later can be five minutes after round one."

Alexis laughed. "Well, good for you, but I need a break." She turned around, sideways, partially hiding her naked flesh from Ash. "Besides, what fun is this if I can't give you anything to look forward to?"

Ash sighed heavily and heaved himself out of bed, eyes scanning the floor for his scattered clothing.

"I guess," he said mournfully, plucking his underwear from a lampshade. "How did this wind up here?"

"Don't question it. Just be grateful," Alexis said, shimmying a pair of jeans over her legs.

Ash turned his socks the right way and jammed his feet into them. As much as it pained him, he began to allow the events of the previous night to recede into a happy memory and turned his attention back to the ship's business. According to their briefing, the next mission was relatively simple: hit the moon's surface and grab a few rocks from the

Sea of Tranquility, not far from where men had first landed over a century before. According to Miranda, this mission should be less complicated than their last one. Moon rocks were a dime a dozen, and only a few people were needed to go to the moon. It was, thankfully, a simple mission plan.

"We're two days away from the moon," he said. "I don't think we really need to rush into the mission, so we should have plenty of time to sim it up."

"Agreed," Alexis said, flipping a T-shirt with a picture of cartoon girl that Ash didn't recognize; she had tan skin, blond hair and a blue and pink sweater. As Alexis spoke, the ship began to wake up with the rest of the crew, with metallic pings filling the hallway. "Have you talked to Blondell or Sierra about the sim package?"

"Not yet," Ash said, as the pings outside began to intensify. "I'm honestly not even sure how much of a crew we're gonna need. It seems like more your responsibility than anything else, since we're gonna need a shuttle." Ash's voice trailed off as he watched Alexis' facial expression freeze and her head tilt, as if she was trying to comprehend something she didn't understand. An instant later, Ash realized what it was.

The noises outside weren't normal.

And then Ash heard the screaming.

"Dammit!" he bolted for the door, grabbing the bat that was propped against the dresser. Ash punched the release on the door. It sprang open just in time for Ash to see a shower of sparks explode across the hallway. Three red bolts of energy followed, closer to the doorway, attracted to the noise. Spinning on his heel, Ash turned around and grabbed Alexis, who was starting to run out of the room. A laser bolt slammed into the doorframe, leaving flames and sparks in its wake.

"Is someone on the ship?" Alexis blared, watching in horror as the flames in the doorway receded.

"All hands on deck!" ordered the deep voice of Valliant over the ships communication system. "We're under attack!"

Ash started inching toward the door again, reflexively

putting an arm around Alexis while he held the softball bat in the other hand. Alexis, however, had other ideas. She ducked out from Ash's arms, moved to her dresser drawer and whipped out an eight-inch hunting knife, removing the blade from its protective cover. Ash raised his eyebrows at the determination on her face. He cautiously peered out the door.

A look to the left revealed no one. A look to the right revealed one of the attackers, clad in a white spacesuit, white coverall and reflective helmet. He – or she – was inching their way toward the Bridge, firing a scattershot of laser blasts as they moved. There was no cover between them, but Ash needed to stop the attacker from gaining those last few yards to the Bridge. A good thirty feet separated the two.

Ash wasn't sure he could close that kind of distance in time. He ducked back into the room and grabbed the closest thing he could get his hands on, a picture frame. With a heave, he chucked the frame in the opposite direction from the attacker, shattering its glass surface on an overhead pipe with a loud crash. Ash ducked back into the room, but the footsteps he heard indicated that his trick had worked: the attacker rushed toward the sound of the noise, firing shots with every step.

Just as they passed Alexis' door, Ash stuck out the metallic bat, aiming for about thigh level. The plan worked and the attacker fell, crashing into the ground with a hollow *thunk,* causing a spider web of cracks to appear in the helmet. Ash raised the bat into the air and with a primal scream prepared to bring it down on the invaders skull . . .

And just before Ash could swing the bat, his attacker winked out of existence, leaving Ash standing, completely confused, with the bat poised over his head. Ash froze, his legs congealing, not believing his eyes. Alexis grabbed a fistful of his shirt and yanked him back into the cabin.

"What the hell do we do?" she said, curly hair flying in every direction.

Ash ran to a door panel and pounded the controls.

"Ash to Bridge. Valliant, the hell is going on?"

"Ash, this is Radar. Those sons of bitches are on the ship!"

"Radar, tell me what's happening!" demanded Ash. "How many are there?"

"Five. One was heading for the Bridge and we don't have time to get to the armory—"

"Alexis and I took care of him. Where are the other four?"

"Cutting through the cafeteria!"

Ash spun around and grabbed Alexis by the hand.

"Come on!" he said. Both bolted at full speed toward the invaders.

"Why the hell are they in the cafeteria?" asked Alexis as they rounded the corner.

Ash plotted the layout of the ship in his mind. The cafeteria was large, one of the biggest rooms on the ship. It was an open space with two doors on each side, surrounded by two narrow hallways. One of those hallways ran north-south, lined by cabins, but the other one . . .

"The Junction Room!" Ash said. "The one heading to the Bridge was a distraction, and they want to avoid the hallways if they can. If they can get to the Junction Room . . ."

Ash didn't need to finish his sentence. Alexis knew exactly what would happen if their attackers reached the room which contained the most sensitive machinery on the ship. Abruptly, Ash skidded to a stop. He and Alexis were at the weapons cache. He ripped the top of the metallic box open and grabbed two weapons, handing one to Alexis and clicking the safety off of his own gun in the process. Ash had never actually fired this model but realized that it was a smaller version of the same gun they had taken with them to Kepler.

Rounding the last corner, Ash and Alexis skidded to a stop in front the door to the cafeteria. Another door to the same room was twenty feet down the hallway. Motioning for Alexis to stand still, Ash ran to the further door, trying his best to block out the metallic pings of the gun and shrieks that followed every blast. There were multiple screams from inside of the cafeteria. How many people were trapped in there? Ash couldn't tell.

There was no time to call for reinforcements. No time for help, and no time for better ideas. More than anything else, Ash realized, as he signaled Alexis with three fingers, was this: he couldn't protect Alexis. They could both die, right then, right there. And the idea of losing Alexis, just when he'd really found her, filled him with a terror so exquisite it was incalculable.

"Three, two, one . . ." Ash dropped his fingers and pounded the door, sending it open in a blur. He burst into the cafeteria, followed by Alexis.

Four white human-like forms advanced toward the back end of the cafeteria. Holding his weapon with both hands, Ash fired at the attackers as rapidly as he could. One was caught squarely in the back and went down. Another series of shots missed just enough to get the attention of the second attacker, who spun around and fired, forcing Ash to dive wildly behind an upturned table. Pinned behind the furniture and gasping for breath, Ash was too scared to peek up and try to get a bead on his target. He could, however, see the volleys of plasma coming from Alexis' side of the room. She had clearly reached her position and was holding her own.

Collecting himself, Ash rose just a hair above his cover, resulting in three rapid-fire bolts catching the surface of the table. Ash was pinned and unable to move without risking exposure. Alexis, as best as he could tell, was firing spasmodically, and it seemed like two different positions were firing back at her. Peeking around the table, Ash saw one of the forms advancing, trying to flank Alexis who was pinned behind a narrow column.

With no choice, Ash made a run for it. He barely missed being shot as a laser bolt whistled past his ear, singeing his hair. Ash ran until his feet skidded out from under him, bringing him to the ground. Firing awkwardly as he slipped, Ash turned his head just in time to see the shots connecting. A second body went down as Ash skidded into a table, his pants slick. Without missing a beat, Ash grabbed the table and flipped it, forming a barrier between himself and the remaining two attackers.

"Hello again!" he yelled at Alexis, firing his gun blindly over the table.

"Shut up and fire!" Alexis retorted, taking her time to aim at the closer of their two enemies.

Ash did the same, and that was when he saw a tall, black girl, stealthily moving from table to column. *Blondell.* Ash hid behind his cover and pounded on the table to get Alexis' attention, pointing at Blondell once he succeeded in doing so. Alexis nodded, understanding. Glancing back over the table, Ash saw Blondell pointing at the attacker closest to her. Ash nodded back and trained all his fire on Blondell's target. Alexis did the same.

Hurdling over the table and leading with her shoulder, Blondell speared the assailant, sending his torso forward and his weapon arcing through the air. At the same time, Ash and Alexis broke cover and aimed all of their fire at the fourth assailant, who stood momentarily frozen at the sight of his cohort being attacked from behind. That hesitation was all that Ash and Alexis needed. Bolts from each of their guns sent him crashing backward, over an upended table. In a flash, both attackers evaporated like a puff of smoke, and the cafeteria was empty again.

Silence fell.

Ash looked at Alexis, then Blondell, who lay on the ground, stunned at her victim's sudden disappearance.

Glancing up at Ash, she mumbled, "Huh?"

Others burst into the cafeteria from both doors: Sia, Radar and Tidus all with weapons drawn.

"It's all right," Ash said. "I think we got them all." He flipped his safety back on and jammed the gun into the waistband of his jeans.

"That's great. Look anyway," said Tidus, gesturing back toward the corner from which Ash had entered the room. "Check over by those tables."

Twitching with adrenaline, Ash nodded.

"Okay," he said, turning around after redrawing his weapon. He broke into a jog and ran toward the door. On the way, he passed Mercury, lying prone on the ground, legs akimbo, a puddle of bright crimson red forming around the

239

spot where her arm had once been connected to her shoulder. Ash froze in abject horror, staring at the warm, advancing puddle of blood, lying perfectly unspoiled on the floor, save for the marks left by Ash's shoes from when he had run through it. Mercury's eyes were panicked, bouncing around the room but always returning to the jagged ribbons of muscles, bones and tendons which tangled uselessly from the stump of her left arm.

"Help!" Ash yelled, his voice chillingly high. He stood, utterly horrified, staring at Mercury's pale face and shallow breathing. Thankfully, his cry had been enough to get the attention of the crew piling into the cafeteria and the scene of the carnage. Echo reached Mercury first. She was the calmest of the entire crew, ripping off her belt and using it as a makeshift tourniquet.

"Mercury? Honey? Stay with me!" pled Echo, lying Mercury flat and raising her arm into the air. "We can fix this! Pike! Wet bandage! Now!"

Pike, dumbfounded, raced off toward the kitchen, just as Valliant came on the ships comms system.

"Ash, get in here, now! This is urgent!" His voice was spiked with excitement more than terror, and Ash didn't sense any immediate danger in his voice. Hearing a commotion behind him, Ash spun around and saw fresh horror: Exodus, immobile, with a small, neat, smoking hole on the left side of her chest. Sia, Alexis and Blondell carried her. Sprinting, Ash joined them, clearing a space on the floor for her body.

"Is she all right?" he asked, voice trembling. Exodus was as still as death as Alexis pressed an ear to her mouth.

"She's not breathing," said Alexis gravely. With ruthless efficiency, Alexis whipped out her knife and sliced off a piece of Exodus' shirt, jamming it in place over the bleeding wound. She interlaced her hands and began pumping on Exodus' chest, counting off quietly.

Valliant's voice came over the comms system again. "Ash, I understand the concern, but your crew has this, and we have no time. Get down to the Bridge. Now."

"Go!" Alexis screamed, pumping desperately on Exodus'

chest. "I got this!" Alexis pinched Exodus' nose and leaned into breathe into her mouth.

Ash leapt up and ran toward the Bridge, doing his best to avoid the various debris strewn around the room and trying desperately to put the bloodshed of the cafeteria out of his mind.

Reaching the Bridge, Ash saw Valliant eagerly leaning over Radar's chair. Radar was animatedly pressing inputs into his blocky keyboard.

"What?" Ash demanded.

Valliant turned around, his face painted with his normal, stoic reaction, which immediately faded when he made eye contact with Ash.

"Ash, my God, what happened to your head?" Valliant gasped, pointing. Ash brought his hand up to the left side of his hair and ran his fingers across it, discovering a groove in his hair where none had been. His hands came back shaking and slightly pink with blood.

"Jesus Christ," he mumbled. As if he hadn't seen enough horror.

Valliant snapped back to his senses. "You're all right, and that's what counts," he said, gesturing down to Radar. "We think we found our friends. And we think we found a way to track them."

Ash looked wildly at Radar. *Was this true?*

Radar gestured enthusiastically to his screen. "This – our radar – works because a pulse is transmitted to an object. The length of time it takes for the pulse to get back to us tells their position." Radar pointed out the window. "So, our aliens are mostly invisible, save for that little shimmer that gives us the vaguest idea of where they are. I can get them for a split second or two – it's happened before – but I think that's only when they go one direction."

"So?" Ash repeated. He was edgy, twitchy, hands sweating, heart accelerating, and he was getting an explanation about how radar worked? They had dragged him away from two dying crew members for this?

"Ash, with two ships, we can track it together," Valliant said, and that captured Ash's attention.

"How?"

"It's not exact, but we can triangulate their position, using both ships as a distance marker and computing the approximate location of the attackers. Do you realize what that means?"

Ash didn't need to think twice.

"Holy crap. We can follow them."

"Exactly!" cried Valliant. "Between the two of us, we can follow these bastards and attack them. And they can't escape this time!"

Ash's mind flashed back to his previous run-ins with the aliens. On each instance, the enemy had run the instant that they had successfully returned fire.

Ash heard wild scurrying behind him, as other crew members ran around the Bridge. They adjusted weapons and checked security feeds, a reminder of what was at stake. Ash had lost one crew member already to these terrorists, and was on the verge of losing another two. But, astonishingly, there were more important matters which now commanded his attention.

As if reading Ash's mind, Valliant said, "Ash, I need you to momentarily put the crew out of your mind. Put everything out of your mind but this. These are the ones who have bombarded the planet – our planet – with a disease that is well on its way to ending humanity. This is a chance to stop them."

Ash swallowed hard.

"We've lost every time we faced these guys," he said. "It was only through blind luck that we were even able to fight them off previously." Terror washed over him, as it had every time he had faced the aliens in combat.

"True," Valliant said. A corner of his mouth turned upward in a twisted smile, one that betrayed a desire for vengeance. "But now there are two of us."

And with that, Ash understood. "So what's the plan? Do we follow them?"

Valliant shook his head vigorously. "Not yet. We wait until they get where they are going and go after them when they get there. We can work out a plan as we travel, and I have an idea . . . but I need to get back to my ship."

"You do?" The idea of Valliant leaving filled Ash with icy terror.

Valliant nodded.

"I'm afraid so, Ash. This can only work if I'm on the *Remedy*. But don't worry. We can pull this off."

Seeing the terror on Ash's face, Valliant guided him to the back of the Bridge, away from the rest of the crew, who were now staring.

Placing a hand on Ash's shoulders, Valliant said, "Ash, you must have more faith in yourself. You have done an incredible job and earned the trust of much of your crew. You've done more than anyone could have asked of you. If you can do a little bit more, we may abrogate the need for you to go to the moon and get the last piece of the Spades vaccine. We may be able to stop this entirely."

Ash tilted his head down, at his feet, feeling for all the world like a small, scared child. "You do realize that this is terrifying, right?"

Valliant stared at Ash with sympathetic eyes. "More than you know. When this is over, you and I will get a beer, and I'll tell you about the past three months of my life, and about all the crew I lost. We've survived on determination and pure will. I will not allow you to suffer from the same doubt that I have." Valliant cleared his throat, trying to banish the emotion from his voice, and stood up straight. "You'll do well. And I'll see you soon. Follow me to the dock."

CHAPTER THIRTY-ONE

Ash and Valliant said goodbye one more time as Valliant boarded his small shuttle. MacGregor, walking slowly, joined Valliant, but Larissa stayed behind.

"Remember, she has military experience, so if you need that level of expertise, you'll have it," Valliant explained. The shuttle's door closed, and the craft flew into the void of space, taking with it the closest thing Ash had to a mentor.

With Radar communicating with his counterpart on the *Remedy*, there was nothing that Ash could do on the Bridge. His next stop would be a painful one. He paused to gather his thoughts outside the cafeteria before entering. Leaning on the door which he had kicked open barely an hour earlier, stalling the unavoidable, Ash came to a solemn realization. Whatever lay behind that door was already there. Standing outside wouldn't change the outcome. It would only delay the inevitable. He opened the door.

The cafeteria was mostly empty. A few feet in front of him lay the mass of coagulated blood, gleaming raw, like a scar on the tile floor. On the other side of the room lay a lumpy mass, covered by a white sheet. And perfectly symmetrical to that, forming the third point of a triangle of pain, sat Alexis, weeping gently into her hands. She looked up, blinking, when Ash entered the room, and without a moment of hesitation, whimpering, stood. Arms extended, Ash stood still, and Alexis walked into his embrace, burying her head in his chest. Muffled by Ash's shirt, Alexis spoke.

"Exodus died," she said. "The CPR didn't help."

The second part of the sentence struck Ash as extraneous. Of course the CPR didn't help . . . another crew member was dead. Another Daniel gone. More blood on his hands.

"I couldn't do it." Words barely audible, Alexis kept talking. "Mercury lived. For now. She had a lot of blood loss though." And then the hysterical sobs began, punctuated by rage-filled curses. "I couldn't save Exodus, god dammit!"

Alexis cried and cried, and Ash, with no idea of what else to do, held tight.

Minutes later (how many, Ash didn't know), Alexis pulled away, wiping her eyes. "So what's the plan, Captain?" she asked, voice strained. "Where we going next?"

Ash simply stared. "Does it matter?" he asked weakly.

Exodus' death felt like a heavy punch to the gut. Two crew members were dead. A third maimed, and maybe dying. The only person on the ship who had any idea of what he was doing was gone. The fate of the world was, quite literally, in Ash's hands, hands that felt impossibly small. And more blood would probably flow.

"It has to," Alexis said, looking off to the side, spitting out the words and wiping her noise with her sleeve. "It has too, Ash, because we're now down two, their deaths will not be for nothing. We're here for a reason, goddammit, so let's finish this."

"We're already there, Lex," Ash said, vision swimming in and out of focus. It was all starting to catch up with him. The day had started with him waking up, warm, naked and comfortable, in the arms of someone he cared about. It had transitioned to a gun battle that ended with unexplained disappearances, blood and gore, and led to the only adult he trusted leaving. *How much am I supposed to be able to take? How am I supposed to do this?* "We're already there. Let's go to the Bridge. I'll explain the plan."

Gently, Ash extended an arm toward Alexis, swallowing and emitting a low groan in the process. He resisted the urge to close his eyes and instead briefly steered his focus inward, if only to stuff his own doubts and fears into a place where they could remain undisturbed. After a moment's hesitation, Alexis' shoulders slumped. She settled into Ash's extended arms, whimpering softly.

Ash explained the new plan as they walked to the Bridge, retracing their steps from earlier in the morning. The atmosphere on the Bridge was deadened, muted, as if a thick woolen blanket had been strewn across the room. Word had leaked out about Exodus' death. No one even looked twice at Alexis' tears as she sat in her seat and firmly grasped her controls. Quietly, Ash stepped behind Radar, who had stopped fiddling with his station and was checking the controls of his weapon, holster unobtrusively slung over his hip.

"Where are we?" Ash asked.

"They're on the move, Captain, and they're heading in the direction of Earth," Radar said, expertly flicking a few switches to bring up a new display. This made Ash pause, horrified.

"Are they about to attack?"

Radar shook his head. "It's too soon. The attack isn't supposed to occur for another three weeks. And besides, if they are, it's already over. We can't do anything about it."

That last sentence gave Ash a bizarre sense of peace. Radar was right, of course. The alien ship was too far ahead. Even at top speed, they couldn't catch up.

"Fair enough," Ash said. "Blondell, you got a course?"

"I do," Blondell said. Her hair was twisted into tangled heaps and smears of blood ran across her gray T-shirt. "I'm coordinating with the *Remedy*. They're going to bounce on a course forty-five degrees down on the z-axis, away from us. They'll jump in and pincer attack at the pre-determined time. I need Alexis to steer us into position and I'll fire."

Ash looked at Alexis, who was holding onto her controls, white-knuckled, her skin the color of paper.

"Alexis?" Ash said quietly.

Alexis hesitated as her hands tightened on the controls, gripping them tightly. After a set of heartbeats, she nodded and steered the ship through space, gently gliding the *Redemption* into position.

"On my mark," said Blondell.

Almost unconsciously, Ash took the time to scan the Bridge, noting the empty seats and missing spaces from when this journey had started. Anton wasn't in his seat, and in all the chaos, Ash hadn't had a chance to check on him. Sia's seat was empty as well. Pike stood near the weapons station, looking confused, unsure about whether or not he should sit in Anton's chair. Robin stood at what had been Daniel's position, his face flushed with shock and adrenaline. Exodus and Mercury's seats were completely empty.

Blondell completed her countdown. "Execute," she said, and the space in front of the ship transformed into a wild stream of colors as the *Redemption* began the next leg of its journey.

CHAPTER THIRTY-TWO

Hours later, Ash was at loose ends, trapped in yet another state of hurry up and wait. With nothing else to do, he roamed the ship, checking for signs of damage after the gun battle. He found plenty of scars and electric burns, but there was no major damage. Ash considered returning to the Bridge, but doing so only brought his mind back to those he had lost thus far. Daniel's larger-than-life smile. Exodus in her dress that somehow looked sexy and goofy at the same time. So Ash wandered from section to section, trying to elude the ghosts of the *Redemption*.

He stopped at Engineering, where he found Jameson and Robin working on engine repairs. Jameson was instructing Robin on what to fix next, guiding him by gently touching his shoulder. It struck Ash as remarkably sweet, and he smiled when he saw it.

Ash jammed his hands in his pockets. "How's it looking?" he asked, startling the room's occupants.

Robin turned around and, seeing Ash, bolted in the other direction without saying a word, disappearing like a feather caught in a violent storm. Ash started to say something, but Jameson cut him off.

"Let him go," Jameson said. "The more time that passes, the more embarrassed he gets. I don't think he fully understands how to deal with this part of himself yet."

"That I can completely understand," Ash said.

Jameson sighed. "Last night, before the attacks, Robin was telling me his story. He's from the U.S., middle America,

I think. I was familiar with it, but never had a chance to hear the horror stories. He said he's always known who he is, but so did everybody else. School was a non-stop festival of teasing and getting the snot kicked out of him." Jameson gestured over to two instrument-strewn seats. Oblivious to the tools, he sat down.

Ash brushed aside an odd-looking socket wrench and followed suit. "I can't imagine what that was like."

"It gets better. I can tell you that," Ash said. "When I came from, at least on my end of the planet. There was still a long way to go, and we weren't there yet. Basic rights are still denied to people like Robin. Like you."

Jameson shrugged, dismissing the information as if he had barely heard it.

"It was Martin Luther King who said, 'The arc of the moral universe is long, but it bends toward justice.' Easy for me to say, though. I'm at the end of the arc. I tell people I'm gay, and no one even blinks. Robin, it's different for him."

"He was treated as sub-human," Ash said bitterly. "I wasn't born until 1998, but I know. And if he came from an area that was, shall we say, less than tolerant . . . it must have been hell. But you must give him some comfort. To know that it will get better."

"To what end?" snapped Jameson, making Ash jerk his head back in surprise.

"What do you mean?"

"Ash, didn't you hear what I said during the presentation?" Jameson leaned closer, putting his elbows on his knees and boring his stare into Ash as he spoke. "The income inequity? The government and business working hand in hand to enrich themselves? Things are starting to look like they did in your time, just before the world fell off a cliff. Many of us at home were starting to worry. There were rebellions. . . ugly ones that had nothing to offer the world but hatred – groups that were marshalling to overthrow the U.G. Even if they didn't know what they wanted instead. They had nothing to offer the world but anger. And they were starting to gain traction." Jameson paused and waved a dismissive hand in the air. "The real resistance groups – the only ones that could make a difference – were stuck in the shadows, operating in brief moments and not earning enough support to overthrow a government that has held people's hands and stoked their fears for decades. Why are we even bothering?"

The words stunned Ash. "I'd never have expected that out of you. You are supposed to be all logic."

"Logic leads to the emotion. Logic comes from facts. And all of the objective evidence shows that the Earth is like a broken song, skipping around the same loop over and over again." Jameson brought a finger into the air and twirled an absent-minded circle. Then, the weight of his rant hitting him, he put his head in his hands, covering his face. "I don't want to see this. Not again." Jameson said nothing else.

Ash paused before putting a hand on Jameson's knee, squeezing tight.

"I don't know your world, so I don't know what's happening. I know you well enough to know that you are right. And I know that . . . that as long as you breathe, there is hope. Personally, or for the planet. The world must be filled with people like you who are capable of incredible things. Surely that, in and of itself, is worth fighting for."

Jameson nodded wordlessly, and the two sat silently for a long time.

Ash moved on a few minutes later, a slowness in his step betraying his feelings of inadequacy, stopping next at cabin number four: Anton's room. Taking a deep breath, Ash knocked on the door.

No answer.

Ash could have, he supposed, opened it automatically. That being said, barging in on the room of someone he had thrown out as captain seemed to be a bad way to rebuild trust. Ash stared at the door, feeling useless, before turning on his heel and moving on.

His feet carried him next to Miranda's science station next to the dock. She didn't look up as Ash entered the room and only acknowledged his presence with a very brief wave before her hand returned to the keyboard.

"What are you up to?" Ash asked. It was a full fifteen

seconds before Miranda responded by dramatically flinging her hands and inhaling deeply.

"Well, nothing productive, apparently," she said. "I have been trying to synthesize the right combination that will let these two elements, plus the moon rocks we're going to hopefully get soon, turn into the Spades vaccine. Hopefully they will be able to figure it out on Earth. But I can't get the formula right."

"What's wrong with the formula?" asked Ash. Miranda shook her head.

"Too many variables. I don't know the molecular composition of the rocks we're going to get. As best I can tell, the moon rocks act as a suspending chemical which maintains the chemical stability of the cure. Without it, we've only got two active ingredients."

Ash raised his eyebrows. "Come again?"

Miranda sighed impatiently. "Every vaccine has been comprised of pieces of the disease. It's a dead or weakened form, but that's how you get vaccines."

Ash's mind whirled as he considered the implications.

"Is it possible that this is why we've run into our friends so close to the asteroid belt and Kepler? They were gathering pieces for the attack on Earth?"

"Makes sense to me," Miranda said. "And it's preferable to the alternative possibility."

"That we're being stalked?" Ash said.

A bitter smile covered Miranda's face. "Yeah, that," she snarked.

A moment of silence passed between the two before the communications speaker in the room came to life.

"Ash? It's Echo," said a disembodied voice. Without the accompanying image that was usually projected of the speaker, the voice sounded tinny. Ash walked over to the system and tapped a button.

"Ash here. What's up?"

"We need you on the Bridge as soon as possible. There's a bit of an emergency," Echo said.

Ash nodded to no one in particular. "On my way," he said, disconnecting the transmission and looking at

251

Miranda. "At least I have something to do."

"What a problem," said Miranda, voice dripping with sarcasm. "Have fun. I'll keep trying to figure out how to integrate these things and give Earth as much of a head start as possible before Spades hits."

"Sounds like a plan," Ash called over his shoulder, breaking into a jog, barely noticing the suspended state of the asteroid they had grabbed on their first full day onboard the ship, a lifetime ago. As Ash ran, he found his mind wandering to the earlier conversation with Jameson. Was it worth it? Everything they were doing? Were they really going to be able to save mankind? Or were they just delaying the inevitable?

The truth, Ash knew, was beyond his grasp. He also knew that slowing down – that giving into the pessimism which seemed so pervasive among those from future time periods – was simply not an option. Perhaps the "current" state of the Earth wasn't reflective of anything that had to do with the environment, with society, with culture. Maybe it was just that everyone had become so hopeless they had forgotten that they had a duty to make things better for the future.

Walking through the threshold to the Bridge, Ash made eye contact with Alexis and noticed a fear in her face that he hadn't seen before.

"What's up?" Ash stopped a few steps into the room.

"Ash, no!" cried Alexis, trying to stand up, but unable to do so with her arms bound to her chair. The sight filled Ash with terror and he tried to run to her. However, a loud crash and crunching pain to the back of his head ended any thoughts of intervention. As Ash fell to the ground, his final vision before the blackness took him was of Alexis shrieking and Echo backing into a corner, one hand in the air, the other clasped to her mouth, while Sia pointed a weapon at her head.

Chapter Thirty-Three

As consciousness returned, Ash's first thought was a wistful one: *I've got to stop getting knocked unconscious on my own goddamn Bridge.*

Without opening his eyes, he took inventory of his senses and situation. His wrists were bound to the chair in which he sat. Without moving, Ash realized from the soft fabric that he was tied to his captain's chair. A creeping, throbbing pain occupied the back of his head, transforming into a starburst of fevered agony whenever he moved. Taking a chance, Ash blinked once, twice, and found that the movement did not cause him paralyzing pain. As his vision focused, his first sight was no surprise: Anton, gun in hand, pointed at Ash's head.

"Hello, Captain," Anton intoned.

Ignoring him, Ash gently shifted his head from left to right, trying to take stock of the situation. Holding weapons at various crew members throughout the room were Sia, Pike, Tidus and two of the last Back Brigade members, Ryan and Louis. Being held at gunpoint were Radar, Blondell, Alexis, Sierra and Echo. Echo was the only one standing, and Pike was pushing her to a chair with the butt of his gun.

Mental inventory complete, Ash looked back at Anton, blinking heavily. He fought the deep fog that threatened to drag him back into the realm of unconsciousness.

"A mutiny? Really?"

Anton's grin broke into a leer, exposing yellowed teeth that seemed to have gotten more rotten since the last time

Ash had seen him . . . when was the last time he had seen Anton, anyway?

A scuffle behind Anton briefly got the Bridge's attention. Echo was resisting being forced into one of the chairs in front of Alexis' station.

"Stop it, dammit!" cried Echo. She held onto the railing, while Pike attempted to pull her away. Watching the thin blond girl struggle, Ash knew what would happen next, and sure enough, moving with incredible speed, Pike whipped his arm and connected his gun with Echo's face.

Ash winced, watching globs of blood splatter from Echo's now-broken noise. Falling into the seat, Echo whimpered and tried to hold her hands across her face. That only lasted a moment, as Pike ripped her hands and pinned them to the arms of the chair, wrapping them cruelly with rope that Ash recognized from their Kepler mission.

Rage piercing through the pain in the back of his head, Ash focused on his nemesis and spoke again. "This is what you have been up to the past couple of days?"

"You really have to stop screwing crew members. You'll pay better attention," Anton said, gesturing to a bound Alexis.

Hearing the remark felt like being stabbed with an icicle. Ash wondered if that was, in fact, the case. Had his relationship with Alexis – the excitement, the physicality, the sense of hope – blinded him to the coup?

"It's been an exciting few days. I'm just grateful you were too busy to notice."

"Fantastic," Ash said. "Really, great job. If you would have put half the effort of organizing this into our mission, we would have already beaten Spades and be having tea with the future President or something. Instead, I'm tied to a chair and more people will die. Really. This is just great." Ash tried to keep the fatalism out of his voice, but it wasn't working. "You want to be Captain this badly? Go ahead. Take it. It's yours. Let's go to the moon and end this thing."

"We're not going to the moon," Anton said.

Ash felt as if an elephant had landed on his chest. "You're afraid," he whispered, feeling the blood drain from his face. "This isn't for power. It's for fear."

"Same thing," Anton snapped.

"You want to end the mission . . . what, because you're afraid of dying?"

"Don't you get it, Ash?" Anton whispered back, leaning so close that Ash felt his hot, stinking breath. "Fear is an incredible motivator." Anton pulled back and addressed the crew. "There's a new Captain and a new set of orders," he said, extending his weapon and spinning in a slow circle. "We're stopping. Now. Blondell, do it." Anton stopped, levelling his gun at Blondell, whose hands were still tied. A moment later, Pike released her bindings, and Blondell slowly keyed in the appropriate command. "Good girl. Now, plot a course for Kepler. We're going back there."

"Back? To Kepler?" Ash blinked and looked incredulously at Anton. "What does that do?" Anton, who had been facing Blondell, spun around so quickly that it actually sent a jab of pain through the back of Ash's skull.

"It gives us time," Anton said. "It gives us the one thing we are missing."

"Have you completely lost your mind?" Ash spat.

"You would know," Anton returned.

Ash sighed, trying to regain his composure. "Anton, think about this logically. I know we have our differences, but you have to know I'm right. This makes no sense. Going back to Kepler doesn't give us any time."

"You know we lost this fight, right?" Anton spat. The declaration seemed to take the air out of the room. Already silent, the remaining sound and air seemed to have spun away, creating nothing but a vacuum which devoured every other noise, save for Anton's labored breathing and frenzied speech.

Feeling the conversation slipping away, Ash said, "Lost? Anton, we're so close. We're one stop away from getting the final piece of the vaccine. Just a few hours and we'll be on the moon, and a day or two after that, we'll be on Earth, helping them develop the vaccine for Spades."

"Do you really believe that?" Anton's face twisted into a rage. "Do you really think they're gonna make it that simple?"

"Who is they? What are you talking about?" Ash countered. He was truly starting to fear that Anton had some sort of break with reality, and the concept was a terrifying one: It meant that someone who didn't have full control over their mental faculties was in control of a powerful warship, capable of saving the planet, and by converse, capable of ending it.

"We are going back to Kepler," Anton said, abruptly changing the subject. "It's a new planet, and a new life, capable of supporting humans—"

"With gas masks! And don't forget about the long-armed aliens! Anton, come on! I understand this . . . why you are afraid . . . but please, listen to me here. Your plan will not save us. It may doom us all."

"It's the only alternative!" exploded Anton, jerking his arms into the air. "It is the only way to keep the human race alive!"

"We can still save our planet!"

"Our planet is lost!" cried Anton, spittle flying from his mouth.

Ash's mind hurried to develop an appropriate response, and that's when he noticed it: Alexis' piercing glare. She had been listening to the conversation with a combination of fear and concern, but her facial expression had abruptly changed. Ash tried to make eye contact with Alexis, but she seemed oblivious, and after a moment, Ash realized that she wasn't looking at him. She was looking behind him.

Tied to the chair, Ash was unable to turn around, but it wasn't long before he noticed Radar's facial expression tighten. Staring directly at Ash, Radar mouthed, *"Keep. Talking."*

With renewed hope, Ash continued.

"Anton, come on, we both know that's not true," Ash said, wishing desperately he could see what was going on behind him.

"Really? It isn't? This is the best chance that humanity has? Us?"

"And Valliant. And the *Remedy.*"

At this, Anton paused and sneered, ever so slightly. "Yes,

of course, how could I forget about your very good friend, Benjamin Valliant." Anton laughed, haughtily, seemingly to himself. "Maybe when this is all over, they can join us on Kepler. We can make a home for them too. There's plenty of room, after all, even for—"

Several things happened at once.

Sia cried "LASER!" and whipped her arms away from Sierra just as a circular blast of blue energy caught her squarely in the chest, sending her flying backward, over a panel.

Simultaneously, two more blasts shot out at Pike and Louis; however, both shots missed wildly and gave the two would-be victims a chance to scurry behind chairs. Tidus and the other back brigade goon each leapt up to return fire, but they missed. Desperate to see what was going on – and to help – Ash began shaking his chair from side to side, trying to loosen it from its moorings. More shots rang out across the Bridge and there was no slowing of the weapon fire. So far, no one else had been hit, but Ash saw Sia twitching. Evidently, she had been stunned, not killed.

A quick movement on his right caught Ash's attention and he stopped moving. His left arm popped loose as his bonds were ripped to shreds by a sharp knife. Using his arm as leverage, Ash turned around to see the face of his rescuer, but whoever it was had moved.

Larissa suddenly appeared on his right, freed his other hand and jammed a weapon in it.

"On me. Now!" she said. Ash followed her in a crab walk to duck behind Anton's weapons platform, keeping his head as low as possible to avoid the circular blue laser shots and the deadly red ones intermixing in a fiery ballet of destruction.

Sparks and small flames flew from the various instruments which were taking the brunt of the weapons fire. Larissa whipped up the air computer, which Ash thought was extraneous until a wild shot ricocheted into the panel, stopping the bolt of energy and evaporating it out of existence. Ash tried to crane his neck around the bulky equipment to find his friends, to find Alexis, but seeing through the storm of weapon fire was virtually impossible. He saw multiple bodies strewn across the floor. Without thinking, he aimed at the nearest location from which red lasers were emerging and fired. He crawled back to Larissa, who appeared to be trying to get a line of sight on a different target.

"What the hell happened?" she screamed at him.

"Attempted coup!" Ash cried back. "Don't ask! Just help me finish this!"

Larissa fired four shots in rapid succession to her left. Ash didn't so much hear the *thump* as he felt it.

"Glad I picked that moment to check on Jameson. Now, how many are there?" Larissa asked.

Ash stared at the body which was a mere five feet from him, and even closer to Larissa. The face was covered by a stray arm, but it could have been any of the guys from the Back Brigade. He saw a small rise in the chest at the same time he noticed a gleaming switchblade in his enemy's hand. Ash realized that Larissa's attack had shaken loose the last strand of Anton and company's moral compass. They were no longer content to take prisoners – they were aiming to kill.

"Four at the most," Ash said, peering over the control panel again. More people were down, and there were moments of silence in between the gun fire, followed by screams demanding surrender from either side. Ash didn't say a word, not willing to give away his position for a useless ultimatum. Instead, he scanned, desperately trying to find a mass of dark, curly hair whipping from side to side.

"Okay, good," Larissa said. "At least two down. You break right. Get to the pilot's station. I've got you. We need to draw them out or this never ends."

"On it!" Ash replied. He fired a couple of shots in the opposite direction and broke into a fast run. It was only five steps to Alexis' seat but the shots began almost as soon as he rose. Ducking and rolling as he moved, Ash heard the muffled scream of someone, and looked up in time to see another body falling. Three to go.

Hearing a shout from his left, Ash whipped around and

saw Alexis, his Alexis, knocked to the ground by a brutal uppercut thrown by Anton. Anton stood over Alexis, eyes wild and gleaming, his hands clutched in tight fists and legs in a fighter stance.

Charging without thinking, Ash leapt off the ground, head connecting with Anton's chest, taking joy in the delicious *crack* as Anton's ribs crumbled underneath Ash's skull. The tackle drove Anton and Ash into Ash's chair, with Ash's momentum pinning Anton against an armrest. Filled with a burning rage, Ash pressed the crown of his head into Anton's injured chest, eliciting delightful cries of pain from his attacker. The armrest inched backward. First an inch, followed by a sudden crash to the ground as it gave way to pressure and dropped to the floor.

Metallic chunks of the chair's armrest flew across the floor. Ash grappled with Anton who landed on top of him. One hand clutching his side, Anton used his free arm to land two vicious blows into Ash's already bruised cheek. Ash's head had felt like exploding the instant it had connected with Anton's chest; now the punches made Ash see paroxysms of light against darkness before his eyes. By the time Anton landed his third shot, Ash was dimly aware that consciousness was slipping away. Again.

Gripping his ribs with one hand and straddling Ash, Anton raised his other hand to deliver another blow. Desperately, lamely, Ash tried to raise his hands to cover his face, seeing Anton through only the smallest slit of light between his swollen eyes.

There was a sound like metal ringing on metal. Anton went very still. He froze, still as a statue before he collapsed, landing face first on the floor next to Ash.

It took Ash a solid ten seconds before he was able to move, but when he did, he gently opened his eyes and focused on Anton's prone body. A massive lump was forming on the back of his head, and an open wound was bleeding profusely. Anton moaned softly and brought his legs up to his chest in a desperate effort to curl into the fetal position. Next to Anton stood Radar, holding a polished piece of the Captain's chair. Radar's knuckles were wrapped

259

tightly around the metal rod. The top of the improvised weapon was slick with dark red blood. Radar, who had been the quietest crew member, so demure that Ash had to give him a nickname because he had been too shy to give his real name. Radar, who had almost killed a man.

The Bridge was silent, with bodies scattered across the deck. A wave of nausea swept over Ash. He keeled over and vomited, tasting the bitter bile as it raced from his stomach to his mouth.

When that was done, Ash stood up, spitting and swaying, attempting to assess the state of the Bridge through eyes that were functioning like deformed kaleidoscopes. There was Pike and Tidus, on their knees, hands being tied up by Echo and Blondell, both of whom seemed to be taking immense joy in their new assignment. Rivulets of blood freely streamed from Echo's nose, falling onto Pike's bald head and into Tidus' perfectly feathered hair, and through it all, Echo was smiling. The rest of the would-be mutineers were unconscious and being roughly awoken from their stun-gun induced sleep by Larissa and Robin. Robin, in particular, was enjoying himself.

"I told Ryan not to try anything funny! I tried to warn him!" he cried.

"Calm down there, space cowboy," Larissa said, trying to keep an edge in her voice and losing the battle against smiling at Robin's exuberance. "You just be glad I came in when I did."

Through his pain addled skull, Ash remembered what he was really looking for: Alexis. Turning around, he found her, sitting on the ground and holding her cheek, which was rapidly swelling. As gently as he could, and wincing at the pain it caused, Ash knelt down at her side. He tried to kiss her gently, but only succeeded in making Alexis groan.

"I appreciate the thought," she said, her voice strained. "But don't do that." Alexis slowly turned her head and noticed Ash's swollen face. "Oh, God! Are you alright?" She instinctively raised a hand to stroke Ash's face, causing him to leap as if he had just been shocked by a taser. Just as quickly, Alexis pulled her hand back.

"Well, this sucks," Ash said, gently placing a hand on his own face, noticing immediately the raw and puffy condition of his skin. Moments later, Echo walked up to the two, handing them both ice packs. Ash noticed that she had her own pressed against her nose.

"This helps," she said, her voice muffled by the pack.

"Thanks," Ash said, placing the packet on his swollen cheek. It was cool, refreshing, and tinged with some sort of chemical smell that Ash couldn't place. "What's in this thing?"

Echo shrugged.

"No idea, but it must be from their time period. Good news is that it's helping." Echo withdrew the ice pack and Ash realized she was correct. The bleeding on Echo's nose had stopped, and the swelling appeared to be reverting. Noticing the look of concern on Ash's face, Echo added, "Don't worry. I'm okay," before matter-of-factly adding, "but I will kill that son of a bitch."

Despite the circumstances, which included unconscious crew and a broken Bridge covered in blood and gore, Ash started to laugh. Even the small movements hurt his face.

Minutes later, the assessment was complete: No one was dead. Ash, Alexis and Echo had taken the worst of the beatings as far as the good guys were concerned. Aside from a few scrapes and bruises, the rest of the crew was relatively unharmed. The mutineers were stunned but slowly regaining consciousness, and Larissa was holding them in the center of the Bridge. With his face still covered in the futuristic ice pack, Ash gathered the remaining, loyal crew, which consisted of Alexis, Robin, Radar, Echo, Jameson and Blondell. Miranda and Sierra, who had missed the entire fight, were brought up to the Bridge.

"What do we do now?" Ash asked. Including himself, there were only nine crew members left who could be trusted; ten, including Larissa, who was currently holding the six mutineers at gun point. "Can we run a ship with ten people?"

"It'll be a stretch, but we can make it," Jameson said. "Blondell, how many hours until we reach the moon?"

"Roughly four, but we can slow down if necessary."

Ash shook his head. "I really don't want to take that chance," he said. "We don't know how stable our attempts at triangulating the terrorists are—"

"There is no stability whatsoever," Radar said. "We sort of have a lock on them, holding steady between the Earth and the Moon, but we're having trouble maintaining the signal. It's a small miracle that we've held on this long."

"Well, then, there're you go," Ash said. "If we lose them now, we may lose them forever, and that's not an option." The assembled nodding told Ash that he had the crew onboard.

"So what's the plan, Captain?" Blondell said. Ash paused, pursed his lips, and spoke again.

"Guys . . . nothing has changed. We still have a mission. The only question is this: can we still fly? The Bridge took a hell of a lot of fire. Robin?" Robin and Jameson exchanged knowing looks. It was Jameson who spoke first.

"We can try to clean up the damage, Ash, but we have no real way of knowing."

"I've gotten good with this, but I can't say for sure that I know these systems one hundred percent," Robin added. "And if we screw this up, we can get killed."

"Our lives are forfeit anyway," Ash said.

Everyone in the huddle froze. "I'm serious. Our lives don't matter. If we die trying . . . we die. Our lives mean nothing compared to the rest of humanity." There was hesitation before the first head started nodding (Alexis', of course), but the rest of the group soon joined in.

"We're in," Echo said, and there were murmurs of agreement.

"I'll do everything I can," Robin said. In a surprising display of affection, Jameson slid a hand over Robin's.

"We both will," he said, voice strong.

Echo gestured over her shoulder.

"What do we do with these guys?" she asked, pointing at the seven mutineers who were in various states of captivity and consciousness.

"We'll need to find a way to lock them up somewhere,"

Ash said. "Jameson, is there a brig somewhere on here?"

Jameson shook his head rapidly. "No, Ash, I don't think the builders of this thing anticipated a full-scale mutiny."

"Conference room," said Larissa loudly, without turning around. Ash's mind whirled.

"One entrance, big enough to hold all seven of them . . ." he mumbled to himself.

"Great for late night rendezvous," mumbled Robin, earning him dirty looks from Jameson and Alexis, as well as confused stares from the rest of the crew.

Ash shook his head. "Larissa, does it lock from the outside?" he asked.

Larissa, attention still firmly focused on the bound mutineers, nodded. "It does," she said. "Ash, you've got master control, so you'll have to reconfigure the lock, but I can walk you through it. Captain Valliant had to do that a couple of times on the *Remedy*."

"A couple of times?" asked Echo.

Ash ignored her. "Fine," he said. He picked up two weapons from the table and handed them to Radar and Echo. "You two, help Larissa march them into the conference room. Larissa, right behind you."

"On it," Echo said, as she and Radar traipsed off. "Come on, jerk-offs! Mush!!"

"Oh, Lord," Larissa muttered, gesturing at the mutineers to stand up.

They did, slowly, with Pike and Sia practically dragging Anton. "Echo, stop slapping Louis with your gun, even though he deserves it. As for the rest of you, any funny business and it's back to the land of unconsciousness. Let's go," said Larissa. Slowly, the group shuffled out into the hallway, and the remaining crew stood alone.

"Well, we know what to do now," Ash said. "Robin, you're in charge. Tell us what we need to do to fix the ship."

Robin, savoring the moment, smiled.

"Let's do it!" he said cheerfully, natural enthusiasm returning as he marched to the nearest smoking panel.

Sensing a movement to his right, Ash looked up and saw Alexis, taking small steps toward him.

"Hallway?" she asked quietly, walking past Ash, toward the door.

"God, yes," Ash said, turning around and following her off the Bridge. A few steps later, they were alone. Sighing heavily, Ash looked at Alexis and said, "It's always something."

"Between getting sucked almost two centuries through time, the deadly space virus, the asteroid belt, freaky aliens and mutinous crew...yep. You're right. Always something." Both chuckled. "You holding up okay?"

Ash shrugged. "At this point, what the hell is left? I mean, really, what else are we going to do? We may all die here today, but it's been like that since we got here. I feel oddly calm about it." Ash paused, expecting a severe reaction from Alexis, but instead, she just shrugged.

"When you accept the worst, there's nothing left to lose," she said. "Sometimes it takes hitting rock bottom to figure that out."

Ash smiled bitterly. "Tell me about it. Still, all things considered, we're alive, in a damaged ship, with half a crew, and maybe on the verge of saving mankind. Yeah, this could be a lot worse."

"And you got laid yesterday," Alexis said. "That's gotta help."

Ash full-on laughed. "It does," he said. The moment passed. "Come here," he said quietly.

Alexis walked into Ash's open arms. Ash held her at arm's length before gently kissing her on the forehead. Alexis murmured happily and folded herself into Ash's chest. They stood there, gently swaying with the rhythm of the ship, and for just a few moments, there was nothing else in the world.

Chapter Thirty-Four

Their plan, Ash realized, was deceptively simple and could go wrong a million different ways.

He had reviewed the final details with Valliant. Despite the wonders of the miracle ice-pack, Valliant still saw the bruising on his face.

"What in hell happened?" he asked. "Anton?"

"Oh, yes, it was a rocking good time. Anton knocked a few of us unconscious and then tried to take control of the ship. That turned into a laser fight."

For the first time, Valliant's composure seemed to crack; his face twisted into confusion, then rage. "He did *what?*" he cried.

Ash dismissed the outburst with a wave of his hand. "Don't worry, it's all good now," he said. "Problem solved. Half the crew locked in the conference room. No biggie."

"I don't believe it!" Valliant cried. "I knew Anton was unstable, but I never dreamed he was so dangerous."

"We have all become professionals at things which are unbelievable," Ash said. "I just hope we can finish this off."

"Well, you've clearly held it together enough. How is the ship?"

"Mostly working. The Bridge took a decent amount of hits during the gunfight, but I think we are okay. Some of the sensors seem to be off, but otherwise we're good."

"Well, you never know when one of those can come back to surprise you," Valliant replied. "Still, it's not like we have a choice at this juncture."

"Amen to that," Ash said. "Believe me, there's nothing more that I'd like to do than to take the time to determine how badly my Bridge is damaged and sim this entire scenario out. The best I can do is have Jameson and Robin run every diagnostic possible and try to fix whatever issues they discover."

Valliant shook his head, slowly, sadly. "Time is a luxury we don't have. Or we may. We just don't know. Our enemies are so unpredictable that we don't have much of a choice, and I'm worried that if they leave the moon, we'll lose them forever."

"Unfortunately, I agree," Ash said. "Even if we can get the Spades vaccine, if they nail us before we make it to Earth . . ."

"Then all of this is for naught," Valliant said. "So, here's where we are."

As Ash explained their next steps to the crew, he saw their faces transform, first to curiosity, then skepticism, followed by outright disbelief.

"We're bait?" Blondell said.

"Bait," Ash replied.

"Like a worm on a hook?" Robin said.

"A worm on a hook with laser guns and torpedoes, but yeah, a worm on a hook," Ash said. "If anyone else has a better idea, believe me, I'm open to it."

Silence was the response.

"Ash, you sure about this?" Blondell said. "Believe me, if this is the plan, I'm in, but there's no alternative?"

Ash shook his head. "The aliens, as best we can tell, have positioned themselves roughly halfway between Earth and the Moon. It is next to impossible to get to the moon without getting ambushed, so that's out. If we try to wait them out, they may just attack Earth, even ahead of schedule. Valliant's ship has stronger weapons and defense capabilities than ours, so we can't be the mouse trap in this situation. We have to be the cheese."

"The cheese?" Larissa said, raising her eyebrows.

"Cheese," said Ash.

"Swiss cheese?" cracked Alexis.

266

"Maybe we go with a cheese with less holes in it," said Ash.

"I like American," said Robin.

"I'm partial to cheddar," said Jameson, making half the remaining crew gasp. "What?"

"You participated in a joke!" Echo exclaimed. "I've never heard you tell a joke before!"

"I'm starting to wish I was back on the *Remedy*," Larissa mumbled.

Ash, smiling slightly and speaking quietly, said, "Thanks, Jameson."

Blondell got back to business. "How long do we have to keep the aliens occupied?" she asked.

Ash's response was less than encouraging. He shrugged, hands open, palms facing the sky. "Valliant doesn't have an exact answer. Long enough to allow him to sneak in."

Everyone groaned.

"Not exactly the vote of confidence I was hoping for," said Blondell.

"That I understand completely," Ash said. "Valliant's going to try to keep his ship no more than ten minutes away and race in as soon as we engage."

"We almost got killed last time," Blondell reminded him.

Snippets of memory darted through Ash's mind. A big man and a big smile, the smell of burnt flesh . . .

"It's different this time," Alexis chimed in. "We're more experienced."

"And I can track them, so they can't attack us completely out of nowhere," Radar said. "That's an advantage we didn't have before."

"Metal Pole Boy is right," professed Larissa, making Radar smile sheepishly. "In all the half-battles we had, we were never able to get a radar lock for more than a few seconds. That's an advantage we would have killed for when we were firing our weapons at them." Larissa stood and pulled her hair back into a pony-tail. "I've had plenty of weapons experience on the *Remedy* – I can make this work."

"Yeah . . . about our weapons," Ash said. "Here's the thing . . ."

267

Larissa closed her eyes and bit her lip, nodding before Ash said a word.

"We can't fire them. At least, not with any real accuracy," said Ash.

That brought an outcry of protests from the crew.

"What?" It was Blondell who was the loudest. "Why?"

Larissa responded. "Because when we fire them and fail to make a kill, they flee. And we don't want them to flee when they can outrun us. We need them dead." She looked over at Alexis. "This one's on you."

"Unfortunately, Larissa is completely correct," Ash said. "We can fire the weapons as long as we don't come close . . . just enough to hold off until *Remedy* arrives. And Alexis, you're going to have to fly like you never have before."

Alexis nodded eagerly, but her smile didn't sync with the rest of her face. "I can do that," she said, forced enthusiasm in her voice. "I can."

Ash couldn't think of anything else to say to Alexis. At least, not in front of the rest of the crew, so he kept moving, following her to her seat as the rest of the crew moved to their stations. "Well, that's the plan. Jameson and Robin, get back to Engineering and do what you can to make sure the Bridge won't burst into flames before we go into battle. Everyone else, get ready."

Alexis strapped into her pilot seat, hands twirling through her hair. Ash watched her intently and couldn't help but notice her head tremble slightly. "You all right?" he asked gently.

"Hell no," she responded. "What the hell's the matter with you? Of course I'm not alright!"

"I know," Ash said. "If it's any consolation, neither am I."

"You're making it worse!" Alexis said, so loud that Miranda and Sierra looked over. She sighed. "Sorry."

Ash shrugged.

"You really think I care that you're upset at a moment like this?" he said, practically laughing. "If you weren't worried, I'd think there was something wrong with you."

Ash paused, thinking hard, before he licked his lips and continued. "I know you've done difficult piloting before. You steered us clear of a battle with these guys. You're a natural pilot, and everyone here has faith that you can do this."

"Thanks, Captain," Alexis said softly.

Ash continued: "And as your . . . umm, let's go with friend . . . you're special. You know that." He put a hand on her shoulder, forgetting his inhibitions, leaned in and kissed her softly on the neck. Who the hell cared if anyone else saw it? They could be dead in minutes. "And I believe in you," he whispered gently.

A dreamy smile came over Alexis' lips.

"Coming up on five minutes," intoned Blondell, interrupting the moment.

Ash pulled back and walked over to his platform, strapping himself into his chair, chuckling slightly as he squeezed the hastily repaired armrest. It had been wrapped in duct tape that looked identical to what Ash would have found in his home time.

"Everyone, hang on tight," Ash said, absently gripping and releasing the arm rests. Silence prevailed, until Ash remembered Valliant's advice from the party: he was the Captain. He needed to speak. Maybe now more than ever.

Yet now, of all times, the words escaped him. Maybe it was the pressure. Maybe it was the fact that death was so close, Ash could practically feel its hot breath on his face. Maybe it was the repeated blows to the head. But Ash was tired. Words failed him.

So all he said was, "For whatever it's worth . . . I couldn't have asked more out of anyone here."

There was silence. No nods of agreement, no cheers of gratitude. Ash wasn't even sure anyone had heard him.

But words didn't matter now, did they?

"Get ready, everybody. One minute," said Blondell.

"Radar, where are they?" Ash asked.

Radar, who was already flicking switches on his computer, didn't bother to turn around in response.

"They're still and holding position."

Ash considered. "Well, maybe we'll get lucky, and they

269

won't know we're coming."

"We've always thought that they had issues with their radar when they went invisible," Larissa added. "Every time they attacked us, if we could get in behind them and stay there, they had a lot of trouble determining our position."

Ash raised his eyebrows. "So we could actually catch them by surprise?"

Larissa nodded.

"If that's the case, Captain, I suggest we go in hot. Outside shot we can blow them up and end this right away," said Jameson, his voice ringing loud over the ship's comm system.

"Agreed," Ash said. "We may only get one shot at this. Larissa, get the weapons ready. Maybe we can fire a killing blow and put an end to this thing early."

Larissa responded by flinging various objects on her air computer. "I'm arming torpedoes now," she said. "If we can catch them in the right spot, maybe we can end this."

"Five seconds," Blondell said. "Four . . . three . . ."

"I love you all," Ash whispered, to no one in particular, feeling equal parts exhilaration and terror ripping through his veins.

"One . . ."

Ash jerked forward as the ship deaccelerated. "Fire!" he ordered, and Larissa punched a fist through her panel just as the ship slowed to a normal speed, but not fast enough, as a stream of laser fire greeted the *Redemption,* spat forth from the nose of the invisible aliens.

"Evasive maneuvers!" Ash said, but it was unnecessary, as Alexis was already slamming her controls forward, flinging the *Redemption* and its crew into a violent dive.

"They were ready for us!" exclaimed Radar as the dive accelerated. "I'm sorry. I couldn't tell!"

"Doesn't matter, track them now!" said Ash, digging his nails into the arms of his chair. "Find them before they find us!"

"Trying!" responded Radar.

Blondell leapt over to the communications panel and spoke frantically. "*Remedy,* get here now. They were waiting for us!" she cried. Earth whirled by the front windows, the Pacific Ocean, Japanese Islands and southeastern Asia briefly whirling by before disappearing out of view.

"They're behind us!" said Radar. "I have them, and they are—"

Ting. Ting. Two sharp bursts connected with the *Redemption's* shields, causing the rainbow hue to the front window and shield system.

"Reverse!" Ash yelled, and Alexis did, yanking her joystick upwards, straining the engines and intensifying the vibrations throughout the ship. "Robin, the left weapons bank?"

Robin responded by taking an open palm to display and smacking it.

"It's no good, Ash, I don't have a clue . . . uh, just try not to rip the wing off, okay?"

"That's some great advice!" Larissa cried. "Firing rear guns!"

Before Ash could say another word, the ship shook with the sounds of its weaponry being utilized. Craning his neck, Ash saw the red dot that was their attackers shimmer.

"Watch it!" yelled Radar. "Don't come close!"

"I know, you moron!" said Larissa, but she nervously wiped her brow as she continued keying commands. "I'm trying to give us a little space."

"Well, they are backing off," Radar said.

"Alexis, can you get us a better angle?" Ash's mind whirled, trying to diagram the fight in his mind. *Screw it,* he thought. "Blondell, Alexis needs to stay away from them . . . what's the best way to do it?"

Blondell, who was wildly flinging around icons on her air computer, used her entire hand to open a new screen and plot out lines of attack.

"Lex, why you are going up?" Blondell asked.

"Get the high ground!" responded Alexis, her voice thick with exertion.

"Huh? Why? This is space . . . high ground doesn't matter!"

Alexis tilted her head to the side, computing the

information, before nodding. "Right, sorry . . . okay, hang on again!" Alexis heaved the controls downward.

It barely gave Ash time to say, "Crap," before he flew toward the front window, saved only by Blondell's outstretched arms.

"Do you ever learn, you freakin' idiot??" she screamed.

"Sorry!" Ash said, tightening his grip. Moments later, the ship's internal gravity compensated for Alexis' maneuvers, giving Ash time to race back to his seat and rebuckle his harness.

"Ash, Jameson here," said a voice in Ash's ear. Ash's skin prickled. From the added echo in his voice, Ash realized that Jameson was talking on a private channel, not one that the entire ship could hear.

"What?" Ash asked, straining to concentrate on the rest of the ship with half of his hearing gone.

"I know Robin can't see it, but the left engine is showing signs of real strain."

"How bad?" Ash asked.

"Bad enough that we could lose it.

"What happens then?"

"Everything gets terrible."

Ash swallowed.

"How much time left?" asked an anxious Alexis.

"Five minutes till the *Remedy!*" said Blondell.

"Move!" shouted a panicked Radar.

Alexis did, returning the ship to a steep dive as three more laser blasts connected with the *Redemption*.

"Shields going critical!" cried Blondell.

"Come on, Valliant," Ash muttered under his breath. Louder, he said, "Reroute all power from the weapons to our shields. Everything we got!"

Larissa responded by sliding her panel back.

"Done!" she exclaimed. "But if this gets so bad that we're about to lose the shield, we may have just lost our contingency plan."

"There is no contingency plan, goddammit!" cried Ash, his face flushing. "It's this or we're all dead! Come on, Valliant!"

272

"I can't make him get here any faster!" shrieked a stressed Blondell.

"I know, I know," Ash said, exasperated. "Alexis, can you get behind them?" This was all going way, way too fast.

"Trying!" Alexis said, playing with the throttle. "If I can just get this to go a little faster . . ."

"Working on it!" said Jameson over the communications system.

"No, no, don't do that, they're turning again, coming in to intercept!" said Radar.

Sure enough, despite the invisibility, Ash could see the distortion of the alien ship starting to glide through the air, accelerating into a steep bank, starting to head back toward the *Redemption*. Terror coursing through him, Ash's mind, seemingly of its own will, returned to their first minutes onboard the *Redemption,* when the crew, without a clue of what they were doing, managed to just barely fight off their attackers. Hell, at the time, they were brand new to the ship. Now, weeks later, with more experience under their belt, they appeared at the edge of defeat again.

And it hit Ash.

"Alexis, belay that last order. Let them in and keep drifting." Ash's voice was calm, confident.

"You want me to do *what?*" Alexis said.

Jameson spoke on a private line. "Ash, what are you doing?"

"Jameson and Blondell, when I give the order, hit the P-B button again," Ash said.

Blondell spun around in her seat. "That button from the start?"

"Yep, that one," Ash said.

"Why in God's name do we do that?" Alexis said.

But, off to Ash's left, he saw Larissa, smiling ever so slightly.

"You never figured out what P-B stands for, did you?" asked Larissa. There was silence. "Parking brake," Larissa said, now grinning openly.

"A parking brake? This ship has a parking brake?" barked Ash.

"That's just what they always called it, there's an engineer out there with a sense of humor, alright?" bellowed Blondell.

"An abrupt stop . . ." said Alexis, her voice trailing off with the implication of what Ash was discussing. "That will activate our thrusters and stop us! It's brilliant!"

Jameson, suddenly understanding, spoke next. "Slowing down is the last thing they'll expect, and we are all out of ideas. Alexis, start the process."

Alexis nudged the joystick upward. Ash tore his eyes away from her and looked to the window, where the shimmer in space was starting to get larger.

"They're accelerating to attack, Ash," Radar chimed in. Ash, desperate to stand despite being strapped in, labored against his restraints.

"Not yet," Ash said, his voice thick. "Radar, as close as you can."

"They're almost in range . . . *now*, Captain!"

"Hit it!" roared Ash. Blondell and Jameson simultaneously slammed the "P-B" button. The ship jolted, and Ash bounced roughly in his seat, but in front of him, the passage of stars in front of the ship had slowed from a sprint to a jog. Meanwhile, the aliens shot past.

"They're trying to turn!" yelled Radar. "But they shot right past us!"

"Full power, Alexis, get us out of here before they can come again!"

"Hang on, we've got company!" said Radar. However, he wasn't looking at his screen. Instead, he was pointing up, as a gray blur slowed, streaking across the sky like the proverbial white knight on a horse. "Here they come!"

It was the *Remedy*.

Without slowing, the *Remedy* fired, simultaneously opening up a barrage of lasers from its nose and wings. Meanwhile, two torpedo's fired from the ships belly. The direct hits were far stronger than most of the glancing blows that the *Redemption* had taken thus far, and Ash felt a surge of hope.

"Turn us, turn us!" ordered Ash. "We've got to help

finish this!"

"They're turning to run!" cried Radar.

"They're not gonna be fast enough!" replied Blondell.

Alexis, sweat pouring down her face and drenching her clothes, body tense with effort, pulled the ship starboard as quickly possible, turning it, turning it, finally bringing the battle into full view. Blondell was right. The *Remedy,* which had been travelling at full speed, was closing on the distortion. At least some of its laser beams had connected, and for the first time, the invisible shield failed the aliens, revealing a familiar, cylindrical body and two triangle shaped wings. The ship stuttered as another barrage of lasers hit.

"Larissa, everything you got!" Ash shouted, standing. Larissa fired a laser blast and torpedo, but it was extraneous. The two torpedoes hit the alien ship at the same time, one toward its nose, the other toward its engine. The ship, already rocked by the earlier laser bolts, faltered. A brief orange glow appeared near the front of the ship. Time locked, the enemy ship frozen as if it was suspended in crystal. The orange flames were sucked inward and the ship collapsed in on itself, imploding in an array of sparks, metal and white gas. A rebound explosion followed, sending swirling debris dancing through space, spinning like ballerinas in a symphony, before disappearing, leaving only the glow of Earth behind them.

The cheers that erupted from the *Redemption's* Bridge exploded with the force of a thousand cannons.

Ash wasn't sure who hugged him first: Robin, Echo or Radar. Blondell didn't move; she simply sat at her panel, hands covering her face, heaving as she sobbed. In his ear, Jameson was screaming something, but what, Ash couldn't tell, because the rest of the ship had gotten so loud that it was as if the entire planet was rejoicing with them, celebrating the fact that their lives, and the lives of countless future generations, had been spared.

Ash, forgetting everything else, stumbled, as if in a dream, five steps in front of him. Alexis was staring in front of her, blinking, her hands held limply at her sides, clearly not believing what she was seeing. She smiled as Ash approached, and in one fluid motion, unbuckled, stood up, and launched herself into his arms. Tightening his grip, Ash pulled back, but only to give his lips enough room to connect with hers. They kissed, passionately.

It's a fairy tale, Ash thought.

The kiss ended and the two made eye contact, laughing. No words were said. None were needed.

With one arm around Alexis, Ash walked over to the communications station, switching channels.

"Valliant, that was incredible timing," Ash said. "Absolutely perfect." There was no response. "We did it, Valliant. We saved the world." Again, nothing. Looking up, Ash spotted the *Remedy*, a gray speck against the blackness of space, flying toward the planet. Without slowing down, the *Remedy* executed a tight turn and began racing back toward the *Redemption*.

Ash, his brows knitting in confusion, said, "Valliant? What's going on? Are there more of them?" The ship grew quiet as the crew stared at Ash. "Valliant? Were your communications systems damaged?" Still, no response. The *Remedy* kept racing, its nose pointing straight at the *Redemption*. Ash quieted. He paused. In a soft, almost pleading voice, he said, "Ben?"

The *Remedy* opened fire, connecting a full barrage with the *Redemption*.

Chapter Thirty-Five

Klaxons and sirens opened up as the *Redemption* shook harder than it ever had. Every crew member who had been celebrating instantly lost their footing and bounced to the ground, careening around the Bridge until the shaking died down. Desperately, they raced back to their stations. That in and of itself was difficult: between the smoke and lack of any light source, save for the stars in front of them and a few randomly illuminated panels, there was near complete blackness on the ship.

"Valliant!" cried a desperate Ash. "What the hell?"

There was no response.

Radar, a bleeding gash running the length of his cheek, pounded on his station. "Radar's out, Captain!"

Everyone seemed to speak at once.

"Ash, engines are going critical. Every gauge I have is redlining!" said Jameson.

"Electrical is failing!" yelled Blondell as sparks flew from panels across the ship.

"We're losing structural integrity!" said Robin, not even attempting to control the panic in his voice. Frantic, Ash pulled himself up and crammed a scream back down his throat at the sight in front of him: Earth, slowly growing larger, filling the window.

Turning back around, Ash tried to pull himself back into his seat, practically willing the rest of the crew to do the same. The movement was difficult; the ship was now lurching, and Ash felt like he was walking up a hill in motion.

What he saw first, however, broke his heart: Larissa, who hadn't moved even after the alien ship had exploded, was free of her seat and raced for the exit.

"Too late for that!" she yelled.

As a violent explosion hit the left side of the ship, Ash knew that Larissa was correct. Sadness gripping him like a vice, Ash spoke quietly.

"You're right," he said, voice drowned out by the panic cascading around him. At the top of his lungs, he screamed, "Everyone, get to the dock! Jameson and Robin, we're out of here, meet us by the shuttles!"

No one needed to be told twice, they bolted uphill, moving toward the exit. Using the beams on his elevated platform, Ash pulled himself up as high as he could. Behind him, he heard Alexis grunting with effort as she attempted to level the ship. Slowly, but steadily, the bucking ship heeded Alexis' commands, and it began to right itself. The floor leveled out.

On his feet, Ash spun around and found a length of discarded rope that he had been tied with earlier. Grabbing it, he raced over to Alexis' station, shoved her hands off of the controls and began to wrap the rope around the steering column. Seeing what he was doing, Alexis jumped up, found another strand of rope, and did the same.

"Auto-pilot down?" she asked, tying her rope against the ship and knotting it as tightly as she could.

"It has to be," Ash replied, mirroring Alexis' movements. "This is the only way we can keep the ship level." Job complete, Ash looked around and saw no one left on the Bridge, save for Miranda, who stood pale-faced next to the exit.

"Come on, out!" Ash ordered, taking the frozen girl by the shoulders and pushing her out the door. This spurred Miranda to movement, and she began to bolt down the hallway. The ship shook intensely as they ran, and more than once, Ash saw crew members fall, only to be picked up by those next to them. Before Ash even realized it, his feet had delivered him and the rest of the crew to an intersection in the hallway:

← Bridge
Cafeteria →
Engineering →
Conference →
Docking Bay ↓
Labs ↓

"Conference room!" Ash said. "Dammit, the other half of the crew!"

The vibrations seemed to be slowing down momentarily; at least for the moment, the ship appeared to not be in imminent danger of exploding. Even so, Ash put a hand on the wall to steady himself. He had bigger problems right now.

"I'll take care of it!" Alexis said, and turned to race down the hallway.

Ash put a hand on her stomach to stop her. "No," he intoned. "My crew. My responsibility. And my hand – I have to open the door to get them out of there!"

"You come with me!" Miranda said, before Alexis could protest. Ash heard the panic in her voice. "I need your help with something!"

Alexis looked at Miranda, confused, before turning to Ash. Ash had a moment to calculate. He knew Alexis' stubbornness and knew how dangerous running to the conference room to free the mutineers could be.

"Go!" he cried.

Alexis nodded. "I'll see you in a few minutes," she said, her voice sounding more like she was giving a command than making a statement.

Ash, his mouth dry, nodded in return, and Alexis and Miranda sprinted down one corridor, while Ash turned down another.

Keeping his head low to avoid the viscous smoke which had filled the air, a jumble of thoughts competed in Ash's tortured mind as he hurried to the conference room. Valliant, his voice steady, orienting them to their mission. Giving Ash advice on how to lead the crew. Reminding him

279

of the importance of making sure his crew felt inspired. Imbuing him with the confidence he needed to lead. Valliant and his crew, now probably dead or worse.

Only one thing makes sense, thought Ash. *The aliens must have beamed aboard and captured control of the* Remedy. *Dammit. I thought we told them to be alert for that.*

Ash reached the conference room door and disengaged the lock without hesitating. The door opened a few inches and froze, its opening mechanism malfunctioning. With just enough room for his fingers to slip into the opening, Ash wrapped his hands around the metallic surface and began to pull.

"Come on, help me, you assholes!" Ash yelled, and soon other hands joined him. Working with the same people who had tried to kill him hours before, the door began to move, eventually giving way for one person to slip through. Gasping, Ash released the door and looked inside the conference room. It was filled with deep, thick smoke, and the entire group was on their hands and knees. Ash saw Pike whimpering in the corner, saw Ryan's eyes swimming as the sweating, weeping boy tried to stay conscious. Next to him was Anton, holding the back of his head, his shirt covered in what appeared to be his own vomit.

"Out!" Ash said, waving his hands frantically. Any threat of danger from the group of mutineers had long since burned away. The people in front of him looked like they were barely alive, let alone capable of violence. One by one, they moved, coughing, spitting and retching as they reached the comparatively fresher air of the hallway and began to run.

"Head for the dock!" Ash commanded, counting off as the mutineers left the room which had nearly proved to be their tomb.

Last to leave was Anton. He glanced up and the two men made eye-contact. Ash saw nothing in Anton's eyes but fear and doubt. The moment passed, and Anton ran, full speed, following the rest of his would-be crew.

During the run to the dock, the ship began to cruelly

shake again, bouncing its occupants around as if they were rag dolls. Ash, his stamina almost depleted, put every ounce of strength he had left into his feet, surrounded by the panicked footfalls and jagged breathing of his crew. The *Redemption,* clearly in its final moments, reminded Ash of a wounded animal that knew its fate but was trying to cling to life.

At last, Ash reached the dock, nearly crashing into Miranda and Alexis as he did so. "Oh, thank God!" Ash cried as he wrapped an arm around Alexis. The two women were covered in soot and their clothing bore scorch marks.

"Ash, we have a problem," Alexis said, gasping for breath.

"No kidding!" Ash replied, pushing both women to the docks.

Alexis spun around and faced Ash. "No, more than this!" she cried. "The damn lab!"

"Huh?" Ash questioned.

"The freakin' vaccine!" cried Miranda.

"We don't have time!" Ash cried. "Besides, it doesn't matter anymore, we killed the aliens!"

"Don't you get it?" said Miranda, her eyes springing tears. "What did I tell you before? *Every vaccine has a piece of the disease in it.*" Not understanding what Miranda was saying, and not really caring either, Ash turned around to Larissa, who had appeared behind Ash.

"All accounted for!" she said. "Let's get on the shuttles. I'll take two, Alexis takes one." Behind her stood the two ships, docking bay doors ready for opening. Most of the crew had split into the two crafts, and from what Ash could see, were strapping themselves into the various seats.

"Good, open the doors once we get into the shuttle!" ordered Ash. Larissa nodded and raced off toward her ship; Ash ran toward his, followed closely by Alexis and Miranda.

"Ash, do you not understand what I am telling you?" cried an increasingly hysterical Miranda.

"There's nothing we can do anyway, Miranda" said Alexis, her voice sympathetic.

The three had moved onto the shuttle and Ash angrily

pounded the controls, causing the ramp to transverse back into the belly of the shuttle.

"Do about what?" Ash asked through gritted teeth. He couldn't believe it; they had come so far. They had won. And the ship was being destroyed because the aliens were somehow still alive on his friend's ship.

Without warning, and with the kind of physical strength that only fear could create, Miranda grabbed Ash by his shoulders and shoved him into a nearby wall.

"Don't you understand?" she said, her voice frenzied. "We tried to remove one of the components of the vaccine, but we couldn't get there, the corridor was impassable. Ash, the two components of Spades were next to each other, and the only thing that could cause them to combine is extreme heat. Like the kind of heat that would be generated from an explosion."

Any outside noise or chatter disappeared as Miranda spat out these words. With a dawning horror, Ash realized what Miranda was saying.

"Spades—"

"Is being created. On this ship. Right now."

Ash didn't pause, didn't hesitate. "Alexis, get us out of here. And arm any weapons we have!" Alexis bolted toward her seat and began to press a series of controls as other crew members filed in behind her. Next to her was Blondell in the co-pilot's seat.

"Blondell—"

Blondell cut Ash off. "Already relayed that to Shuttle Two, they're doing the same." Ash nodded and stood between the two chairs as Alexis feathered the throttle and gently guided the shuttle out of the docking bay, and out of the *Redemption*. Watching the rear on a nearby display, Ash saw the second shuttle follow closely behind.

Once clear of the *Redemption,* Ash yelled, "Go back and open fire!"

"Calm down, Ash!" said Blondell. "We have to get clear enough to turn and start a firing run or we'll crash into the ship. No sense in getting all of us killed."

A horrific thought flashed through Ash's mind.

"Can we kamikaze this thing into the *Redemption?*"

Alexis and Blondell caught their breath, but before either could say anything, Larissa's voice piped in over the communications system.

"No, Ash," she said. "I thought of that as we were running. We looked at the same thing on board the *Remedy* when we were doing a threat assessment. There's no spot that any shuttle could hit which could cripple the ship, and it's not possible to stop the *Redemption's* momentum short of destroying it. Running into the ship would be like hitting a space station with a pellet gun." Ash nodded and pushed the black thought aside.

"We have bigger problems," said Blondell, urgently turning a dial and bringing up her weapons display.

Ash followed her gaze to a nearby radar screen, and instantly he saw what she was looking at: a large red dot, signifying the *Redemption,* was moving away from the shuttle in a hurry. It seemed to be gaining speed as moved toward the nearest target that was exerting gravity: Earth.

"Can we catch it?" asked Ash.

"Worth a shot!" said Alexis. "Blondell?"

"We're clear! Execute the turn."

"Shuttle two, get in behind me," said Alexis, dabbing at her eyes. Ash glanced again at the radar screen and saw that the *Redemption* had somehow gained more speed, and with it, more distance. A dawning realization began to sink in.

Banking hard, the shuttle craft turned sharply to the right. Ash allowed the gravity to press him into the wall, his right arm dimly reaching for a handhold on the roof. He felt his head bouncing uselessly against a panel. A fog closed in on his chest, solidifying behind his ribs and spreading upward, a column of pain, thick as concrete, solidifying in his every vein.

"We did this," he said quietly. No one else heard him. He had become spectral. His actions now belonged to the ages.

The shuttle stopped turning, and Larissa's shuttle did the same to his right. "Fire!" commanded Alexis, and Blondell did fire, depressing two buttons on a nearby control panel. Small green jets of energy shot out from both of the shuttle's wings, but the lasers uselessly disappeared well before reaching the smoking, accelerating carcass of the *Redemption*.

"Everything we've got to the engines," said Alexis, but her voice had already lost its fervor. Indeed, the opposite of what Alexis had commanded seemed to be happening: The ship was slowing down. Alexis glanced toward her right. "Blondell?"

In response, Blondell flipped multiple switches and pressed another button. Her weapons system folded back into the main controls.

"Too late," she whispered quietly, and Alexis hung her head. "This ship is meant for short hops and defense, not attacking a major starship. We depleted its fuel cells. They'll recharge, but we can't catch the *Redemption.*" Silence fell, as Ash, Blondell and Alexis uselessly turned their heads upward, watching the *Redemption* speed toward Earth.

Like a comet flung across the evening sky, with a smoky tail and fiery corona, Ash's ship and humanity's last hope moved closer to the planet. The rest of the crew, having heard the entire sequence of events and having been advised about the status of Spades from Miranda, crowded the front of the ship.

"There it goes," said Robin quietly, watching the *Redemption* fall. Faster and faster the ship sped as Earth grew nearer and nearer. Ash watched the ship career through the stars and was struck by the fact that this was the first time – and the last time – that he had ever looked at it from the outside. He hadn't realized just how big it was; at least two football fields long and as tall as a three-story building, with wings that looked to be the size of a baseball diamond. Three engines – all aflame – glowed in the rear of the ship, blue plasma evacuating from various compartments, creating an intermingling of flames and which would have been stunning under any other set of circumstances.

The ship was almost in the planet's upper atmosphere, careening toward the Pacific Ocean. It was a sight that looked hauntingly familiar to Ash. It took him a moment before the recognition hit him: He was looking at an altered angle of the same video Valliant had shown him and the rest of the crew the very first day they were onboard the *Redemption*. This was it. This was Spades crashing into the Pacific Ocean. The land masses looked a little off, like two pictures that had merged together wrong, and Ash realized that it was because he was three weeks earlier than the original attack was supposed to take place.

Suddenly, as if captured by an invisible force field, the *Redemption* straightened and a halo appeared around it. The ship became smaller and smaller as it accelerated toward planet Earth.

"It's caught in the planet's gravity," Jameson said quietly. "It should impact in a few minutes."

"My God," mumbled Blondell, followed by a sniffle.

"Will we see it crash?" asked Robin quietly. "Will we see it hit?"

"I don't think so," Jameson said.

The *Redemption,* now directly over Japan, became smaller still, shrinking to the size of a pinprick, its mass obscured by gray clouds and blue ocean. It fell into a cloud, disappearing . . . then nothing.

In his mind's eye, Ash still saw the *Redemption* continue to fall, gaining speed while belching smoke. At long last, its tortured flight would end, reaching the embrace of the warm Pacific. And inside its very bowels, two components that were never meant to touch would combine, forming the deadliest disease in human history, and in so doing, doom the entire human race.

A silence, thick and viscous as oil, spread across the shuttle. There were no sounds, save for the soft beeping of machinery, the gentle hum of the engines and the sporadic hacking cough of Pike.

Ash, his head and heart heavy, kick-started his brain into thinking of the next step. Crushed though he was, maybe there was hope still. Looking up, he saw something that he hadn't noticed before.

"The *Remedy!*" he shouted, so loud and abruptly that half of the crew jumped. There, floating gently above the planet, was the *Remedy,* silent in the distance. Ash thrust his hand forward, turning on the communications system. Perhaps Valliant and his crew could still be saved. Perhaps there was still a way to stop Spades on Earth before it reached a critical level of virility.

"Maddox to *Remedy,* come in *Remedy.*" Silence was the response. Was it possible that Valliant had wrested control of his ship back? "Valliant, this is Ash. Come in, please." Ash's voice was pleading, beseeching.

"*Remedy* here," said a deep, steady voice that Ash instantly recognized.

"Valliant!" Ash cried, relief flooding his voice. Ash forgot about the impending destruction of his ship, forgot about his latest brush with death, forgot about Spades, and was simply grateful to hear Valliant's voice. "Ben, are you all right?"

There was silence on the other end for a good ten seconds, as if Valliant was trying to figure out what to say. When he did finally respond, it was with the most horrifying sound that Ash had ever heard in his life.

Laughter.

It started small, almost like a chuckle, but gained intensity and momentum as it continued, eventually evolving into a manic, deep cackle that sounded utterly uncontrollable and comprehensively horrifying. With that laughter, Ash realized what had happened, realized, at long last, that he had been played the fool.

"You son of a bitch," Ash said in a quiet voice.

The laughter continued. Valliant seemed not to have heard.

"Ash, I'm so sorry," he said, in a voice that sounded surprisingly apologetic. The rest of the shuttle craft's occupants looked on in horror, staring at the communications unit as if it contained Spades itself. "It's been extraordinarily difficult for me to keep all of this straight. Please try to understand, if you were me, you'd be laughing too."

Ash swallowed hard, the words hitting him like an anvil. Gently, Alexis reached up, wrapped her free hand around

Ash's arm and squeezed tight. No one else on the ship moved.

"You did this?" Ash said. There was no ire in his voice; just pure, unadulterated disbelief. He looked around the crowded shuttle to try and read the facial expressions of the rest of his crewmates, which ranged from Blondell's dumbfounded disbelief to Miranda's hard anger.

"Oh, Ash," said Valliant, his voice cool as ice. "I've been doing this from the very beginning. Every step you've made, every single fight, from the moment you had the good fortune to find us, that was me. All me."

"What the hell?" boomed Ash, pounding as hard as he could on the panel.

"Ash," Blondell said quietly, warningly.

"Captain Maddox, you must gain control of your emotions. That's one of the reasons this was so easy," said Valliant, a steel edge having snuck into his voice. "My God, a hero complex and an insecure personality can be manipulated easier than tricking a child into believing in Santa Clause."

"Fooled into this? Why? Why would you want to end humanity?" In Ash's mind flew images of history's worst villains: Hitler. Mao. Stalin. Pol Pot.

Benjamin Valliant?

"Do you not pay attention, *Captain* Maddox?" asked Valliant, oozing contempt. "What did you learn when the sissy ginger and the Amazonian briefed you about Earth?"

Blondell drew in a deep breath; Jameson stood stock still.

Ash, desperate to learn what he had been tricked into, thought back to that day in the conference room, before that conference room had meant so many other things.

"That Earth was saved?"

"No, you optimistic simpleton," Valliant said. "That Earth was doomed again. Do you learn nothing from history? From the fact that we were, once again, destroying our own planet or oppressing the vast majority of humanity for the benefit of a miniscule few? That we were repeating the same mistakes that we have made over and over and over again, extending the suffering of countless billions?"

The puzzle pieces clicked for Ash.

"You wanted to end all life to stop the suffering of some?"

"Of almost all!"

Horrified, Ash followed the thread of logic. "So someone told you that Earth had problems and you decided that it was time to end the Earth? And wait a minute. How the hell did you know how bad things are? You decided to end humanity based on a briefing?"

"A briefing?" said an incredulous Valliant. "Oh, of course, you assumed that we were like you, from different time periods. Another weakness of yours. You can't see differing perspectives. We're not scattershot like you. All of us were sent backward from one month after Spades hit."

Gasps escaped from the shuttle crew, and another realization hit.

"You saw all of this," Ash said. "All the problems of Earth, all the problems of society—"

"Yet another gift pissed away," said Valliant. "The U.G. is so wrapped up in their quest to enrich themselves that they completely miss how infiltrated their whole society and military is." Valliant's last statement brought more questions.

Trying to ignore the stinging insults, Ash spoke again. "So why didn't you just get the Spades pieces and crash your ship?"

"Think three-dimensionally, boy," said Valliant. "That wasn't our mission. We were supposed to stop the other ship from hitting the planet in the first place."

Ash's mind went blank.

"We were the failsafe," said Jameson quietly.

"Very good, red!" screeched Valliant.

Jameson put his hands over his eyes, vision having become too much effort. "Ash, Valliant was the first mission. And he failed. Intentionally."

"We were sent here a month ago to stop the *Edwards* from crashing into the planet," Valliant spat. "Clearly it must have worked."

"Huh?" That came from Blondell. "Oh. Wait. In the original time line, after the *Remedy* was sent back in time and the alien ship hit the planet with Spades—"

"The Unity Government realized that the *Remedy* had failed," continued Jameson, his voice thick. "So they sent us back to try to stop the *Edwards* as well."

Ash sat, dumbfounded, until his mind stumbled to the next question.

"What in hell is the *Edwards?*" he asked. He paused, until he felt like he had been hit with a truck. "Oh, God. That ship. That ship from the very beginning. The one we blew up."

"Well done!" cried Valliant, sounding genuinely proud.

"We actually did what we were supposed to do? We completed our mission?" asked Alexis in disbelief.

"You did," said Valliant. "We didn't stop you in time – in my version of history, Spades came when the *Edwards* crashed onto Earth."

Ash hissed a sharp breath of air as his mind reeled back to the video Valliant had shown them during their first conversation. "You lied to us," he blurted, feeling ridiculous even as the words left his lips. "You said it was an alien ship."

"Alien to you, certainly," responded Valliant, a smile in his voice. "But, Maddox, as a Captain, you must have been impressed with the way my crew reacted. Almost instantaneously, Larissa began to hack into your computers, uploading the mission profile." In disbelief, the entire occupants of Shuttle One looked to toward Shuttle Two. Larissa had gone completely silent. "From there, it was just a matter of making you collect the components and bringing you back here."

Miranda leaned into the communications panel.

"That still doesn't explain why the aliens went after Earth in the first place," Miranda said. "It doesn't explain why any species would travel so far to eliminate another planet."

"You still think those were aliens?" For what seemed like an eternity, Valliant paused, and when he spoke again, he sounded so idealistic that Ash could practically see the stars in his eyes. "We begged them. So many of us. We begged them not to meddle with time in order to, quite literally, fuel their own greed. To expand their power. But no. The corporate cartel that served as our Government insisted that local resources were running low. It was *safe,* they said. It was *secure,* they said. That was it. That was all the proof I – we – needed. If our society was so greedy that we were willing to muddle with time, then humanity was no longer deserving of continued existence."

Ash was about to sputter out a series of questions, until Jameson leaned over and flicked the mute button.

"So much of this makes sense now," he said. "Ash, there are no aliens. There never were. The aliens were us. They were humans that they had sent back in time."

A montage of thoughts ran through Ash's mind. An asteroid that looked like it had machinery. A man-made, symmetrical hole on Kepler, one that he had mistaken for an exit.

"They were mining," Ash gasped, bringing a hand to his mouth. Jameson nodded gravely.

"Mining for fuel," he said. "Sent back in time in order to bring the resources to the present-day Unity Government."

"And when they returned to Earth, they brought Spades with them," completed Alexis. "Ash, it all makes sense."

Ash stood still, fighting his way through the turmoil in his mind, before reaching for the mute switch again.

"Except one thing," he said. "Valliant, who the hell was trying to kill us the entire time?"

"Think, Maddox," responded Valliant, voice thick as syrup. "You already know that the Unity Government can travel through time."

Oh. "Son of a bitch," Ash muttered.

Valliant laughed coldly.

"When their first two options failed, they sent a third ship. A warship, to kill both of us. That obviously didn't work out too well, now did it?"

Jameson looked down and cleared his throat before speaking

"There will be no other ship," he said. "We would have

seen it by now. That's it. The Unity Government is out of options, out of resources and out of time. They have to live with the disaster they created." For a long time, no one spoke. Not even Valliant.

Finally, quietly, Ash asked, "Can we do anything?"

Blondell shook her head. "We're dead if he wants it," she said quietly.

Ash heaved a deep breath. "So, now that you got that off your chest, is this the part where you kill us?"

"Kill you?" said Valliant. "Are you kidding? I know the range of those ships you're on, and I know your own limited abilities. I'm not going to kill you. You were the Captain of the ship that just committed the greatest atrocity of all time. You go to Earth, Captain Maddox. You pay the price for your crimes, and you explain to the Unity Government why *your* ship that *you* lead just doomed the planet. You will not see me again. Valliant out."

The connection cut abruptly as the *Remedy* raced past the two floating shuttles. Leaning forward, Ash activated the rear monitors, just in time to see the wake of the *Remedy* as it rocketed into the depths of space.

"Where do we go now?" said Echo, her voice quiet as death. Ash stared out the window, his breath coming in jagged rasps.

"Where else can we go?" he responded, barely above a whisper. He looked at his doomed planet. "Let's go home."

CHAPTER THIRTY-SIX

Valliant was right. The two shuttles couldn't go anywhere else. Both ships had limited capacity for flight. As a result, Alexis and Larissa put the shuttles down on the first spot of solid land they could find. As best Ash could tell, they were on a small, uninhabited island in Japan. Nothing else was in sight besides blue sky, blue ocean and a scar of smoke to the east, signifying the spot where the *Redemption* had crashed and delivered its deadly cargo to the world. Ash sat on the beach of the island, hugging his arms around his legs, his chin tucked between his knees, trying to make his body as small as he felt.

He had been sent to save the world. Instead, he had doomed it.

Behind him, gentle footsteps, barely audible over the crashing of the waves. Ash didn't need to turn around to see who it was.

"Hey," said the quiet voice.

Ash thought about responding with a "Hey back," but couldn't muster the strength to get the words out. There was a gentle rustle of sand as Alexis sat down next to him and wrapped an arm around his waist. Ash sunk his head deeper between his legs.

"I don't deserve that," he said, his voice muffled.

Alexis snorted. "This was supposed to happen. All of it. From Spades to the *Remedy* to the *Redemption*. You know you can't blame yourself."

The lapping of the ocean strobed melodically, relaxingly,

back and forth, back and forth, its creamy froth stopping just short of Ash and Alexis.

Ash lifted his head up and stared into the distance. "On an intellectual level, I think I understand that. But emotionally? I feel the weight of the world." Ash moved his hands off of his legs and gripped the warm sand, enjoying its coarse feel, wondering how much longer he would be able to enjoy it. Where was Spades? How nearby was it? Could it touch them here? Was their time limited to breaths, to heartbeats, instead of days, weeks and years?

Alexis gently rubbed Ash's back. "There are no words," she said solemnly. "There is literally nothing I can say that can relieve you of that guilt. The only person who can do that is you." She sighed. "The way I figure it, you have a choice."

"Yeah?" Ash said. "What's that?"

"You've beaten depression before, right?"

Ash snorted. "I've lived with it. I've functioned with it. I wouldn't say I've beaten it. And sometimes it's certainly kicked the ever-loving crap out of me." He paused. "Why? What does that have to do with anything?"

"I think that everyone gets that far down. So far down, so deep in your own sadness that you think you can never get back up," Alexis said. "When you get there, you lose hope. You decide life isn't worth living."

"You become like Valliant," Ash said bitterly.

Alexis tilted her head. "Exactly. Was he right?"

"Of course not," Ash snapped.

"Why?" asked Alexis.

Ash paused, thoughtfully, before responding. "Because as long as you breathe, you have hope," he said gently, letting the words hang in the air.

Alexis said nothing else. She simply tightened her grip around Ash's waist, leaned over and kissed Ash's forehead. Ash closed his eyes at the comforting sensation, feeling the warmth spread from his head to his toes, and finding himself undeserving of such grace.

"I wish I could make you whole. Change your mind. But you know no person can do that alone. Even you can't do it alone."

Ash took a deep breath.

"I know," he said. He stood, brushing the sand off of his pants. "Come on. Let's get back to everyone else." Extending a hand, Ash pulled Alexis up, and hands still linked, they walked back to the shuttles and the rest of the crew.

***

Ash and Alexis arrived back at the shuttle site to find the crew in various states of awareness. The limited supplies that were on the shuttle had been inventoried and organized. A few small fires burned and some members of the crew sat in groups of twos or threes, chatting quietly or crying silently.

The only person missing was Larissa. She sat fifty yards from the rest of the crew, even facing a different direction. Upon hearing movement behind her, she slowly turned, and jerked when she spotted Ash and Alexis approach. After a moment's hesitation, she stood and walked quickly toward them. Hearing movement, Blondell and Radar closed ranks on Ash, as if worried Larissa might throw a punch or worse.

Reaching Ash and his hastily assembled guard, Larissa stopped. "I'm sorry," she spluttered.

Ash was stunned. "What?" he asked.

"Sometimes...you get so mad that you forget what you are fighting for. And what is really important. Mors Certa wasn't supposed to be like this. It was supposed to bring down the U.G., not the rest of the world." The words tumbled out of Larissa's mouth as if they were running downhill. She stopped, took a deep breath, and ran a hand through her hair before continuing. "I knew it would be bad. I knew people would die. But I assumed that the ends would justify the means." Larissa stopped again. "Please forgive me. Please. I didn't realize what I was doing, and I was wrong. I'm so sorry."

Ash stared at Larissa, blinking, in disbelief. Looking at her pleading eyes, Ash almost felt as if he had her life in his hands. Larissa, who had helped stop the mutiny and saved his life. Larissa, who had participated in the great deception that set the crew of the *Redemption* on a path that led to a crash landing on Earth, and in so doing, had likely doomed the planet.

Ash walked passed Larissa, but reached a hand up and squeezed her shoulder, holding his grip for a moment before moving on. Whether it came from strength, mercy, compassion, exhaustion or confusion, Ash didn't know. Maybe a little bit of everything.

Ash found one of the fires and sat down, joining Robin, Radar, Echo, Jameson and Blondell. Jameson had an arm around Robin, who looked peaceful as he rested on Jameson's shoulder. Blondell sat, absent-mindedly throwing small pebbles that were scattered around the camp fire. The group had been talking, rehashing and reanalyzing the conversation with Valliant. Ash suspected that they had been doing that for some time.

"What I still don't understand is why the U.G. didn't send a message back in time," said Radar. "Something like, 'Hey, watch out for that ship that's gonna kill you all!'" Radar paused to grab a fist-full of sand and throw it at the fire. It disappeared in the gentle wind. "God, I wish I had hit that son of a bitch with a metal rod when I had the chance."

Giggles circled the group.

"Maybe they did," Jameson said.

"Maybe they did send a message?" Ash asked.

Jameson nodded. "Perhaps they did, and it failed. Or, maybe Valliant was able to intercept the message before it arrived at its destination. Let's not assume Valliant told us everything he knew, or that we fully understand time travel."

"Fair point," Ash said. "Hell, I still don't understand why they grabbed us. Why'd they take kids from the 1990s?" Ash gestured toward Robin. "And why did they take teenagers from all different times?"

"I have a theory about that," said Jameson.

Ash sighed. "I had a feeling you would. Spill it."

"I think the Unity Government knew more than Valliant gave them credit for. Yes, they could have assumed that Valliant failed because the mission simply didn't succeed.

But follow the logic here. You're the Unity Government. You send a ship back in time to stop a deadly disease, and if it works, you'll know right away, because everything on Earth would have changed. But if it fails, nothing changes . . ."

"And the ship should be around to be debriefed," Alexis said, finishing the thought.

"And when they weren't, and there were no signs of its destruction, the Unity Government realized something went wrong. To be safe, they changed the mission profile. But to be really safe, they also changed the composition of the crew."

"Younger kids," Ash said. "From different time periods. Change of perspective."

"And with enough variety that all points of view would conflict with each other. There'd never be a chance for any sort of conspiracy, as well as a low enough information level that it would have been impossible to make any deductions like the *Remedy* did."

Echo finished. "No way that what happened onboard the *Remedy* could be repeated."

Ash ran a hand through his hair.

For a solid five minutes, the group was silent, each lost in their own thoughts. No one spoke again until Jameson said, "There's one thing that I still don't understand."

"Just one thing?" Ash said.

"Well, one in particular," Jameson said.

"Fire away," replied Ash.

"The coordinates," said Jameson. Ash scrunched up his face in confusion, trying to recall what Jameson was talking about. Like a bolt, it hit him.

"The coordinates," Ash echoed, thinking back to their first few hours on the ship. "The three digits which led us to the *Remedy* in the first place." Jameson nodded.

"Exactly," he said. "Who put them there, and why?"

"Well, duh, it had to be the *Remedy,*" said Radar.

Jameson forcefully shook his head. "Couldn't have been. Remember? When Valliant spoke. 'From the moment you had the good fortune to find us.' He had nothing to do with those coordinates."

"He could have been lying," said Blondell.

"Sure," Jameson said. "But I don't think so. There may have been things Valliant was hiding. But you heard that rant, same as I did. He was just so impressed with himself. He wanted us to know how smart he was. If he had done that, if he had fooled us into finding him, he would have told us."

"Jameson, what are you saying?" asked Robin, now sitting up straight.

"I really don't know," Jameson said, with uncharacteristic befuddlement in his voice. "But whatever happened here, there's more to it. More pieces to the puzzle of Spades and the Unity Government. The only thing I can deduce is that someone, somewhere, wanted us to find the *Remedy*. And from there, you'd have to assume that it was someone who had access to the *Redemption* before we arrived, which, at least theoretically—"

"Would only be the Unity Government," said Alexis.

The group let the weight of what Alexis had said sink in.

"Someone in the U.G. wanted us to find the *Remedy*," said Blondell.

"Or someone in the U.G. wanted the *Remedy* to find us," countered Jameson.

"Yeah, but which one?" asked Robin.

No one answered. No one could.

Ash paused and looked around at the assembled masses. His crew – well, they weren't really his crew anymore – was intermixed now, mutineers and loyalists, bound together by having become unwitting participants in the biggest mass murder of human history. Ash stared at friend and foe alike: Pike, laid out in the sand, groaning, a hand on his chest. Mercury, looking dazed and lost, a stump the only part of her ruined left arm that remained. Miranda, lying flat on the ground, weeping softly. Larissa, only her back visible, weighed down by the shame of what she had and had not done.

Alexis, burrowed into Ash's chest, with the slightest of smiles on her face. Still hopeful, after all of this.

As the group sat and time drifted on, the harsh light of

the sun dimmed to a dull yellow, and the overlapping sounds of waves gently washing ashore intermixed with seagulls and quiet conversations. Ash closed his eyes and allowed the sound to take him away, drifting pleasantly, almost forgetting what had happened and every mistake he had made.

It was a soft, mechanical rumble that brought him back.

Ash's eyes snapped open and he came back to full awareness. Everyone else was staring up, where two large, black machines hovered over the beach, silhouetted menacingly against the deep blue sky. They were the shape of helicopters, but that was where the similarities ended. There were no external rotors keeping the machines afloat. Squinting, Ash saw two holes in each side of a flat panel, whirling softly against the dying light of the evening sun.

Simultaneously, a dozen figures materialized on the beach. They took a moment to orient themselves, when one suddenly pointed in the direction of Ash and the rest of the crew. Everyone was standing now, staring anxiously, running worst case scenarios through their minds.

Ash felt oddly at peace. At this point, what was the worst that could happen? It wasn't like he could doom the planet again. The warped thought brought a smile to his face.

The figures ran toward the crew. They were large, fast, and clearly armed to the teeth. Dressed in dark black armor. Weapons drawn. As they approached, Ash heard their voices clearly. And they were pissed.

"Hands up, hands up!" they cried, voices overlapping. Looking back up, Ash noticed something he hadn't seen before: a large infinity symbol on the side of the helicopter, with a "U" and a "G" in the loops.

Ash took Alexis' hand and raised it into the sky, raising his other hand at the same time. Alexis did the same. Ash felt the rest of the crew behind him, mirroring his actions.

"Hands up! Hands up!"

Alexis looked up at Ash, her face slightly confused. "Ash?" she said.

Ash looked back at her, and the slightest of smiles played across his face. Seeing his confidence, Alexis smiled back.

298

Ash winked.

He released Alexis' hands and stepped forward, slowly, making sure to keep both of his hands in the air. The group of troops was on him now, a dozen of them, forming a semi-circle, weapons drawn, ready to fire. Ash walked into the center, feeling alert. Ready.

Had he made mistakes? Sure. But what the hell difference did it make now? All that mattered – all that would ever matter again – would be the day ahead.

In a confident voice, Ash declared, "I'm Asher Maddox, Captain of the U.G. *Redemption.*" He tilted his chin up with an air of defiance. "What do you want to know?"

The End

Acknowledgements

With this leg of the journey completed, I've learned something very important: My name may be on the front of the book, but no author has ever written alone.

First and foremost: To Maer Wilson and the crew at Ellysian Press, including Joseph Murphy and Jen Ryan. Your edits made *Redemption* such a stronger product, they made me a better writer, and they gave Asher Maddox a better chance to have his story told. Maer, as long as I live, I will never forget sitting in a diner outside of Harrisburg, about to order a piece of cherry cheesecake, getting an Email from a publisher, thinking it would be a rejection, and then the world changing when I realized it wasn't. Thank you from the bottom of my heart for this chance.

Once again: To Brenna, Auron and Ayla. To my rock, Brenna, I cannot imagine a world without you, and *Redemption* wouldn't be what it was if not for countless late-night talks about Ash, Alexis and the rest of the crew and their story. You've pulled me from the darkness countless times, and I hope to be worthy of your love. To my hope and inspiration, Auron and Ayla, everything we do, it's for you. You are my hurricanes, my road runner and my wrecking ball, and there isn't a moment where I am not thinking of you. Words aren't enough. They never will be.

Next: To Mom, Dad, Jack and Cindy. Forget the love and the care you provide to me, just for a moment. Forget the logistics. Thank you for loving my wife and kids the way you do. That, alone, gives me what I need. Thank you for everything you have ever given me. Now that I'm a Dad, I understand so many things so much more.

To my sister Becky: Thanks for letting me follow in your footsteps as the family writer. It is my pleasure and honor to be the flip side of the same coin. Keep being brave, you Brooklyn hipster.

Thank you to Uncle Bob and Aunt Colleen! Your advice got me through publishing the first book, and what you taught me remained for this one.

To my best friend, Pete, and my mentors, Jenn Mann and Tony Iannelli. When I decided to go public with my own story, you realized, long before I did, that I had something to say and it would change my life forever. Thank you for helping me find my *Redemption*. You've all done more good for me then I can calculate – provided support in the darkest of hours, helped me find jobs and launched various levels of my career. I'm not here if not for any of you.

As a politician, I get paid to serve the people, but anyone with half a brain knows that we're just the mascots. Thank you to the incredible staff of the 132nd Legislative District: Jean Creedon, Geoff Brace, Nancy Loch, Hank Beaver and Kira Zickler. Your dedication to the public reminds me of the importance of my job each and every day.

To Drs. Stein and Salas, my therapists. At different points in my life, you saved it. I have no words to express my gratitude for your advice, kindness and support.

To the random schmuck on Facebook who changed my life. I made the decision, as a public official, to go public with my own 17+ year with depression on August 11, 2014. The day before, I read you say words to the effect of "So sad Robin Williams committed suicide. He just needed to pray to Jesus more!" Your ignorance made me realize how far the world had to go in terms of dealing with mental illness, and inspired me to publicly discuss my own depression and anxiety for the first time. That, in turn, led to *Redemption*. It's a rare moment to be grateful for someone else's ignorance, but I will be forever thankful for yours.

To Robin Williams. Yours was a life well lived, and I hope to be part of a positive story of those influenced by how it ended.

To the people of the 132nd Legislative District, who have given me the honor of serving them. I wake up every day distinctly aware that I get to be your voice, and this book, I hope, is part of that effort. I hold a lot of titles in my life, but one of the ones I treat with the most reverence is State Representative and public servant. Thank you for this responsibility.

To everyone who has ever suffered, ever felt lost, scared

or alone. As you almost certainly figured out after reading this, depression, anxiety and I are intimately acquainted. Those two illnesses are constantly running in my background like an app in an iPhone. I won't say I've figured out how to beat them. I don't think I ever will. But I will say that I've learned how to manage them. How to live my life, to make it a good one, despite their presence. I hope that the struggles of Asher Maddox and his crew have helped you realize that, whatever you pain, you can be a hero. This book was dedicated to my wonderful wife, my little boy and my little girl, the light of my life. But it another way, if you have ever suffered, this one is also for you.

About the Author

Mike Schlossberg has been a writer since he wrote his first short story in eighth grade, a *Star Wars* fanfiction. While he claims it was terrible, the creative passion followed him into adulthood.

Serving as a State Representative in Pennsylvania, Mike has had the chance to make a difference. The problem closest to his heart is mental health, where he strives to break the stigma surrounding those who suffer from mental illnesses and give them hope. For Mike, this issue is personal, as he has been treated for depression and anxiety related disorders since he was 18. It was this desire to help which drove him to write *Redemption,* his first novel, but not his first book. That honor goes to *Tweets and Consequences*, an anthology about the varied ways elected officials have destroyed their careers via social media.

When not writing, Mike plays video games (both modern and old school), watches anything related to the Muppets (specifically *Fraggle Rock*!), reads, attempts to get to the gym, and calls his constituents on their birthdays.

Mike lives in Allentown, Pennsylvania, with his wife Brenna and his two wonderful children: Auron, born in 2011, and Ayla, born in 2012.

To contact the author

Mike is an *avid* social media user who uses Twitter way too much. To connect with him, visit:

http://www.mikeschlossbergauthor.com
https://mikeschlossbergauthor.com/blog/
https://www.facebook.com/MikeSchlossbergAuthor/
http://www.twitter.com/MikeSchlossberg
https://www.instagram.com/MikeSchlossberg/
michaelschlossberg@gmail.com

Also from Ellysian Press

The Boogeyman by Lillie J. Roberts

The nightmare begins...
Two girls lost on a lonely country road.
One killer thrilled with an unexpected opportunity.
Two families desperate to find their lost children.
One girl...lost
One girl remains...
Until a young boy joins her...

And discovers the Boogeyman is real.

Exiles of Forlorn by Sean T. Poindexter

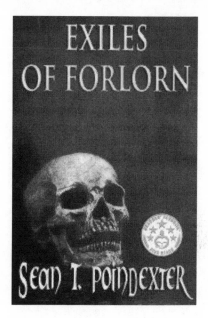

It all began when the old man died.

On a ship of exiles bound for the edge of civilization, he passes on his life's work to a band of youths. He gives each of them a piece of information that leads to a mythical treasure.

The five friends – the lord's son, the soldier, the thief, the beautiful river pirate and the wizard's apprentice – all agree to join the hunt.

They arrive on the shores of Forlorn eager to begin their journey, but find a community plagued by threats from pirates and man-eating giants. The friends must choose to either stay and help those who have taken them in or to venture into unknown lands in search of a prize that may not even exist.

Either choice promises excitement, danger — and death.

Relics by Maer Wilson

Most of Thulu and La Fi's clients are dead. Which is perfect since their detective agency caters to the supernatural. But a simple job finding a lost locket leads to a big case tracking relics for an ancient daemon.

The daemon needs the relics to keep a dangerous portal closed. His enemy, Gabriel, wants the relics to open the portal and give his people access to a new feeding ground – Earth.

Caught on live TV, other portals begin to open and the creatures of magic return to Earth. The people of Earth are not alone, but will soon wish they were.

When Gabriel threatens their family, Thulu and La Fi's search becomes personal. The couple will need powerful help in the race to find the relics before Gabriel does. But maybe that's what ghostly friends, magical allies and daemonic clients are for.

When the creatures of myth and magic return to Earth, they're nothing like your mother's fairy tales.

ABOUT ELLYSIAN PRESS

To find other Ellysian Press books, please visit our **website**: (http://www.ellysianpress.com/).

You can find our complete list of **novels here**. They include:

The Elohim Legacy **by Sean T. Poindexter**

Kālong **by Carol Holland March**

Marked Beauty **by S.A. Larsen**

Dreamscape **by Kerry Reed**

The Rending **by Carol Holland March**

A Deal in the Darkness **by Allan B. Anderson**

The Will of the Darkest One **by Sean T. Poindexter**

The Tyro **by Carol Holland March**

The Shadow of Tiamat **by Sean T. Poindexter**

Muse Unexpected **by VC Birlidis**

The Devil's Triangle **by Toni De Palma**

Moth **by Sean T. Poindexter**

Premonition **by Agnes Jayne**

Exiles of Forlorn **by Sean T. Poindexter**

Relics by Maer Wilson

A Shadow of Time by Louann Carroll

Idyllic Avenue by Chad Ganske

Portals by Maer Wilson

Innocent Blood by Louann Carroll

The Boogeyman by Lillie J. Roberts

Magics by Maer Wilson

The **Ellysian Press Catalog** has a complete list of current and forthcoming books.